SHALE

THE BURNS SERIES BOOK 3

M.M. HOLT

ISBN: 9798587093669

Contents

Dedicated to the continuing struggle against
the Accord of Nations.

WARNING

'SHALE' is the third book in the Alex Burns series. It continues the story from the preceding novel, 'PROTOCOL.' If 'SHALE' is your first encounter with Alex Burns, please turn back. Read 'PROTOCOL' before you take another step. Consider also reading Book 1, 'Fifty Degrees South,' as well. It's dangerous to lose your way in the hostile world of the Accord of Nations in the year 250, AONE.
You have been warned.

PROLOGUE

I RAISED THE spear to the sunlight. It was over eight feet long, thin but stubbornly rigid, and it glittered like no metal I had ever seen before. It also seemed to emit a crackling hum, like an electrical cable.

It looked deadly too. The tip was sharp to touch, and the spear's shaft was light. In the right hands it could be wielded to cut, smack, and bludgeon, or just twirled around to create a diversion before the next stab.

But I had never fought with a spear before. I'd never even held one, not even in the combat simulator back at AONS Harmony in AON sub-territory California. Spears were not part of a modern arsenal of weapons, of course. Not just because they were primitive, but because they were symbols of male power; and male power was responsible for all the trouble in the world. Every Accord member knew it.

But this wasn't the Accord of Nations.

It wasn't even Earth.

And for a hundred thousand light years in every direction, I was the only human male alive.

I stood in a dusty clearing in the middle of a dense, tall, alien forest. The strange trees loomed on three sides, thick and green, and full of screeching birds I could neither see nor imagine. To my right, a tall, gray cliff dominated the clearing. At its base was a series of caves in which my hosts lived.

On my left was a sight that would strain the tolerance of the most dedicated Navy Spirit officer. A thousand bear-wolf monsters, known as Goths, howled and roared at me. They bared their teeth and unsheathed their claws, and they slashed at the air with great swipes. They were in a frenzy, a rage. They growled a single Goth word over and over. 'Gwanta!' they growled. 'Gwanta! Gwanta! Gwanta!'

Gwanta, the god of the Goths. Gwanta, the god of war and of vengeance.

The roars echoed off the cliff face. They bounced back across the clearing as if the cliff itself wanted vengeance, as did the forest and the sky. The whole Goth land called to Gwanta, beseeching him to avenge the terrible wrong done to the Goth nation by the strange alien creature from across the galaxy.

I raised a sleeve to my face and wiped away the sweat dripping into my eyes. I grabbed the collar of my soiled, blue Navy Working Uniform and peeled the shirt from my clammy back. Then, I reached up to my nose and pushed the small breathing device deeper into my nostrils, shoving it all the way until it hit cartilage. I didn't want it coming loose when the fight began, and I didn't want to smell the reek of the planet's foul air.

Then, I lowered my arm and gripped the spear in what I thought was the most natural way, left hand on the middle to guide the sharp tip, right hand on the lower third to provide the power. I twisted my boots around in the dust until I found a fighting stance. Then, forcing down the fear smoldering in my stomach, and closing my mind to images of claws and teeth tearing at my uniform, I raised the spear and leveled the quivering tip at my opponent.

Ten yards away, swaying on his hind limbs, the Goth warrior Granak glowered down at me. At the sight of the raised spear, he barked in disgust. Granak required no spears. Not at all. He had all the weapons he needed built in. His claws were as big and sharp as fruit knives. His canine teeth were as long as my hands. He was many times my weight, at least twice my height, a yard wider, and his hide was as thick and tough as old carpet.

He panted at me, his long, red tongue dripping saliva to the dust beside his hind paws, twelve feet down. His genitals swayed obscenely beneath him, and his sewage breath reached across the ten yards between us, like an advanced fighting force. That breath of Granak's was so foul, it could kill a man all by itself—if the man ever allowed him to get close enough.

The sight of him drained my courage. How could I ever hope to defeat a creature so enormous? How could I win with nothing but my boots, my wits, and a primitive weapon I didn't know how to use? Worse! How could I defeat such a creature when he was fighting for his king, his god, and the pride of his nation, while I was fighting only for myself?

The answer was that I couldn't—not without a miracle.

Standing there in the heat and dust, I asked myself the questions I'd struggled to answer all morning. How had I allowed this to happen? How did I end up in this nightmare? How was it that I came to be clutching a spear in the middle of an alien forest, fighting a monster on a planet one hundred thousand light-years from Earth?

And not just any planet, either. This was the planet Rome itself, the home of Octavia and her alien nation, the nation moving its enormous warships into formation around Earth while I stood with the spear, the dust, and the overwhelming odds of defeat.

But, of course, I knew how this situation had come about. No matter how much I shook my head, I knew all too well. I had chosen to be here. I had chosen to go with the Goths. Me, and no one else. It was a wrong choice, a stupid choice, the worst decision possible. Only a fool would have made it. A fool or someone out of his mind. But that's what I'd done. I'd chosen the Goths. Now I faced the terrible consequences.

'What are you looking at?' I shouted across the sand to Granak. His ears sprung up and twitched towards me like turret guns. He couldn't understand me, of course. Only Karz, the she-Goth interpreter understood a few words of Accord languages. But Granak got the gist. He knew a taunt when he heard one. He must have heard hundreds or thousands of taunts from enemies whom he soon ripped to pieces. Now, he faced another enemy, and another opportunity to rip and tear all over again.

As if hearing my thoughts, he smiled. The black seam lining his immense snout curled, revealing more of his teeth and brown gums than I wanted to see. Then, he snorted and sneezed with a great shake of his head before ducking his eyes under a wipe of his forelimb, and settling back into swaying tall in the sun with his ears twitching and his claws sliding in and out of their dark sheaths.

And so, we waited for some signal to start. The alien sun beat down, my eyes stung with sweat, the spear tip quivered and glittered. Meanwhile, the Goth mob howled, and my arms and legs, already tired from carrying the planet's heavy gravity, trembled with exhaustion and fear.

Come on, I thought. Let's get started. Let's get this over with, for better or worse.

But Granak was in no hurry. He looked casually at one shaggy shoulder, then dug his snout into his fur, checking for something, bites from alien bugs, or the bones of his last meal, or his last victim. Who could tell? His long shadow stretched towards me over the dust, revealing an enormous creature apparently eating itself.

Finally, Granak looked up from his fur. He lifted his snout to the chanting mob and bared his teeth at them and nodded a few times. Then, as if reaching a decision, he turned back to me, dropped from his great height, flopping down onto his four dinner-plate-sized paws, lowered his head, and charged.

I didn't need the Goth mob to tell me the fight had begun. They had dropped their chant of Gwanta. Now they howled and bayed in a raucous free-for-all. Baying for blood. Baying for death. My blood and my death.

There could be no getting out of it now. Minutes ago, I might have wanted to run or protest or plead, to drop the spear and beseech the Goth king to pardon me, but those doors were now shut. There could be no going back.

Granak's shadow came bounding over the dusty ground towards me. His breath shushed from his open snout in rasping puffs. His black eyes gleamed. His dark fur shimmered. And his haunches drove him forward with astonishing power, like a charging buffalo, like a truck made of muscle, bone, and hate.

This is it, I thought. This is how it will end. I'll die with my head crushed like a piece of fruit, my ribs cracked and pulled apart, and my guts ripped out and dragged in the dust for the entertainment of a howling mob. That's how it will go. That's how it will end. And it will be all my own fault.

So I waited with the spear tip trembling five feet in front of my sweating face.

Soon, the edge of Granak's hysterical shadow reached me. I gripped the spear tighter, leaning forward, anchoring my boots deeper in the dust, bracing myself for the terrible impact.

All right. Here we go, I thought. Here we go. You won't survive, but at least you'll die fighting. You have failed yourself. You have failed your people, and you have disgraced your family, but you'll die with a weapon in your hands. At least you'll have that. A sailor's death in battle. At least you'll have that.

But what I couldn't know was that fate had something else in mind. I would soon make a discovery that would change everything, and that this ordeal of man against monster would lead to a weapon that could defeat Octavia and save the Earth and its people from invasion and annihilation.

If I survived the day.

If.

But with every bound of that horrible shadow, the 'if' grew bigger. On it came, till the 'if' was like another enemy itself, in partnership with Granak, the monster.

And then, all too soon, the shadow rushed over me. The hot, foul breath hit my face, and the thick yellow claws came slicing through the poisonous air.

PART ONE:
INCARCERATION

'There are no such things as aliens. There is only diversity and greater diversity.'

Amendment to the Accord of Nations
Constitution
Year 250, The Accord of Nations Era

1

TWO WEEKS EARLIER
Accord of Nations Navy Brig
AON Navy Ship, Schumer
Sub-territory California
Accord of Nations Territory USA
Year 250 in the Accord of Nations Era

They made their move in the mess hall at five p.m.

The four of them pushed back their chairs and stood up, rising above the other prisoners hunched over their trays. They reached into their blue smocks as they rose, keeping their eyes on me at my table at the mess hall's edge.

The one hundred and forty-eight other prisoners stopped talking. Their recyclable cardboard spoons froze between their trays and their open mouths. They nudged each other and whispered. Something was up.

Without saying a word, the prisoners pushed

back their chairs and rose from the tables like a silent blue wave. Then they crept away to the edge of the hall. None of them said a word, but their faces said plenty. In the Accord, violence was almost never seen. Now, it had shown up to entertain them, like an action movie screened with dinner.

This was my first day in the main brig at AONNB Schumer. I had just been released from a month in the medical wing recovering from injuries sustained in AONT sub-territory Hong Kong. Following that, I had spent a second month in a brig known as Re-Orientation. The Re-Orientation brig was designed to treat the really bad cases: the one who needed severe reminding of the Accord of Nations' values.

But now I was out.

I had wanted to re-enter the main brig as a nobody not the infamous traitor, Lieutenant Alexander Burns. I had my reasons. I wanted to be left alone till I could think straight. But now, I faced the first of many violent encounters.

The four guys and I remained alone, like the last five players in a game of musical chairs. Just them and me. The four of them stepped from behind their tables and crept towards me, fanning out in a crescent, covering off all routes of escape in case I got up and ran—in case I called out for the masters-at-arms.

But the four guys were wrong. I wasn't going anywhere.

I had been eating my first meal out of Re-

Orientation. The dinner, as expected, met all the Accord dietary mandates. It was all tofu, soy milk, and kale. Meat never appeared on the menu. Meat was banned. So was fish. So was chicken. The AMA—the Accord Medical Authority—had ruled that non-vegan diets were dangerous, especially for males. Meat-based diets increased toxic masculinity, which urged males to compete with each other. The AMA could never allow competitive urges—not for military personnel.

So, meat, fish, and chicken were out. Tofu, kale, and soy milk were in. The AMA's plan had worked. Males in the Navy fought much less— and not just because the diet denied them protein for muscle growth. Soy milk also increased the body's levels of estrogen, the female hormone. The AMA was delighted. Eventually, it recommended that every male in the Accord should drink a pint of soy milk a day.

After twenty-six years of life and a battle with an alien invader, I had discovered the truth about soy milk and kale, just like I had discovered the truth about the Accord of Nations and everything it said was good for people. Kale and soy milk sounded healthy, but tasted like cold defeat. The same with the Accord's motto of T.E.D. It sounded virtuous but was in fact just another way to coerce, control, and silence people.

Not that any of those discoveries would help me.

The four guys had withdrawn their hands from

their smocks. Their right hands were clenched into fists. The fists clutched small shivs, each poking two or three inches above their thumbs.

Their left hands were empty. Each guy held them out from their sides, palms open, as if they needed to balance themselves—as if they were experienced fighters. What a joke! Almost no one in the Navy knew how to sail a boat. They almost certainly didn't know how to use a knife, or a shiv, or their fists. They only knew about fighting as a concept, not from any experience.

If they tried anything on me, I would have to give them a crash course in real-life combat.

Then again, things might have changed while I'd been locked up. The aliens had arrived, and I was a known traitor. The public probably hated me; the prisoners probably hated me the most. And their hatred might give them powers they never knew they possessed.

I sat still at my table, watching the four guys creeping closer, and working out which one I would hit first. One of them stood over six feet, almost as tall as me. His or her arms extended far. That could be a problem. Long arms with a knife must be handled with care. I decided I would hit this tall guy or girl or girl-guy first.

The other three were shorter. The stocky one on the far left glared at me the hardest of the three. He was the leader, maybe. I would hit him second. The other two guys seemed less committed. Their shoulders angled slightly away from me. The same with their feet. Like they weren't sure of themselves. I would work out what to do with them when the time came. With luck, they would run away.

When they loomed six feet from my table, the four guys stopped and stood in their knife-fighter's stances. They crouched and shifted weight from one foot to the other, their free hands twitching, like the gun fighters shown in the documentaries about the decadent pre-Accord Old West.

Their blue prison smocks displayed the usual insignias. Each wore a patch reading AONNB Schumer, which stood for Accord of Nations Navy Brig Schumer. The other patches stood for their names and their crimes. The name patches read Schiff, Redondo, Das, and Fung.

The four of them were a Navy Spirit fantasy of diversity made of several genders, four ethnicities, and a disability. Das's left earlobe was missing. Navy Spirit would count that as a hearing-related non-ability. All of them wore shaved heads. The patches naming the reasons for their incarceration all said, 'HC,' which stood for 'Hate Crime,' which could have been for anything from saying there were only two genders to misusing someone's preferred pronouns.

My own name patch read 'LIEUT ALEX BURNS.' The crime patches read, 'TR (Treason), FTOO (failing to obey an order), T (theft), I (insubordination), AM (attempted murder), and O (for othering the Romans and their enemies, the rabid Goths, with whom they shared the planet Rome).

The four guys now fanned out in a crescent around my table, almost like real fighters. I slid my metal dinner tray of kale and soy milk closer to my chest, and kept my hands on the tray's edges, ready for when the moment came.

'T.E.D.,' I said, pronouncing each letter clearly: tee, ee, dee for the words tolerance, equality, and diversity.

'Nice try.' This was the stocky one named Schiff.

'Did I say it wrongly? Have the words changed? This is my first day back.'

'We know who you are,' said Schiff. 'We know what you did.'

'Yeah? And who are you?' I said. 'Or who are you supposed to be?'

'You let all of us down,' said Schiff. 'You embarrassed us in front of the intra-galactic visitors. Now you've got to pay for your mistakes.'

I nodded at the HC patches on their smocks. 'What crimes did you guys commit? They must have been bad. What did you do? Say that men can't get pregnant? Or maybe that there are only two genders? What was it?'

'Big man,' said Schiff. 'You think you're brave saying things like that about Accord values?'

I reconfirmed my decision to hit Schiff second.

Around the mess, the blue ranks of prisoners watched and waited. Their soy milk and kale were forgotten. Now they hungered for a fight, to see toxic masculinity in action.

'Don't do it guys,' I said. 'You'll regret it.'

'"Guys?"' said Schiff. 'Did you just call us guys? You sound like some pre-Accord toxic male from the movies. What exactly shouldn't we do, traitor?'

'Whatever it is you're planning,' I said. 'That's what. Give it up. I don't want to fight the Accord. I don't want to fight you guys, either. So go back to your tables and eat your soy and kale, and I won't say anything more about it.'

'Or what?' said Fung, the tall guy with the long reach.

'Or I'll break the Accord value of tolerance and then I'll break your faces.'

I'm not normally so aggressive. I'm usually a mild kind of guy. I have to be pushed to lose my temper. I made the threat about breaking faces to avoid a fight not start one. But the threat didn't work. The four guys simply smirked and stood their ground.

'If you haven't noticed,' said Fung, 'there are four of us and only one of you. We're armed. You're not. And no MAs are gonna save you—not for the next five minutes. That's right. No MAs. That's because even the guards hate you, Burns. So, for the time being, it's just you and us.'

I was about to say that fighting alone against the odds was my usual way of combat. Hadn't they seen the news about me on Unity TV? But before I could speak, someone else spoke first.

A voice behind me said, 'Look here, dickheads. Now, there are two of him.'

The four guys flinched. They hadn't expected anyone to step forward from the huddle along the edge of the mess hall. They probably hadn't expected to be called dickheads, either, which was a very pre-Accord-era insult. But they smiled. Maybe whoever had spoken wasn't much of a threat. I didn't turn around to check. I didn't want to give any opportunities for Schiff, Das, Redondo, and Fung to lunge at me.

Instead, I said, 'Whoever you are, stay out of this.'

Then, I heard the voice say something I couldn't believe.

'You are not alone, Lieutenant. I can help you.'

2

'Thanks,' I said. 'But I don't need your help. This is my fight.'

'It's everyone's fight,' said the voice. Then the speaker stepped up beside me. He was a male, about twenty years old, dark skin, shaved head, about five-eight at the most. He swam in his blue prison smock, barely filling out the sleeves and pants legs. A guy like that wouldn't be able to raise a fist, let alone swing it at anyone. But he typified Accord of Nations Navy personnel: thin from the vegan diet, and not the least bit threatening.

'It's better if you leave this to me,' I said. 'But thanks.'

'Fighting alone is too hard,' the kid persisted. 'You're just one guy.'

'Just stay back. These guys won't be much trouble.'

'No need. They won't touch me. I'm higher on the Oppression Hierarchy than any of them—

way higher! I'm a non-abled, AONT African transgender man who suffers mental health problems because of transition remorse. My Oppression Hierarchy ranking is on the moon compared to theirs. Hit me? They wouldn't dare.'

But just as these words came out, Fung, the tallest of the attackers, made his move. He had no problems with my place on the Oppression Hierarchy, which was at the bottom. To him, I was enemy number one, a male descendent of the pre-Accord West, so any attack on me was fine, and the more violent, the better.

He lunged with his long right arm like a fencer thrusting a foil. He had style. He stayed elegantly side and raised his left arm behind him like a scorpion's tail, which I guess was supposed to intimidate me. Clearly, he was begging to be humiliated.

As the lunge came in, I gripped my metal tray and flung it up to my right. The bowls of tofu and kale, and the cup of soy milk, all rose with the tray. By the time they left the tray's metal surface, they traveled at an impressive velocity, like projectiles. The kale and tofu hit the would-be fencer in the face and chest, splattering his blue smock with green and white slop. The cup of soy milk followed, hitting him square in the forehead and sending up a plume of white. I followed through with the tray, turning it and swinging it down onto his shiv hand, deflect it away from my chest.

The shiv's blade made a great scratch on the

tray's face, and Fung found himself overreaching, off-balance, and blinded by the oily soy milk. I stood up to my full height, let the tray drop, raised an elbow, and slammed it down into the back of his neck. He hit his head on the table edge and fell to the tiles. Then he lay still among the table legs.

'Nice work!' said the kid.

'Stay back,' I said.

I turned my attention to the next guy, the one with the patches that read 'Redondo,' and 'HC.' I had planned to hit Redondo last, but now I changed my mind. He or she stood next in line, so it made sense to hit him before the others. If I had tried to reach past him to the guys called Das and Schiff, I would have exposed my right side, and I would have been fighting three guys at a time instead of just one.

Not a good idea.

So, I swung my left fist at Redondo's throat while he gawped at Fung on the tiles. The fist struck hard, bending his neck cords like bowstrings. He clutched his throat with both his hands, almost cutting himself with his own shiv. Maybe he'd never been hit before or never expected a punch to hurt so much. All of which meant he gave no resistance when I swung my right fist into the side of his face.

As my knuckles hit, his jaw twisted on its hinges. It slid sideways, out from beneath his upper teeth. He let go of his throat, clutched his face and stumbled backward. The stumble turned into a stagger. He staggered once, twice. He bumped the edge of a table, sat down on its top and slid off onto a chair. Then, he slid to the mess hall's blue tiles, and lay there, kicking his legs around. Everyone has a plan, my fight instructor once said, quoting some pre-Accord bruiser, until they get hit in the throat.

Now only two guys stood beside my table: Das, the guy missing an earlobe, and Schiff, the mouthy leader. Das backed away, holding his trembling shiv with two hands like a pistol. He backed through the tables all the way to the ranks of blue-smocked prisoners standing at the mess hall's edge and then merged into the mass of them where I couldn't see him anymore. So much for conviction, I thought. So much for courage. So much for Accord Navy training.

Schiff and I watched him go. Then, we turned to face each other, the last two guys in the fight.

'Don't even think about it,' I said. 'You won't be joining your brave friend over there. Not any more. Not before I kick your ass. And if you drop your shiv and give up, I'll kick your ass even harder.'

Schiff stayed quiet. His face did all the talking. It told me he wouldn't fight, but had no clue what to do instead. Then, he turned and made a run for the edge of the mess, shoving two tables out of the way before I headed him off. Then he ran back the way he came. I followed. It was like herding a sheep. But before I could catch him, he grabbed the kid, smacking the protesting arms away. Then, he pulled him by the loose smock and put the shiv to the kid's throat.

'Oh, I see,' I said.

'See what?'

'When you're in danger of having your head kicked in, it's OK to use violence on someone further up Oppression Hierarchy.'

'Just hit him,' said the kid. 'Don't worry about me.'

'I will. You can depend on it. I'll hit him so hard I'll knock him back to the pre-Accord era.'

But Schiff just smirked. Then the smirk broadened into a smile.

'What's so funny?'

'You'll see.'

'See what?'

An alarm sounded. As with all AONNB alarms, this one was in the form of a non-threatening, three-toned chime, like a summons to dinner. The alarm chimed twice and the mess doors swung open and a stream of prison MAs rushed in. The MAs belonged to the section of the Navy dedicated to enforcing the Navy Spirit Code. They streamed in, upending tables, yellow stun guns raised, all of them shouting 'Get down! Get down!' like there was an actual riot going on, not a dust up between three guys.

But despite all their shouting, they ignored the prisoners cowering around the edged of the mess hall. They also ignored Schiff and the kid. Instead, they kept the stun guns leveled only at me, and me alone.

Schiff pushed the kid away and shouted, 'The traitor Lieutenant Burns oppressed me. Me and three other Accord members.'

The kid pointed at Schiff and said, 'No. It was him and two other guys that attacked Lieutenant Burns first.'

But the MAs weren't interested.

'Get on the floor, Burns!' said the MA sergeant. 'Get on the floor and put your hands behind your back!'

This was an order I was to hear over and over for the next two weeks. Get on the floor. Face the wall. Put your hands up. Drop your weapon. Submit to the Accord. All the variations. I would end up making a pledge never to submit to those orders again, as long as I lived. But these were early days, and I owed the Accord at least a soybean of respect.

Before I could respond, the stun guns fired. At a range of two yards, not even the MAs could miss. The first bolt struck my back. My muscles locked, and I sunk to my knees, and then toppled forward, bending to the forces of the Accord of Nations and its Navy Spirit Code of conduct.

That's when I heard Schiff call out, 'Wherever they put you, Burns, remember this: there's always going to be someone like us ready to get you. You can't beat us all.'

As I lay with my cheek on the cold blue tiles, I thought of all the obstacles ahead of me. How could I ever fight the Accord? And where would I ever find a weapon that could drive Octavia and her invaders from the earth?

The answers were that I could never defeat the Accord and that no weapon known could come close to defeating Octavia.

And after all they'd done to me in Re-Orientation, why should I even try?

3

They dragged me away. Four MAs picked me up by the arms, pulled me out of the mess hall, and marched me along one corridor, then another corridor until we reached a section of the brig known as Toxicity. We stopped outside a cell with an open door and they pushed me inside.

'Not one day, Burns,' said the MA with a name patch reading CORP TARRANT. 'Not one day out of Re-Orientation and you're oppressing people. Didn't you learn anything?'

'Plenty,' I said. 'I learned all about electrodes and electric shocks.'

'Good,' said Corporal Tarrant. 'You can think about them while you wait in solitary for your court-martial.'

He slammed the door closed. Seconds later, a slot opened. Corporal Tarrant's eyes re-appeared.

'T.E.I.D., Burns,' he said.

'Don't you mean T.E.D?'

'No, Burns. I said T.E.I.D.'

'What's T.E.I.D?'

'You'll find out,' he smirked. Then the slot closed.

No sooner had the door's bolts shot home when two TV screens lit up on the cell's wall.

One of the TV screens displayed the Oppression Hierarchy, listing all the oppressed groups, from non-abled, transgender women of color to the very bottom, to my own group—the one that never changed position. The other screen displayed the 24-hour Unity TV news channel.

Well, I thought, sitting down on the cell's hard bunk. At least, I can catch up on the news.

The clock in the corner of the TV screen was 5:28 p.m., two minutes to go before the next news cycle. The news anchor read out the last story. The Accord had formed a new committee to tackle the high incidence of sexism in dog parks. The committee's aim was to stamp out systems of patriarchal oppression in canines.

The clocked ticked to 5:30 p.m. The news anchor smiled and said, 'Stand by for the latest headlines,' and then the Accord anthem played over an image of the rainbow and dove flag rippling in slow motion. Then the screen flicked to a different news anchor. The chyron said the newsreader's name was Ecology Quinn. Ecology Quinn wished me T.E.D and began reading the top stories.

The first story epitomized the Accord. It was about transgender women in sport. According to the report, every female sports team was now one hundred percent transgender women. In other words, every player on the women's teams was a former male.

As a result, the biological women players had claimed discrimination under the Accord of Nations Constitution. But transgender women were also women just the same as biological women, and anyone who said anything different went to jail. The claim posed a problem for the governing body of women's sport, the AONWSA.

After weeks of deliberation, the AONWSA had failed to reach a decision. So, it dodged the problem by appealing to the Department of Diversity to make a ruling. The Department of Diversity solved the problem by banning women's sports completely—not because transgender women were biologically male. Never because of that. Oh, no. Instead, the department said the real problem, the root of it all, was the concept of sport itself.

Sport, the department ruled, was a tactic used by pre-Accord Western imperialists to oppress women and minorities. Sport ranked teams in order of their competency. Measuring people's competencies was unfair. Everyone knew that. Ranking people according to their competencies was even worse. The only way to rank people fairly was in the order of oppression. So, the Accord Department of Diversity reached an inevitable decision: it banned women's sport completely.

Ecology Quinn then read out the other leading stories. These also epitomized the Accord. They included stories about pay gaps, man-spreading, mansplaining, the importance of eradicating toxic masculinity, racism, intersectional racism, changes in the Oppression Hierarchy, new groups added to the Oppression Hierarchy, new definitions of old groups on the hierarchy, white fragility, and the importance of vigilance at each former nation's border to make sure anyone who wished to enter a nation could do so without hinderance.

The next story reported on the upcoming court-martial of the traitor, Lieutenant Alexander Burns. In the unlikely event that viewers had forgotten about Lieutenant Burns, Ecology Quinn reminded them that Burns had disgracefully 'othered' the intra-galactic visitors in AON sub-territory Hong Kong two months previously. The tall, fair-haired navy officer, who bore a resemblance to a well-known action film star, also breached many of the Navy's codes of conduct. Now, in a first for Unity TV, the court-martial of this traitor would be broadcast live around the Accord so that every Accord member could watch justice in action. No footage of the actual 'othering' event was shown.

Then the next story came up. This was one really got my attention.

This story also concerned AON sub territory Hong Kong. The report showed footage of an AON Navy Prison brig. The brig was AONNB

Kwok. The cheerful reporter said that the brig had received a secret visit from 'our intra-galactic friends, the Goths, the same visitors who had impressed everyone two months ago with their strong culture.

The reporter stood outside the exterior walls in which deep scratches had been gouged, some of them as tall as the reporter herself. She cheerfully called these marks 'cultural expressions of friendship.'

The report then showed grainy CCTV footage taken by night cameras. The footage revealed the enormous Goth bear-wolf creatures rampaging through the prison corridors. Some of these creatures walked on hind legs as they passed the cameras; others ran on all fours, their great backs arching, their fur shimmering, their heads tossing, and their snouts pressed to the floor and the walls as they searched for something.

Or someone.

I watched the rest of the report and wondered.

Then the next astonishing story came up.

The breathless reporter, a woman called Diversity Valdez appeared. She wore short hair, no makeup, no jewelry, and had crooked teeth. She was a typical Unity TV news reporter.

'T.E.I.D,' she began. 'That's soon to become the new greeting for everyone in the Accord. Just thirty minutes ago, Accord commissioner and chairperson, Daniel Genet stood here on the famous Steps to Equity in front of the Accord headquarters in AON sub-territory Los Angeles to make the historic announcement. The Accord, he said, would soon elect its first intra-galactic commissioner. The new commissioner would be none other than Admiral Octavia Caesar from the planet Rome.'

The screen flicked to footage of Commissioner Daniel Genet themself behind a lectern. Commissioner Genet said, 'Our wonderful Accord values will soon transcend time and space.' When the applause died down, Commissioner Genet stepped away from the lectern. And then, after the briefest pause, Octavia herself stepped forward and took the commissioner's place.

There she stood, as beautiful as ever. Her light brown hair was swept up into a bun shape. She wore subtle makeup and a flesh-colored sheen on her lips. She wore a sexless blue Accord smock, but somehow it drew attention to her slim neck and the swell of her bust.

This should have caused outrage around the Accord. Earth females never allowed breast supports to constrain them. Breast supports were the epitome of pre-Accord male oppression. But Octavia was from a different culture. She could dress however she pleased.

And just as on the rainy rooftop in AON sub-territory Hong Kong two months ago, I was excited by the sight of her. I knew that a shape-shifting monster lay beneath the flawless skin. But I also remembered her waist in my hands and her lips whispering in my ear.

'I am,' Octavia said, her voice echoing on the Steps to Equity, 'deeply honored by Commissioner Genet's words. Let me assure the people of the Accord that I will honor my new role and work to ensure that Accord values are not only upheld by the peoples of Earth but also by my people from the planet Rome. And so, for the first time, I say to you, the new greeting of the Accord of Nations.' She paused, smiled, and said, 'T.E.I.D. Tolerance, equality, and intra-galactic diversity.'

Octavia lowered her glittering eyes, then turned her beautiful face and her irresistible smile to the camera and the audience of billions.

'For you,' she said. 'For you.'

And then I felt the strangest sensation. Octavia seemed to gaze from the screen directly at me—here in my cell in the Toxicity section of the brig at AONNB Schumer.

Then, as if to confirm my thoughts, she winked. Her left eye slowly closed, her long eyelashes swept down and up again, like a beautiful fan. No, It wasn't a nervous tic. It was a wink. An actual wink! Nobody had dared wink in living memory. Winks were a dangerous form of sexual harassment. Every school-age Accord member knew it.

Then Octavia smiled into the camera, and her voice spoke in my mind.

'See, Alex. It's happening. I'm taking control without a shot being fired. And your government is helping me bring about its own demise, just as

I said it would. All in the name of tolerance. So, you're too late, my darling. All your heroics were for nothing.'

She touched her hair and smiled, revealing perfect, even teeth, and watched me with one eyebrow raised.

I got up from the bunk, walked to the cell door and pounded on it until the slot opened.

Corporal Tarrant's eyes appeared.

'How can I change the channel?' I said.

'You can't.'

'Then, switch it off. I've seen enough.'

Corporal Tarrant's eyes crinkled at the corners.

'Can't do that, Burns, and we can't turn down the volume either.'

'Does Navy Spirt know you're torturing inmates with noise?'

'Navy Spirit recommended it, Lieutenant.'

I gave the door a punch. The crinkles deepened either side of Corporal Tarrant's eyes.

'This is how it's going to be now, Burns. It's never going away and you're never going to get out. Your days of othering visitors are over.'

4

Two days before my court-martial, a visitor came to my cell.

It was eight-thirty in the morning, just after the breakfast of soy milk and kale. The Unity TV 24-hour news was still blaring away. The other screen still displayed the live Oppression Hierarchy.

Overnight, the Oppression Hierarchy rankings had changed. The group for LBT women had dropped two places. The reason: an LBT actress had benefited from unearned privilege. She was cast in the role of Octavia in the upcoming mini-series, 'Intra-galactic Diversity,' which would screen on Unity TV Entertainment.

Meanwhile, in other news, the Goths had made another 'visit' to the Accord, this time in AONNS Harmony, sub-territory California, my old base. During their visit, the Goths had once again displayed their strong culture, by knocking down several base personnel, placing a huge paw on their chests, and sniffing them, which was obviously a form of greeting. Security cameras captured footage of the enormous creatures raging along Navy Way, snuffling at each building's entrance, apparently hunting for something.

Or someone.

After watching the story, I couldn't help but wonder what the Goths were doing. Their connection to both AONT sub-territory Hong Kong and the navy base in AON sub-territory California was a single person: me. But why would they hunt for me? Why was I the object of so much rampaging and snuffling and gouging and knocking down of personnel?

Suddenly, an alarm sounded. The volume on the TV dropped and the slot in the door slid open. Corporal Tarrant's eyes were there.

'Get up, Burns. They're coming.'

'Who's coming?'

'Shut it. Face the window. Put your hands behind your back.'

There was that command again.

I stood up and faced the window. The MAs came in, handcuffed me, and added a manacle that tethered me to the wall. They left me looking through the tiny window at the sky and at the teardrop-shaped alien craft hovering high in the clouds.

Out in the passageway, footsteps approached—several pairs, moving fast with one set distinct among the clop of the rest. The footsteps stopped outside the cell door. The MAs called out 'T.E.I.D.' Then the distinctive steps came inside and clipped up behind me.

'Turn around, Burns,' said Corporal Tarrant. 'No sudden moves.'

So, I shuffled around until I faced the door.

'Hello, Lieutenant,' said Captain Odilli of Navy Spirit.

This was not going to end well.

5

I hadn't seen Captain Odilli since the debriefing room on AONNS Accord Values in the sea south of AON sub territory Hong Kong—just before the incident with Octavia at the harbor's edge.

Her head only reached high as my shoulders, but the thick captain's epaulets, and the large Navy Spirit crest swelled her presence. She didn't smile, but one corner of her mouth curled up as if she enjoyed the sight of me in a prison uniform.

'We're going to talk about your court-martial,' she said.

Behind Captain Odilli stood three other personnel. Two of them wore AONN MA seagoing patches, which made them different to the usual land-based MAs. Their appearance was typical: their arms almost burst from their shirt sleeves; their necks swelled as wide as their jaws; they waddled instead of walked; and their faces radiated hostility. They stood either side of

Captain Odilli, glowering at me while clenching and unclenching their fists.

I stole a glance at their hips to determine their sex, or what their sex might have been, once upon a time. It wasn't idle curiosity. I wanted to know how hard they could hit me. Both of them saw me looking and clenched their fists even harder.

Captain Odilli watched me, her mouth a smirk. 'You don't need to know their names, Burns. Just call them Lieutenant Stunning and Corporal Brave. Stunning and Brave—that's all you need to know.'

I made no reply.

'And this,' said Captain Odilli, waving a hand at the smaller figure to her right, 'is Lieutenant Ricci.'

Lieutenant Ricci seemed to identify as a female. She stood about five-seven with her dark hair cut short, like every other female officer—but with a difference. Her hair was thick on top and not shaved on the sides. She had brushed it forward to create wispy curls in front of her ears. She resembled a pixie—a pixie forced to dress in a Navy Working Uniform and boots. A pixie! No doubt, she would hate the comparison if she knew about it. Pixies and other characters from pre-Accord-era children's books were banned because they promoted belief in superstitions. When Lieutenant Ricci she saw me looking, her face flamed.

'Now listen, Burns,' said Captain Odilli. 'What I'm about to say might even be of benefit to you.

It might be an opportunity for you, but only if you're willing to cooperate with us. If you cooperate, allowances can be made.'

'Allowances, sir?' I said, using the traditional pronoun. Once, I would have taken care to use 'per' or 'zer,' or whatever Captain Odilli had chosen for that particular week, but those days were over — and to my surprise, she didn't seem to mind.

'Yes, allowances, Burns. Instead of spending the rest of your life in a Navy brig, you might receive a shorter sentence. Say, twenty years, instead of sixty or eighty.'

I said nothing. I had already guessed what my 'cooperation' would entail.

'First, you must plead guilty to the one hundred and forty code violations you made in AON sub-territory Hong Kong. No bargaining. No concessions. Second, you must make a public statement, a confession that you will read aloud at the court-martial. You must make no mention of invasion or use the word 'alien.' You will say that your actions occurred when you were non-sanity-abled because of the stresses of your mission to the Roman Friend Ship.'

'That's it? Nothing more?'

'No, there's one more thing.'

'And what's that?'

'You must make a gesture of contrition.'

'A gesture?'

'It's nothing too unusual for you, Burns. Given your year of birth, I'm surprised you haven't undergone this procedure already.'

'What concession?'

'You must apply to Navy Spirit for gender reassignment.'

Her eyebrow rose. I kept my face blank. I ignored the tiny snorts of Stunning and Brave and whatever expression Lieutenant Ricci wore.

'You can even go straight to the reassignment surgery today. Then it will be done.'

I said nothing, and kept my face a stony blank.

'It isn't open for negotiation, Burns. You either accept the terms and get out of prison in twenty years or you stay toxically male and die in AONNB Jenner. Well?'

'No.'

'I see. You need persuading.'

She glanced over her left shoulder. Corporal Brave nodded. She brought her hands around from behind her back, stepped around the captain, and waddled across the cell, massaging her right fist into her left palm. Without stopping, she drew back the fist and swung it into my prison NWU, just above where a belt buckle would normally be.

'Ooh,' said Corporal Brave, resettling the knuckleduster. 'You're harder than most, Lieutenant. I like that.'

'I don't think I heard you, Burns,' said Captain Odilli. 'What was your answer again?'

When my breath returned, I said, 'No. I'm not changing genders, and I won't alter my story. I know what I saw in AON sub-territory Hong

Kong, and I heard what Admiral Octavia told me about her plans She used the word invasion. Not integration. Not harmony. Not inclusivity. Invasion.'

Captain Odilli pointed at Lieutenant Stunning, who stepped forward to join Corporal Brave.

'Your toxicity is speaking for you again, Burns. I thought for a moment you said no.'

Lieutenant Stunning stepped behind me, put an arm around my neck, and held me in a lock while Corporal Brave rained punches on my stomach, face, and groin.

Meanwhile, Lieutenant Stunning, her chin resting on my shoulder, kept up a commentary while he comrade's fists flew.

'How's that privilege now, huh?' she or he whispered to the back of my ear. 'How's the privilege now?'

Fortunately, the punches weren't earth shattering.

When Lieutenant Stunning and Corporal Brave stood back and massaged their fingers, Captain Odilli said, 'What's that, Burns? I didn't hear you.'

By this time, blood drops fell from my nose to the blue tiles.

'Let me out of these handcuffs and I'll show these two Accord members all about the words stunning and brave.'

Captain Odilli smiled.

'Hold him again.'

She walked forward till she was a foot away

from my face.

'You can't win, Burns. Don't even imagine that you can. The prosecuting JAN lawyer for the court-martial will be Captain Diana Nolan. She is best in the military. She's from a family that can trace its line back to actual pre-Accord revolutionaries—all the way back to Ariel Hoskins. Navy Spirit chose her for that reason, as a way of demonstrating the Accord's ascendancy over traitors. Captain Nolan will destroy you, Burns. She'll destroy you and your case in front of the entire Accord. Did I tell you the court-martial will be broadcast on Unity TV?'

I made no reply.

'Then, after you're locked away in AONNB Jenner, we'll still find extra ways to punish you. These meetings with Lieutenant Brave and Corporal Stunning might continue. We can schedule them until you die or go mad. That's what you're facing, Burns. Fifty years in AONNB Jenner at least. It's a fate worse than death.'

She turned around and took two steps towards the cell door. The prison MAs waited on the outside, standing at attention. At the doorway, Captain Odilli said, 'You're being transported to AONNB Holder tomorrow. You have twenty-four hours to change your mind.'

She stepped through the door. Then she came back.

'There's one thing more, Burns. Not that it matters to your sentence, but I'm curious about it.'

I kept quiet.

'Tell me why,' she said. 'Why did you do it?'

'As I told you, Captain, Octavia is an invader, not a friend.'

'That's not what I mean. I mean, why you? What made you think you had to be the one? Why did you think you were some kind of savior? Why bother ruining your career when the odds were so against you succeeding?'

I thought for a moment. Before Re-Orientation, everything had seemed so clear. I had wanted a mission. I had gone to the alien ship. I had heard Octavia's plans. What I did afterward in Hong Kong seemed natural. I hadn't wanted to be a savior. I just wanted to stop the invasion.

After Re-Orientation, that feeling had gone. I still thought Octavia was an enemy. I still knew the Accord was bad, but now, I was just angry. Now I just wanted to fight. If that meant fighting Octavia, so much the better, but I couldn't explain more than that. I was an angry man, a toxic male, just like the Accord said.

'Answer the Captain,' commanded either Stunning or Brave.

I looked up. They all stood watching me. Captain Odilli, Stunning, Brave, and Lieutenant Ricci.

But I said nothing. I had nothing to say.

'Did I say fifty years in AONNB Jenner?' said Captain Odilli. 'Better make it life.' And she turned and walked away, her footsteps clopping down the passageway. Stunning and Brave offered me one last smirk each and waddled to the door after the captain.

Lieutenant Ricci stayed where she was.

'Ready, Lieutenant?' Stunning called to her.

'Leave me alone with the prisoner for a moment.'

Stunning smiled and waddled out. Now, Ricci and I were alone. She took two slow steps towards me and reached into her pocket.

She's going to pull out a knuckle-duster, I thought. She wants to get in a punch of her own, to have something to brag about to her friends.

'You too, Lieutenant?' I said. 'Going to strike a blow against the patriarchy?'

Ricci said nothing. The hand came out of her pocket, but it didn't hold a knuckleduster. It held a phone. She raised it up and squared it in front of my face. The camera clicked. The flash went off.

She looked at the screen, then turned it around and held it in front of my face.

'You should look at this. You'll find it interesting.'

I kept my head down. I wouldn't give her the satisfaction. I had other things to think about, like what I would do to Stunning and Brave if I ever escaped.

'Lieutenant, did you hear me?'

She pushed the handheld in front of my face. I saw the image. It wasn't a snap of my cut eyebrows and bleeding lips, but something else: a photograph of a message written on a slip of paper. The lettering was all in capitals.

The note read, 'You are just one man, but you are not alone. We are many. At the court-martial, wait for the prosecution to speak, then follow the woman in red to freedom.' The note ended with a curious sign-off that read 'U.D.A.'

Lieutenant Ricci said, 'A disgrace, Lieutenant Burns. That's what you are.' Then she turned and walked from the cell.

The next morning, before dawn, the MAs showed up. They swung open the cell door, shouting and swearing at me to get up. Then, they handcuffed me, marched me out of AONNB Schumer, shoved me into a prison van. Then, they drove to an airfield, and put me aboard an AON Navy helicopter. Before we took off, they injected me with a drug that knocked me out.

I woke to the bleak walls of a different cell in the Accord of Nations Navy Brig Holder, fifty miles inland from the AON sub-territory California coast.

After a dark and disturbing dream.

6

I was in my childhood home — Kresta, my mother's house. The one with the blue walls.

My father, Cal was there. He and Kresta talked in the kitchen. I was in the next room with my toys, the navy battle ship Cal gave me. I had the ship patrolling the room. The talk in the kitchen grew louder.

'Alex doesn't need it, Kresta,' said Cal. 'He's six. It's obvious he's made his choice.'

'But you know how it goes,' said my mother. 'Nothing's obvious until the Accord says it is. Did you read the letter? They're very specific.'

'Alex wants to be a male, not female. He's not like other kids.'

'You don't know what he wants.'

'He told me, and it's clear he's male. He only plays with the dinosaur toys and toy ships. Dinosaurs and toy ships, Kresta. That's what he likes. He's fascinated by them. He'd play with toy guns, too, if they were legal. That's how male he is. Dinosaurs, guns, toy ships—what more evidence do you need that the kid is

a male?'

'We have to stop using "He," said Kresta. 'The letter from the Accord says we have to use "They" until he decides his own pronouns.'

'He likes the old pronouns, the traditional ones. He, him, his. He likes being male. He likes the way he was born. He's made his choice. He wants to be a boy. He wants to grow up to be a male. I don't care what the Accord says.'

'Read the letter again, Cal. Under the new quota, too many male children were born in Alex's birth year. The Accord says it's about maintaining diversity. The AONT USA population is forty percent male, and that's too high. Too many males and the Accord's harmony is threatened by male toxicity. It's at risk of reverting to pre-Accord era values.'

'He's not changing.'

'You weren't listening. It's not about what he wants. It's what the Accord says must happen.'

'No. The kid is male and he's staying male because he wants to stay male.'

'I don't want him to change either, Cal. I just want him to be happy. But in the end, it's not up to any of us. It never is. It's what the Accord wants.'

'I'm not going to ruin to his future, Kresta.'

'His future, Cal? His future? If he's going to have any chance of living a normal life, let alone a successful life, we've got to do what the Accord says.'

'Alex is different.'

'It happens all the time, Cal—all the time, in every city and every town, all over the Accord, as you well know.'

'It doesn't happen to my son—our son.'

'Don't call him "son." Call him "Accord member," Cal.'

'Call him "son," Kresta.'

'Are you sure this isn't about you, Cal?' Kresta said. 'Are you sure it's really about Alex, and not about your pre-Accord family? The stories your father told you?'

'They're not stories.'

'They're not facts, either.'

'I don't care. Alex is staying a male child, and he'll grow up to be a male adult. It's his right.'

'His right? His right, Cal? What rights do people have in the Accord? He doesn't have a choice. Neither do we. Dr. Iqbal says they want to see Alex next week about the conversion. It's not up to us.'

'No. No conversions—not for our son.'

'Careful, Cal. You know what can happen if you speak too loudly.'

'You're as skeptical about the Accord as I am, Kresta. Don't deny it. You always were—even more than me. What's changed your mind?'

'I'm just being realistic, Cal. No matter what we want for Alex, we have to be realistic about the world and what it takes to live in it. The Accord is not going away anytime soon. If we don't cooperate, it will force Alex to change.'

'He's our son, Kresta. We owe him the chance to decide for himself, to be himself, to be who he is meant to me.'

'You're not listening, Cal. We live in the Accord, not in your daydreams. I know we both want the best *for Alex, but there's only one way he can have a future.'*

7

Two days later, at nine-thirty in the morning, after the prisoners had recited the Accord pledge, my cell door at AONNB Holder clanged open and no less than five MAs stood outside. Two held stun guns; one stood with a handheld; two held handcuffs and manacles. One threw a blue, camouflage NWU at me, both jacket and pants.

'Put them on,' he said.

'Why? Am I going into combat?'

'Just put them on, Burns.'

'The Navy Spirit Code is clear,' I said. 'It states that personnel must wear service dress uniforms at courts-martial, not work uniforms, not battle dress uniforms. Even you should know that, Sergeant.'

'Courts-martial? Don't you mean "court-martials?"'

'That's the way you say it.'

'Insistence on pre-Accord grammar is an oppressive act, Burns. It's also another code violation—as you should know.'

'Add it to the list, Sergeant.'

The MA sergeant turned to one of the armed men beside me. 'Corporal,' he said. 'Like we discussed.'

'Yes, sir. Like we discussed.' The corporal unholstered a green stun gun.

'Last chance, Burns,' said the sergeant.

I stood up and took off the prison smock, and pulled on the NWU. I didn't mind. I wore the black boots and the blue camouflage jacket and pants almost every day. I ate, studied, worked, and trained in them. I'd worn them on the mission to Octavia's ship. I just didn't want to give the MAs the impression I would co-operate with them.

Once I was ready, the MAs told me to hold out my hands. They clipped on the cuffs, then told me to stand still while they applied manacles to my feet. Then they linked the cuffs and the manacles with a light chain.

Once they'd trussed me up, the lead MA turned to someone I couldn't see. 'All right,' he said. 'The prisoner is ready.'

In walked a Navy Spirit officer. She had the usual short hair, the usual razor-sharp side part, the blue smock. She also carried a document satchel, which she opened. Then, she took out a pen and clipboard.

'Captain Odilli asks if you've changed your mind. Say the word and we'll get the message over to Captain Toth.'

'Who is Captain Toth?'

'He's from JAN.'

JAN stood for Judges Advocate Navy, the section that handled the defense of sailors in courts-martial.

'Have you changed your mind, Burns?'

'Not a chance,' I said.

'I'll give you one more opportunity, Lieutenant. Say yes. It could save you decades of jail time, maybe more. Captain Toth's a competent lawyer.'

'Did he volunteer for my case or was he ordered?'

'No one is stupid enough to volunteer for your case, Burns.'

'It's still no,' I said. 'Make sure Captain Odilli hears.'

'She'll know,' the Navy Spirit officer said. She nodded to the MA sergeant, who saluted and turned back to me.

'Let's go, Burns. The whole Accord is waiting for you.'

We walked in a procession out of the cell. The four MAs walked either side of me like motorcycle outriders. The guy with the handheld walked backward in front of us, keeping the lens on the prisoner.

This strange procession passed through the various buzzing doors, clunking locks and beneath the posters reading 'Tolerance, equality, diversity,' and new banners reading 'T.E.I.D.'

We passed by the signs posted around every AON Navy base: signs such as, 'Check your privilege at the door,' 'Words are weapons,' 'Feelings are facts,' 'All cultures are equal,' 'Truth is a construct of the oppressive pre-Accord West,' and 'Pre-Accord-descended lives don't matter.'

Finally, just before the exit, a large poster read, 'There are no such things as aliens. There is only diversity and greater diversity.'

The exit door buzzed and clunked open. Light and cold air surged in. The MA with the handheld shivered as he backed outside. I squinted at the daylight and followed him into the cool air.

And the commotion.

From overhead came the thump of helicopters. Along the brig's walls, armed MAs patrolled. Each carried a rifle, the same PQ47 rifles carried by the prison MAs at AONNB Schumer.

In the distance, more MAs held back a crowd of civilians. Behind them, several Unity TV vans pointed their satellite dishes north, south, and east. And above everything, a net of Roman teardrop craft hovered below the clouds like giant gray raindrops.

Ahead of us, I saw our destination, the AON Navy aircraft hangar. By the size of it, the hangar usually sheltered the large Oneness cargo planes —the planes used to resupply Navy bases around the Accord, which resupplied the AONN ships on their various goodwill missions.

Today, the hangar would be a courtroom.

The procession moved off. We trudged and clanked over the blacktop and stopped in front of a door near the hangar's northern end. Eight more MAs waited there, four with sidearms, four with PQ47 rifles, all with holsters in which stun guns waited. Three Judges Advocate Navy personnel stood waiting in dark blue JAN smocks. One wore an earpiece. Another held up a camera. The third stood at the entrance, a hand on the door lever.

'T.E.I.D.,' said the senior MA and saluted the JAN officer. Her name patch read CAPT AL SARARI.

'T.E.I.D,' Sergeant, said Captain Al Sarari. 'Here's the procedure: You wait two minutes for my order. Then you go in.' The captain's face hid beneath the peak of her cap, but she soon raised her chin to inspect me. Her expression said she would like to murder me in my manacles. We looked at each other a moment, then she touched the earpiece and turned away.

'Copy that,' she said into the air, and turned to the MAs. 'Sergeant,' she said.

'Sir?'

'Now!'

The MAs on either side of me stiffened. They stood to their full height, which was about as high as my neck. The JAN officer at the entrance pulled the lever and the door hinges creaked. Warm air flowed out, followed by the murmuring of many voices. The murmurs faded to whispers and what sounded like the creaking of many seats.

'Move!' said the MA to my left.

The manacles rattled as we shuffled through the door and into the hangar.

There were fifteen minutes to go before the mayhem.

8

On the hangar's front wall was the largest Accord flag I'd ever seen. The dove and the rainbow stood as high as two people. The flag itself could cover a tennis court. It left no room for any other flags—not even the Accord of Nations Navy flag, which sulked on a side wall.

The hangar was swollen with people. There must have been two thousand people inside, all dressed in Accord smocks colored blue, green, and rainbow, all sitting on rows of seats so that each row looked like a squashed rainbow itself. The air was thick with whispers and murmurs. The odor of many bodies fed on tofu and kale was strong and sour.

At the back of the hangar a bank of TV cameras swiveled on their tripods. As I entered, the cameras swung left and right, scanning the crowd. At least two aimed their lenses at me. Beside them, Unity TV reporters mouthed words into headsets.

Surrounded by my escort, I shuffled across the gray concrete floor. The manacles rattled in the silence, and the heavy cloth of my NWU rustled way too loudly. No one booed or gasped, but several people coughed, and in every row of seats, people strained their necks for a better look.

The MAs led me to a bench facing the flag. A JAN officer in a blue smock sat behind it. His name patch read CAPT TOTH. My defense counsel. The MAs pushed me down into a seat, then swaggered away to the edge of the hangar. Then, they turned and glared at me, their hands on their holsters.

'Morning, Lieutenant,' said Captain Toth, as if we already knew each other, as if we'd already met to discuss my case.

'How long will this take?'

'Not now, Lieutenant,' he whispered. 'We can talk during the recess.'

'But how long?'

He sat back and looked at me. 'First of all,' he said. 'It's "sir," and secondly, I don't like your attitude, Lieutenant. If I were you, I'd showing a little more respect and a lot more remorse. I was told about you. They said your mind was affected by what happened in AON sub-territory Hong Kong, but they didn't tell me how much. Now, I can see for myself. Let me tell you something. This is not a pleasant situation for me either, Lieutenant. You think I like this? Do you think I want to be the guy defending you?'

On a raised bench beneath the flag sat a row of

twelve Navy captains. Usually, twelve captains sat only when a Navy ship had been lost, but Admiral Zhou must have ruled that for my case, the full complement was necessary.

Some famous faces graced the bench. I saw Captain Jarndyce, known throughout the service for her daring exploit of running down a boatload of hostile anti-vegans trying to flee AONT USA by sea to AONI Haiti.

I also saw Captain Abbasi, whose example inspired a generation of captains for his dedication to achieving Oppression Hierarchy representation on his ship, the AONNS Ocasio-Cortis. The entire five thousand sea-people aboard had been recruited in exact proportion to the Oppression Hierarchy's weighting for them.

However, the AONNS Ocasio-Cortis sank just one week into its voyage. Its engines failed in the AONO Pacific and waves tossed it onto a reef near the AON island of Progress, which in the pre-Accord had been called Guam. The incident report concluded that the crew was short on engineers. Normally, the loss of an aircraft carrier such as the Ocasio-Cortis would result in a court-martial for Captain Abbasi. However, the Navy made a special exemption because achieving diversity was considered a higher value than achieving seaworthy competence.

I also saw Captain Paine, my former commanding officer at AONS Harmony. Zee's lip's were pursed. Zee would never forgive me for scuttling her chance of promotion to admiral.

Beside Captain Paine sat Captain Odilli of Navy Spirit, a smirk on her face as usual. She was no doubt savoring the thought of my gender reassignment surgery in AONNB Jenner and the beatings from Lieutenant Stunning and Corporal Brave.

Captain Abbasi pressed a button on the bench. A gentle chime sounded to bring the court-martial to order. Chimes had replaced the previous practice of raising a wooden gavel and hitting a small wooden block. This was for the usual reasons: gavels striking blocks evoked painful cultural memories of pre-Accord Western oppression.

The chime sounded three times, and the hangar quietened down until there was no sound except the rasp of hemp smocks. Captain Abbasi switched on a microphone and said, 'This court-martial will now begin,' but before he could continue, a commotion broke out at the back of the hangar. The entire audience rose from its feet and stood as three people made their way down the central aisle.

Captain Toth nudged me to stand. I soon saw the reason. The three people entering were Admiral Khan, and no less than two Accord Commissioners: Commissioner Daniel Genet and Commissioner Rowena Martin.

Once the three VIPs sat down and the crowd had settled, Captain Abbasi cleared his throat and spoke. He said that the court-martial was convened under AON Navy regulations to hear the charges against Lieutenant Alexander Burns (O-3). Lieutenant Burns was accused of one hundred and forty Navy Spirit Code violations. He then called on the prosecuting JAN officer, Captain Diana Nolan to name the charges.

Until this moment, the proceedings had seemed surreal. It hadn't been a week since the electrodes were pulled from my head. Now, I was in a hangar of two thousand people and subject to the gaze of Accord TV viewers from AONT Greenland to AONT New Zealand. My mind was unfocused, disbelieving, and charged with directionless anger.

But when Captain Nolan stood, my attention snapped into focus. It concentrated on her and nobody else.

She rose from the bench on the opposite side of the aisle. She walked with long strides into the space between the row of captains and the rest of us. She wore the dark blue smock and sexless blue pants of the Judges Advocates Navy, but on her the pants behaved differently to the way they behaved on most people. On most people, they hung like floppy bags, hiding every body part, but on Captain Nolan the uniform lengthened her legs, highlighted her slim waist, and suggested a bust.

The result was that Captain Nolan drew the hated male gaze like a magnet. Not just mine, either. Beside me, Captain Toth gawped and every male MA's head followed her like an automatic laser sight.

'Honorable Captains of the Accord of Nations Navy,' she said to the bench. 'It is my unpleasant but necessary duty to read out the Navy Spirit Code violations committed by Lieutenant Alexander Burns.'

'Please proceed,' said Captain Abbasi.

I didn't listen. I watched Captain Nolan instead. I couldn't help but wonder why someone so beautiful would want to put me in prison for decades; and why someone so intelligent could believe all the Accord lies.

And I thought that way right up to the point when she walked up to me and leaned down till her face was inches from mine. As she spoke about one of my code violations or another, she reached up and brushed an imaginary strand of hair from her face. The gesture cooled the heat of her animosity. But not for long. The temperature soon rose.

'It's unfortunate,' Captain Nolan said, 'that someone to whom the Accord and its Navy have given so many opportunities, should abuse those opportunities so much.' She mouthed these words with such contempt, it seemed for a moment she was talking about someone else, but then she stood in front of me and raised one long arm in its baggy sleeve to point at me. 'There,' she said, 'there is the living example of privilege inherited from the pre-Accord West, an example that we must punish to the limit of the Navy Spirit Code.'

Then Captain Abbasi said, 'Captain Nolan,

proceed to the evidence of the first code violation.' He frowned at his notes. 'The code violation of "Intimidating a superior officer with his oppressive male height."'

Captain Nolan nodded gravely.

'Certainly, zeer,' she said, and walked to her bench where she rifled through some notes. Then, she turned once again to the captains and opened her mouth to speak. But, before she could utter a sound, the hangar door swung open and clanged into the wall. Everyone turned to look at it and the bright rectangle of sunlight.

The first stage of the pandemonium had begun.

9

Two thousand faces turned to the door.

A masked gunman, dressed in a khaki battle dress uniform, stepped inside. He held a PQ47 rifle to his chin and swung the muzzle left and right, shouting at the captains on the bench to get down.

More gunmen followed. They came through the door, one after the other, all with PQ47 rifles raised and swinging. All of them shouted, 'Get down! Get down!' and all wore the same plain khaki battle dress, not the usual green and brown pattern worn by the AON Army.

It was an astonishing sight. Raids like this did not happen in the Accord, not even from climate change deniers—and this was a raid inside a guarded Naval base. All of which raised an obvious question: How had they gotten past the MAs?

'What's going on?' demanded Captain Nolan. She was still standing at the head of the gallery, commanding and magnificent in her floppy smock. 'What do you think you're doing?' she shouted at the twenty, now thirty gunmen. 'This is a naval court. Get out. Now!'

But they did not get out.

Instead, one of them pointed his PQ47 at her. 'You too, Captain,' he shouted, but Captain Nolan didn't move—not until the gunman pushed the muzzle into her smock and forced her back to the prosecutor's bench.

Meanwhile, more armed personnel entered the hangar through the back entrance. Same khaki masks; same old-fashioned khaki uniforms. They ranged along the walls with their PQ47s threatening the panicked audience, shouting at them to get down. The audience was quick to obey, ducking beneath the backs of the seats in front of them.

'Who are they?' Captain Toth whispered.

'How should I know, Captain?' I replied.

Once the shrieking audience was silenced by threats and shoves, and one epic burst of gunfire into the hangar's roof, the stage was set for their next move.

And then it happened. With everyone waiting, a woman in a cap and red mask stepped through the hangar's forward door. She carried a pistol instead of a rifle, an AONN Empathy, a point three-eight caliber officer's weapon. She walked straight across the concrete following the same line I had walked fifteen minutes before and then stood in front of me and Captain Toth.

'I know that walk,' wailed Captain Odilli from the bench. 'I know who that is.'

Under her red mask, the woman shouted, 'Shut her up.' Then she called to one of the gunmen. He brought over a set of bolt cutters. 'Stand up, Lieutenant,' she said.

'I advise you not to have anything to do with these people, Lieutenant,' said Captain Toth.

'Shut up,' said the woman. 'Move it, Lieutenant.'

I clanked to my feet and the guy cut the manacles at my waist, hands, and feet. The chains clattered to the concrete floor.

'Thanks,' I said.

'You read the note?' the woman said.

'Yes.'

'You see this?' she tugged at her red neckcloth.

'Yes.'

'Then you know who I am. I'll explain about the rest later. For now, we better get going. Come with me.'

'Sorry, Lieutenant,' I said. 'I'm not going.'

'You what?'

'I'm not going with you.'

'You're not serious. We just busted in here for you.'

'Sorry, Lieutenant, I'm not going anywhere.'

She blinked over the red mask.

'Why? Because of your councillor here? Don't be stupid. This is your chance. We're offering you freedom.'

'I'm not leaving, Lieutenant. Not yet.'

Now her forehead creased as she blinked even more. She looked at the concrete floor, then at the gunmen ranged around the hangar, and the people cowering in their seats. From outside, a three-toned chime sounded.

'Your mind is more damaged than we were told, Lieutenant.'

'I don't know anything about that.'

'Trust us. We're on your side. We're against the Accord, the same as you. We're a resistance movement.'

'How did you get inside the brig?'

'What?'

'How did you do it? How did you get inside?'

'I'll explain later. The short answer is that the MAs were called away to some disturbance, but for now we've got to move before they get back.'

'No. How did you get inside this brig? What kind of disturbance? How did you know it would happen?'

'There's no time, Lieutenant?'

'Make some. Show you're serious and not some Accord ruse for the cameras?'

'You have to trust us, Lieutenant.'

'Show me you're serious.'

'How?'

I looked at the twelve captains cringing in front of the gun muzzles.

'Shoot Captain Abbasi,' I said. 'Call him by his real gender first. Then shoot him.'

'Shoot Captain Abbasi?' Lieutenant Ricci repeated. 'Is that all? Why don't we shoot

Captain Nolan, too?' she taunted. 'Or how about Commissioner Genet, say? We'd have to be serious to do that, right?'

'Right. Commissioner Genet would be even better.'

She didn't move.

'Well, Lieutenant Ricci,' I said. 'What are you waiting for?'

One of the gunmen came over.

'What's the hold-up?'

'He doesn't believe us. He wants proof.'

'What proof?'

'Proof, Adams. Proof. You've heard the word before.'

'So give it to him.'

Lieutenant Ricci turned around.

'Corporal Nevis!' she yelled toward the bench.

'Yes, Lieutenant,' answered Corporal Nevis, standing behind the row of captains.

'Shoot Captain Abbasi.'

'What?' said the corporal.

'You heard me. Shoot Captain Abbasi.'

'Kill him?' said the corporal.

'You just presumed the captain's gender,' said Lieutenant Ricci. 'You're halfway there. Now shoot.'

'Shoot him where? To kill?'

'In the leg.'

The corporal took a step back and raised his rifle. Captain Abbasi shriveled. 'Please,' he said. 'No!'

'Do it,' said Lieutenant Ricci. 'Do it, now!'

The corporal closed one eye and dug his chin into the stock.

Everyone waited. The corporal nodded to himself, holding an internal conversation in his mind, persuading himself to pull the trigger.

And then it happened: the second bizarre event of the morning.

Before Corporal Nevis could fire his weapon at Captain Abbasi, the hangar swung open a second time and clanged into the hangar wall all over again.

The corporal raised his chin from the rifle. Captain Abbasi took his hands away from his head and his groin. Lieutenant Ricci turned away from me to look at the door. So did the guy she called Adams. What was going on? Was it the MAs? Would flash-bangs and tear gas come bouncing in, followed by yet another entrance of swinging weapons?

And then, as if things weren't strange enough, they soon turned stranger than anyone could imagine.

A great roar surged through the doorway and echoed around the hangar.

At the bench, Captain Abbasi flinched. The rest of the captains ducked.

'What's going on?' said Captain Toth somewhere beside me.

'No idea,' I said, but that wasn't exactly true.

I watched the door and the reactions of the gunmen. They backed away, slowly at first, then quickly, before they gave up, turned and ran to the far side of the hangar beneath the AON Navy flag.

Then, the door's rectangle of light was blocked from top jamb to threshold with dark, shimmering fur, like the edge of a great dark pine forest had been shoved against the hangar's outside walls.

And a second growl sounded so loud and close, that the whimpering from the audience stopped completely and for a moment the only sound was of someone being voluminously sick.

10

The growl was not like a lion's roar. It was more like a bear's growl: a long, throaty bass note that rattled the rivets in the metal walls. And then things got worse. A thick stench wafted through across the concrete, an intense odor of rotten meat, wet fur, and sewage.

Then the doorway flashed with light as the furry hide blocking it moved away. Moments later, a dark beast's head pushed through, followed by huge shoulders too wide for the jambs. Shaggy forelimbs stretched forward and fruit-knifed-sized claws slid out from massive paws and gouged furrows in the concrete.

The whole shaggy mass jerked one way, then the other, the creature's head threw itself from side to side, buckling the door jambs. Then, with one shocking burst of strength, the creature pulled itself through the door and into the hangar.

Once inside, it swung its head left and right,

just as the gunmen had done with their rifles. Then, it stood on its hind legs, raised its shaggy bulk to twice the height of the cowering MAs, and sniffed the air, the great black flukes of its nostrils flaring outward with each intake of breath.

At the doorway, another monster scratched and clawed at the concrete floor, dragging itself through the buckling doorjambs. Once inside the hangar, it lumbered up beside the first creature, and rose on its hind limbs, revealing a vast fur-covered underside, and enormous male genitalia. Then it tossed its snout, snuffling at the fetid air. Behind it, a third creature writhed at the door.

'The visitors from the news,' said Ricci. 'What are they doing here?'

'How should I know?' said the guy beside her.

'But what are they doing here?' said Ricci again. 'And how did they get in?'

'May the Accord values protect us,' said Captain Toth.

Behind us, the two thousand Accord members found themselves caught between Accord values and their own instincts. They wanted to be tolerant and inclusive. But they also wanted to run for their lives. They stood up but stayed put. They put their hands over their mouths but then pulled them down. Some pulled their rainbow smocks over their heads, as if the colors and symbols of the Accord alone could protect them and save them from othering anybody.

But when the two Goths dropped to their four

giant, shaggy limbs and charged, everything changed.

The crowd panicked. People scrambled over their seats and their fellow Accord members. They pushed and shoved their way to the aisles, and climbed over each other to reach the back of the hangar. There was no time for Accord values any more.

Monsters were among them.

At the front bench, the panel of captains cowered. Captain Abbasi and Captain Paine clutched each other, their faces rippled by fear. Captain Odilli clung to the sleeve of the gunman behind her, who clutched his weapon. The rest hid themselves under the bench. None of these esteemed captains, the Navy's finest leaders, could utter a word as the beasts raged through the crowd, tossing Accord members into the air like shreds of smocks in the wind.

I watched the chaos from the defendant's bench, trying to stay calm. If I hadn't seen the Goths two months earlier on Octavia's ship, I might have panicked like the rest. Instead, the Goths gave me an idea. This raid was my chance to escape—a genuine chance, not the fake escape offered by Lieutenant Ricci and her resistance group.

But my mind was full of questions. Could I get out of the hangar? Could I slip past the MA patrols? How would I get over the walls? Would the Goths provide a big enough distraction? What about the Unity TV helicopters? And if I escaped both the Navy and the Accord, what then?

Don't think too much, I told myself. Don't think too much or you won't do anything at all. Especially, don't think the thought that's growing in your mind.

The thought that the Goths hadn't just shown up to create chaos.

They were hunting for someone.

And I began to suspect who that someone might be.

11

But I couldn't leave just yet.

I turned to Lieutenant Ricci.

'Get under the bench.'

'What?'

'Get under the bench. Fast as you can. Or they'll claw you in half.'

She didn't move, so I stepped forward, grabbed her shoulders, and pushed her down. In doing so, I broke a Navy Spirit Code violation as serious as misgendering an Accord commissioner, but it saved Lieutenant Ricci from a dose to true diversity. No sooner had I finished pushing her under the bench when a Goth skidded by, its yellow claws spraying chips of concrete.

Lieutenant Ricci's hand was at her throat.

'That's why,' I said.

I turned to Captain Toth. 'Now you, Captain. Under the bench.'

'It's "No, sir," Lieutenant.'

'Just get under the bench, sir.'

'No, Lieutenant. These are our intra-galactic friends. They're behaving this way because, at some point, we have othered them. It's our fault. If we could dialogue with them about Accord values, especially tolerance and inclusion, they would understand what the Accord is about and then they would stop expressing their culture in this manner.'

'Sure, sir,' I said, shoving him down. His bold talk meant nothing. Like everyone in the Accord, he was so totally indoctrinated, that he believed that Accord values would protect him from danger, like a shield. 'Stay out of sight, sir, I told him, 'or they'll tear your head off before you can say "intersectionality."'

'Lieutenant Burns, you should,' he began, but a stomach-churning scream from the back of the hangar silenced him, and he shut his mouth and sat still, like a cornered animal.

Welcome to reality, Captain.

Next, I checked for Captain Nolan. After what she said about me, she was the last person in the Accord I should have helped, but I couldn't watch the Goths tear her apart. I scanned the seats around her bench, but she wasn't there. She must have panicked with the rest of the crowd. Either that, or she'd already fallen victim to the claws and the teeth.

I scanned the hangar's mid-section. Goths smashed their way through seats and tables, and charged at Accord members, knocking them down, and pinning them with their paws. But amazingly, they didn't kill anyone like they did when fighting the Roman Marines on the Excidium. Back then, they knocked the Marines down and ripped off their armor and tore their insides out. This time they didn't want to kill their victims; they wanted to smell them.

All over the hangar, Goths tripped up fleeing humans with a swipe of their paws. Then, they pinned them to the concrete and sniffed faces, armpits, and crutches. Then, having sniffed, stomped off in pursuit of other victims.

Maybe they're searching the Accord Commissioners, I thought. Commissioners Genet and Martin were somewhere among the panicked audience. They were the most likely targets, right? But I knew this was a lie as soon as I thought it. As much as I wanted to deny it, I knew for whom they searched.

Then, as if reading my thoughts, the Goths stopped rampaging. A loud bark sounded above the growls and the mood in the hangar changed. It was like a drop in atmospheric pressure before a storm. The cavernous hangar was now silent except for hoarse breaths from the Goths and whimpers from stricken humans.

The Goths looked about, sniffing. Their ears twitched in various directions. After a few seconds, they located the originator of the bark. He stood on his hind limbs twenty yards to my right, sniffing at me so hard that he swayed with the effort. Then, he raised a paw and pointed at me and barked a second time, and what seemed like a forest of great bear heads turned from him to me. After snuffling their way through thousands of human smells, they had finally found the one scent they wanted — the object of their hunt.

Instantly, I dropped beneath the bench. Lieutenant Ricci crouched there, her red mask off, and her pixie face frowning.

'What's happening? Why have they stopped?'

'I'm going. Thanks for bolt cutters.'

'Going where?'

'Out of here.'

'You've changed your mind?'

'No. This is about the Goths. It's me they want. No one else.'

'What? Why you?'

'I'm not sure, but I can guess.'

'What are you doing to do?'

'I'm going to get out of here?'

'Where? The hangar? The base?'

'All of it.'

'But you'll never escape alone. It's madness. It's your toxic masculinity talking. You're not thinking straight.'

'Like I said, I can try.'

'Let me help you.'

'You and your resistance? No thanks. I'll get further on my own.'

'You're just one guy, Lieutenant. You know that, right?'

'So they say.'

'Then, take this.' She held out the Empathy 38

pistol.

'You keep it.'

'You don't have to fight alone, Lieutenant—not now and not against the Accord.'

'Sure,' I said, getting up. 'Stay here till they follow me out.'

'Burns, wait!' she said, but I was already walking away.

Around the hangar, the humans lined the walls, cowering like children in their colorful smocks. No one spoke. No one moved in case they caused a furry ear to twitch in their direction, or a snout twelve feet in the air to aim its black flukes at them.

They had no need to worry. Every Goth's snout was busy aiming itself at me. Every ear too. And every eye. They locked on me like lasers. The giant heads moved with every step I took. The nasal flukes flared and the dark eyes shone like moist dark plums. For the moment, the Goths remained where they stood on two legs or four. How long until one of them barked or howled and they all came running?

What a sight they were! The size of them! The claws, the teeth, the thick, shaggy fur! Monsters! —that's what they were. No invented term like visitors or intra-galactic friends, or extra-diverse beings could change the truth. They were monsters—like you always dreaded.

And now they moved. Here, a giant paw raised and padded on the concrete. There, a head descended from the height of two men to just one. They looked like a forest of giant bushes coming alive and moving out.

I made no sudden moves. I didn't want to trigger a stampede. There were things I needed, like a gun. I stepped to the bench under which the twelve captains cowered. Captain Odilli was there on her knees. There was a discarded PQ47 beside her. I reached down to grab it. She raised a protective arm, thinking I would hit her.

'T.E.D., per,' I said. 'I guess the gender reassignment surgery will have to wait.'

For a moment the fear left her face. The old smirk returned. 'You can't run away, Burns. You're in a Navy brig.'

'We'll see, Captain.' I would have said more, but I noticed the rest of the captains flinch at something behind me.

'We'll see,' I said again. Then, I picked up the rifle and turned back to the Goths. They had crept forward, stalking across the concrete, climbing over the creaking seats, their heads lowered, their eyes and snouts always on me.

I raised the rifle to my chin and backed towards the door. The Goths altered their course to follow. I drew them towards me, like hauling a net from the sea.

Twenty steps from the door, the Goths' moods changed. They picked up their pace from a creep to a walk, and then from a walk to a trot and finally to a charge. Giant shoulder joints plunged and rose beneath the shimmering fur, and massive hind quarters drove the creatures forward.

I should have felt terror. Instead, I felt an almost forgotten sensation instead: freedom. For the first time in months, I was free—free of the cold cells, the tight shackles, the rubber stick pushed between my teeth, and the warm electrodes on my temples. I was free of the orders to face the wall, to get on the floor with my hands behind my head. And for a moment, I was a free of anger and resentment. I stood on the threshold. Liberty waited just beyond. Now I had to make sure I didn't lose it ever again—not to the Accord, not to the Goths, not to Octavia.

The rifle in my hands would help.

It would have to, because I couldn't reach the door before the claws of the first Goth struck.

12

The PQ47 rifle was the standard weapon for the AON Army, the Marines, and the Navy MAs. It worked fine if you could shoot, which ruled out most people in the military.

However, a shot from a PQ47 wouldn't stop a Goth. It took at least three blasts from the heavy Roman rifles to knock one down. To a Goth, a shot from a PQ47 would be an irritation, a bug bite.

But a well-aimed shot to the right body part might cause a Goth to slow down. I raised the rifle and settled the crosshairs on a giant snout. It was soon lost amongst the mass of fur and tossing heads and I couldn't find it again.

I looked up from the sights. One giant with dark red fur pulled himself free and came bounding ahead of the rest. I brought the crosshairs onto this creature's face, then lowered and raised the muzzle in time with his plunging head. I squeezed the trigger. The rifle bucked early. The shot raised a tuft of hide. The Goth kept coming. I aimed and fired twice more, missing both times.

On the fourth shot, the Goth's snout plumed pink mist, then plunged to the concrete. The rest of him pitched forward—fur, legs, rolling belly— all of him, tumbling and skidding. The Goths behind tripped up, tumbled over, and blocked the Goths stampeding behind them. They piled up into a rolling hill of fur while their claws raked the air, scrambling for purchase.

But not all the Goths.

The rest came on, forking around the hill of their comrades. They were even more frantic to reach me, but now I had a precious few seconds of extra time.

I slung the rifle's strap over my back and ran to the doorway. Once outside, I slammed the door, then sealed it with the steel lever.

Then, to my horror, I remembered the people I had just locked inside. In my rush to get out, I had forgotten them. Should I go back? Maybe I should go back. But already, the thumping and scratching on the door had begun. There could be no going back without being captured by the Goths. I hoped I was right: that the Goths hunted only one human.

Me.

With the roars growing louder, I turned to my next move. I'd escaped the Goths for the moment, but I hadn't escaped AONNB Holder or the Accord. Any second, I expected a shot to ping on the hangar behind me, or some barking loudspeaker to order me to drop the weapon and lay on the ground with my hands behind my head—as usual.

So what to do next?

My mind raced over the options. Maybe I could climb the brig wall and escape into the forest in the west. Maybe I could steal a car and ram the gate. Maybe I could hide on the grounds and escape at night. But all these options seemed impossible and no other options came to mind— that is until I heard the thumping overhead.

I looked up. A Unity TV helicopter hovered high above the hangar. The sun glinted on the camera lens aimed from the cabin. A helicopter, I thought. A helicopter—what if I could steal a helicopter? There were two helicopters in the air, but there were also several on the ground inside the brig.

A helicopter might be the only way over the brig's high walls. But how to steal one? And how to fly it? And then, where would I go? To the forest, to the mountains, to the sea? I had too many problems to solve, too many decisions to make, and so little time. And after months inside the brig, and so much Re-Orientation, my mind was sluggish.

And that's when, in this moment of weakness, as if listening to my thoughts and waiting for its chance, a familiar voice spoke in my mind.

'Hello, Alex,' it said. 'Did you think I'd forget you?'

13

I knew that voice.

It was the same feminine voice with the same pre-Accord accent and the same tone of dry amusement.

Octavia's voice.

'Do you think I could ever forget, Alex?' The voice spoke in my head, like I was wearing earphones. 'I know you can hear me,' the voice said. 'I know you think your mind is playing tricks, but this time, it's me.'

I said nothing. I had to think about getting out.

'Why don't you answer me? They gave your mind electric shocks, Alex, but they didn't shock your tongue.'

I shook my head. I had to move away from the hangar door. I had to get undercover. Any moment, the shots would come. The loudspeaker would bark. I had no time for whatever this was.

'I know it's difficult, Alex. Take a moment. I can wait. But don't take too long. You know what's coming, don't you? You know what will happen when they break down that door. I understand, Alex. Really I do. Let me reassure you. This is not a Navy Spirit program in your brain. I'm not Captain Paine nor Captain Odilli speaking. I'm exactly who you think I am?'

I tried a new tactic. I pictured a stone wall, high and rough, the same wall I'd pictured to block out the shocks during Re-Orientation.

But none of these tactics could block the images that came welling up from my memory. Images and sensations of Octavia, her beauty, her femininity, her blue uniform glistening with raindrops on the roof of a skyscraper in Hong Kong. Her wet fingers on my cheek.

'I'm not going anywhere,' said Octavia's voice. 'I'm never going away, not from this planet, not from you.'

What do you want?

'That's better. There's no need for aggression, Alex. I am not your enemy. I like it when we're friendly together, not fighting each other.'

Well, if you want to be my friend, get out of my head. Get out of my world. Get out of my world's government. Take your soldiers, spaceships, and these Goths, and get away from this planet. Find somewhere else. This can't be the only planet out there.

'Now is not the time, Alex. "Out there" can wait. For now, you are in danger. You need my help.'

I don't need anyone's help—not yours, not the

Accord's.

'You are wrong. You will be recaptured. You will be maimed or killed. No, my dear. You need me.'

The Goths—what do they want with me?

'Good question, Alex. They might want you for many reasons. One of their priests might think he received a message from their ridiculous god. It might be because they remember you from the raid on the Excidium. The Goths aren't rational, Alex. They exist to fight. That is all. They share the same planet as we Romans, but that is where the similarity ends. They are uncivilized, not to be engaged. But there is no need to worry, Alex. I can help you. My ships are nearby. Look up at the sky. See the ships in the clouds. I will order one to descend. Just say the word.'

Back at the hangar door, the walls bulged and the deep chorus of roars swelled inside. They made me recall Octavia in the form of a building-sized monster, stomping through the rain beside the harbor in AON sub-territory Hong Kong.

'I'll take my chances,' I said.

'You have no plan. And failing to plan means planning to fail.'

'If you want to save me, why didn't you help me in prison?'

'How do you know I didn't? Why do you think they released you before they could destroy your mind completely?'

'You got me out?'

'I know you too well, Alex. You won't accept

my help—or anyone's help. You won't even accept help from *him*. But now things are different. You must trust me.'

'Him? Who is him?'

'You know who I mean.'

But I didn't.

'Why don't you just capture me yourself?' I said. 'Why don't you destroy the Goths with your ships? Why don't you knock down the walls of this brig? Why do you want me to ask?'

'You really don't know the reason?'

I said nothing.

'I want to help because you asked me, Alex, not because I coerced you. I don't want you to come to me as a prisoner. That wouldn't be a true meeting of souls. One of your philosophers said that in your pre-Accord era. You must ask me, Alex. You must ask me freely.'

'I don't need your help. I can escape these Goths. I can defeat them. I can escape the Accord too. I don't need your help or anyone else's.'

'You will lose, Alex,' the voice replied. 'Accept my offer. Accept my friendship. Accept it now before it's too late.'

Up in the sky, the black ships hovered, ready.

'Time is running out, Alex,' said Octavia's voice.

Behind me, the door hinges rattled. More growls joined the chorus.

So what to do?

'Say the word, Alex. Say it willingly. Say it now.'

No sooner had these words entered my mind when a final whomp sounded behind me. The door swung out, clanging on the hangar's outside wall. Then, a giant brown snout pushed through the opening, followed by two giant, furry limbs, preceded by long, yellow claws.

'Too late,' said Octavia's voice.

14

I turned to face the monstrosity at the door.

The Goth watched me as its claws gouged furrows in the concrete. Behind it, in shadow, the other Goths waited their turns.

They will capture you, Alex. They will claw you. They will kill you.

So what to do?

Across the brig's grounds towards the exit gate, the MAs took up positions behind cars, light towers, and small buildings. They crouched down with their faces behind the rifles. More MAs crept up behind the two AON Navy helicopters I saw earlier.

Two AON Navy helicopters.

No sooner had I thought the word 'helicopter,' when an idea formed in my mind. If I could stay ahead of the Goths and somehow avoid the MAs, I could get to a helicopter, start it up, and fly out.

It wasn't much of a plan. But my sluggish mind wouldn't give me more, and any plan was better than being clawed to shreds, or worse, captured.

But how to make it happen?

Get moving, I thought, and take it from there.

I stepped away from the hangar wall and across to a metal storage building. It provided cover from the MAs—at least for the moment. That left the other problem: the massive Goth dragging its bulk through the doorway inch by inch.

Maybe I should slow him down a little.

I raised the PQ47 and aimed at his snout.

'Stop, now!' I shouted, 'or you'll die before you gain one more inch.'

Instead of stopping, the creature writhed, pulling itself harder, while bellowing and moaning. Its thick fur squeezed through the door, springing up as it slid free. The sight of it reminded me of a caterpillar.

Did these creatures understand anything other than their own growls? They must have at least some intelligence. How else could they bring a spaceship across the galaxy? How else could they organize their attacks?

'Understand?' I shouted.

But the Goth's face said nothing. Its tongue lolled and its eyes shone as its claws gouged the concrete and its head writhed left and right, up and down.

So, I squeezed the trigger.

The rifle bucked. The shot hit the Goth in the neck. Then, I fired a second shot into the snout itself. The creature's head thrashed, but its claws still gouged the concrete. Then, the gouging dwindled and the great furry carcass remained stuck in the door, blocking the beasts behind it.

For now.

I ducked around to the far side of the small building. Then, I set off towards the AON helicopters. I stayed between the MAs and the Goths. One of the MAs might actually be able to aim and hit me, but they would never risk shooting a visitor. That would mean othering them.

The brig public address system came to life. The four tones of the xylophone sounded, and then a harsh female voice echoed around the walls. 'Attention, Lieutenant Burns!' the voice commanded. 'This is AONNB Holder MA Captain Drogba. You are ordered to put your weapon down, then drop to the ground with your hands behind your head. If you do not comply with these instructions, then according to the AON Navy Spirit Code, we may use force or any other means necessary to subdue you.'

But I had already made my choice.

Now I was going to live with it.

15

Thirty seconds later, I had crossed thirty yards towards the helicopters. That's when the first shot snapped in the air above me and struck the hangar wall with a hollow 'tonk.'

More shots came: a snap in the air to my right, followed by another thunk into the hangar. Then, a snap low to my left followed by a 'ping' as the shot ricocheted off the concrete. I ducked. Then, I zigged and zagged, going left, going right, making myself a moving target in two dimensions.

But no bullets hit. No sharp pains. No smashed bones. No face plant into the tarmac.

Maybe they only wanted to warn me.

To increase the odds of reaching the first helicopter, I fired two shots on the run, both at the windows of two cars the MAs sheltered behind. The shots did some damage. The windows exploded in an impressive shower of glass.

'Stop and drop to the ground, Lieutenant

Burns,' came Captain Drogba's voice over the PA system, but it didn't sound so confident anymore. So, I kept on zigging and zagging, getting closer to the cars and the helicopters. The thirty yards turned into twenty yards, then ten. And then I was crouching behind the canopy of the first helicopter.

But by then the shooting stopped altogether. The MAs had lowered their weapons, which didn't make sense—not even for incompetents like them. Minutes later, I would soon find out the reason. But In the meantime, I turned my attention to the next problem.

The AONN Helicopter was a Dove Of Peace model. Like all military ships and aircraft, it had a name painted on its side. This one's name was Elizabeth Wherren. I'd heard of that name somewhere—maybe in a Navy Spirit historical intersectionality course.

Not that it mattered anymore.

I climbed into the Elizabeth Wherren's cabin, placing the rifle on the seat beside me. To my left, the MAs aimed their rifles, but still did not shoot.

So, I confronted the helicopter's controls. The various levers and throttles were unfamiliar. I had trained to fly Navy Slingshot jets, but not. The two had little in common. But I had flown in helicopters plenty of times as a passenger on Navy training exercises, and a pilot had given me a long turn at the controls.

Once.

That was two years ago at AONNS Harmony. I

hadn't landed the helicopter. I'd controlled it at a low altitude with a Navy pilot beside me.

That would have to be enough.

The first thing I noted was the button labeled 'IGNITION.' That was a relief. Then, I tried to remind myself of the other controls and their functions: the anti-torque pedals for rotating the helicopter clockwise and anti-clockwise; the cyclic control or 'stick' between my knees for motion forward, reverse, to port and starboard. The collective control, as they called it, was like a handbrake lever between the two seats. It made the helicopter climb and descend. The throttle was a twist grip on the collective with a governor switch at its tip to remove the need to adjust the engine's speed.

So far, so good.

Now to get going.

I flicked the 'FUEL' switch to 'ON,' turned the throttle to ten percent, and pressed the ignition. The Elizabeth Wherren whined. The rotors turned and threw shadows along on the ground. The battery gave way to the engine, which took over with a growl of its own. Behind me, the tail rotor spun in time with the main blades. I increased the throttle to eighty percent.

Almost there.

The public address system came to life again.

'Lieutenant Burns, step out of the aircraft.'

Now the MAs stood up. They raised their weapons to their chins and watched me over their sights, yet they didn't fire. It was like they expected me to give up, or maybe they aimed at something I couldn't see.

Meanwhile, the Elizabeth Wherren whined louder. The rotors turned faster. The cabin vibrated. How long until it could lift off? A minute? Two minutes? Would the thing ever leave the ground?

I raised the collective in hope, but we stayed firmly put.

'Come on,' I said to the Elizabeth Wherren. 'Come on.'

Outside, the MAs backed away again. Maybe they knew something about the Elizabeth Wherren I didn't—that it needed fuel, or couldn't fly, or had some kind of anti-theft device.

And then I discovered the real reason the MAs hadn't fired.

It began with a roar so loud it drowned out the engine's thump.

'Come on,' I shouted at the Elizabeth Wherren. 'Get me out of here.'

But the only answer were more roars, barks, growls, and the snare drum roll of claws on concrete as a wave of shimmering fur and bared teeth surged outward from a gaping hole in the hangar wall.

'For God's sake,' I said, using the forbidden phrase from the PAE. 'Move!'

The cabin shuddered. The whine gave way to a pulse. I lifted the collective again. 'Move!' I shouted. 'Move!' But the Elizabeth Wherren stayed anchored to the tarmac.

Meanwhile, the Goth wave rolled on, a red-furred beast leading the charge. The beast's head plunged and its back arched as it charged towards me. The other Goths charged behind it. Their expressions were even madder than they looked inside the hangar—if that were possible.

'Come on!' I shouted.

Then, to my relief, the Elizabeth Wherren rose. First, one skid came off the concrete, then the other skid reluctantly followed.

Up we went, as high as four yards.

But it was too late.

The Goths were upon me.

The leading Goth leaped. Its head appeared beside the cabin and the claws clanged down onto the skid. The head dropped from view, but the Goth's claws had done some damage. The helicopter pitched down to its right. The rifle slipped in my lap and I had to release the controls and snatch it before it slid from the canopy. The chopper righted itself but not before another creature banged onto the skids. The Elizabeth Wherren lurched like a drunk.

'What do you freaks want?' I shouted, and for a moment almost reprimanded myself for othering the Goths by the use of the word 'freaks'. Indoctrination dies hard, and I'd had a lifetime of it, the full measure, and then extra doses because of my supposed privilege. 'What do you freaks want?'

No sooner had I finished yelling when I heard an almighty bang.

It sounded like a lawnmower driving over a rock. The tail rotor had thumped into a Goth who had leaped too late or too soon and in the wrong direction. I heard the yelp and saw the poor beast's ruined snout.

Meanwhile, the helicopter reacted as expected. Without its rotor to counter the force from the main blades, the cabin began to spin, slowly at first and then faster. The grounds of the brig swirled past. I saw the hangar, the walls, the cell blocks, the hills and forest beyond, the hangar again, the cell blocks, the hills, the forest. I pressed the anti-torque pedals, but the wrong one. The cabin kept spinning. The grounds of AONNB Holder whirled past, over and over.

But at least we climbed—up and away from the hysterical mass of fur and teeth below.

By now the MAs had finally had been ordered to act. They could shoot without hitting the Goths. I still didn't believe they would actually fire, and I kept on believing it right up until the first bullet pinged off the canopy. Not good. One of these guys might aim for me and hit the fuel tank.

I pressed on the anti-torque pedals—right foot down. The cabin spun faster. I pressed down with my left foot. The spin slowed. Gently, I thought. Gently now. I pressed and pushed until the spinning stopped. Then I nudged the cyclic forward, and the helicopter stumbled away from the rifle shots and the boiling sea of Goths.

Up and out we went. The Elizabeth Wherren's

nose pointed south while the body slid west. It was like a horse determined to go its own way, no matter how hard the rider turned its head. Seconds later, with more gentling of the torque pedals, the nose swung to the right direction: to the hills in the west, where the dark blanket of the forest already reached out to me, and freedom waited.

Freedom waiting.

Nice dream, I thought. Nice dream.

16

Below me, the gates of AONNB Holder opened.

The MAs slung their rifles and ran to a row of Progressive four-wheeled drive vehicles. They climbed aboard and then the Progressives jerked to life, wheeled around, and streamed through the gates. Then, they bounced across the road into the field opposite the brig.

Next came the Goths. Like a stampede of giant buffalos, they charged through the gates, bounding on all fours, their backs arching, their heads rising and plunging, their long red tongues flopping like scarves.

High above them, I held onto the cyclic with my right hand and the collective with my left and I pressed the torque pedals with my feet, trying to keep the Elizabeth Wherren nosing in the right direction, and at an altitude low enough so that I could ditch if something went wrong.

The radio came alive.

'Lieutenant Burns,' it squawked. 'This is Captain Drogba. You are now endangering civilian lives. Repeat. You are endangering civilian lives. Descend immediately and land your craft in the nearest safe space, then step outside and lay face down with your hands behind your back. Do you copy? T.E.I.D.'

That command again.

'Do you copy, Lieutenant Burns? T.E.I.D.'

I let go of the collective, pulled the headset from its clip and put it on. Then I clutched the collective again before the helicopter could drop.

'Copy that,' I said. 'Over.'

A pause and then the voice came back on.

'The correct form of ending your message and respecting the Accord is T.E.I.D., Lieutenant. T.E.I.D.'

'It's the correct form if you believe in the Accord, Captain, not if you don't. Over.'

'You are ordered to reduce your altitude, Lieutenant, and then land in a clear, safe space. I repeat. Do you copy? T.E.I.D.'

'Copy that. Over.'

'I do not see your altitude decreasing, Lieutenant. T.E.I.D.'

'Correct, Captain. Over.'

'Are you still refusing to comply? T.E.I.D.'

'No, Captain. I'm just asserting my right not to be oppressed. Over.'

'You are a cisgendered straight male descended from the pre-Accord West, Lieutenant. You know nothing of oppression. You know only privilege.

Land the helicopter, now! T.E.I.D.'

'No,' I replied. 'The chopper stays in the air. Over.'

'"Chopper" is a pre-Accord word forbidden by the Navy Spirit Code for its phallocentric associations in AONT Britain, Lieutenant. You should know that. T.E.I.D.'

'I don't care. It's a chopper, Captain. Chop—er! Over.'

'You're making things worse for yourself, Lieutenant. You're still young. Don't waste your life. Surrender now, while the Accord can show you mercy. T.E.I.D.'

But I ignored her. I kept on sliding west towards the hills and the forest. The forest! It reached out to me, drawing me to its dark reaches. Somewhere under the trees freedom waited. I would find it. I just didn't know how.

The radio squawked yet again. Captain Drogba wasn't finished. She began ranting about the need to rid the world once and for all of toxic masculinity like mine. It was dangerous, unpredictable, and worst of all, it was intolerant of the new intra-galactic friends.

I couldn't debate her and fly a damaged helicopter, so I tuned out for what must have been minutes and listened to the engine. The rhythmical thump was so soothing after all the gunfire and growling.

When I tuned back in again, Lieutenant Drogba was still talking.

'What makes you think you're an expert on the

pre-Accord era, anyway, Lieutenant? The pre-Accord era was nothing but the West oppressing everyone else. That's a fact. Period. Every history book says so. T.E.I.D.'

'What?'

'I said you don't know any more about the pre-Accord era than the rest of us, Lieutenant. You're deluded. T.E.I.D.'

Maybe I hadn't tuned out after all, or maybe I'd been arguing with her while my mind was elsewhere. But Captain Drogba had a point. What did I know about the pre-Accord era? I'd done the courses and watched the movies, the same as everyone else. That was all.

But then again, that wasn't true either. Someone had told me about the pre-Accord era. Someone had explained that the pre-Accord era was much better than the Accord commission said. Who was it? When had they told me? If only my mind would obey me, instead of fighting me, like an inner enemy.

'Do you copy, Lieutenant? T.E.I.D.'

An alarm sounded in the headphones. It was another four xylophone tones designed not to startle. I looked out to port and then at starboard. For the first time, I noticed the two Unity TV helicopters. They thumped either side of me. Cameras aimed their lenses at me from their cargo sections. Beside them, reporters talked into headsets. As I watched, the pilots made thumbs-up signals at me. Then both helicopters climbed, taking their cameras and reporters with them.

That's strange, I thought. Then I saw the reason why.

The forest rushed up at me.

I lifted the collective. The engine groaned, the nose lifted, but the forest's green canopy kept boiling up. And then a new problem arose. The helicopter resumed its slow rotation. I saw AONNB Holder in the distance, then the hills and forest rolling away, then AONNB Holder, then the forest again and the rising hills. And all the while the xylophone alarm played the four tones in my ears.

Better do something, Burns, I thought, or this escape of yours is finished.

Keeping the collective raised and the cyclic steady between my knees, I stamped on the anti-torque pedals. Neither would move. I stamped on the right pedal, then on the left. Nothing. Then, the left pedal crunched under my boot, dropped to the cabin floor, and stayed there.

'Do something, Burns,' I shouted, but there was nothing I could do but hang on.

The forest swelled closer, like a green wave. The Elizabeth Wherren skimmed over it, gliding like a dragonfly, but within seconds her skids touched the top leaves, then dropped beneath them.

At first there were only mild snags, like someone tugging on a shirt sleeve. But then the snags became pulls, and the pulls became yanks, dragging the nose to port and then starboard. Creaks and scrapes sounded on the cabin's underside and then, suddenly, the Elizabeth Wherren pitched forward so far that the forest reared in front of my eyes, and the rotor blades chopped into the canopy, churning up leaves and twigs like a lawnmower.

Seconds later, there was a sickening crunch. The rotor blades shattered. The engine stalled, and the rotor hub spun naked until it whirred to a stop. Then everything was suddenly and strangely quiet. All I could hear was the ticking of the dead engine, the comic squelch of my NWU pants on the seat, and the echoes of weirdly nonchalant bird calls, as if the birds hadn't heard a thing.

But from then on, it was all down.

The Elizabeth Wherren paused for breath then dropped. It thumped down into the thick branches below, shrieking and moaning as metal and perspex scraped against wood. Then, the slide turned to a plummet and I thought we might fall all the way to the dappled ground, but by then, the branches were thicker, more able to bear weight. After one last great crunch, the Elizabeth Wherren stuck and held.

For now.

I waited in the shuddering cabin, one hand on the hatch edge, the other holding the rifle, not daring to move in case I caused another slide. Beneath me, I could see leaves and twigs twirling to the forest floor. Each took four seconds to descend before lying hitting the ground and lying down. Either side of me, the branches holding the helicopter's weight were as thick as my legs. They looked sturdy, but would they hold? I decided they wouldn't.

By then, I noticed something else. Something far more dangerous. The unmistakable sound of a trickle from the fuel tank.

Not good.

All Accord helicopter engines ran on carbon-based fuel. Despite the promotion of electric engines, Accord scientists hadn't been able to progress them to aircraft. The scientists had, however, achieved impressive levels of diversity in their engineering departments.

I reached across and slid open the port hatch. Then, I grabbed the rifle and began climbing across the seats and onto the cabin's upper side. As I did, the radio squawked into life.

'Lieutenant Burns,' said Captain Drogba. 'We see that you are down. Do you read me? Acknowledge. T.E.I.D.'

But my debate with Captain Drogba was over.

I reached for a branch outside the canopy just as the chopper slid once more, bulldozing away from me towards the earth.

'Lieutenant Burns,' squawked the radio. 'MA detachments are in pursuit. You are ordered to…'

But that was all I heard before the Elizabeth Wherren fell away, groaning like someone in pain, and landed upside down on the forest floor. Then, just like in the movies—the ones about the war against the pre-Accord powers—the fuel tank exploded. Orange and black flames bulged out, sending up a blast of heat, followed by chips of wood and thick black smoke.

I held onto the branch, cursing.

The smoke and flames would signal my exact position to anyone within twenty miles.

17

I clung to the branch, dangling above the forest floor until my boots found a second branch thick enough to take my weight. I stood squinting against the smoke, holding my breath, trying to think. Then, an ominous crack sounded beneath my boots, and the branch slumped with a great shimmer of leaves and I dropped into the smoke feet first, the rifle clattering behind me.

Two seconds later, I arrived at another branch. My boots missed it, but my crutch did not. Take that, toxic masculinity. Then, this branch also cracked and dropped away. Down I went again until I grabbed a third branch and hung on, my palms cut, and the rifle swinging from my shoulder.

Below my boots, the tree trunk glowed orange, and the leaves curled and blackened. I wouldn't be able to hang around for long.

I squatted and launched myself out through the smoke towards a sturdy branch on the neighboring tree. My left hand hit the branch palm first, then grabbed and hung on. Then, I reached up with my right hand to get a better hold.

But my left hand slipped, and I fell like a trapeze artist who has missed the catcher's outstretched hands. Down I went—all the way to the lower branches. They smacked and tore at the blue cloth of my NWU as if taking revenge on me for the neighborhood on fire. I hit a thick branch chest-first, knocking the wind from my lungs. Then, I bounced back from the branch and fell feet-first to the earth. My right ankle twisting with a sickening wrench.

But otherwise, I was intact.

I got to my feet and hobbled away from the burning wreckage. Then, I leaned against a tree and thought about what to do next. I had to keep moving, but how far could hobble before the MAs showed up and found me? I guessed I could hide until dark, eight long hours away. Maybe by then the Goths and the MAs would give up.

But two problems remained: the Unity TV choppers. They were back, hovering either side of the column of smoke. Their cameramen aimed their lenses at me once more, and the reporters' mouths flapped, no doubt describing the action for the Accord-wide audience of billions. Maybe, I should get rid of them first.

I hobbled to where the most sunlight hit the forest floor and the view above was clear. I leaned against a tree to take the weight from my right boot. Then, I raised the PQ47, and aimed it at the lowest of the two choppers.

The crosshairs slid over the Unity TV livery and the name, 'Unity 38.' Then they settled on the reporter's mouth opening and closing behind the ball of her headset microphone. When she saw the raised PQ47, her mouthed moved faster.

As I expected, the chopper turned its head and thumped away. I fired anyway—two shots. I aimed the first into the tail boom. No damage done, except for a bullet hole in the paintwork. I fired a second shot. Bang! I scanned the tail boom but found no second bullet hole. Instead, chips of blade fluttered from the tail rotor. Seconds later, the tail boom swung around. The reporter stopped talking. The camera man put down his weapon and held on as the chopper spiraled over the trees like a wounded mayfly and disappeared from sight.

I lowered the rifle. How had I missed so badly? Maybe it was the wind? It must have dragged the shot to the right and into the rotor. That had to be the reason. I was too good a shooter with too many high-scores in the combat simulator to miss so badly.

But it wasn't the time for analysis.

I lifted the rifle's sights onto the second helicopter, the one emblazoned with the words Unity 19. Unlike its wounded pal, Unity 19 had stuck around. Its cameraman aimed his lens down at me. The reporter's mouth flapped behind the microphone. Both saw the rifle. Both carried on filming and talking. They could have been reporting the morning traffic in AONT sub-territory LA. Maybe they thought the chance to film the fleeing traitor, Burns, was worth the risk of being shot.

They would soon find out.

The distance between me and the chopper was far, maybe a thousand yards. Not an easy shot—not firing at a moving target in the sun and a cross-breeze. I settled the sights on the tail boom. I squeezed the trigger, the muzzle climbed, I saw clouds for a moment, then I settled the sights on the tail boom again, and squeezed the trigger a second time. The shots echoed through the forest, and I saw the two bullet holes appear in the paintwork.

But the chopper stayed put.

Then, the pilot did something either foolish or brave. He rotated the chopper till it faced me. Now, my only possible targets were the front of perspex bubble or its underside. The pilot's face smiled in the rifle's sights. I dare you, the smile said. Shoot to kill or get running.

Obviously, the guy hadn't heard about my marksmanship in Hong Kong. That must have been something the Unity TV reports left out.

So, I fired at the cabin's underside, far enough back to avoid hitting people, but close enough to give them a taste. I squinted through the sights. No bullet hole was visible in the cabin. I ranged the sights over the passengers. To my horror, the cameraman had slumped halfway out of the hatch. His camera dangled on its strap, yanking on his neck. The reporter's mouth stopped moving and she grabbed his shoulders, trying to pull him inside.

Seconds later, the pilot turned the chopper's head to the east. The reporter struggled to bring the camera guy inside the cabin. The camera itself slipped from his shoulder. It fell a long time before it plunged into the trees.

I lowered the rifle and let it slip to the ground.

Not good, Burns. Not good shooting. Even worse result. You probably just added a human death to your tally. An innocent death, too.

I slumped against the tree. What on earth was I doing? Did I actually think I could get away from the Navy and the Accord? Was it worth someone's life? And what if I did escape? What then?

Maybe I should have given up then and there. I should have sat down against that tree and waited for the MAs. Then, I should have submitted to the court-martial and gone to jail. Who knew what might happen! Maybe there'd be a revolution—a revolution by an actual rebel force, not the joke force of Lieutenant Ricci and that guy Adams.

I sat on the ground among the writhing tree roots, drew my knees up, and watched a bug explore the camouflage pattern on my right pants cuff. The bug crawled over the regions of blue and gray as if it were on a mission itself. It moved with purpose. Its feelers swirled around like it was gathering information and relaying it to the bug headquarters.

The bug reached the cuff's edge and fell to the dirt and the pine needles, and I fell into a state of hopelessness, overwhelmed by thoughts of anger, fear, and loneliness.

Maybe I should just sit and wait after all.

Minutes passed and the sense of hopelessness grew around me like the night. But then, I sensed something. It was signaling to me from beyond the treacherous thoughts. Signaling like a small light on a dark sea. I wasn't alone. Someone had told me something about myself. Someone who watched me from far away. They had said something about never giving in, about fighting on, and persevering no matter how bad things seemed.

But who was it? And what did they mean by fighting on? Fighting on for what? Escaping the Accord without plans? It didn't make sense.

I tried to remember all that had happened in the months before Re-Orientation and the electric shocks. I remembered Octavia, dangerous and beautiful in her blue uniform in the rain. I saw the dark, metal canyons inside her ship, the Excidium. I saw ranks of gray Marines with their weapons, and three monstrous Goths, howling and rabid, biting at their bleeding wounds. Then, I glimpsed the wooden deck of a pre-Accord warship at night, rising and falling on a dark sea. A tall figure stood by the mainmast. He spoke to me from the gloom. I couldn't hear him, but the sense of what he said reached me. Stand up. Get moving. Get moving. Now.

And then I awoke to a noise from deep in the forest. A terrible roar, like a wave rolling through the trees.

I stood up. Shook my head. Winced as my right ankle complained.

Then I got moving. I hobbled away from the tree, slinging the rifle over my shoulder, feeling more determined with each step.

But then I stopped and looked around. Which direction should I go?

To the north, there was more forest and then the city of AON sub-territory Omar. That was no good. To the west, over the hills, lay the AONO Pacific. That sounded more promising. If I could reach it, maybe I'd find a boat. Maybe I could sail it away to the far side of the world.

The roar came rolling through the forest once more.

So, I turned and hobbled west, pushing up the nearest slope, ignoring my right ankle and its complaints. Never give in, I thought. Never give in. Keep thinking that thought: 'Never give in.' Don't think at all about what the Goths will do if you're caught.

18

After five minutes slogging up the slope, I heard the roar again. That's when I realized I could never outrun the Goths. They would track my scent and catch me. Nor could I escape the MAs—not in daylight. They would soon launch their own aerial search.

I had to change tactics.

So, I turned and hobbled back along path I'd just taken. I might have been a sailor, but I knew this old survival trick, to double back and create a trail that led nowhere.

A hundred yards along the track, I picked out a tree, an AON sub-territory Californian Nye Pine, formerly known as a Monterey Pine. It would provide good coverage. More importantly, I could reach the lower branches from a standing position.

I reached up and got both hands on the lowest, thickest branch, and hauled myself halfway up when I felt a jab in my back. The kind of jab made by a small steel circle.

'Think you can hide up there, Lieutenant?'

I didn't move. I couldn't move. Both hands were busy clutching the branch.

'You think you'll escape those MAs? No chance. The visitors? Even less. Probably none. It's hopeless, Lieutenant. Now, let go but keep your hands up.'

I let go and dropped to the ground, landing on my good ankle.

'Now take three paces away from me,' said the voice. 'Nice and slow.' I took three paces back and waited. 'Now turn and face me,' said the voice.

The guy was about my age or slightly older. He was short and unshaven, which implied he was a cisgendered male, though of course, you could never be sure. I'd have to play the pronoun game to find out.

His uniform was khaki. Not an MA uniform. He wasn't from the AON army, either. There were no stripes or patches to indicate his rank or his name—and the uniform was a style from decades ago. Obviously, he was a guy from the joke resistance group.

'You can put your hands down now,' he said, slinging his rifle.

'You were at the hangar with Lieutenant Ricci,' I said.

'Right. The hangar. Now, we better get going. They'll be here any minute.' He began to walk away.

'Hold on,' I said. 'Go where? And who are you exactly? And how did you get here so fast?'

He stopped, put his hands on his hips, and examined some clouds in the sky before looking at me with his head tilted.

'You think we're some hobby group? Is that it?'

'Maybe. Or some kind of mock resistance group.'

'We're bigger than you think, Lieutenant. More competent, too. You already met our guy in AONNB Schumer. Remember?'

'The kid in the mess?'

'Right. The kid in the mess. You can thank him later. Now, come on. We've got civilian-plate Progressives waiting on the other side of that hill.'

'I already told Lieutenant Ricci I didn't want any part of your resistance or rebel group or whatever you call it.'

'You think we're fake? You think we're not serious?'

Behind Adams, five more resistance members came out from behind the trees, all armed with PQ47 rifles, all dressed in the same old style, blank khaki. Lieutenant Ricci came up and stood beside Adams. Were they a couple? Did the hostile Adams run his hands through the pixie hair each night?

'More trouble?' Ricci said.

'He still thinks we're not legit. Well, if we're so fake, Lieutenant, why are we helping you escape? Why don't we just capture you and hand you over to the MAs?'

It was a good point, but no matter what he said, there was no way I would go with these two. Call it intuition. Call it stupidity or pigheadedness or foggy thinking, but I knew not go with them. Somehow I knew.

'What's it to be, Lieutenant?' said Ricci. 'You come with us and stay free or go it alone and find yourself back in handcuffs. That's if those visitors don't get to you first.'

'No.'

'No? Again? You're kidding, right?'

'I don't need any help.'

'Sure you don't,' said Adams. 'How far do you think you'll get on one leg? Guys!'

Two males stepped forward, shouldered their PQ47s, and stood either side of me, offering supporting hands.

'I'm not going.'

'Yes, you are,' said Adams.

'No,' I said, keeping one hand ready to swing the rifle around.

'It's true,' said Adams. 'You actually think you'll escape. Don't you?'

'Listen. I don't know what you or your group is about, but if you want to help me, create a diversion. Draw the Goths and MAs away from me in the wrong direction.'

'You think they still won't find you? You think the MAs won't track you from the air, or that the visitors won't sniff you out?'

'I'll take my chances.'

'You can't succeed on your own, Lieutenant,' said Ricci. 'You have to trust someone eventually. You're just one guy.'

'So everyone keeps saying.'

The distant roar sounded again. This time, it came from the direction of the smoke. The Goths must have been close to the helicopter wreck.

'We've gotta go,' Adams said, 'or we'll all be caught too.' He began backing away, shaking his head. The other guys followed him. Lieutenant Ricci lingered. She reached into her jacket and pulled out her handheld.

'Take this.'

'Why?'

'It's for when you change your mind. Our number is in there.'

'So is the handheld's tracing chip.'

'Take it anyway. You can always dump it, but if you're smart, you'll call us.'

I took the handheld and put it in my jacket.

'Thanks, but I don't need it.'

Lieutenant Ricci began walking away. Then, she stopped, turned.

'U.A.D.,' she said. 'We'll meet again.' And then she followed the rest of her 'resistance' into the trees.

I watched them go, then turned and looked for a different tree. Fifty yards away, the forest thickened and darkened. There, I thought, and hobbled over to it. I found another Nye Pine with low branches and pulled myself up until I was sitting on it.

But that's when I heard a different set of footsteps crunching on the pine needles.

It was the first of the MAs.

He or she or they must have arrived with the pursuit vehicles. They must have stopped at the burning helicopter wreck. Now there were searching the area.

As much as I could tell, the MA was a she. She wore a peaked cap that hid her face, but I could see hip swell at the base of her smock.

She held the PQ47 level at her chin as she crept through the trees, swinging the barrel left and right. It was a good impression of somcone who knew what they were doing.

I crouched above, keeping still, working out what to do next, hoping that she would walk away.

But when she got to within yards of my tree, she stopped and listened. She crouched and turned a full circle, sweeping the forest with the rifle's sights. Then she took a few steps back and repeated her sweep. There was a radio mike clipped to her collar.

She lowered the rifle and reached for talk button on her microphone. Was she about to call her pals? I couldn't wait around to find out. So, before she could speak, I dropped from the tree, landing on my one good foot and then rolling to take away the momentum. Then, I was up and had my arm around her neck with my other hand around the rifle's muzzle.

'Drop it,' I said to the back of her head. 'Don't

say a word.'

She or he or they fought back. She swung an elbow up at my face, stomped at my feet, back-kicked my shins, and a whole lot of other fighting tactics, but she didn't succeed. She was strong. I was stronger. Toxic male stronger. I saw each move coming a mile away and dodged it. Then, I tightened my grip on her neck.

She dropped the rifle to the ground and clawed at my arm.

'Scream or make a noise and I'll keep choking.'

She stopped clawing.

'Blink twice if you understand.'

She blinked once, twice.

'I won't hurt you, but I am going to gag you and tie you up—with your belt if you're wondering. Don't worry. Fifteen minutes and the others will find you.'

She wheezed something.

'What was that?'

'You're too late.'

'We'll see about that,' she said.

I began dragging her to the nearest tree, but before I could reach it, I heard a twig snap the whisper-quiet wheels of an electric Accord Progressive surged over the rise. Three more Progressives rolled behind it. All were loaded with MAs. The MAs held their weapons level, like they knew how to use them.

There was a captain in the lead Progressive, stripes on her sleeves. Once the car stopped the captain said, 'Let the private go, Lieutenant

Burns.'

I kept hold of the private's neck, thinking fast.

But before I could come up with a plan, the MAs jumped out of the vehicles and surrounded me, their rifles aimed at my head. I knew they still wouldn't be able to shoot with any skill, but at close range, and with so many rifles, not even they could miss me—not even with their squirming comrade as a shield.

I released the MA. She clutched her neck and ran through the ring of her comrades. Then, she turned and scowled me like a hurt child.

'Now drop the weapon,' shouted the captain.

I kept the weapon on its strap over my shoulder.

'Didn't you hear me, Lieutenant? Are you deaf as well as toxic and male? Drop the weapon. Now!'

I stayed put, my mind racing, my attention on the trees, the hills, the trembling hands of the two MAs on my left.

'It's too late, Lieutenant,' said the Captain. 'There's no way out. Not this time. It's over.'

I thought of the words 'Never give in.'

Yes, but what use is telling yourself to never give in when thirty rifles are trained on your head? Maybe it's time to concede that the MA captain might be right: that this time, there really was no escape.

But against all logic, I couldn't surrender. Not yet. I don't know why, but I sensed there must still be a way out of this mess. I didn't know what

it was. I only knew it was possible.
    And for better or worse, it was on its way.

19

This group of masters-at-arms had been chosen with the usual regard for the Oppression Hierarchy. Looking around the twenty faces squinting over their rifles, I saw a wide spectrum of genders, disabilities, and ethnicities. Naturally, the commander was from the highest O.H. rank, which offered me hope that he or she or they might be incompetent and therefore likely to mess up. The name patch on the commander's smock read CAPT DRISCOLL.

Captain Driscoll stepped down from the Progressive. She took a moment to check me out, scanning me up and down, no doubt comparing me to the guy in the movies I resembled—the actor who always played the role of the pre-Accord bad guys. Then she said, 'Drop the weapon, Lieutenant. Don't think you can bluff your way out of this a second time. Don't think we won't use deadly force either. There are no visitors around anymore, so we don't have to watch our aim.'

I looked at the captain's determined face and then once more at the thirty guns pointed at me, and let my rifle slip to the ground.

'Good. Now step away. Take three steps to the side and no more. Hands up. Keep them up. Move it, Lieutenant. We don't have time for toxic male heroics.'

I stepped to the side.

'All right,' said Captain Driscoll. 'Private Adhanom! Grab the gun.'

A short guy with square, black-rimmed glasses, stepped forward and dragged the rifle away by its strap.

'Excellent. Now drop to your knees, Burns,' said Captain Driscoll. 'That's right. Your knees, just like a straight male should.'

But I stayed put.

'Your knees, Lieutenant. Now!'

I didn't move. I knew that if I dropped to my knees, there's be no more chances.

'No,' I said.

'What was that, Lieutenant?'

'You heard me.'

Captain Driscoll considered the situation. Maybe more force was necessary. She probably didn't like using force. No Accord member did. But with an infamous, toxic male, extreme measures were justified. There was also that distant roaring in the forest to consider. The Goth visitors would arrive any minute. And then what? She could never use force on *them*. Not ever. That would be othering them—othering a group in the highest rank of the Oppression Hierarchy yet.

'Corporal Chan!' she shouted.

'Yes, zer,' said one of the MAs.

'Private Yalta.'

'Yes, zer.'

'Force that prisoner to his knees, then cuff him and get him into the Progressive. Move it! Now!'

'Yes, zer. The steel cuffs or the rainbow hemp cuffs?'

'What?'

'Steel or rainbow, zer?'

'Rainbow. The more the better. Come on now! Let's go! Get him cuffed and loaded.'

Corporal Chan and Private Yalta came forward. Corporal Chan carried the rainbow ties. He walked around till he was behind me. Private Yalta stood in front, holding his weapon.

'Lower your hands, Lieutenant,' he said. 'Place them behind your back and drop to your knees.'

'No.'

'Do it, Lieutenant. Do it, or we'll hurt you.'

'You touch me, you'll know about it, Corporal.'

'Corporal Chan!' yelled Captain Driscoll. 'Why are you waiting? Force him to his knees! Use the weapon. Hit him with the butt. Come on! Let's move it.' Then she turned back to the Progressive. In the passenger seat, a guy nursed a laptop computer. 'How far now?' she said.

'Half a mile, Captain. Three or four minutes at the most.'

She turned back to me and the corporal and the private. 'I said cuff that prisoner now, Corporal!'

'Yes, zer,' said Corporal Chan. He reached out and grabbed my right arm from behind. His first mistake. He should have kicked the back of my knee, causing it to buckle. Then he should have kicked me in the back to force me to the ground. But that would be expecting way too much of AON Navy training.

I turned around, my left hand already clenched into a fist. I hit Corporal Chan in the throat. Not the hardest I could hit. It was my left fist after all. But it made solid contact. Then, I followed up with my right fist. Corporal Chan's mouth didn't have time to open in shock before the punch hit the side of his head.

As he fell, I turned to Private Yalta and his rifle. I knew he wouldn't shoot. He'd probably never shot anything other than a target in his life, and not many, either. He held the butt high like he was going to club me. Another mistake. He should have jabbed at my face and then clubbed the back of my head. But he didn't. Now he was vulnerable. I put one hand on the rifle muzzle, the other on the stock, and twisted.

The rifle fired. The shot went away through the trees. Birds scattered. I gave Private Yalta a head butt. His hands leaped to his face, and he backed away.

Now, I held the rifle.

Captain Driscoll shouted at the MA beside her. 'Shoot the prisoner in the leg.'

The MA flinched. Would he shoot? Probably not. Could I aim the rifle and hit him before he fired? Definitely. But could I then take out all his comrades? Probably not.

I let the rifle slip to the ground, but I hadn't surrendered. Not yet. I hung on, not knowing why.

In the distance, the rumbling grew louder. The guy with the laptop said, 'Two minutes now, Captain.'

A sharper edge came into Captain Driscoll's voice.

'Private Lewin. Private Bedi. Private N'Dichi. Private Tsang.'

'Yes, zer.'

'Yes, zer.'

'Yes, zer.'

'Yes, zer.'

'The four of you cuff him. And for the Accord's sake, let's get out of here.'

'Yes, zer!' they said in unison.

They dropped down and came towards me.

'Private Alawi! Private Abbas! Help Yalta and Chan into the cars.'

'Yes, zer.'

'Yes, zer.'

Then the four privates circled me, like the four points on a pre-Accord clock face, but they still hesitated. Like their comrades, they didn't have a takedown plan.

'Now!' yelled Captain Driscoll. 'Fast as you can. Now!'

The guy behind me kicked the back of my knees. I swung an elbow back at him, but he had seen what had happened to Private Chan and ducked out of the way. Then the other three tried their moves. Three sets of hands reached for me. One set grabbed my throat. Two sets grabbed each of my wrists.

I raised a boot to kick the stomach of Private Bedi, but suddenly, everyone stopped moving, including me.

The Goths surged over the rise. They rose up like a wave of fur, teeth, and claws, rolling over the slope and down around us. I thought they might even roll over the top of us, but they spread left and right, encircling the MAs and the Progressives. Then, the roaring and barking ceased, and the Goths swayed on their hind legs, panting and drooling. They formed a giant wall around us, like we were in the center of a large hedge maze.

The young MAs raised their quivering rifles. Each of their faces said he or she wanted to run, if only they could. But there was no way through the encircling monsters. The Goths stood too tall and too wide. Their teeth were too big; their claws were too long, and they exuded a scent heavy with threat—threat mixed with the reek of sewage. There were a frightening, astonishing presence.

But the greatest shock was yet to come.

A smaller Goth wearing a red neckcloth was there in the circle. This same Goth dropped to all fours, lumbered forward, stood on two hind legs, sniffed at the MAs on the left and right, then sniffed at Captain Driscoll.

And spoke.

20

'We take him,' the Goth growled and raised a paw at me. 'We take him.' The MAs stood opened-mouthed. No one knew what to say. No one knew what to do. They stood still and silent, like dummy soldiers.

The Goth growled a second time. 'We take him,' she growled, keeping her paw up. 'HIM.'

Still, no one spoke. A radio squawked. The MAs flinched. The Goths' ears all twitched towards the Progressive with the guy hunched over his lap top. He looked up like he'd been caught drawing obscene pictures of the Accord commissioners. The Goths' ears didn't point at him for long. They soon flicked back to the female Goth with the red neckcloth.

'Him,' the Goth growled again. 'We take him.'

She looked around the astonished MAs sniffing deeply at each trembling rifle muzzle and each shaking head. No one dared reply.

A large, male Goth with dark red fur broke

from the ranks of encircling monsters and lumbered forward. He growled something to the Goth with the red neckcloth. She growled something back. Then, the large Goth swept the MAs with a great wave of his paw and issued three loud barks.

Captain Driscoll hadn't said a word. She stood frozen like the rest of the MAs. Her eyes had locked on the large Goth, but not on his face or teeth or claws, but on his heavy, shaggy, pendulous male genitals.

The rest of the MAs followed her gaze. They looked at the Goth's hind legs. Then they looked away, then looked back again. Then they looked at each other, then looked away again.

How could the Goths be so brazen? How could they be so obviously one sex or the other? It defied everything the Accord had taught. Sex was fluid with an infinite number of shades from male to female, not one thing or the other. Everyone knew it. Everyone! And yet, right in front of them was this large and threatening display of binary sex organs. Worse! They were male.

The smaller, female Goth tried once more to communicate with the stunned Earth creatures. She swept the group with her snout, sniffing at each MA all over again. This time she sniffed longer and deeper at each one, her chest swelling and her nasal flukes fanning. After several long sniffs to confirm her choice, she returned her attention Captain Driscoll.

'My leader say not…,' she growled and raised

a paw at the rifles. 'We want,' and pointed her paw at me. 'We take.'

Still, no one spoke. The MAs looked sideways at Captain Driscoll. She raised one hand to her face. She saw the MAs watching her, and dropped the hand to her hip where it sought her pocket before forming a fist and resting on the webbing of her belt before dropping back to her side. Eventually, she found her tongue.

'You know one of our Accord languages?' she said.

The Goths said nothing.

'Your cultural sensitivity is appreciated. In the name of the Accord we wish you our values of tolerance, equality, and divers...'

'Not understand,' growled the Goth.

'We have a diverse range of languages,' continued Captain Driscoll. 'So, if you prefer to switch to ...'

The Goth shook her head.

'Not fight,' she growled. 'Not fight. My leader say we take him,' she raised the same giant paw all over again. 'Him. We take him.'

'You want...him?' Captain Driscoll said. 'You want the prisoner? Lieutenant Burns?'

The Goth cocked her ears but said nothing.

'Yes, Captain,' said the MA with the name patch reading N'Dichi. 'That's what she... I mean... the visitor said. She doesn't want to fight us. She wants Lieutenant Burns.'

Captain Driscoll found some words. 'Shut it, private. How do you know this Goth person identifies as a female?'

'Not fight,' the Goth growled again. 'We take.'

Captain Driscoll said, 'Intra-Galactic friends! First things first. Before we discuss the prisoner, may I ask your pronouns?'

'Not understand,' growled the female Goth.

'OK,' said Captain Driscoll. 'OK, that's fine. Totally fine. We'll keep everything simple so we won't offend you. My pronouns are zee and zer and zoo. That's all I think we'll need, and please, don't think I meant anything by the pre-Accord word "zoo."'

The female Goth shook her head even more. Beside her, the giant Goth leader growled. Then a third Goth lumbered forward. He had a long scar down his snout. He too growled, waving his paw at Captain Driscoll and then at me. Then the female Goth with the red neckcloth said, 'My leaders both say we take now. We take now.'

'With respect, intra-galactic friends,' said Captain Driscoll. 'This male is our prisoner. This is our planet, and so we…' She paused and frowned. The hand went up to her face again. Perhaps she realized for the first time the contradiction in the Accord view of borders. There were no borders between nations, of course. Everyone knew that. But now she had to enforce some kind of planetary jurisdiction. Something didn't make sense. Did planets have borders? Could borders be actually good?

'I'm sorry,' she stammered. 'I am being territorial. It's totally against Accord protocol. We have no borders on our planet. You are welcome in the name of diversity, which we value highly, but this is the Accord of Nations. I have my orders from the Navy. He is our prisoner.' She pointed at herself and then at me.

The Goth with the red neckcloth growled to her leader. He growled in reply, louder this time with a great upward toss of his snout, like he hadn't chased all this way to be told what to do.

He rose on his legs, his pendulous genitals swaying beneath him. Captain Driscoll and every MA looked at them. Then they looked at the trees, the sky, and the clouds. The Goth growled. The Goth with the scar growled as well. Other Goths from around the circle growled, filling the forest with deep, rolling echoes.

'My leader say take now,' growled the female Goth with the red neckcloth. 'Now.'

'I'm sorry, intra-galactic visitor,' said Captain Driscoll. 'He is our prisoner.' She turned to the four guys beside me. 'Private Bedi!'

'Yes, zer.'

'For the Accord's sake, get the prisoner in cuffs, and let's get out of here.'

'Yes, zer.'

The four MAs glanced warily at the Goths and then back at me. Private Bedi stepped forward, palms up.

'Don't try it,' I warned. 'If I don't kick your asses, these guys will.'

Private Bedi said, 'Come on, Lieutenant. You want to go with us instead of. . . the visitors,

137

right? Ready, guys?'

The four MAs seized me. Two grabbed my hands. One kicked the backs of my knees. The other threw an arm around my neck. I got one hand free and swung it at Private Bedi's face. He clutched his nose and staggered backward. The other MAs hung on to my neck and arms. They actually climbed on me, using their weight to bring me down. After a last shove, I slumped to the forest floor.

Down there, the earth radiated sweet pine scents. Above me, the Goths traded growls. Then, I saw black paws and yellow claws churning the leaves, and the human hands let go of my neck and arms. I stood up to find myself surrounded by towering Goths and cowering MAs.

'Raise your weapons!' shouted Captain Driscoll. 'Aim at the big... at the large visitor!' The remaining MAs each raised a PQ47 at the Goth leader. For a moment, there was silence: not a growl, and not a word from Captain Driscoll. Only the forest spoke. Trees sighed, birds twittered, the fire crackled beyond the hill. And in the distance, beside a large tree, Adams, Ricci, and their 'resistance' group watched on. When Adams saw me look his way, he beckoned me with his right arm.

Meanwhile, I stood there in the middle of this bizarre standoff, trying to think of a way of turning it into an escape. And then, right on cue, right in the middle of all the uncertainty, a voice spoke in my mind.

'Alex?' it whispered.

No, I thought. Not now, not here.

I tried to imagine the wall I had used to survive Re-Orientation, a wall, steep and stony, glistening with raindrops, blocking everything out.

But the voice flowed through it.

'I can help you, darling. I can help you out of this. I can save you from capture. You need me. You're injured. You're tired and confused. Accept my help, Alex. Say the word and I will get you out. My ships are above you. My Marines can be there in minutes. They can fight off the Goths and scatter the humans. I can save you from this. You need my help.'

Get out of my mind. Get out! All I want is for you to be gone—you, and the Goths and your armies. Everyone.

'That will never happen, Alex. Better to accept that truth, and then to accept my help. I am here. My armies are here. Soon there will be more. Your planet will no longer belong to you or your people. There will be nothing you can do.'

I shook my head. I saw the Goths, the MAs, Adams, and Ricci. Then, without thinking, I followed an older instinct—one that needed no words, no argument, no persuasion.

Only action.

I dropped to the ground and before either the Goths or the MAs could move, I grabbed the discarded PQ47 rifle. I raised the muzzle, aimed, and shot Captain Driscoll in her right arm. Then, I swung the rifle and shot the Goth leader. I aimed for his neck, but I hit the top of his shoulder. He barked but otherwise remained unaffected. So, I fired a second shot. It hit his shoulder again, raising a tuft of thick fur. But once again, he shrugged it off as if it were a fly.

Then, with the rifle shot echoing through the forest, I turned and bolted—sprained ankle and all. I didn't know where I was going. I wasn't thinking straight. I was going away. That's all. Away to where I could be alone and recover. Anything to get away from the Accord, from T.E.D., from the Goths, from Octavia, and conflict. I had to get somewhere I could breathe and think. Just that. Breathe and think and remember.

But I was soon overtaken and surrounded again: Goths on one side, MAs on the other. I raised the weapon and swung it from Goth to human and back.

'Drop the weapon, Lieutenant, while you can,' said one of the MAs.

'My leader say not hurt,' growled the Goth with the red neckcloth.

'There's no escape, Burns. One way or another, we'll get you back,' said the MA.

'My leader say we go now,' said the Goth. 'Go now.'

I turned to the Goth with the red neckcloth. 'Where? Go where?' I said.

'Go Gwawanath,' she said. 'Go king. See our king.'

'Don't even think about it, Burns,' said the MA.

'Gwawanath? What's Gwawanath?' I said. 'Is it

a ship?'

'Alex,' said the voice in my mind. 'Don't talk to them. Let me save you. I'm here but you have to ask me. You have to ask.'

'No,' I said.

'We go ship now,' said the Goth.

So much had happened in the last two months. My career was over, my mother dead, and my father's whereabouts still unknown. I faced a jail term of decades, and my comrades had turned into my enemies. Worst of all, Octavia had gained power with the Accord's support, dooming its people. And so, I came to a decision. *The* decision. Not a considered decision, not a wise decision.

'You fight?' I asked the Goth with the red neckcloth. 'You fight Octavia?'

'You are being deceived, Alex,' said the voice in my mind.

'You fight Octavia?' I said again.

The Goth with the red neckcloth shook her head.

'Not understand.'

'Fight Romans?' I said. 'Fight Romans?'

She growled to the Goth with the scar. He growled back at her. Then she lowered her great snout to me.

'Fight Ranawah,' she growled.

'Fight Roman leader?'

'Fight Ranawah leader. Very fight Ranawah leader.'

She watched me.

'OK,' I said.

'Not understand.'

'OK,' I said again. 'I go with you. Fight Ranawah.'

'Gwah,' growled the she-Goth, which I guess meant 'yes,' or 'understand,' or 'good choice.' Who cared as long as they could get me out of there and let me enjoy some form of freedom on the right side of the struggle? Yes, that's what I told myself in my delirious state. The Goths weren't the Accord. They weren't Octavia and they weren't prison. They were unknown. That was the price of carrying on.

'Big mistake, Burns,' someone said. Maybe it was Captain Driscoll, maybe an MA, maybe the clear thinking part of my mind.

I stepped back to give myself room. The pine needles crunched beneath my boots. Crunch! Such a friendly, reassuring sound. Such a sweet, pure scent. I stepped further back. I could have kept going. I could have stepped all the way to the ocean. The ocean!—how peaceful it must be. How vast and empty and quiet! Not an MA anywhere. Not an Accord value. Not an alien of any kind. Just the sea and peace.

But then I heard a growl, and a great, soft-hard paw smacked me on the head.

Once, twice.

I heard a shot fired, growling and shouts.

Then light exploded in my head and I saw no more.

I had chosen the Goths.

But what I didn't know was that by going

away from Earth and Octavia, by traveling all the unimaginable distance to the far side of the galaxy, I would discover a secret that would change everything.

For better or worse.

PART TWO:
THE GWANTASNARR

'There shall be no travel in space. Space travel and space exploration are aggressive acts of the pre-Accord West. Their practice leads to colonization and oppression.'

Amendment to The Accord of Nations
Constitution
Year 250, The Accord of Nations Era

21

We were driving in my father's car. Just him and me. He wore his dark blue AON Navy uniform. It always made him look bigger than normal, which was big already. I think we were driving home from my school.

'Do you ever have dreams, Alex?'

'Sometimes.'

'Do you remember them?'

'No.'

'Not any dreams? Not one?'

'Maybe for a little while. Then I forget them. There was one about a dog.'

'A dog? What happened?'

'I don't remember, dad. I forget.'

'If you remember any of your dreams, you'll tell your dad, right?'

'Sure, dad.'

He liked me to call him 'dad' even though my teacher said mom or dad were bad pre-Accord words.

We drove on. I think we were near Kresta's place.

'What about you, dad? Do you have dreams?'

'Sure. Plenty of them.'

'What happens?'

'Good things.'

'Like what?'

'Things about our family. Things your ancestors did in the pre-Accord era.'

'What's an ancestor?'

'Someone from your family that lived hundreds of years ago, before the Accord.'

'What things did they do?'

'Good things. Your ancestors were very brave. They helped people.'

'My teacher says that families are bad and that the pre-Accord era was bad too.'

'Not all the people were bad. Your ancestors were good people. Many of them were in the Navy, like me. They sailed in big ships, Alex. They fought in dangerous battles. In those days, the navies were different. The world was different.'

'My teacher says we're not allowed to know about the pre-Accord era. We're not even supposed to talk about it.'

'But would you like to know about it? Lots of interesting stuff happened back then, Alex.'

'I don't know, dad. The teacher said they didn't believe in T.E.D. back then. That's bad, right?'

When we were near Kresta's house, my father became very serious.

'Listen, Alex. You know those pills that Dr. Iqbal gave you?'

'They taste like dirt.'

'I want you to do your dad a special favor.'

'What favor?'

'Don't swallow the pills.'

'But Dr. Iqbal says if I take them, I'll help the Accord. Kresta says I should do what he says.'

'I know, Alex. I know. Your mom means well. She wants the best for you, the same as I do. We both want the best for you. But we don't agree on what that is— the best for you, I mean. Your mom wants you to be what the Accord wants.'

'She says the Accord always knows best.'

'I know she does, but I want something different for you.'

'What different?'

'I want you to be yourself, who you're meant to be, not what the Accord says you have to be.'

'Kresta says not to call her "mom."'

'Alex, I'm serious. Throw the pills away. Throw them down the sink. But don't tell your mom. If she wants to watch you swallow them, hide the pills under your tongue and spit them out later.'

'I don't know, dad. It sounds sneaky. Dr. Iqbal says if I don't take them it's bad for the Accord.'

'It's only for a little while, Alex. Only till I work something out. Then, there won't be any more pills and no more instructions from Dr. Iqbal or anyone else.'

'Work what out?'

'It's a secret.'

'What are you going to do?'

'Just see some people and do some things.'

'What things?'

'They're secret too, but they're good things that'll help you. I know someone who can stop the pills.'

'What about mom? What about the Accord?'

'Don't worry, the Accord will take care of itself.'

'What about mom? Does she know what you're doing?'

'Whatever happens, Alex—even if it's something bad, it won't be because of anything you did. Will you remember that?'

'What won't, dad?'

'Whatever happens.'

'But what will happen?'

22

Acceleration.

That's what I sensed when I woke up.

Acceleration.

Rapid, erratic acceleration.

It threw me forward and back across a deck of some kind.

Right and left.

Up and down.

In darkness.

I couldn't see my legs. I couldn't see my hands, but I could feel the thick cloth of my NWU against my skin, thank goodness, and the hard, cold metal of the deck or floor beneath me. That was something.

Strange noises accompanied each lurch and plunge. I could hear creaking metal joints and clanging hatches or doors. Occasionally, a loud bang would sound too, and I would be thrown up from the deck or floor completely.

Underneath this cacophony, a deep bass note droned, like a never-ending groan. I thought I might be back in Re-Orientation with the Navy Spirit doctors and their rubber bite sticks and electrodes.

But then, I smelled it: the reek of wet dog.

And then I remembered.

I had chosen the Goths.

When the lurching and pitching stopped for a while and I could finally sit still, I took stock of myself. I checked my arms, legs, feet, chest, and head. My ribs burned. My neck refused to let my head turn right, my right ankle complained at each touch. Then there was my head! It swam with pain like an anvil had swatted me.

I had chosen the Goths.

But the strongest sensations were of the usual kind: thirst and hunger. The last meal I remembered was the soy milk and kale in my cell at AONNB Holder before the court-martial. My throat felt dry and my stomach growled deeply— like a Goth. I also needed the head.

'Hey!' I called to the dark. 'Anyone here?'

My voice echoed back at me.

'Hey!' I shouted again. 'Who is in charge here?'

There were no answers except the creaking metal, the clanging doors or hatches, and bass note drone.

'Hey!' I shouted once more.

And waited.

Seconds later, a door in the bulkhead or wall opened. Weak blue light shone in. I squinted until my eyes became used to the light. The room or cabin in which I found myself was about the size of half a tennis court. No furniture. Shelving ran along one wall. Two dirty mattresses lay at one end. Both the bulkheads and the deck were dark gray metal.

I turned to the door. It must have been almost twelve feet high. A shaggy figure stooped beneath the head jamb, blocking most of the weak light, and forming grotesque silhouette.

'Where are we?'

The Goth lowered its enormous head and replied down at me with four barks that sounded like 'Gwah. Gwah. Ban hah gwah!'

'Where am I? Where's the interpreter—your female friend with the red collar?'

The Goth scratched its arm and sniffed at me.

'The interpreter.' I circled my neck with a free hand and pulled at an imaginary neckcloth. 'Where's the interpreter and where is the head?' I mimed an action that even a great alien oaf would understand.

'Gwah!' the creature growled. 'Gwah!' Then it raised a paw and slammed the door.

'Gwah,' the creature roared as it lumbered away.

Gwah—what could a word like that mean? For certain it didn't mean, 'Yes, I understand. Great to see you again. Do you need any help standing up? No? Then, I'll be right back with the interpreter. Is there anything else I can do?'

More likely it meant, 'I'm coming back with a few pals to slice you open and stir up your insides.'

I sat back in the dark. How on earth had I gotten myself into this mess?

But I knew exactly how.

I had chosen the Goths.

23

First things first.

I tried standing.

This was easier said than done. With the floor lurching and my ankle throbbing, I couldn't stay upright. So I sat back down and waited.

And tried to think.

How on earth had the Goths brought me here? Carried me on a shaggy back like a sack after annihilating the MAs? And carried me where? Where had they hid this ship? In the forest? Or had they used a shuttle to go between Earth and wherever it waited? Why hadn't the Romans stopped them? There was so much I didn't know and so much to find out. That's if the Goths didn't kill me first.

And a voice whispered in my mind, 'Or eat you.'

A lever clunked, and the door swung open. The weak blue light shone in from the corridor. Another shaggy figure stood silhouetted in the light. This figure stood about ten feet tall, not twelve, but it still ducked its head to look inside.

'You wait,' came a growl. It must have been the interpreter—the female with the red cloth around her neck.

'You wait,' she growled again. 'Ranawah outside.'

'Where am I?' I climbed to my feet—my foot.

'You wait. Ranawah fight us now.'

'Where are we?' I tried hobbling towards her.

'Ship. You wait.'

'Ship? What ship?'

'Go Gwawanath,' came the reply.

Gwawanath—that unpronounceable word she had growled in the forest.

'Where is the ship?'

'You wait. Friend.'

'Friends? Great. We're friends, but I need to know where we are, and I need.' I mimed what I wanted. 'Now!'

'No now. Ranawah outside. Later. Come back later. Friend.'

'When later?' I shouted. 'Where are we going? Where are the Ranawah? Is Octavia there? Is Ranawah leader there?'

But all the interpreter would say was, 'Go Gwawanath.'

A second shaggy figure loomed behind her. It too growled—but its growls were lower and reinforced with threat.

The shorter creature reached out a paw to close the door.

'Wait? Your name? What's your name?'

The interpreter waited a moment and then growled, 'Karz.'

'Karz?' I said, lowering my voice to mimic hers. 'Karz. Thank you. I'm Burns. You must' but before I could continue, an awful bang sounded deep in the ship, and the great oafish Goth behind Karz slammed the door shut, sealing me back into darkness.

For the next thirty minutes, I waited while the ship banged and lurched and rolled all over again. Outside, in the passageway, alarms rang, and a loudspeaker barked and growled. What were the Goths doing during all this rough flying? Were they fighting the Romans? Or were they on the deck, hanging on like me?

And then the lurching and the banging ceased. Soon after, the door opened again and Karz loomed once more in the doorway.

'Ranawah gone,' she growled. 'Now, you.' She pointed a great paw down the passageway.

I got up and limped to the door.

'You go him.' Karz sniffed at her large Goth escort.

'Go with him? To the head?'

Karz raised a paw, pointing down the passageway.

I hobbled out of the door and followed the shaggy back of the lumbering Goth. Forty yards along, he stopped beside another open door. Inside was a cabin, lined with the same dark metal as mine, but with wide holes in the deck out of which a powerful stench radiated.

'There?' I said. 'Go there?'

'Gwah,' the Goth replied.

It could have been worse. So, I hobbled inside. The large Goth swayed in the passageway.

'You going to watch?'

'Gwah,' he growled, and then stood at the open doorway, sniffing at me with his great snout. Privacy must not be part of the Goth culture, I thought. Either that or this oafish creature wanted to watch me.

When we stood in the passageway again, the Goth pointed back towards the cabin or cell where Karz waited outside the door. Her paws were clasped demurely in front of her.

'Talk now,' I said to her.

'No. You there.' She raised a paw at the door.

'No, Karz.' I shook my head for emphasis and crisscrossed my arms. 'Not there. No more dark. Talk now.'

'No talk. You wait.'

'No. Tell me where we are going.'

'Go Gwawanath,' she replied.

'And where is Gwawanath? Or what is it?'

'You there first.' She tilted her head down at the doorway.'

'No. No more. Take me back. Go Earth. Fight Romans. Fight Octavia.'

'You wait. You friend.'

'Friends don't lock friends in the dark.'

Her ears flattened.

'Friend,' she growled and pointed once more into the cabin.

I looked inside. A figure sat on a mattress in the gloom: a human figure.

'Friend,' growled Karz.

'That's no friend.'

'Friend.'

'Not them. They're no friend.'

'Talk later,' growled Karz. 'Later talk.'

The 'friend' on the mattress was none other than Captain Diana Nolan, the woman who wanted to put me inside AONNB Jenner for eighty years.

'Friend,' growled Karz.

'No, Karz. Not friend. Very not friend.'

24

Seconds passed in the dark. Neither of us spoke a word. I silently seethed. Captain Nolan breathed short, shallow breaths.

But at first, I decided to be friendly.

'So they got you, too?'

More seconds passed. Then Captain Diana Nolan spoke. 'I'm the superior officer here, Prisoner 548B. I'm from the Judges Advocate Navy, not the regular Navy, as you are, but you must address me as an officer. You must salute me as one too. And when you salute me, you must use the proper salutation.'

'T.E.D., Captain. How's that?'

'It's T.E.I.D., Lieutenant. It's not official yet, but the Accord Commission has allowed its use by AON Navy personnel. Don't forget it.'

I had been wrong. Captain Diana Nolan wasn't in shock—not even close. I didn't know whether to be impressed or to write her off as being like Captain Toth, by which I mean she was so deluded by the Accord that she believed its values would protect her no matter where she roamed, even if that roaming took her into a cell in a ship crewed by Goths.

'We should drop the protocol, Captain, given where we are.'

'As far as you are concerned, Prisoner 548B, the Accord's laws and customs still apply. You are in the Accord of Nations military, as am I. So, you will address me according to my rank. You will also use my preferred pronouns, as required by the Navy Spirit Code and the Accord Constitution.'

'The Accord? You think we're still in the Accord too?'

'It's not "you," Prisoner 548B. It's yinz.'

'Yinz? That's a new one.'

'Even so, you will use it.'

'Come on now, Captain. There's no need for us to play the pronoun game. This isn't a competition to get higher on the Oppression Hierarchy.'

'My other pronouns are ker and dee, Prisoner 548B. You will address me properly, or the number of your code violations will increase.'

What a joke! I had so many code violations already that it wouldn't matter how many I added. I could add hundreds and it would make no difference.

'You know where we are, ker, right?'

'And where's that, Prisoner 548B?'

'You really don't know?'

'You tell me.'

'We're on board a vessel controlled by the bear-wolf aliens known as the Goths.'

'"Bear-wolf aliens?" That's two more code violations in one sentence: an insult and a phrase that both others and disrespects our intra-galactic friends.'

'Well, that's what they are, ker: bear-wolf aliens. You can call them anything you like— puppy dogs, teddy bears, furry friends—but they are still aliens. They're twelve feet tall, covered in fur and reek of garbage. They have enormous teeth, and six-inch claws, and they have kidnapped both you or yinz and me, and haven't told us where they're going, except to someplace that has a name that sounds like someone coughing their guts out.'

Captain Nolan remained silent in the dark.

'Also, this ship has just suffered an attack from what they call the Ranawah, which is their name for the Romans, whom you also call intra-galactic friends, but who are actually aliens as well as invaders and monsters in disguise. If I were you, Captain, I'd be thinking about getting out of here instead of standing on Accord protocol and insisting I use your pronouns.'

Her clothing rustled in the dark.

'I have a weapon aimed at you, Prisoner 548B. If you try to touch me, I will use it.'

'You think I'll attack you?'

'Item 17C of the Navy Spirit Code requires a third person to be in a room whenever a cisgendered male is in the presence of a female-identifying Accord member. The code is there for a reason, Prisoner 548B. It's there to protect those who identify as female from toxic males such as you. I repeat, I have a weapon.'

'Aren't you a cisgendered female, a real female, not a female identifier?'

I heard what sounded like an attempt to cock the weapon.

I said, 'It's not me you should point your weapon at, Captain. It's our intra-galactic friends out there.'

'Right now, Prisoner 548B, I'm concerned about the Navy Spirit Code. That is all. The Code comes first. Everything else follows.'

'That doesn't work on me anymore, Captain. I've discovered the truth about Navy Spirit and the Accord.'

'You forget that you attacked Admiral Octavia. You shot her several times, Prisoner 548B.'

'She is a dangerous invader leading an invasion force. Invaders must be repelled.'

'Admiral Octavia is about to become an Accord Commissioner, Prisoner 548B. It's not an invasion when she and her people are welcome.'

I tried to think of something to say—something about handing a gun to your own executioner. I wanted to tell this ridiculous JAN captain that she was wrong, but nothing came. I was tired and hungry, and it had been a long day.

Instead, I said, 'It's not me who you should fear, Captain. I won't attack you, but our furry friends might, and they will do worse than you can imagine.'

'No, Prisoner 548B. You are wrong. You assume that everyone not from the Accord is dangerous. These intra-galactic friends are an oppressed group, and like all oppressed peoples we must view them as Accord members in waiting. They integrate to our values naturally when we tolerate and accept them. There are no enemies of the Accord. There are no aliens or invaders. There is only diversity and greater diversity.'

'No enemies at all? Not ever? Not even ones who want to kill and enslave us.'

'The Accord's enemies are toxic masculinity, patriarchal oppression, and the oppressive values of the pre-Accord West.'

'You keep on believing that, Captain.'

'I do. I will, Prisoner 548B.'

'And while you're tolerating these monsters, I'm going to get us out of here.'

She made no reply, but the cloths rustled once more and I imagined her holding out the weapon in the dark. Then, I made a mental note to disarm her of it when the lights came on.

For the moment, I left her alone and began searching the cabin, running my hands over the cold metal bulkheads, feeling for a switch or a catch that would open the door.

After a few minutes, I asked the question that had been forming in my mind since the moment I saw Captain Nolan on the mat.

'How did the Goths capture you, anyway, Captain? And why?'

She shot back a reply. 'How I came to be here is not your business, Prisoner 548B.'

'OK. It's none of my business, but do you have any idea why?'

'I could ask the same question of you, Prisoner 548B. Why are you here? How did you come to be aboard this ship?'

'That's easy. I chose to be here.'

'You chose to be here?'

'The Goths offered me a chance to fight against Octavia. I know it sounds like a strange decision to make, but I was under pressure and my mind... my mind is not quite the same as before Re-Orientation.'

'You chose to be here? That seems a strange choice. They have you locked in this cabin.'

'I made the wrong choice. That's why I am getting out.'

'Getting out? Out of this ship? Or out of the Accord?'

'Both.'

'You think you'll succeed all by yourself?'

'You know what they say: if you never try, you never know.'

'Where exactly do you think you will go?'

'Like I said, I'm getting out of this cabin first. Then I'll work it out from there. If you like, you can help me.'

'No, Prisoner 548B. I'll do no such thing. I am going to put you into AONNB Jenner for the rest of your life.'

'You could just say no thanks.'

'Politeness is for my friends.'

I shook my head in the dark. I already had an enemy inside my mind. I didn't need an enemy on the outside too. I just hoped she'd keep out of the way when any fighting began.

'Once last try, Captain. If we're going to be in this cabin together, we might as well get to know each other. They told me you come from a famous Accord family.'

'Who is "they," Prisoner 548B? "They" is an old-fashioned preferred pronoun.'

'Captain Odilli of Navy Spirit. She told me you could trace your ancestry back to the pre-Accord revolutionaries, all the way to Ariel Hoskins himself.'

'My family is my business. On occasion, it is the business of the Accord Commission. It is never your business.'

'My family fought on the other side—in the revolution, I mean.'

'I have read your file, Prisoner 548B. I know who you are and where you came from and what your parents did.'

'Our ancestors might have met in battle. Imagine it.'

'Ancestors and family lineage are concepts the Accord will eventually remove from the public consciousness. They convey unearned privilege. What is important is how closely an Accord member observes Accord values in the present.'

'But the Accord commission likes your family, right? They like its values and achievements. I'll bet your family has been in the Accord power structure for centuries.'

'My family played a special role in the Accord's foundation. Your family supported evil pre-Accord Western powers. That is why your family is shamed as an example of oppression and unearned privilege.'

'Are you saying that your family has enjoyed no privileges? How many senior Accord positions have they held? How many deputy commissioners or heads of departments?'

'None of that matters, Prisoner 548B?'

'Your family seems to have enjoyed unearned privileges for years. Surely that matters.'

'What matters, Prisoner 548B, is what the Accord Commissioners say matters. That is all. It doesn't matter what you or I think or what history says or books say. Only what the Accord says.'

At those words, I knew there was no hope for her. So I gave up and went back to searching along the bulkheads. You couldn't argue with the Accord. It didn't allow arguments based on reason and logic. You could put-forward the most well-reasoned argument in history and still lose the debate because the Accord said you were privileged.

I found nothing along the bulkheads except the cold gray metal. So, I gave up and sat down to think. That's when the growling outside the door began. The Goths were back, and they would soon explain my fate.

25

The door clunked open. The weak blue light flowed in. I glimpsed Captain Nolan on her mattress with her long legs folded beneath her, like a collapsed fawn. She turned a glare on me that could have reversed the ice growth in the AON Arctic circle. I noticed her hands were empty. She must have hidden the pistol in her smock.

I turned back to the door. Two enormous Goths loomed in the passageway. Karz, the interpreter, swayed in front of them, her paws clasped over her chest. All three sniffed from Captain Nolan to me and back again as if they expected to find us on the same mattress, as if Captain Nolan had been captured to act as my mate.

My mate!—the idea would have driven Captain Nolan to the limits of outrage. She would have screamed patriarchal oppression so loud the rivets in the bulkheads would shake loose and the Goths would have to clamp their paws over their flattened ears.

But the idea of mates might have been fine in Goth culture. Their males did all the fighting and the Goth leader was male. Maybe they had very pre-Accord ideas about the roles of the sexes. They wore nothing but their fur, so each Goth's sex—in the pre-Accord use of the word—was on constant display.

Of course, Captain Nolan would never acknowledge this meaning of the term 'sex.' Never. In her view, there was no such thing as someone's sex, only the much vaguer word 'gender' and all the many variations of gender between male and female, which every Accord member learned at school was as infinite as the stars.

I turned to face the three Goths. The two tall males growled low, threatening rumbles interrupted by deep sniffs. I could see the tips of their yellow claws sliding from their fur sheathes.

'Easy, guys,' I said. 'Only want talk.'

'Don't say "guys," Prisoner 548B.'

'Go now,' growled Karz.

'Go where?' I said. 'Earth?'

'Not,' growled Karz.

'Then where? Fight Ranawah?' I said.

At the word 'Ranawah,' the two big Goths snorted and tossed their snouts.

'Not,' growled Karz. 'Go captain now.'

'I'm coming too,' said Captain Nolan. She got

to her feet and stood erect and tall, her face radiating assertiveness. Her hand reached up and brushed away the imaginary curl. Then, she said, 'I'm the superior officer. I will speak to your captain.'

Karz sniffed at her, then sniffed me.

'Friend not come,' she growled. 'No friend.'

'I am coming too,' Captain Nolan repeated, stepping forward. 'You do not represent the Accord, Prisoner 548B.'

'This is not about the Accord. They're here for me. They captured me. You are here because you…'

'I will ask the captain why I'm here, Prisoner 548B.'

Karz growled again. One of the two large Goths ducked his head under the door's top jamb and came lumbering inside, then towards Captain Nolan. I stepped in front of him and held up my palms. 'Stop there, friend.'

The Goth stopped. He looked down at me over his long snout and sniffed at each of my hands. Then, he lifted a paw to shove me out of the way, but before he could reach me, I stepped inside the paw's arc, reached up, and grabbed the shag of his chest and yanked down on it so hard that I felt the thick hide lift from the hard muscles beneath.

'Karz, order your friend to back off,' I shouted.

But Karz said nothing. The Goth lumbered forward, dragging me with him. He would not stop. That was clear. So, I lowered my shoulders, shoved one boot behind me, and dug in. It was like pushing a car—a great, furry twelve foot Accord Progressive with first gear engaged.

He kept on coming. My boot gripped, slid, and gripped and slid all over again, making a comical squelch on the deck. It didn't slow the Goth down a bit. On he came. My fists dug deeper into the fur. I felt the Goth's hot breath on the top of my head. Then he stopped.

I expected a swipe loaded with claws to rake my back, or maybe even a bite on my arms, but by then, Karz had piped up from the doorway. The Goth growled a reply, then stepped back. I let go of his fur. My hands were greasy with Goth oil.

'Friend,' growled Karz and began lumbering down the passageway.

The big Goth rumbled at me.

'Are you OK?' I said to Captain Nolan. She stood against the bulkhead with her hands over her face. She dropped them, stood to her full height, and brushed the non-existent curl away from her eyes.

'What did you say?'

'I asked if you are all right.'

She sniffed. 'The savior complex is a well-known manifestation of toxic masculinity, Prisoner 548B.'

'The savior complex just saved you from a paw swipe.'

'I disagree. The intra-galactic friend sensed my acceptance of him.'

'He also sensed the urge to swat your head off.'

'You do not know that, Prisoner 548B.'

'No, but I had a good idea.'

'I think you have come to believe your own press, as they say.'

'What?'

'You fantasize that you are the film actor you are said to resemble: the tall, fair-haired actor who always plays the role of villain in the films about the pre-Accord.'

'I do not. I don't even know the guy's name.'

'How else can you explain this display of what he would call gallantry, but which we now identify as the worst manifestation of maleness and an attempt to subjugate those who identify as female.'

'You could just say thank you.'

'Why should I do that? You did me no favors. If anything, you offended our intra-galactic friends by presuming they were hostile. In doing so, you set back my attempts to be inclusive and introduce him to Accord values.'

'Oh, so you think he wanted to shake your hand? Or give you a hug? Take a look at him, Captain.'

We both looked across at the giant Goth. He swayed by the door, listening, one ear turned to Captain Nolan, the other aimed at me. When he saw us looking, he rumbled threateningly from his great height. Then, he raised a paw and swept it towards the door, as if shooing us out. Captain

Nolan stepped past him and through the door, as confidently as an Accord commissioner. The two Goths' snouts tracked her, sniffing deeply. I hobbled after her, out and down the passageway. The Goths hulked after us, exchanging rumbles.

After we had walked the passageway for fifteen minutes, I called out to Karz's shaggy back.

'Karz, where is ship's captain?'

'Go captain,' Karz growled.

'I'll do the talking, Prisoner 548B,' said Captain Nolan.

I ignored her. 'Where is ship in space, Karz?'

Karz growled a word I didn't understand.

We reached the end of the passageway and passed through another door into a wide, open deck area. Sprawled across the deck, hundreds of Goths lay on mattresses. As we entered, they rolled over and sniffed us. Their snouts jerked up and down. Their nasal flukes flared. They snuffled and rumbled and growled. All of them were huge, all of them were males, except for a handful of females.

Many were eating. They gnawed on gray bones that looked like the femurs of large animals. Some of the bones ended in tufted hooves. The Goths watched us over their meals, the black hems of their snouts rippling. Don't worry, guys, I thought. I don't want your dinners. Even so, I knew that eventually, I too might have to gnaw a rancid bone. So would Captain Nolan. That would be something to look forward to.

Further forward, we walked past a wide viewport on the port side. It revealed nothing— not Earth, not the planets, not the sun, not even the stars. Only darkness. The sight of all that nothingness made my predicament clearer. I was on a space vessel in the midst of hundreds and possibly thousands of hostile monsters, far from Earth and freedom.

Go Gwawanath.

'Where are we, Karz?' I said.

'Ship,' said Karz.

'No. Where in space?'

'Did you not hear my order, Prisoner 548B?'

'OK Captain, so you ask where we are?'

She didn't reply, nor did she express alarm at being in space or aboard this alien ship. Her self control was impressive—either that or her belief in the protective qualities of Accord values was beyond the usual level of madness.

We passed through the forward door, out of this stateroom and into another passageway. At its end, Karz stopped and growled to another enormous male Goth guarding yet another door. The Goth sniffed at me and sniffed Captain Nolan. He took a long time to be sure of her scent, if that's what he was doing. Meanwhile, Captain Nolan said nothing. She just kept her noble chin high and her gaze above his heavy maleness swaying between his hind quarters. She looked into the distance, as if she were gazing at a distant mountain peak and the rest of us weren't there.

The guard at the passageway's forward end also sniffed at Captain Nolan. Then he growled to Karz. Karz growled in reply. The guard growled a second time. They both growled together. The Goth thumped the door with one great paw. He waited until a thump sounded on the other side, and then, using a forelimb, pushed the door lever down. The door opened. The Goth lumbered aside to allow us through.

'Gwah,' growled Karz.

'Gwah,' the guard growled in reply.

'Gwah,' growled the two Goths behind us.

We entered a small stateroom made of the same gray metal. It was dominated by an image on the forward bulkhead of a shaggy, Goth-like creature, standing on its hind legs, its sex prominent, its fur glistening, its expression serene. One of its paws held a black sphere. The other was raised with its claws extended. A blue halo glowed behind its head. Above it hovered three symbols like the writing from AONT China in the pre-Accord era.

Around the bulkheads, several female Goths gnawed on more bones. Their snouts rose and sniffed as we entered.

In the center of the stateroom lay two more mattresses, each stained with yellow and brown smears. On the first mattress, three male Goths sat on their haunches. I recognized the big, red-furred Goth, the one Karz called the leader. Either side of him sat two other Goths: a smaller Goth and the angry brown Goth with the scar on his snout.

They leaned forward, sniffing and snuffling at our hair, ears, and uniforms. In the sitting position, their teeth were level with Captain Nolan's face. The sight of Goth noses so huge and close, and the blast of the Goths' breaths, so full and foul, was a test of anyone's composure, but Captain Nolan did not take a step back. She stood her ground and even managed a strained smile.

'Gwah,' growled Karz.

'Gwah,' growled the three Goths. Then, every Goth in the room growled in unison till the noise was so loud I couldn't hear my own thoughts. When they calmed down, Karz lowered a paw at the mattress. We sat down, relieved to be away from the three probing snouts. Instead, we found our faces level with the Goths' shaggy chests, and only a foot or so above their squirming laps. And coming at us, like a thick wave, was the reek of wet dog.

When we were settled, the captain growled the strange word, 'Gwah,' and every Goth's ears stood to attention. The meeting, or whatever this was supposed to be, was about to begin.

26

Captain Nolan spoke first.

'Karz, please tell your leader that I am Captain Nolan of the Accord of Nations Navy. Please add that I greet him in the names of tolerance, equality, and intra-galactic diversity.'

The Goth leader turned to Karz and growled. Karz said, 'My captain say you not speak. Only him.' She tossed her snout at me. 'Only him.'

'You might not realize, intra-galactic friend,' said Captain Nolan, 'that on Earth, we are not simply men or women, "him" or "her." There is a spectrum of…'

The Goth captain growled. Karz growled too. They both growled together.

'Not speak,' said Karz. 'Only him.' This time, she raised a paw and pointed at me.

Captain Nolan did not give up. She attempted some Goth-speak.

'Please tell captain I bigger leader than Burns—than him.' She pointed at me with a slender hand. 'I speak first.'

Karz growled to the captain. The captain growled in return.

'Only man speak. Not you. You his...' and she growled a word I couldn't understand.

I turned to Captain Nolan. 'I think you better listen to Karz, Captain. Goths know nothing about the Oppression Hierarchy.'

'We must explain it to them, Prisoner 548B. Everyone must know, especially intra-galactic friends.'

The Goth leader growled louder. Then he raised a paw and pointed at the painting of the serene Goth on the bulkhead. Then he growled again, his shaggy, red fur shaking.

When the growling died down, Karz said, 'My leader say god Gwanta want female not speak. God Gwanta everything to Gwanath people.'

'Gwanta?' Captain Nolan asked.

'Gwanta.' Karz dipped her head reverently at the painting of the serene Goth with the black sphere and the halo.

'They're serious about it, Captain.'

'I can see that, Prisoner 548B.'

'For the sake of tolerance, how about leaving the talking to the male, just for this meeting?'

Captain Nolan nodded up at the three Goths, pursed her lips, and reached for the imaginary curl over her forehead.

'In the interests of tolerance, I will respect your culture.'

'Not understand,' said Karz.

'I agree that I will allow Lieutenant Burns to

speak.'

'Not understand,' growled Karz.

Captain Nolan sighed. 'Not speak you. Only he speak.' She pointed at me.

'Not understand.'

Captain Nolan drew a breath and said, 'Just don't say anything that others them.'

Karz growled to the leader. The leader growled in reply. The Goths on either side of him growled. Then the Goths at the entrance door growled. One Goth's growl would trigger the next until they were all howling and growling like a wolf pack in forests of far north AONT Canada.

The growling ceased, and the sniffing began again. The leader and the two other Goths leaned down from their great height, aimed their snouts at us and sniffed with short upward tilts of their heads. Even Karz leaned down and sniffed. It was like they wanted to confirm that our scents were the same as five minutes ago.

Then, when the last sniffs were complete, the captain growled long sentences to Karz, who translated, and I began to understand what these giant, violent creatures intended for me.

Joining them in the fight against Octavia was the least of it.

27

First, Karz introduced us.

'This, leader, Captain Gwawn,' growled Karz. 'This second leader, Glathaw.' She pointed at the Goth to the captain's right. 'This third leader, Granak,' she raised a paw at the Goth on the captain's left, the angry one with the scar on his snout.

I nodded up at them. They sniffed at me. Granak sniffed the longest, leaning down to push his scabrous snout into my hair. Then he sat upright and nodded to himself and then to the captain and Glathaw.

'Karz,' I said. 'Please ask captain when go Earth?'

Karz growled something to the captain who growled back at her.

'Captain say not.'

'Not what?'

'He say he see you.'

'See me?'

'He see you.'

'See me where?'

'See you Ranawah ship.'

'Ranawah ship?'

'Ranawah ship.'

I thought for a moment. By 'Ranawah ship,' he must have meant Octavia's ship, Excidium, the ship to which I had been ordered by the Accord to welcome Octavia to Earth. This was the same ship in which I'd fired a Roman weapon and killed at least two Goths.

I remembered it clearly: the large rifle in my grip; the blasts smashing the Goths in the snouts and shoulders; the Goths dying in agony, biting their wounds, and their claws driving them around in circles on the deck.

Captain Gwawn and his two lieutenants watched me from above, their snouts twitching.

'Ranawah ship?' I said cautiously.

'You on Ranawah ship growled Karz.'

'Yes,' I said.

She growled this to the captain. He growled in reply. Granak, the one with the scar, growled louder, nodded his head several times, and inhaled deeply, puffing himself up with indignation.

'My leader say you fight Gwanath people. Yes?'

'Gwanath?' I said. 'What is Gwanath?' I wanted to clear up the meaning of this word once and for all. Karz raised a paw at Captain Gwawn, Glathaw, and Granak, then at the guards swaying on the haunches at the door, and at the female

Goths on the mattresses.

'Gwanath,' growled Karz

The growling began all over again as the Goths confirmed they were indeed Gwanath. When they settled down, Karz said, 'Captain say you shoot Gwanath on ship,' she growled, holding up her paws to mimic firing a rifle. 'You kill Gwanath.'

I kept my mouth shut, knowing that I also killed at least two more Gwanath back at AONNB Holder.

'He smell you.' Karz raised a paw at Granak. 'He smell you. You shoot Gwanath. Kill Gwanath. He smell you.'

Granak glared at me. The other Goths remained silent. The atmosphere seemed to change, as if the pressure dropped.

'You shoot!' growled Karz. 'Granak smell you. Same now. Smell never wrong. Never wrong.'

I kept quiet.

'He smell you,' growled Karz a second time. 'Same smell. Smell not wrong.'

And Granak sniffed me all over again, the flukes of his nostrils flaring wider. Then he turned to Captain Gwawn and growled.

'Same smell now,' growled Karz. 'You shoot Gwanath people.'

They sniffed at me accusingly. I saw the yellow tips of Granak's claws inch from the sheaths in his paws.

'Tell captain that Goth… Gwanath people attack me,' I said. 'Attack. Want kill me.'

This was half right. I hadn't been certain they were attacking, but I shot them anyway, killing them before they could reach Captain Le Seaux and Andrew Chen.

'You kill Gwanath,' Karz growled. 'Now, we take you Gwanath king.'

'What?' I said. 'Not understand.'

'Gwanath king. We take you Gwanath king. Go Gwawanath.'

'What about fighting Romans… fighting Ranawah and Ranawah leader Octavia?'

'Go Gwawanath.'

'Why?'

'King say what happen you.'

'Like a court? The king wants to pass judgment on me?'

'Not understand.'

Captain Nolan spoke. 'I can't allow this.' All the Goths sniffed at her, but she carried on undeterred. 'We punish Burns,' she said. 'We punish him on Earth.' She pointed at me. 'We punish him for shooting Gwanath people.'

The captain growled and turned to Karz.

'Leader say go Gwanath king.'

'In battle,' I said, 'everyone kill everyone.'

'Yes,' Karz growled. 'My leader say Gwanath like fight. Gwanta like fight. We fight no rifle. No rifle. Fight like…' and she pointed at her left paw, then her claws, then her teeth. 'Gwanath kill you. You kill Gwanath. OK.'

'Shoot OK?' I said.

'Shoot OK.'

Now I was confused. They liked killing. They understood about killing and being killed in battle. What was the problem?

Then the answer came at last.

'You,' Karz growled. 'You kill Gwanath prince. Gwanath king son. Prince. You kill prince.'

'I shot a prince?'

'Prince. King Gwantalan son.'

So, I had killed a prince. That was why the Goths didn't care about the shots at AONNB Holder. Those Goths were soldiers, commoners. But back on the Excidium I had killed the king's son, the Prince of Goths, or whatever title they might have given him.

Around the stateroom, every Goth watched and sniffed me: Karz, the captain, Glathaw, Granak, the guards, the females on the mattresses with their bones. Even Captain Nolan turned and looked at me. I half expected her to sniff me too.

'What will king do?' I asked.

Karz growled this question to Captain Gwawn. He sniffed at the painting of the Goth holding the black sphere. Then he growled his response.

'My leader say king ask god Gwanta. King very Gwanta. All Gwanath very Gwanta. Gwanta say what happen you.'

At the sound of the name Gwanta, every Goth in the stateroom made a bow at the painting. Then they barked three times.

'What they say, Karz?'

She pointed with her right paw at her own snout, then her left paw. Then she repeated the three barks.

Paws, claws, teeth. It must have been some kind of philosophy, or battle cry, the equivalent of T.E.D. Whatever it meant, it didn't sound good for me.

'What Gwanta say?' I asked, pointing at the painting of Gwanta myself, but then withdrawing my finger when Granak began to rise from the mattress.

'Gwanta like kill,' Karz said. 'Gwanta very like kill.'

'Kill? No. I say sorry, king. Accident. Mistake. Mistake.'

'Gwanta like kill,' said Karz. 'King Gwantalan like kill. Gwanath people like kill. All like kill.'

The bizarre and dangerous state of my predicament sank in. I had chosen to go with these Goths because I was tired of fighting the Accord and Octavia, and because I had nowhere to run. Now, I would pay the price. I was damned whatever I chose to do.

'Where king?' I asked.

'King in Gwawanath.'

'Obviously, Gwawanath is the name of their home planet, Prisoner 548B,' said Captain Nolan.

'How far Gwawanath?' I asked.

Karz sniffed quietly for a moment, then she said, 'Gwawanath…' and raised a paw and swatted the air several times.

'How far?'

I thought for a moment, remembering what Octavia told me about her home planet, Rome, the one she shared with these Goths. Rome orbited a star on the far side of the galaxy, but how far away was that?

'How long Gwawanath?' I asked again.

Karz shook her snout. She turned to the captain and growled a low growl. The captain raised a paw at the forward end of the room.

'We ask pilot,' said Karz.

'Pilot,' I said. 'Pilot of this ship?'

'Ask pilot,' growled Karz.

'Please ask pilot.'

Karz growled to Captain Gwawn. The captain growled to Granak. Granak barked, then stood and lumbered to the secured door at the forward end of the stateroom.

He growled to the guard standing outside the door. The guard thumped on the door with one great paw. Then, after a few moments, the door swung inward. Granak stood far too tall to go through it, so he lowered his head beneath the top jamb and growled. A long growl replied from inside.

Granak lumbered backward to make way. I expected another shaggy form to come crouching through the door.

Instead, a beautiful Earth woman stepped out.

28

The woman was tall, fair-haired, and dressed in an olive-green uniform, form-fitted to reveal a slender figure, just like the uniforms worn by Octavia's crew on the Excidium. Yet, unlike the confident Excidium women, this pilot was meek. Her hands were clasped, her gaze on the deck.

She could only be a Roman—a Roman wearing the same Earth disguise as Octavia, a Roman in human form. But what was she doing aboard a Goth ship? Romans and Goths shared the same planet but were enemies.

'Pilot,' said Karz. 'Ranawah pilot. Ship.'

Towering over the pilot, Granak growled down at her. To my astonishment, the pilot opened her mouth and growled a reply. A beautiful human face and a terrible animal growl!

Karz translated. 'Pilot say Gwawanath far.'

'How far?' I asked.

Karz growled at the pilot, who growled back at her. More growls were exchanged. 'Not know words. Pilot speak.'

We turned to the beautiful woman. Without looking up she spoke in English, and in the same pre-Accord era, AONT USA accent as that of Octavia.

'From the ship's current position,' she said, 'the distance to Gwawanath is approximately one hundred thousand light-years. This is taking into account both the diameter and the width of the galaxy, which we must traverse on a diagonal course.'

Just like that. And it had me wondering. Why didn't the Goths rely on this woman to translate? Why did they use Karz?

'So how long will it take to get there—to Gwawanath?' I said.

'Presently, we are standing off Earth's solar system. We have not fully accelerated. You will know when acceleration begins. I recommend you take precautions.'

'Acceleration?'

'Acceleration is not quite the right word to describe what happens when we cross the galaxy, but it is a good approximation. It might be more precise to describe it as extreme acceleration. Yes, acceleration in the extreme. Very hard for most life forms to endure. You will feel powerful forces, especially as Earth people. You must prepare before acceleration.'

'So how long?' I asked. 'How long to cross the galaxy to Gwawanath.'

'It is not so simple. The galaxy is rotating. Your sun itself is moving at five hundred thousand miles each Earth hour. Gwawanath is situated on the galaxy's far side. It is moving at an even higher speed than your sun. To reach it, we must allow for both the distance and the motion of the points of origin and destination.'

The stateroom was silent. Every Goth seemed fascinated by the weird language. Their snouts constantly sniffed; their ears flicked to the pilot and then to Captain Nolan and me. Sometimes the ears moved independently of each other and faced different directions.

'So how long? How long to cross the galaxy—to Gwawanath?'

'Two Earth days.'

'Two Earth days! Two Earth days for one hundred thousand light-years! That's impossible.'

'Knowledge of pre-Accord space travel is forbidden, Prisoner 548B,' said Captain Nolan. 'How do you know about light years?'

The pilot spoke again. 'Our ship, the Gwantasnarr was attacked and damaged by Roman forces as we left Earth. We have just completed repairs—the other pilots and I. She then growled to the Goths, who sniffed in reply. 'We can now make the crossing. However, the Lovelorn…' She paused and corrected herself. 'I mean Admiral Octavia and her Ranawah forces are still in pursuit—even now.'

And no sooner had the pilot finished speaking when there was a crash in the stern. We were all jolted from the mattresses.

'What was that?' I asked.

Karz sniffed. 'Ranawah.'

A thump sounded on the door aft. The guard thumped back. The door opened. A Goth entered and growled several times to the captain.

'Ranawah ship come back,' growled Karz.

The Goths all climbed onto their hind legs. The room filled with their bulk. They growled at each other. Then, they turned toward the painting of the god Gwanta and barked the three curious words, lowering their heads as they did so. Then, they stood up, turned, and lumbered to the passageway, roaring the word, 'Gwah!'

The captain turned and growled at Karz.

'My leader say now you.'

'Now me? Now me what?'

'Leader say you fight for Gwanath people. Fight Ranawah. We tell king you fight Ranawah.' She tossed her head. 'Fight Ranawah for Gwanath people. Maybe Gwanath king like. Maybe Gwanta like.'

'Gwanath king like?' I said, hoping that she would add the words, 'Not kill.'

She sniffed me again and said, 'Gwah.'

The door swung open once more, and another Goth entered the stateroom. He growled to Karz, who growled back.

'Ranawah coming!'

Everything was happening way too fast: the accusation of murder by Granak; the news we were about to travel to Rome for my trial; the pilots being Roman. And what did the pilot mean

189

by referring to Octavia as 'The Lovelorn?'

I would have to find out.

In the meantime, yet another Goth came lumbering through the door. He growled at Karz, then lumbered over to me on his hind limbs. He cradled something in his shaggy paws. It was one of the long Roman rifles. He opened his arms and let the rifle drop. I caught it before it hit the deck.

'Use kill Ranawah. You kill. King like. Maybe not kill you. Or maybe Ranawah kill you, so no need go king.'

I held the rifle in my hands. It was the same type of weapon I had fired at Octavia. I should have been pleased to hold it again, but now it seemed like a burden.

'Put that weapon down, Prisoner 548B,' said Captain Nolan. 'I order you not to join this battle.'

I looked at her squarely in her light blue eyes. 'I don't want to join it, Captain,' I said, 'but I also don't want to die.'

She began to speak, but I ignored her. I turned and hobbled after the shaggy backs and shuddering rumps of the Goths.

No, I didn't want to die. I was tired and angry. I felt the battle against Octavia had been lost and Earth had gone mad. I was uncertain exactly what mattered any more, and what I should do, but for the moment, I could agree with myself that I didn't want to die.

Not yet, anyway.

29

In the passageway, the roaring became so loud it drowned out the clanking and banging amidships.

We reached the passageway's end and burst into the large stateroom. Inside, hundreds of agitated Goths hulked around on their hind limbs, like a dark forest in a gale. They bayed and growled. They lumbered in a circle, snarling at each other, waiting for a command to attack. 'Gwah!' they roared. 'Gwah!' Thankfully, they ignored me—or didn't see me, or couldn't smell me. I stuck by the bulkheads to avoid each giant rump, flank, and paw.

At a roar from Captain Gwawn, the mass of Goths swirled out of the stateroom into the passageway aft. On their four limbs, they flowed like a river of fur. They surged down the passageway's length growling 'Gwah!' and 'Gwanta' and the three words Karz had spoken to the painting—the words I thought were paws, claws, and teeth.

The river of Goths poured into a cargo hold where hundreds more Goths roared as they entered. Then the combined force massed in front of a large port, roaring at whatever lay on its far side. Some even reared up and raked the metal with screeching claws. The Goths weren't just eager for battle; they were frantic for it. They were rabid.

What lay on the other side of the port? Were the Roman Marines crouched and waiting with their rifles? Could events have moved so fast? Could a Roman ship have pulled alongside and grappled us while we talked in the forward stateroom? Or was it the other way around? Had the Goths grappled the Roman ship?

And then, there was a larger question. Why did the Romans bother with these raids? If the Goths were such a nuisance, why didn't they just blast their ships from space and be rid of them? Why risk the lives of their Marines in bloody skirmishes? And why hadn't they eradicated the Goths from their shared planet—or at least forced them to stay put where they couldn't do any harm? And then there were the questions about the Goths themselves. Hadn't they used explosives to attack the Excidium?

The more I discovered about Octavia, the Romans, and their co-inhabitants of Gwawanath-Rome, the more mysterious and troubled their world seemed. One day, I thought, I'll find the answers to all these questions—maybe from the pilots, maybe from Karz, or maybe from Octavia herself.

If I survive long enough to ask.

In the meantime, I had to survive the next hour. I hadn't been away from the Accord for a single day and I was already caught up in a battle and accused of murdering a Goth prince. What would happen the next day and the day after that? When would it all end?

'Gwah!' roared a Goth beside my ear. I stepped out of its way, back to the forward bulkhead. I didn't want to be crushed beneath four thousand hubcap-sized paws. I had to stay alive long enough to fire at one of the Marines. Not only that, I had to make sure the Goths saw me firing.

Then the port opened, revealing a tunnel or a bridge leading to the enemy vessel. The Goths surged into it, growling and clawing. Some went on four legs; others went on two. All of them lusting to fight with paws, claws, and teeth, to fight and kill for their nation and their god Gwanta, the god Octavia had called ridiculous.

When the last of the Goths had jammed themselves inside. I followed, unslinging the rifle, my right hand clasping the stock, my left keeping the muzzle raised and ready. I had no tactical plan other than to find a place from which I could shelter and shoot and show willingness to kill Romans.

And then to stay alive.

At the bridge's end, I hobbled into a living nightmare. The Goths, unafraid of the rifle fire, roared into heavy volley blasts from Roman

Marines. By the time I arrived, the Romans had knocked the first wave of Goths to the deck where they writhed and clawed the gray metal. The rest of the Goths bounded over them, only to be smashed down in turn.

The Roman rifles inflicted horrific injuries. Goths with shattered limbs ran in tortured circles. Others bit their wounds or dragged themselves toward the enemy by their front paws, their useless hind limbs smearing a thick trail of guts and glistening blood.

It was appalling. This was no way to fight a battle. This was no way to defeat Octavia. This was no way to win a war. The only thing it was good for was dying in battle. Maybe that's all the Goths wanted. Maybe that was all Gwanta demanded of them: death by paws, claws, and teeth. Maybe it didn't matter whether the battle itself had any objective. It was insane.

But not all of the Goths died. Led by Granak, many Goths escaped the blasts and reached the Roman Marines. The Marines stood almost as tall as the Goths themselves. Even so, the Goths knocked them down and tore at their armor with violent raking swipes. Then, they tore at the gray flesh beneath and eventually at the swirling brown viscera. They tore and ripped and stomped and bit and raised their bloody snouts and howled until they were driven away by rifle blasts from other Marines.

From behind the barricade of a fallen Goth corpse, I crouched down, raised my rifle, and picked out individual enemies. The blasts knocked each Marine down, but not out. They stood too far away, and their armor was too thick. Still, the blasts smacked against the armor with deep clangs, flinging each Marine from his feet or spinning him around till he faced the wrong direction.

As the battle raged, the number of Goth corpses piled up on the deck, but so did the numbers of disabled Marines. The fighting remained intense. So, I continued to fire. I knocked down a Marine who had singled out Granak with his rifle. I blew away the arm of another Marine before he could pull his rifle's trigger. And in one shot, I knocked the helmeted head from a sniper. He had fired two shots in my direction. Both had hit the Goth corpse, blasting it into bloody chunks, so I had to get up and run to find another one.

I fought without passion. I was like a mercenary from the pre-Accord era, fighting for money, not for principles or nations. I wanted to stay alive. I wanted to prove to the Goth king I had helped his army. That was all. But with each shot, I wondered about that too. What if I survived the trial? What then? Would life even be worth living in an Accord controlled by Octavia?

It was the wrong moment to have no aims in life. I shook my head free of bad thoughts. Concentrate on this moment, I thought. This moment and nothing more. That's all you have.

Through the rifle's sights, I saw three Marines

turn their guns my way. Maybe it was now my turn for some volley fire. But I fired first. The shots scattered the Marines in great clangs of helmets and shattered weapons.

So far, so good—but I knew it couldn't last for long. Word must surely pass around about the sniper who fought for the Goths.

Soon, the next Goth corpse exploded in front of me. Chunks of furry hide windmilled into the air, and dark red Goth blood splattered on the deck. I clambered away and ran to the next Goth corpse. There was one twenty yards away, but before I could hobble to it, I was knocked to the deck— not by a rifle blast, but by a tackle from an unseen Marine. I spun onto my back, rifle ready, but then a heavy metal boot clomped down on my chest, pinning me to the deck. A metallic hand smacked away the rifle muzzle, then gripped it, so I couldn't swing it back to fire.

It was a Marine who had appeared from nowhere. He loomed over me, his boot on my chest, like a pre-Accord knight standing over his vanquished foe. I expected that boot to clomp all the way down through my ribs, crushing away my life. But instead, the Marine leaned down. The metal helmet loomed in front of my face. Then, the helmet's guard rose, and inside, was a dark, featureless face.

'Hello, Alex,' said a voice. There was no mouth, yet the direction from which the voice came was from within the helmet. 'So now you are fighting with my enemies. You are testing my patience, my dear.' This was Octavia's voice, of course. The last thing I wanted to hear. 'What have you got to say for yourself?'

'You are an enemy of the Accord.' I said. 'That's why I'm fighting you.' I didn't want to tell her my actual reasons for being there.

'That's not what your government believes, Alex. Remember? I'm going to be the first Intra-galactic commissioner.'

'You deceived the commissioners.'

'I disagree, Alex. It's not necessary to deceive them. They can't see anything except what they want to see, which is a fantasy of a future that can never exist. Not that it matters. I don't need them in order to realize my plans, but their folly will make things easier.'

'Realize what plans?'

'Oh, you know, the landing of my forces and ships, the occupation of your cities, the annihilation of your people, the destruction of your forests tree-by-tree, the transformation of your seas, rivers, and mountains, the smashing of your monuments, the eradication of your fauna. I can go on.'

I nearly said the words, 'Not while I'm alive.' Then, I realized how pathetic they would sound. Instead, I said, 'Are you here on this ship? Are you here now or is this another of your telepathy tricks?'

'No, Alex. I am far, far away.. Further than you can imagine. I ordered this rendezvous between the Goths and my Marines so that I can help you, and to repeat my offer. I can still bring you to me. Think about it. If you're with me, we can plan a future together. All that destruction doesn't have to happen, Alex. The mothers don't have to lose their children. The children don't have to watch their parents killed. The forests don't have to burn. Not if you ask me to spare them. All you have to say is that you'll board my ship and come to me of your own free will. Your own free will, Alex, not because you are forced.'

'And what if I don't?'

'Then I will abandon you here, and then the Goths will take you to Rome, and their ridiculous king will put you to death in the name of their laughable god in front of their preposterous hordes.'

'You know why they are taking me there?'

'Even across the whirling voids of space, Alex, I can still hear.'

'Captain Gwawn says it's a trial, not an execution.'

'Come now, Alex. Trials are for civilized people, not a rabble, not howling mobs. Why squander your life dying in the dust on the far side of the galaxy, when you can sit beside me in triumph on Earth?'

'No.'

'Just say the word, Alex, and it all stops. Your imprisonment, the destruction of your home, the pressure of this boot on your chest which I feel is about to crack your sternum. All of it. This is your last opportunity. I'm running out of patience.

Come with me now. Yes or no?'

'No.'

'What was that? I didn't hear you.'

'I said no.'

'Then, take your chances with the filthy Goths.'

The face guard snapped closed, the helmet went back, and the armored shoulders rose. The boot on my chest withdrew and clomped onto the deck. Then, the Marine stood still among the fighting, as if waiting for Octavia to depart its consciousness. It stood oblivious to the Goth bounding at it and also to the barrel of my rifle swinging up from below. Then, it jolted alive, just in time. It turned to face the Goth, and raised its weapon to fire, but by then I had pulled the trigger. The Marine's helmet exploded just as the Goth's claws hit its chest.

Both Goth and Marine toppled to the deck. The Goth tore at the Marine's breast plate, ripping apart the chest and flinging out the entrails, unaware that the Marine was already dead. When it raised its head, the Goth's snout was covered in gore all the way from the black nob of its nose to the fur around its mad, shiny eyes. Then it turned its head at the sight of me and bobbed down on its front limbs, ready to leap again.

In its battle mania, it must have thought I was another Marine. I raised the rifle and leveled it at the red roof of its panting mouth. I didn't want to fire, but I wasn't going to be torn apart, either. For two seconds, the Goth remained in its crouch.

Then a great, throaty bawl came from somewhere to my left. The Goth's ears twitched. We both looked around. Goths were turning and lumbering towards the bridge-tunnel leading back to the Gwantasnarr. The battle was apparently over. The Marines must have withdrawn to their ship.

I looked back at the Goth. It was still looking at me. Then its head jerked with a violent sneeze, and after it had recovered, it licked some gore from its shoulder, and then licked its forelimb like an obscene and monstrous cat. It took its time. Then, it stood on its four paws and lumbered away. 'Gwah,' it said as its great flank slid by, like the side of a ship.

I stood and waited till the last of the Goths had trudged into the tunnel, leaving their slain or dying comrades behind. Then, I hobbled after them. I felt raw from the battle and overwhelmed by all that Octavia had told me about her plans for Earth. I was sick with images of forests ablaze and cities in ruins while the Accord commissioners congratulated themselves on their tolerance. I was tormented with the knowledge that by saying yes to her offer, I could prevent the destruction.

Instead, I had said no.

As I limped down the tunnel, I was sure I had made a terrible decision. Worse! I had made it for the wrong reasons — because of pride and a selfish urge to defy Octavia with the misguided thought it was the right thing to do. If I had put my pride away, I could have saved the Earth. Surely, that was the right thing to do, wasn't it?

'Gwah!' roared the Goths.

What did they care about the Earth and the Accord? Nothing. All they cared about was their mistaken belief they had won a battle, that they had fought bravely with paws, claws, and teeth, as Gwanta commanded. This thought made me feel even worse, and the rifle and the weight of my irresponsible and selfish choices became unbearable.

And yet, somewhere, like that small light on the sea at night, was a sense of something else beyond these dark waves of doubt. I wasn't sure yet what it meant, only that now I had chosen my course—for whatever reasons—that I should carry on, and maybe, just maybe, despite overwhelming odds, something might turn out for the better.

I had to keep thinking that, or I might never survive what happened next.

30

'Why won't you take the pills that Dr. Iqbal gave you, Alex?'

We were at Kresta's house. I was about to leave for school. She had been talking on her handheld. 'Alex, I asked you a question.'

'But I'll be late.'

'This won't take long.'

I waited at the door with my school bag.

'Dr. Iqbal knows, Alex. He knows you're not taking the pills. He says you're not showing any progress.'

I said nothing.

'Why aren't you taking the pills, Alex?'

'I better go or I'll miss the Accord pledge.'

'The pledge can wait.'

'But the teachers get angry if we're late.'

'This is more important. Put down your bag.'

I dropped my schoolbag on the floor and sat on the stool near the window where I could watch the street outside.

'You feel sick?' 'Is that it? The pills make you sick?'

'They taste like dirt.'

'Well, swallow them with soy milk, like I told you.'

'I don't like soy milk.'

'You're not usually like this, Alex. What's going on?'

'Nothing.'

She considered me for a moment. 'It's Cal, isn't it? He told you not to take the pills.'

Through the window, I saw two Accord members I knew. They were walking on the street on their way to school. They didn't have to take pills. Only I did.

'Listen, Alex. Cal means well. He wants the best for you—like I do.'

'That's what he said.'

'We both do. It's just that we have different ideas. I want you to have the best future in the Accord. That's why I want you to take the pills. If you don't take the pills, it'll be hard for you. Really hard, Alex. You'll understand that one day and you'll thank me.'

'Cal says he wants me to be myself—what I'm supposed to be. He says our family is supposed to be in the Navy. It's always been in the Navy. He says that's more important than the Accord.'

Kresta sighed. 'Cal's head is full of dreams, Alex. Dangerous dreams about the pre-Accord era, and you know how bad that was. What Cal wants will harm your future. The Accord knows best, Alex. Cal doesn't. He'll only get us into trouble with the Accord. Big trouble. You don't want that, do you?'

'No.'

'If you take the pills, Alex, you can grow up to be anything you want. You can work as a Harmony Officer. You could work at one of the big departments *in AON sub territory Los Angeles like I do.'*

'Could I be in the Navy?'

'The Navy is not good for you, Alex.'

'But can I?'

'We'll see. There are a lot of other things you can do, once you take the pills.'

'But Cal says if I take the pills, I won't be who I'm supposed to be. I won't be a boy.'

Kresta frowned. 'It mightn't seem like it Alex, but in the Accord, it's much better to be female. Kids like you have been turning into females for hundreds of years. Don't they teach you that in school?'

I watched through the window. The other young Accord members were gone. Kresta came back with the pills. She held out a glass of soy milk.

'But what about the things Cal said?'

'Cal,' said Kresta, 'is going to find himself in trouble.'

31

The dream would not let me go. I tried to wake from it, but it tugged on my arm pulling me back down.

Eventually, my senses took hold and hauled me away to the present, all the way to the terrible now.

I woke in darkness to all the hated sensations. I smelled the rank air; felt the sagging mattress; heard the droning engines; and recognized the terrible regrets crouching around me like tormentors, each chanting, 'All will be lost and you have done nothing because you don't care.'

Then, the dream let me go and I sensed the cabin in the dark and the rustle of clothing a few feet from my head.

'Where am I?'

'Don't come near me, Prisoner 548B. I am holding the Equality 38.'

'The what?' I said.

'The gun, Prisoner 548B.'

'We're back in the cabin, right?'

'You really don't know?'

'What happened?'

'The acceleration, as our intra-galactic friends call it. That's what happened.'

'I only remember the battle. What happened after that?'

'The acceleration happened. The pilots started it while the battle was ending. Must have been a mistake.'

'And?'

'It was violent and sudden. It flattened our intra-galactic friends against the bulkheads. Their groans and whimpers were very distressing for them and for me. Then the ship seemed to flex. It's difficult to explain and I won't waste words on you, but the light seemed to bend.'

'And what happened?'

'You blacked out very early, Prisoner 548B.'

'Me? I don't believe it.'

'Why not? You think you're invulnerable? You think you're stronger than someone who identifies as female?'

'Yes, for certain. I mean no. Are we still accelerating?'

'I don't think so. The engines have stopped.'

'I can still hear them.'

'I mean they have stopped making the noise they made during the acceleration.'

'So where are we?'

'You think I can read the pilots' minds, Prisoner 548B? I don't know where we are, but my guess is that the acceleration is over. That's all.'

'Over already? So, that's it? We're here. We're on the other side of the galaxy, a hundred thousand light-years from Earth? Just like that?'

'I don't know, Prisoner 548B.'

'How did we get back here in this cabin?'

'Our intra-galactic friends must have carried us.'

'How long has it been? How long have I been out?'

'I am your superior officer, Prisoner 548B, not your keeper.'

'Guess, Captain. Please.'

'A day. Perhaps longer. I was unconscious too. I woke before you did. That was a long time ago.'

I sat and thought for a moment. Gradually, the details of the situation returned. They showed up like shameful messengers in the dark: Octavia's invasion plan for Earth; the trip across the galaxy; and the Goths's determination to put me on trial for the murder of their prince. Then there were my own personal shames: my hopelessness and my damaged mind.

'If only we could get out of here,' I said.

'I agree, Prisoner 548B. Your court-martial on Earth is not over. It must go ahead until we convict you of all your one hundred and forty Navy Spirit Code violations.'

'You still think there will be a court martial? You still think life will go on after Octavia lands her ships?'

'Of course. Admiral Octavia will acknowledge

our inclusiveness. And, after what you did to her, she will applaud our prosecution of you.'

'From what Octavia told me, there won't be any people left on Earth to do anything, let alone hold a court-martial.'

Captain Nolan made no reply. I imagined her sitting in the dark, her long legs collapsed beneath her, and the pistol rigid in the air.

'You have forced me to withdraw and aim the weapon, Prisoner 548B. I know where you are, and no matter how quietly you move, I will still know your location in this cabin. And if my first shot misses you, the following shots will not.'

'Didn't anyone ever warn you about the danger of firing weapons on submarines and space ships?'

'Your voice tells me your location, Prisoner 548B. If I fire, I won't miss. You can be sure.'

I sighed a weary breath. What if I could escape from all this? What if I could get away from the Goths and Captain Nolan, and this trial, and the ship, and the Goth planet? What then?

The thought almost made me laugh. What if I actually managed to get out of the cabin, open a hatch, and jump into space, what then? Would I walk back across the galaxy, camping along the way? Perhaps I could ask Captain Nolan to join me. And what would be the use if the Earth was nothing but a scorched territory controlled by aliens?

Even so, surely there must be something I could do, something to avoid the trial, or something to survive it. And then, if I were free again, well, what then? I didn't know the answer, and my mind said nothing at first, and then something, like that faint, distant light glimpsed by a sailor alone on a dark and stormy sea, when all seems lost and nothing but hope remains. Stay alive, it signaled through the gloom. Stay alive, it blinked over the endless peaks of the dark waves. Just stay alive. You never know what might happen.

Hope, I knew, wasn't much of a plan and yet what else was there?

'Maybe I can talk to the pilot,' I said without realizing I was speaking aloud.

'Why?'

'What?'

'You said you wanted to speak to the pilot.'

'Did I?'

'Yes, Prisoner 548B. Why do you want to speak to the pilot?'

'To find out what happens next—at the trial.'

'Why should the pilot help you, Prisoner 548B?'

'Maybe she's a prisoner too, like us, or like me. You saw how she behaved in the stateroom. She cringed like a captive.'

'You are presuming her gender, Prisoner 548B.'

I sighed. 'Was there ever a time when you didn't speak that way?'

'Speak what way, Prisoner 548B?'

'Like the Accord Constitution, Captain? Were you actually ever a child who had their own dreams and thoughts?'

'My childhood is my own business, Prisoner 548B.'

'Don't you have any thoughts that aren't about the Accord? Don't you think about food or travel or, I don't know, about a life partner?'

'I am the same as anyone else. I have my private wishes and interests but they are no business of yours.'

'I give up. I think you actually are the Accord, Captain. If the Accord turned into a person, it would be you, right down to your short hair and floppy smock.'

I tried to stand but had to sit down again when the blood rushed from my head. After a minute I tried again.

'What are you doing, Prisoner 548B?'

'I'm getting up.'

'Why?'

'Because it's something, that's all, and something is supposed to be better than nothing. Isn't that what people say?'

'I still have the weapon. I am aiming it at you.'

'Are you sure you know where to aim?'

'As I said, I can locate you by your breathing.'

'I don't care. Shoot if you want, Captain. But make sure you finish me if you do.'

'Something has happened to you, Prisoner 548B. You have lost your attitude. It's hard to believe you are the same rebel who violated so many Navy Spirt codes.'

'In those days,' I said, 'there was something to

fight for.'

A growl came from outside in the passageway followed by a metallic rasp as the door lever rose. Then the door swung open. Blue light shone in. I squinted at Captain Nolan on the mattress. Her hand covered her face against the light. Her long legs were collapsed beneath her, as before, but once again, no pistol.

She saw me looking, scowled, and raised a hand to the brush away the imaginary curl. As usual, she was beautiful. It was remarkable. There wasn't a line of tiredness on her face—not one. It didn't seem possible, and must have been one of the side effects of delusion.

'Take your toxic male gaze off me, Prisoner 548B.'

I turned back to the door.

Two huge Goths swayed in the passageway, glowering down at us.

Karz swayed in front of them.

'Go now,' she growled.

'Go where?' I said. 'Go Earth?'

She shook her head.

'Gwawanath here now.'

'Gwawanath?'

'Gwawanath there.' She raised a paw at the passageway bulkhead.

'It's obvious she means her home planet, Prisoner 548B.'

'Go Gwawanath,' rumbled Karz. 'Go king.'

Yes, I thought, and to my end.

32

We trudged along the passageway. Karz lumbered in front, the two male goths hulked behind.

'Gwawanath,' growled Karz. There was a new lilt in her heavy lumbering.

'Gwawanath,' growled the Goths behind us.

'Gwawanath,' they all growled together.

'Gwawanath,' came distant growls from forward in the ship.

The pilot, I thought. Maybe I can get to the bridge and ask the pilot about the trial.

'Gwawanath,' growled Karz a second time.

'Gwawanath,' growled the Goths behind me.

'Gwawanath,' came the growls from forward in the ship.

After fifteen minutes of trudging and growling we reached the door leading into the large stateroom. The guard on duty growled 'Gwawanath,' and Karz and the Goths behind us growled 'Gwawanath,' and reply. Then they all howled and growled till both Captain Nolan and I had to cover our ears.

Then, the guard stepped back, pulled on the lever with his enormous paw and shoved the door open.

Inside the enormous stateroom, we found a hushed and reverential scene. The Goths had left their mattresses and the detritus of their meals. Now they swayed on their hind legs at the viewports, like a great, black, furry forest in a breeze.

'Gwawanath,' they growled.

Closest to the viewport, in the best position, stood the leader, Captain Gwawn. His two lieutenants, Glathaw and Granak, swayed either side of him.

'Gwawanath,' roared Karz as she entered the stateroom.

'Gwawanath,' roared the Goths behind us.

'Gwawanath,' roared several Goths here and there.

'Gwawanath,' roared the captain, Glathaw, and Granak.

They were hugely and obviously delighted and awed. They panted, their tongues lolling from their maws. Granak seemed the most delighted of all. He actually seemed to smile, which I had never seen any Goth do. But when he caught me watching him, the smile vanished. The slight, pleasant curl on the dark hem of his lip flattened and rippled. Then, he drew it back to reveal the knives of his teeth. He even held up a paw and extended his claws.

'I get it,' I said. 'I don't like you either, pal.'

Apart from Granak, every other Goth swayed in a state of pleasure, or in a trance. They sensed their beloved planet was nearby, even though the viewport showed nothing but the black void of space. They swayed left and right, their snouts raised, sniffing. Every so often, they would look at each other and growled, 'Gwawanath.'

Then, the gravitational forces inside the Gwantasnarr shifted. The ship turned to starboard. Both Goths and humans took a step toward the viewport to keep their balances. And after we all stood upright again, we saw the immensity of an enormous sphere loom into view.

'Gwawanath,' the Goths roared. 'Gwawanath! Gwawanath! Gwawanath!' They roared the planet's name over and over. Then, they uttered something that sounded like a collective sigh, a long 'Gwahhhhhhhh.'

Even Captain Nolan deigned to say something about the sight of the great planet.

'T.E.I.D.,' she whispered. 'T.E.I.D.'

I thought I should say something too, but anything other than T.E.I.D. So, I joined with the Goths and said, 'Gwah.' I dreaded what the planet meant for my future, but there was no escaping the fact that it was an astonishing sight, a truly amazing feature of the universe, right outside the viewport.

Back on AONNS Harmony, I had a Slingshot instructor named Gorski who told me about the relative sizes of Earth and the sun. 'You could line up a hundred Earths, side by side,' Gorski said, 'and they might only just reach across the sun's diameter. Imagine it. But the impressive thing about the sun is that it's so big you could fit over one million Earths inside it. That's how big the sun is. One million times the size of Earth. Maybe bigger.'

'How do you know?' I said. 'Those are forbidden pre-Accord facts. They're locked away in the Accord Space Agency library. No one but Accord commissioners can access them. How do you know how big the sun is?'

Gorski gazed at the sky and said, 'Ask me no questions, Lieutenant Burns, and I'll tell you no lies.'

Back then, the sun's enormity had been difficult to imagine. Now, the sight of the planet Gwawanath put the sun and Earth in perspective. It filled the viewport, looming over the ship, making me feel as insignificant as dust.

And then, as if to emphasize the planet's scale, two moons raced across the surface—mere dots against the background of swirling clouds and patches of green, purple and brown.

'Gwah,' sighed Karz.

'Gwah,' sighed the other Goths around her.

'Gwah,' sighed the Goths on the starboard side.

Gwawanath was such a disarming sight that Captain Nolan lost her hostility. She stood awestruck, almost reverential in her demeanour. She brushed the imaginary curl from her face and actually leaned into me so that her shoulder was against my elbow and her fair head made a slow arch towards my upper arm. 'Isn't it wonderful, Alex?' she said, but without looking at me. It was bizarre. For a moment, I thought she might reach across and take my hand. Foolish thoughts, Burns. Foolish thoughts. You ought to know better. Captain Nolan only wants to be close to the Accord Constitution. Not you. Definitely, not you.

I put all thoughts of Captain Nolan aside and concentrated on the astonishing view outside. As the planet's surface rolled by, it brought mountains and seas into view. A green swathe appeared, like a gash cleaved by an axe in the planet's side. Streaks of clouds rolled with it. The moment this green section appeared, every Goth in the stateroom dropped to the deck with a thump. Then, with their snouts to the metal, and their enormous rumps in the air, they roared. 'Gwanta! Gwanta!'

Two Goths unseen shoved me and Captain Nolan down till our faces hovered over the deck, which reeked of Goth paws. We kowtowed there for minutes while the Goths roared, 'Gwanta! Gwanta!' and 'Gwawanath.'

Only when the green swathe had rolled out of sight did the Goths climb back up to their hind limbs.

Karz came lumbering over. Her paws were clasped in front of her and her great eyes shone.

'Gwah,' she growled.

'What is that green section, Karz?' I asked.

'Not understand,' she said softly. And then she said, 'You like Gwawanath?'

'Yes,' I lied. 'Like Gwawanath.'

'Gwah,' she replied.

'What is the green part?'

'Home,' she growled. 'Gwanath people home. King Grantalan home. Gwanta land.'

'When go Earth?' I said, though I knew it was hopeless to ask.

Karz shook her head. 'Go king,' she growled sweetly, as if 'go king' should be a reason to be cheerful. 'Only go king.'

She turned back to the view of the planet. Around her, the other Goths swayed.

Go Gwawanath, I thought. Go to my death having failed to do anything about Octavia.

'What was that Prisoner 548B? What did you say about Commissioner-elect Octavia?'

'Nothing.'

'It's amazing,' she said, now swaying like a Goth before the planet. 'So beautiful, don't you think?'

'Sure,' I said.

That's when I slunk away from that gathering of swaying Goths. I had one last idea. Just one. I might as well try it. After all, what did I have to lose, except my life?

33

I scanned the stateroom.

From port to starboard, every Goth faced the viewport, swaying on his or her hind legs, rumbling softly.

I threaded between them. A minute later, I reached the forward bulkhead. Then I entered the passageway. The soles of my boots squelched on the metal deck, but no guard barked, and no alarm sounded. There were only growls of adoration for Gwawanath from astern.

I reached the door at the passageway's forward end. Again, no Goths were on duty. So, I pulled the lever, opened the door, and stepped inside. The stateroom was empty. There was nothing but mattresses, discarded bones, and the god Gwanta watching me with his claws unsheathed.

To the right of him stood the door leading to the bridge and the pilots. Again, no guard was on duty. So, I walked across the stateroom and stood before the door, listening for any approaching growls or the scrabble of claws on the metal deck, but nothing came, so I raised the lever and turned the wheel. The door unsealed, and I pushed it gently open. Then I stepped through the doorway and onto the bridge.

Inside, the bridge was dominated by a wide viewport with a spectacular view of Gwawanath. The planet loomed even larger than it had in the stateroom, if that were possible. Beneath the view sat not one, but two pilots, both in human form, both female and thirty-something, or at least disguised as female and thirty-something. I knew enough about Romans to conclude that their real ages could have been anything—centuries, maybe, and probably millennia.

The two pilots sat at a large panel on which screens displayed Gwawanath crisscrossed with lines of longitude and latitude. Around these screens, hundreds of tiny lights blinked like a miniature galaxy. A third pilot stood behind the other two. She must have been the officer of the deck, or the officer who 'had the conn,' as the pre-Accord navy would say. She was the officer in charge of directing the ship's movements.

The fair-haired pilot from earlier sat nearest me. The other helmsman had red hair. The woman at the conn had darker hair. All three wore dungaree overalls rather than Roman gowns or naval uniforms.

'How did you get in here?' said the dark-haired pilot. 'Where is the guard?'

I ignored these questions. Time was short. 'What will happen to me?' I said. 'Down there?'

The tiny lights blinked. The planet rotated. The two pilots at the controls turned to look at their superior officer. She spoke a second time. 'Where is Captain Gwawn? Where is the lady... where is Karz?'

'We have time,' I said. 'They're still gawping at the planet. So tell me. What will happen?'

'Janasta, alert the captain,' said the dark-haired pilot.

Instantly, Janasta, the fair-haired pilot, reached for something under the control panel. A purple light blinked on the wall. An alarm sounded deep in the ship: a kind of clicking sound.

'Wait!' I said. 'You don't need to do that. Just a few questions.'

'I disagree,' said the commanding pilot. 'There is plenty of need. We must either put the Gwantasnarr into orbit or overshoot.'

'But why alert the Goths? We're all in the same boat, aren't we?'

'The same boat, Lieutenant?'

'Prisoners. We're all prisoners. You three, Captain Nolan, me.'

The great planet loomed closer. The alarm light blinked. The first angry growls sounded astern.

'Prisoners, Lieutenant? Far from it. Far, far from it.'

'Then what? Aren't the Goths your enemies? They attack your ships. They kill your Marines.'

'We are defectors, Lieutenant, defectors from our people. We choose to be on this ship. This ship is a Roman ship which we stole for the

Goths.'

'Defectors? Why would you defect?'

'Not everyone in the Roman world approves of our leader's actions. Many of us reject them. Serving the Goths is one way of fighting back, and of freeing both our own people and the Goths.'

'Your leader? You mean government?'

'Leader, Lieutenant, not leaders, not government.'

'Octavia?'

'She prefers her navy rank of admiral, but she is the sole leader, the dictator—the tyrant, Lieutenant. Her real name is Sinistra, not Octavia. The Goths have a name for her too, in their own language. They call her Lanalan. It is not a complimentary name.'

'Please, while there's time, tell me what will happen to me down there on Gwawanath.'

'No,' said the dark haired pilot. Open that door, Lieutenant. By now, Captain Gawn and Lieutenant Granak will assume you are trying to avoid your audience with King Gwantalan.'

'Of course I am. The king is going to kill me. Didn't you hear Karz? "King like kill."'

'Kill is an exaggeration, Lieutenant. King Gwantalan is the ruler of a military race. He will determine your innocence or guilt by military inquiry. He won't just kill you. He'll allow you to prove your innocence.'

'Prove my innocence? How?'

'In a contest, Lieutenant—a physical contest,'

said the fair-haired pilot. 'Like jousting in the Middle Ages.'

'Jousting? Middle Ages? What are they?'

'They existed in your pre-Accord era.'

'But what were they?'

'No time, Lieutenant,' said the dark-hair piloted. 'Janasta, help Lieutenant Burns to return to Captain Gwawn.'

Janasta swiveled her chair. She took her left arm from where it had rested on the control panel and clasped it in her right hand, as if holding a sprained wrist. Then, her left arm swelled, bursting through her shirt sleeve, growing and flattening into a blade. Then, she stood and advanced across the deck, raising the blade to a height level with my neck.

'You could have just asked nicely,' I said.

Before Janasta and her blade reached me, I stepped forward and grabbed her arm just above the elbow and forced the blade down. Undaunted, she bent her knees and placed her right arm on the stern bulkhead and shoved me away with alien strength.

Then, her right arm extended to the door and pulled the lever down. As the door swung open, the blade shrank. I released her arm and then we both stood there, me with my hands balled into fists, she with a ripped uniform.

'All that just to open the door?' I said.

A torrent of growls surged inside. Granak's head dropped below the top-jamb and filled the doorway with fur and teeth.

The pilots responded with rapid growls of their own. Granak listened, twisting his head left and right. Then he growled in reply, his breath fouling the air.

'What did he say?'

The dark-haired pilot said, 'I have informed Lieutenant Granak that you came here to get a better view of Gwawanath, Lieutenant Burns. I told him we pressed the alarm trigger by mistake, thinking you came to attack us.'

'Thank you, but what did he say?'

'He says the sooner he gets you to Gwawanath the better for every Goth. He says they are leaving for the planet surface immediately.'

'Now?' I asked. 'They're leaving now—just after we arrived.'

'Yes, Lieutenant. The captain is ready to board the dropship.'

'The dropship? What's a dropship?'

'To take you to the planet surface.'

'But what is it?'

'A dropship is like a launch in your terminology. It's small, rapid vessel.'

'But why the rush?'

'The rush, Lieutenant, is because the Captain and Lieutenant Granak were friends of the prince you killed. They are eager to see King Gwantalan administer justice.'

I turned to Granak. He glared down at me again. I could guess how he wanted to the king's justice to be applied.

'One last question,' I shouted over the growls.

'Not that it matters anymore, but you called Octavia a different name before the acceleration. What was it?'

'The Lovelorn,' said Janasta, adjusting her ripped sleeve. 'We called her The Lovelorn. That's the best approximation in your language.'

'Why?' I asked. 'It's so strange. Why the Lovelorn? It's such a… I don't know… such a pre-Accord word.'

'It's because of a mission she undertook to explore your planet, and an infatuation with a Roman naval lieutenant named Ranant?'

'Who?' I said. 'What happened?'

But Granak growled at them from his great height, and the pilots turned back to the controls without saying any more.

34

'See you when I get back,' I said, attempting a joke. It failed. The pilots' faces were blank. Maybe they had no sense of humor. Maybe they regarded me as already dead.

I stepped back into the small stateroom. Lieutenant Glathaw and five other Goths swayed there, some on all fours, others standing on their hind limbs, all of them sniffing at me,

Granak came out of the bridge and roared. The Goths shut their maws instantly and flattened their ears. Then they turned and lumbered toward the passageway, growling to the painting of Gwanta as they passed it.

Granak gave me a shove, and I joined the Goths filing from the stateroom. Resistance, I knew, would be useless. So, I trudged along with a shaggy rump at eye level and a ferocious breath on the back of my neck. No escape possible. The time had come to 'Go Gwawanath.'

It had all happened so fast. Two or maybe three days ago, I had languished in a court-martial in an aircraft hangar at AONNB Holder, now I walked the deck of a spaceship on the other side of the galaxy, about to be tried for murder by a race of monsters.

How futile my life had become! And how fast! Two months ago, I had woken up from the dream of the Accord's lies, now I was being sent to my death unless I survived a contest—whatever that might be.

Probably it would be a fight. A fight!—that was a consolation. It was better to die on your feet than to live on your knees. Someone had said that to me once, but I couldn't remember who.

We rumbled along the passageway and into the next stateroom, the one with the viewport of Gwawanath. The rest of the Goths had ceased their adoration of the planet. Their attention was now on the lumbering procession, and the puffed-up figure of Granak. He must have thought the audience needed a show of Goth pride because I felt a great shove on my shoulders followed by the inevitable growl. I stumbled forward but kept my feet. I turned around to find Granak's snout level with my nose.

After my failure with the pilots, I felt in no mood to be pushed. While Granak glared, I raised my fist and swung it at his snout. I made good contact, right into the scar. The punch shoved his lip, if that's what it was called, right back over his enormous and slimy teeth.

'Gwah!' I yelled at him. 'Gwah!'

I knew it was a mistake. I knew it wouldn't help my case. But once again, my mind was not thinking straight, and now it was too late to take the punch back.

The stateroom fell silent as Granak brought his head around. The flukes of his snout flared in front of my eyes. Down on the deck, the yellow tips of his claws appeared.

Karz came up beside us, growling. Captain Gwawn lumbered up too. He got between us and roared in Granak's face until Granak backed away. Then, Captain Gwawn turned and roared some kind of announcement and the whole stateroom descended into another song or roar or battle cry that was so loud, the hull of the Gwantasnarr rang with snarls and barks and howls.

Eventually, the captain calmed the Goths down by roaring out the king's name, Gwantalan, several times, followed by Gwanta, and what I imagined were the Goth words for kill or not kill or maybe another cry of paws, claws, and teeth.

Captain Nolan came over. She stepped carefully through the Goths, ducking under each enormous forelimb and sliding past each massive flank, and then ducking again as the snouts probed downward to sniff at her.

'Where did you go?' she asked.

'The bridge.'

'Why?'

'To ask the pilots about the trial.'

'And you left me alone?'

'I left you with our intra-galactic friends,' I said.

'You still left me.'

'Are you saying an Accord female needed help from a male? Don't let Navy Spirt hear you talk that way, Captain.'

'What's causing so much growling?'

'We're about to go down to their damn planet.'

'How?'

'By dropship. That's what the pilots said. It's probably their name for a cutter or a launch.'

'You mean we're not landing this ship, the Gwantasnarr?'

'Doesn't look like it. Maybe it's not built to land.'

'By why now? Why this minute?'

'Your guess as good as mine. The Goths don't plan. They act on impulses and urges... and grudges.'

'What will happen?'

'The pilots say they'll take me to the Goth king. And then he'll try me, possibly by contest.'

'Contest? What kind of contest?'

'I don't know, but it won't be a game of pin the tail on the unicorn.'

Karz lumbered up.

'Go Gwawanath,' she growled.

'Is there nothing we can do?' said Captain Nolan.

'Go Gwawanath,' growled Karz. 'Go King.'

She clutched something in her forelimbs. It was one of the gray bones I'd noticed earlier. Strips of gray meat and stringy sinews dangled from it.

'Eat,' said Karz.

'No thanks. Not for me, but maybe my friend wants to eat.'

Karz turned to Captain Nolan with the bone. 'Eat.'

Like most Accord members, Captain Nolan was almost certainly a vegan. She might never have tasted meat in her life. She might only have known soy milk and kale and bean sprouts. Now, a putrid, half-gnawed animal femur was inches from her nose. 'No,' she said, and then when she had regained her composure, she added, 'No, thank you, intra-galactic friend.'

'Gwah,' said Katz.

Then, Captain Gwawn growled, and the procession trudged off again. This time, the captain lumbered in between me and Granak. We reached the aft of the stateroom and entered the passageway. Captain Nolan followed somewhere behind.

'Come with me,' I called to her over the shaggy backs. 'Be my defense lawyer. Karz can translate.'

'Not,' growled Karz. 'Not friend. Only you.'

'Friend help.'

'Not,' repeated Karz. 'Only you. Not friend.'

'Did you hear?' I shouted back to Captain Nolan.

But she was too far back, or maybe one of the Goths had blocked her. The last thing I heard her say was, 'T.E.I.D, Lieutenant Burns. May the Accord's values protect you.'

But I knew I'd need a lot more than Accord values.

We lumbered along the length of the ship, past the doors of cabins, through holds, armories, and more staterooms—all of them empty. The Romans might have used them when they had the ship, but not the Goths. All they needed were their mattresses, bones, meat, a picture of Gwanta, and their paws, claws, and teeth.

'Must fast,' Karz growled. 'Must fast.'

'Why?'

'Go Gwawanath,' she growled. 'Goth land.'

'Pilots come too?' I asked. 'Pilots translate.'

'Ranawah cannot go Goth land,' Growled Karz.

'Ranawah… cannot go Goth land? Why? Because of the war?'

'No,' growled Karz. 'Land not like Ranawah. Land hate Ranawah.'

'The land doesn't like them?'

'They not like land.'

'Why?'

'Land kill Ranawah.'

I guessed she meant the land or the air was poisonous to Romans.

'Can I breathe there, Karz?'

'Not worry,' she replied.

'Land not like me too?' I asked. 'Land kill me too.'

'Gwah,' said Karz. 'Not know.'

'You don't know? But I could die.'

'Gwah,' said Karz.

We burst from the passageway into a large

staging area at the Gwantasnarr's stern. Several Roman teardrop-shaped ships floated above the deck. These must be what they called dropships. We lumbered towards one ship closest to the stern. As we approached, a hatch opened, and a gangway slid out. The Goths lumbered up the gangway, roaring and calling out 'Gwawanath,' as they went.

Inside the ship was an area large enough for several Goths to lie on the deck. I saw a bench for the human. The Goth soldiers shoved me toward it, and then Karz climbed in.

'No pilots here either?'

'Pilot on Gwantasnarr. Ranawah people not go Goth land. Goth land not like.'

'Will king kill me?' I asked again, hoping for a different answer.

Karz nodded, then shook her head. 'King kill. King not kill.'

'Contest? King contest?'

'Not understand.'

The other Goths growled at her. Karz growled back at them. Then the Goths turned to me and growled something that could have meant, 'You killed our prince.' Then they all began sniffing again with great tosses of their snouts.

Granak, who had disappeared, now came lumbering across the deck towards us. Just great, I thought. Now I'll have him to worry about too.

'Gwah!' the Goths growled.

'Gwah,' growled Granak.

Karz pushed a paw towards me. She dropped a

small object into my lap. Not a piece of bone, but a white clip. 'Pilots say put here.' She raised a great paw to her snout. 'Here.'

The port closed, and the craft rotated on the deck until it faced aft. An enormous port opened at the ship's stern, revealing the yawning blackness of space outside. We drifted across the ramp and through the port until the Gwantasnarr floated behind us, and we entered space, suspended over a drop into black infinity.

Come on, I said to my sluggish mind. Get me out of this. Get me away from here. Or make my death quick.

But my mind was empty, just like the vacuum of nothingness surrounding us. I was alone with the Goths and my fate.

'Gwah,' roared Granak, and the shuttle dropped away.

35

The dropship landed on the part of the planet marked by the great green swathe. It lowered itself into a dusty clearing surrounded by tall trees with towering green trunks and a thick canopy that blocked the sun and turned the forest floor beneath into shadow.

The Goths roared as the gangway slid out. They bounded through the port and down into the clearing onto the cherished surface of Gwawanath. They charged around, churning up the dust. They chased each other in the circles. They charged at each other, head to head, and then veered off at the last moment, snorting. Even Granak forgot his anger and joined in. The scene was like a great Goth picnic.

But not for me. Picnic was the last word I would have used to describe my first minutes on Gwawanath. As the Goths charged about, I staggered down the gangway, carrying the new gravity. I felt as if I had pulled on a backpack filled with weights and then strapped more weights to my thighs and feet. My hands felt like sacks of sand, and my head lolled on my neck as if I wore a helmet made of heavy metal.

Then there was the air. Thick and putrid, it smelled like the Goths' own breaths, like rotten meat mixed with sewage. It was humid and hot. Each breath seemed to fill my lungs with slime. And no matter how far I pushed the small breathing device into my nose, the air remained rank and unbreathable. I crouched on the gangway's edge, one boot in the dust, and one hand on my chest, trying to breathe.

'Gwah,' growled Granak. He had broken away from the rest to lumber over and sniff at me.

Gwah yourself, I thought. You actually like this air. You've had centuries to get used to it. I'm going to take my time. It's not as if I want to hurry to this trial or contest or whatever it is.

Karz bounded over and nudged her snout in between us, then warned Granak away with a growl of her own. She crept closer to me, sniffing my face carefully.

'Thank you, Karz,' I wheezed.

'Gwah,' she rumbled softly.

More Goths crept over, all sniffing. They sat on their haunches with their heads tilted to one side, like giant, baffled dogs. Why couldn't I breathe? What was wrong with their home planet's wonderful air? They sniffed even more when I doubled over, dropped to my knees, and retched into the dirt.

Not a good beginning—not at all.

And things got worse. In my sickened state, my traitorous mind showed up, right on cue. End it all, it said. Why prolong the pain? Why keep yourself alive? The Goth king will have you killed anyway. You'll die in agony. So, just get it over with. Air this foul will kill fast. Pull the device from your nose and breathe deep.

And on it went while I retched and gasped and my vision swirled and my head throbbed. Pulling out the breathing device might be a good idea. After all, I was alone on an alien planet. The planet was an unimaginable distance from Earth. My chances of getting home were almost zero. And what would I find if I somehow got back anyway? I should just get it over with. I should just reach up and pull out the device and suck in enough of the rancid atmosphere as my lungs could hold.

But something far away on the rolling ocean of my mind signaled to me. It flashed like a small and distant light on a stormy sea in the blackest of nights. Keep going, it signaled. Don't give up —not until you know more about your fate. Just hang on. Just hang on. Keep going. Don't give up.

So I did. I hung on. I breathed as slowly as I could, swallowing hard, fighting my heaving stomach, fighting the traitorous voice in my mind which threatened any moment to whisper its poisonous thoughts.

Then I sat up, lifted each of my arms. They were heavy, but I could move them with more freedom. Maybe I was acclimatizing to the gravity. A few minutes later, I climbed to my feet and took a few steps.

This was enough for Captain Gwawn. He was eager to get going. He growled to Granak who growled at the rest of the Goths who sniffed one last time, then turned and lumbered away across the clearing towards the forest edge. Karz got to her four limbs. 'Go forest,' she growled. 'Not hot. Go slow.'

So, with a swirling head and heavy legs, I dragged myself across the dust and followed the shaggy rumps into the woods.

Once inside, I found Gwawanath easier to bear. The forest was dark and cool. The air was moist and refreshing and the ground soft under my boots. The light filtered down in shafts from the green canopy above, and winged insects, stirred up by the big Goths, flitted in and out. As we went further, strange calls echoed in the depths and every so often, I heard timber crack and large objects fall.

As far as I could tell, our direction was toward a tall, gray bluff. It loomed dark and craggy through the gaps in the canopy. I imagined the Goths' home was its base and we would eventually reach a clearing where they lounged in the dust, their great genitals flopping about, chewing on their bones and scraps, dreaming of dying in battle for Gwanta, and getting up only to defecate and copulate.

In other words, I imagined they lived the same as they behaved on the Gwantasnarr.

'Gwah,' rumbled Captain Gwawn, as if he knew what I'd been thinking.

Gwah yourself, I thought, and we trudged on.

Every so often, something crashed through the forest out of sight. A creature or creatures fled, snapping twigs and startling curious birds from the treetops. At the sound of them, the Goths twitched their ears and swung their snouts around to sniff. Some even climbed to their hind limbs and sniffed all over again.

'Gwah,' Lieutenant Glathaw growled.

'Gwah,' growled Granak.

'Gwantalan,' growled Captain Gwawn.

I checked my watch. Forty minutes had passed. I felt better—not great, but not sick. The urge to vomit was still there, but retreating. I could breathe, more or less, and my muscles complained less about the extra weight. Twenty minutes later, I could lift my mind from bodily matters and place my attention on what I'd seen so far.

First, I thought about the Goth land. From the Gwantasnarr's viewport, this part of the planet looked mostly green and forested, but the rest of the planet was purple or brown, like fields of lavender and desert. The purple and brown areas must have been where the Romans lived.

Did that mean the air was toxic over there too, in Roman land? And did the Romans ever venture into these forests to attack the Goths? Why did they allow the Goths to attack them in space when they could kill them here on

Gwawanath? Like so much about the Goths and Octavia's people, this new information raised more questions than answers.

Twenty minutes later, the trees thinned out. Giant paw tracks appeared in the moist soil. The Goths raised their snouts and sniffed. One or two issued what sounded like happy barks. Minutes later, we emerged into a great clearing beneath the towering gray bluff.

I had been right about the caves. There were dark mouths every ten yards along the base of the bluff. Goths of all sizes padded in front of them. Goth cubs, if that's what they could be called, conducted mock fights in the sand, rolling around like and biting at each other. As we approached, all Goths, young and old, stood on their haunches to sniff at us, and more Goths lumbered out from the caves to join them.

In the middle of the row of caves, four enormous Goths guarded a large central opening. They swayed and sniffed as we came closer. Then, one of the Goths dropped to all fours and lumbered inside. Surely, I thought, that cave must be the residence of the Goth king.

But for the moment, the king stayed out of sight. The king's subjects did not. They massed on the dusty ground. There must have been thousands of them, both male and female, all sniffing, all tossing their snouts. Soon, they all began roaring. Several dropped to all fours and charged out to greet us. Goths from our group also dropped to all fours and charged across the dust to meet them in return.

Captain Gwawn stood on hind limbs, like he was about to make a speech.

'Gwah!' he roared.

'Gwah!' the Goths roared back.

'Gwantalan!' roared the captain.

'Gwantalan!' the Goths roared back.

Then, the captain raised a paw at me and roared a word that sounded like 'Hunrunahurr.' The Goths roared louder.

'What they say?' I yelled to Karz.

'Not talk,' she growled.

The roaring stopped, and there was nothing but silence. Seconds later, every Goth turned to face the large cave entrance. Then, they dropped to all fours and lowered their heads to the ground. Their snouts pushed into the dust and their rumps rose high in the air. A big paw shoved me down too. The paw belonged to Granak, of course.

'Gwah,' he warned.

'What's happening?' I said to Karz.

'Not talk.'

'Is it King Gwantalan?'

'Not talk.'

'What will he do, Karz? What Gwantalan do?'

But I already knew the answer.

'King kill,' she growled, annoyed. 'King not kill.'

'What about the contest?'

'Not understand.' Karz pushed her snout further into the dust.

'Karz, what about the contest?' I said, but she flattened her ears.

After a few seconds, the ears rose upright again.

'King kill,' Karz growled softly. 'Kill not kill. Only Gwanta know.'

King kill or king not kill.

I would soon find out which it would be.

36

After a minute or so, a single bark echoed along the bluff and the Goths lifted their snouts from the dusty ground. The growls began again, but they were different to the howls and barks of the crew on the Gwantasnarr. They were grander, more reverential—growls for royalty, maybe. The growling grew so loud I couldn't hear my own thoughts, and even Karz pinned her ears back against the noise. Then, after one final, deep bark out of sight, the growling ceased once more and silence filled the clearing, except for the strange noises echoing around the forest.

Then, every Goth dropped to the ground once again and pushed his or her snout into the dust. A powerful roar growled something from the direction of the large cave, and the snouts rose again. The thousands of Goths lifted their heads, climbed to their hind limbs, and craned their great necks to get a better view.

'Gwah,' whispered Karz.

King Gwantalan stood at the entrance to the

large cave. Like Captain Gwawn the king was a giant, red-furred Goth. Red seemed to be the color of high rank. He stood surrounded by an escort of males, each wearing a red neckcloth, the same as the cloth worn by Karz. Otherwise, the king was like any other Goth male. He had the same bear-wolf appearance, the same massive body, the same twitching ears.

Behind the king, a banner displayed an image of Gwanta, the same as on the Gwantasnarr. Gwanta held the black sphere beneath the Goth characters for paws, claws, and teeth. Behind this stood an image of another Goth standing on his hind limbs with his claws unsheathed. He too wore a red neckcloth.

'Who's that, Karz—in the painting?'

'Grawth,' she growled.

'Who?'

'Grawth.'

'Who?'

'Prince.'

Beside the king stood his first minister or highest-ranking noble or whatever a king's first lieutenant was called. The lieutenant stood on his hind limbs and addressed the mass of swaying Goths. He growled for several minutes. I could hear the words Gwantalan, Gwanta and Grawth.

When he had finished, Captain Gwawn lumbered forward. After a few steps, he dropped onto his four paws. Then, after receiving a bark from the king's lieutenant, he addressed King

Gwantalan himself in a series of low deferential rumbles.

'What's he saying?' I whispered to Karz.

'Not talk,' she warned.

Captain Gwawn barked and growled and coughed. The king and his courtiers listened in regal silence, their ears upright. Every other Goth remained quiet, except for the gurgles of stomachs and some epic sneezes. Finally, after Captain Gwawn had growled for several minutes, he turned and pointed at Granak who had been sitting on his haunches and nodding.

Granak lumbered forward and stood beside Captain Gwawn. He growled and barked and hooted and sniffed the air. Then, he raised both his paws, palm up, in front of his face, like he held a rifle. Then he turned and sniffed at me and uttered an accusatory bark. Then, for the third time that week, the gaze of many large, dark eyes turned my way.

At this point, a great paw shoved me in the back. I stepped forward, holding my chin high, or as high as I could manage. When I was ten yards away from the king, one of his courtiers growled, and I stopped. Then, I said what I thought a person should say in the circumstances. I didn't care that the king wouldn't understand.

'Your majesty, I hope you might allow me to speak for myself.' The king said nothing, but his ears pointed forward, and he cocked his head on its side like a twelve-foot-tall dog. So, I continued.

'The truth is, I didn't know the prince attacked me. Shooting him was an accident. I thought he was one of the regular soldiers. Would you allow me the assistance of the interpreter, Karz? I can explain better if she translates. Captain Gwawn, need Karz.' I turned and pointed at Karz.

The king growled. The captain growled. The king growled more. The king's lieutenants growled. The captain growled again, this time at Karz. Karz crept forward and stood beside me. She added more growls. Then the king stood up on his hind limbs, growled at his lieutenant, who growled at the captain, who growled to the escorts, who shoved me forward until I was about three paw swipes away from the king himself.

With his lieutenants beside him, the king leaned down from his great height and sniffed me. He sniffed at my head, my armpits, and my crutch. Then he stood upright, growled to the captain, who growled to the king's lieutenant. The lieutenant lifted his head and howled long and hard at the mob of Goths watching on.

The Goth mob responded with thundering howls of their own. Then the king and his subjects howled together. I couldn't tell if all the noise signified triumph or grief, or maybe just the fun of howling. As usual, once one Goth started, they all did. And as far as I could tell, none of the howls sounded friendly.

When the howling and growling ceased, the Goths all sat down on their haunches. The king growled to the lieutenant who growled to the captain, who growled at Karz, who turned to me. She growled as if I could understand, holding her paws, pads-up for emphasis. She stopped growling, barked to clear her throat, and began again.

'King angry,' she growled.

'Does he know… accident?'

'Not understand.'

'King angry, yes?'

'Yes, angry.'

'Angry with me?'

'Yes.'

'I talk king. I tell him. Accident.'

Karz shook her head.

'Only Gwanath people speak king.'

'OK. I speak you. You speak king.'

'King not want. King not happy.'

How could I ever put my case forward?

I tried again.

'Tell king, accident shooting prince. Accident. Understand? Accident.'

'King know battle,' growled Karz. 'Everyone fight everyone. Gwanath fight Ranawah. Ranawah fight Gwanath. You fight Ranawah. Prince fight you. King know. King know.'

'So king know mistake?' I tried.

'King angry,' Karz growled.

So what now?

The king swung his head from Karz to me, his ears twitched, his nose flukes flared, his great shoulders swayed. He growled a low and ominous growl, and I guessed the inevitable decision had come.

Karz said, 'King decide.'

'Just ask him to make it quick, Karz,' I said. I was relieved to know my fate at last.

'King say not kill you for kill prince.'

'He what? King not kill me? He not kill me?'

'King say not kill.'

'Not kill?'

'Not kill.'

I could hardly believe it. After all the growling, it wasn't possible that he would release me, not in front of the baying mob of his subjects. But apparently he had done just that. I had survived. I was alive. 'Thank you,' I said. 'Thank you. Please tell the king I am grateful.'

'Not understand,' growled Karz.

'Tell king, I thank him. Tell king, sorry, and I thank him.'

She shook her head.

'King say he not kill you.'

'Yes, I understand.'

'Not kill you.'

'I know, I know. Please tell him thank you.'

'Other Gwanath people kill you.'

'What?'

'Other Gwanath people kill you.'

'Other Gwanath people?'

'In fight.'

'In fight?'

'In fight.'

I almost slumped to my knees. The pilots on

the Gwantasnarr had warned me. Now, my fate would be decided by a contest.

'What fight, Karz? What fight?'

Before she could answer, the king growled again. His lieutenants growled too. Captain Gwawn growled next.

'What are they saying?'

'Pick fighter.'

The king's lieutenant raised a paw and pointed. Granak lumbered forward. He stood before the king on all fours, lowered his snout to the ground, then got up and stood on his hind legs. The king addressed him with several regal barks. He ended with several nods and a look to the side, as if to indicate he would say no more.

Then, Granak turned to face me.

'What now, Karz?'

'You fight Granak.'

'Fight Granak. But not want fight Granak.'

'Fight Granak. If you win, king say not kill. Happy.' She was smiling as much as a Goth could smile, which wasn't much, an open maw, the tip of a long red tongue.

'How fight?' I said, knowing the answer already.

'Fight Granak.'

'Yes, Granak, but how fight?'

'Kill.'

I looked at Granak. He too smiled at me—as much as he could, which was even less than Karz's smile. He panted extravagantly, his tongue out and dripping hot saliva. The drops plopped into the dust.

'Gwah,' he rumbled, then ran his tongue around the edges of his black maw.

'Fight where?' I said.

'Fight here,' growled Karz. 'Here.' She waved a paw at the dusty ground in front of the king. Then she waved a paw at the vast crowd. 'Gwanath people see. Gwanath people like.'

The crowd of Goths pressed towards us, a great forest of fur, paws, claws, teeth, stench, and moist heat.

'How can I fight Granak? Not fair fight?'

'Not understand.'

How would I explain this?

'No claws.' I held up my hands. 'No teeth.' I pointed at my mouth. 'No height.' I drew a breath and stood as tall as I could. I pointed at Granak. 'He big teeth, big claws, big height. Not fair.' I would have added 'gravity and poisonous air' too—if I knew how.

Karz sniffed quietly at me for several seconds, then turned and growled to the captain, and then the sequence of growls went up through the hierarchy to the king who sniffed and then growled some kingly decision to his second in command, who growled to a Goth behind him, who turned and loped into the darkness of the cave.

'What now?'

'You wait.'

The servant reemerged, clasping something across his chest.

It appeared to be a grey rod or staff.

Or spear.

He presented it to the lieutenant who showed it to the king, who sniffed it and growled assent.

Then the lieutenant showed it to the captain, who also growled. Then he showed it to Granak, who shrugged as if it made no difference to him. Then the captain brought the spear over to Karz, who sniffed it and nodded. Then the captain dropped the spear to the dust in front of me, just as the Goth soldier had dropped the alien rifle back on the Gwantasnarr, two days and a lifetime ago.

I reached down and picked it up.

It was lighter than it looked, made of a blue-gray metal, the same color as the rocks on the bluff behind us. The spear's tip was sharp, but the spear itself was not much thicker than a broom handle and was around eight feet long. It looked like it would break easily when bent. It also seemed to emit a low hum, like an electric motor, but with the mob of Goths rumbling so much, and my heart thumping in my ears, I couldn't be sure.

One thing was obvious: the spear was too light to stop Granak—even if I knew how to use it.

'Fight with this?' I said. 'I can't fight with this?'

'Gwanath land,' Karz growled, nodding at the spear. 'Gwanath rock. Gwanath land. You fight?'

Gwanath land, I thought. Really? How had the Goths been able to melt their rocks into a spear with no technology? It was another mystery that would have to remain unsolved, at least for now, and maybe forever.

'Fight now.' Karz swung her snout towards the scar-faced Granak.

'Karz, the king can't expect me to fight with this.'

But Karz had already backed away, making room for the contest.

'Can't fight,' I called.

'You fight Granak,' Karz called back. 'Or you fight them.' She tossed her head at the huge pressing mob of Goths who growled and rumbled and drooled in a thick wall on the hill.

I weighed the spear and looked up at Granak. He looked back, extending his long, curved claws.

There was no escaping it now.

37

Granak was a monster.

He stood twice my height, three times my width, and many times my weight. His canine teeth stretched as long as my fingers. His claws extended as long again—all four sets of them, including an extra claw, hidden in fur near the 'elbow' of each limb. This extra claw resembled the dewclaws on dogs and cats on Earth, but on Granak the dewclaws were like scythes.

Worst of all, Granak had a lot at stake. He had the Goth prince's death to avenge. He had the pride of the Goth nation to restore. And he was a warrior with a reputation of his own to preserve. He could never allow himself to suffer defeat—not in front of his king and his peers, and never to such an unworthy opponent. How on earth was I going to fight him, let alone kill him?

I remembered how the Goths fought the Roman Marines on the Excidium and in the recent battle on the Gwantasnarr. Their tactics were to knock the Marines to the deck. Then, they used their weight, claws, and strength to tear open the armor and helmets, then tear the Marines' guts out and keep tearing until the opponent died through evisceration.

All of which implied the first tactic for surviving a fight with a Goth was to keep your distance, preferably with a large rifle. At all costs, you must keep away from his slashing claws, and never allow him to knock you over and bear down on you with his impossible weight.

So much for staying alive. What about killing a Goth with a spear? Back on the Excidium, it took three blasts of a Roman rifle to even slow a charging Goth from his gallop. It took even more blasts to end his life. So, how many jabs of a spear would it take to pierce a Goth's hide? How deep would the thrust have to go to kill him? Which organ would the spear tip have to stab? And how could I find that organ inside the Goth's enormous, blood-filled body?

Well, I had better do something. I took up a fighter's stance: left foot forward, right foot behind. My left hand held the spear in the middle; my right gripped the bottom third. One hand would guide the spear's tip; the other would provide the thrust. Both hands would haul the spear back in if I thrust it too far. At least, that was the plan.

Granak sat on his haunches watching me with his wet, dark eyes, each set deep in the regions at the base of his long, thick snout. Each eye caught the sunlight, adding a menacing gleam to the coldness lurking within them. There was no mercy there, and no fear. There was only the certainty of the soldier with superior weapons and the skill to use them.

'When start?' I called to Karz.

She stood to the right of the king and his escort, her paws clasped in front of her chest, as usual. She twitched her ears at the king and at the mob. At the highest pitched howls, she shook her head. She knew the fight wasn't fair. Every Goth knew it, but only Karz might have cared.

'When start?' I called again.

'King say,' she began, but the growling mob drowned her out. 'King say,' she called.

'OK,' I called back.

So I waited with the quivering weapon. Granak waited with his paws, claws, and teeth. The mob growled louder and louder until they sounded like thundering surf about to crash down from the hills.

Hurry up, I thought. Let's get this over with—for better or worse.

And then the roaring of the mob ceased. It was replaced by heavy Goth panting and strange, whip-like bird calls from the forest.

King Gwantalan stood on his hind limbs with his great forelimbs spread wide, scanning the adoring mob. Then, after a brief sneeze, he lifted his snout to the sky, opened his maw, and let out a howl that echoed off the gray face of the bluff and caused the courtiers behind him to flatten their ears. The howl rose in pitch to a high, ear-piercing note, at which point it ceased, and the courtiers' ears sprung upright again. Then the king lowered his snout, sniffed at the two fighters standing before him.

And barked.

Instantly, the mob roared. Granak dropped from his sitting position to all fours and snarled. Karz called out to me from the side. It might have been a bark of good luck. It might have been a warning—or a farewell. I didn't have time to ask because the time had finally arrived.

The fight had begun.

Granak watched me, swaying on his paws. He didn't advance. Maybe he wanted me to strike first. But I stayed put with the spear tip raised at his snout. We watched each other for several seconds. Then, Granak lost his patience. He lowered his head and charged, and came surging across the dusty ground like a great furry army tank.

He came within a yard of the spear's tip. He rose on his hind limbs, his great genitals flopping. I thrust the spear at his shaggy guts, but before the tip could reach him, he swung his right paw, and swatted the spear tip away, creating a clear run at me inside the spear's range. I quickly retreated, reeling the spear tip back in until it overtook Granak. Then, I took up a new stance with the spear tip raised at his snout. Then, we both stood watching each other, reassessing our tactics.

The Goth mob roared. It sounded like laughter.

Well, that was something. Maybe they had a sense of humor. Maybe Granak had done something funny. He was big, but also slow. Maybe I could use this weakness to get behind him where I could jab at an exposed flank.

As if hearing my thoughts, Granak shambled towards me, slower this time. I backed away but kept the spear tip quivering and level with his head. He batted it aside and charged. But I skipped to the left, out of his way. He barreled past, unable to slow down, then skidded to a stop in the dust. He spun about. Then, he charged straight at the spear's tip, batted it away, and rolled on by while I stepped aside once more.

Then we resumed our start positions.

Three more of these exchanges followed. Granak charged. I thrust the spear at him. He batted it away but kept on charging at me while I stepped out of range before he could rake me. Then, he thundered by like a shaggy buffalo.

Neither of us scored a hit. No flesh was pierced. No hide was stabbed. The score was nothing to nothing. But then on the last exchange, as Granak thundered by and I slipped left, I jabbed him hard in the rump. The tip went deep into his fur. I felt it go at least an inch into his hide. The shock of it made him scoot, clenching his bottom like a dog with piles. This changed things. When Granak turned to face me again, he paused and stood panting, his red tongue lolling and drooling, and a new, menacing gleam in his eye.

He'd discovered something. It had taken him a while, but now the penny had dropped. He had a new understanding and a new plan. He came forward, taking his time, placing his paws carefully in the sand. He was going to delay his charge till the last second when he could work out which way I would move.

He approached the quivering spear tip, staying just out of thrust range. Then he dropped his snout and sniffed. His nose flukes flared and his ears came forward. I sensed the new tactic in play. He wouldn't charge until he knew he could follow me and pin me before I could bring the spear back between us.

But in this small pause, fear chose its moment to act. It whispered in my ear. You can't keep this up forever. Sooner or later, you will tire, you will trip, and you will fall. The spear will not help you. Granak will drop on you like a monster and the claws will come slicing for the blue camouflage cloth that hides your guts. Better to drop your weapon and give up. Maybe Granak or the king will show mercy.

I shook the voice from my head. It might have talked sense, maybe even a lot of sense, but it was also an enemy, and I had enough opponents to battle that afternoon.

So, I shook my head and flung the voice from my mind, and returned to the sight of the monster snuffling in the hot air, six feet away from me.

I had decided what to do next. I would teach

Granak a lesson about spear tips and pain. As he sniffed and watched me with his gleaming raisin eyes, I drew the spear tip back, took a step forward, and jabbed at the bulb of his snout.

That small jab changed everything.

38

I intended to jab Granak lightly, with just enough force to remind him how much the spear could hurt. A small prick into the sensitive knob of his snout might be enough. Then, I assumed he would lose his temper and charge again. But that's not what happened. As I jabbed with the spear, Granak flinched, and the speartip slid along the length of his snout, all the way to its base.

And into his right eye.

The tip went in—way in. It hit the bone at the back of the socket with a stomach-churning crunch that vibrated along the shaft and into my hands. Granak flung a paw in front of his face, but not before I saw clear fluid squelch outward and splash into the dust in several sickening plops.

I withdrew the spear, pulling white chunks and fluid with it. Granak swatted the spear but hit only air. He squinted at me with his one good eye. Then retreated in a hurried shuffle, his paw pressed tight over his face. Then, he stood on three limbs and lowered his head in the dust and moaned.

The howling Goths in the mob remained silent and open-mouthed. There wasn't even a sneeze or a bark. The king's lieutenant shuffled closer to the king. The king himself stood up on his hind legs and strained his neck for a better view. Karz clutched her paws, her snout swinging left and right. Captain Gwawn, standing to the king's left, growled something out to Granak, but Granak ignored him. He raised his head and looked at me with an intensity that made my damp and clammy shirt feel cold.

I tightened my grip on the spear, thinking fast. I had scored a point and then lost the advantage. I should have taken a step forward and struck again before Granak could compose himself. I should have jammed the spear into his neck or his shoulders, or gone all the way and shoved it deeper into his eye, all the way to his brain, if he had a brain, but I had been too appalled and too slow. Now Granak was wounded. Worse! He was embarrassed.

He dropped onto his four paws and crept toward me, his claws long and yellow against the grey dust.

Karz called out, 'We stop. We stop. You say…'

But the captain growled at her and she ducked her head, admonished.

Granak circled me, just out of range of my spear tip. A direct assault would meet with a jab to the chest or head. He had to get inside the spear's range and then follow me when I stepped out of the way.

As if reading my thoughts, he charged, received a jab in the neck, batted the spear aside, and kept on charging. He came inside the spear's range, but I was fast enough to reel in the shaft and then aim the tip at his face. So, he retreated and began circling me, going one way, then turning and padding the other, watching and waiting for a moment of weakness.

In the silence, the intimate sounds grew loud: my heart thumped; my boots squeaked; and my hands rasped on the spear's shaft. Meanwhile, Granak's breathing became hoarse; and his great paws padding in the sand made a deceptively gentle whisper. But beneath it all, another sound was deafening: otherworldly drone of hate.

In this same situation, the Accord Commission would call for tolerance and understanding, for compassion—to request dialogue and mutual understanding. The Accord, I thought, would die disemboweled with its guts soaking red and brown in the sand.

But not me. Not if I could help it. I might have struggled against my treasonous mind urging me to kill myself before the fight, but at this moment, I wanted to end the contest like a soldier. To die on my feet, never in an act of surrender. At least I could do that.

As Granak circled me, I rotated with him, step by step, facing him at all times, like I imagined dancing might have been in the pre-Accord era, with both dancers face to face, complementing each other's movements, female and male. But this was no time to daydream about pre-Accord gender relations. This was reality. This was life and death.

If only I wasn't so tired. If only I wasn't so sick of it all. If only my mind worked like it used to work. But there was no time for self-pity. There was only time for Granak.

He tried a new tactic. He feinted left. He drew the spear tip with him. Then he lunged right, then left again, until the spear tip could not keep up and he could come inside the spear's range. On his third feint, it worked. He rushed along the spear's shaft, coming for me. I stepped backward to open up the distance between us, trying to gather in the spear and shove the tip back in his face, but my lame foot would not obey me, and I tripped and fell onto my back.

The spear's blunt end hit the ground and bounced out of my grip. Before I could grab it again, a ton of shaggy fury descended on me.

Granak didn't slash my throat as I thought he might. Instead, he brought his weight down on my chest, his giant paws slammed onto my ribs, pinning me to the ground. He watched as my breath went out and would not come back in. He didn't even notice my hands tearing the fur on his forelimbs, his chest, and his barrel-thick neck. Instead, his maw opened and his tongue lolled. He was more like a friendly dog than a killer. Just a friendly, monstrous dog—crouching over me in the dust on an alien planet, far, far away.

I tried to breathe, but my lungs would not obey. I tried again. But each time I tried to inhale, my chest squashed further down, and the monstrous, lolling tongue dripped closer. And then my vision blurred and my heart thumped louder in my ears.

That's when a human voice spoke in my mind.

Then out spake brave Horatius, The Captain of the gate.

It was a deep, male voice, speaking in a strange accent.

To every man upon this earth, death cometh soon or late.

Some kind of poem—a poem from the pre-Accord-era.

And how can man die better than facing fearful odds, for the ashes of his fathers, and the temples of his gods.

'Who are you?'

But all the while, Granak bore down harder, forcing the air from my lungs, bending my ribs. The roar from the mob swelled around me into a chant, a single Goth growl, repeated over and over.

Then the sound faded away, replaced by the shush of water. The image of Granak grew dark until his shaggy head resembled a black cloud in a night sky.

And then I slipped far, far away.

39

I was no longer on the far side of the galaxy, crushed into the hot dust of Gwawanath. Instead, I lay on a wooden deck at night. Above me, masts and sails rose high into the dark, and shrouds creaked and strained. I was on a ship, the kind that sailed in the forbidden, pre-Accord past, centuries ago. The voice continued in its deep and strange accent. This time it was outside my head, speaking nearby.

'Who are you?' I said. Then, I saw the man standing on the ship's quarterdeck, leaning against the taffrail. He wore a great blue coat with a golden epaulet in each shoulder.

'Were you listening, Alex?' he said. 'I don't think you were. So, I'll recite it again. You might find this particular passage useful, especially given your present situation. Listen carefully to the words.'

He cleared his throat and began again.

Then out spake brave Horatius,

The Captain of the Gate:
'To every man upon this earth
Death cometh soon or late.
And how can man die better
Than facing fearful odds,
For the ashes of his fathers,
And the temples of his gods.

He appeared to be an older man—in his forties, maybe. But his face was familiar. I had met him before.

'Is it not inspiring, Alex? The words come from one of the greatest poems about courage ever written. It has been an inspiration to me and to those of us in the service. Over the centuries, it will offer comfort to countless others as well— until your own century, of course, when it will be banned by your government. Did I tell you how important it is to know your nation's history, Alex? A man who doesn't know his history is easy to push around. That's why your government forbids the study of the past. If you don't cherish your history, you don't know who you are, or where you're going, and why should or shouldn't go there.'

'Who are you?'

'And if you knew history, you'd also see the irony about the poem. It's about ancient Rome, Alex, the historical Rome, the Rome on Earth, and a battle between ancient Romans and an invading army. The real Rome, Alex, not the place in which you presently find yourself, nor soon won't find yourself, unless you pull yourself together, young lieutenant of the Accord of Nations Navy. Of course, the poem is not exactly appropriate to your circumstances, sure, but I'm a man of the sea, not of books. But like many men who fight, I have memorized this poem. I can recite it when necessary. True, it was written after my time, but then, as we discussed once before, Alex, time doesn't always…'

'Who are you?' I said for the third time.

'You don't know? You really don't know.' It sounded like 'noo.' He stopped and shook his head. 'So, we will have to go over it all again? God's blood! It's like teaching reefers the knots. They never learn the first time, nor the second. They only learn when they see that proper knots can be the difference between life and death.'

'What?'

'Not "what," Lieutenant. I have put men to the cat for less. I think you meant to say, "I beg your pardon, sir?" Or perhaps, "I beg your pardon, Captain Burns."'

'So where are we, Captain Burns?'

'We're aboard a ship of war, and not just any ship of war. This is His Majesty's Ship Hemera, one of the finest ever launched. She has a crew of six hundred, and carries seventy-four great guns that can smash a mountain into the sea—or so I like to say. She's ordered to your part of the world, Alex. We're at war. Who would have thought, eh? Now sit up, laddy. Don't insult the dignity of the King's ship.'

I sat up and looked around. In my naval career, I had rarely been aboard a patrol boat, let alone a frigate, let alone an aircraft carrier. I'd walked the Slingshot-covered deck of the AONNS Accord Values for just three days. The HSM Hemera was something else: a great, square-rigged warship from the pre-Accord era. The gunwales were lined by heavy cannons on oaken carriages, held in place by rope tackles. The three masts were so tall they rose out of sight into the dark; and high up, between the sails, bright stars throbbed. Somewhere up there, Gwawanath orbited its sun.

The sight of this ship was like a tonic. It healed me. I climbed to my feet. My ankle obeyed me. My ribs ceased complaining. My uniform smelled clean. I felt strong and tall again. My mind was clear. I knew this was a dream, yet it was so vivid. The air was salty and fresh. The roll of the ship was so reassuring, like I'd lived in this world before.

I turned to the tall figure in the great blue coat with its ranks of brass buttons, its bright white lapels, and two golden epaulets. I knew what those epaulets signified: the rank of post-captain, a senior position in pre-Accord navies, the equivalent of a colonel in the army, an exalted rank.

There was something else too. His face, or rather my face. My own face gazed back at me—but with a short beard and a scar on its left cheek. The man looked at me and smiled.

'Now, you remember,' said Captain Alexander Burns of the Royal Navy.

'Some,' I said.

'You will. Give it time.'

'I'm afraid, Captain, that I don't have time to give.'

'No, not much,' he conceded, 'not much at all, but you have enough. There's always time if your mind is right.'

'My mind, sir, is…' I didn't know what to say next.

'Your mind. Yes, I know what they did.'

'No. My mind is not… my mind is… not the same. I can't think straight and when I stop thinking my mind seems to turn on me, like an enemy, a terrible enemy.'

'I know, Alex. It was very cruel. It is a curious feature of your world that people talk about togetherness and understanding and progress, but out of sight, act like barbarians.'

'How much time do I have?'

'It's six bells in the morning watch. The dawn is coming… from over there.' He nodded to the darkness over the port side. 'It will come racing towards the ship like thunder out of Africa. That's how much time you have.'

I looked up between the sails at the twinkling stars.

'I'm dying,' I said, 'or, at least, I am about to die. Every second I stand here, grim death creeps closer to me in that dusty clearing. Oh, grandfather, the things I have seen, the things I have done. So alone and so lost.'

'That's a little dramatic,' said my ancestor, 'but not unfair. You're up against it. No doubt about it. You're sailing along a lee shore. However, I think it's more the case that you are not so much dying, as allowing yourself to be killed, Alex, just as you are allowing yourself to be defeated—in life.'

I shook my head.

'I'm one man against a monster. A monster many times my size—one that has me pinned to the ground. And up there, it's just me fighting against a whole government, and an entire race of invaders, and everyone in the Accord. Only me. It's impossible to fight all of it.'

'I am not referring to them, Alex. I am referring to your soul, your spirit, if you prefer that term. You are from a time in which souls and the Almighty are no longer regarded… nor even known. Am I correct?'

'My spirit's fine, whatever that is.'

'No, it is not fine. You have lost your way. And not just because you're somewhere up there,' he nodded at the stars and then down at a glass cabinet lit by a small lamp. 'You've lost sight of this,' he said. 'Your compass. You can't see it. You don't know why you're fighting at all. You're just plodding forward on instinct and bitterness. That's why you're pinned to the dust by a monster from another world.'

'I know. I chose the Goths. The wrong choice.'

'No, the right choice,' the man corrected me. 'A foolish choice, but the right choice, Alex.'

'No.'

'Oh yes. Sometimes, Alex, the wrong ship will take you to the right port. You couldn't do any good in that forest with all those enemies competing for you—not for something as important as the thing you must do. Escape was the only choice.'

'What thing? What must I do? I'm just one man. I can't do anything—not even for myself, and certainly not for the world. And why should I do it, anyway? What reasons could justify waging a one-man war?'

'What made you wage it before—back there in that city, in that harbor in China? Why did you fight? What were your reasons?'

'I failed. Totally failed. Octavia is alive. She's going to be an Accord Commissioner. She's going to land her forces. The world is lost. And no one wants it to be any different. The people want their own enslavement—or don't have the courage to resist. They don't care whether they're controlled by the Accord or Octavia, so long as they don't have to think, so long as they're "safe." How I hate that word. "Safe"— how I hate it. For them, freedom is too hard; it's the greater enemy. Comfort and "safety" are more important than freedom.'

The captain paused, drew a breath.

'Aye,' he said, 'but they also don't know what's coming? And it's not everyone who thinks that way either. Is it? Some people resist.'

'I don't care. I can't even think about it. They

messed with my mind. They damaged it.'

'Aye, but they didn't kill your mind either. You're still in charge, mostly. You can be in charge again. You're not meant to be like this, Alex, and you can't be like this. Not ever, and not now.'

'Is that more Burns family destiny, stuff? A-riamh deiseil—the Burns family motto?'

'Yes. Your family destiny. You are meant to wage this fight just like your ancestors have fought. Call it the family trade.'

'The family trade? You mean every Burns generation wages some kind of war? For what? I'm just a guy. One guy. One guy alone. One guy about to die.'

'You're not alone. You've never been alone. Not here and not out there.' He pointed over the taffrail into the gloom. 'Eventually, you've got to trust people and to lead them. You…'

But I interrupted him. I wanted to listen, but I didn't have time. The dawn always came. Always. For better or worse. And the dream always vanished just as I reached for the knowledge to save myself.

'You want to help me?' I said. 'Then get the monster off my chest. And if you won't do that, help the monster finish me once and for all.'

'You don't need my help.'

'Then what do I do? Tell me! What do I do?'

On the horizon, a fringe of gold burned. The gloom faded. For the first time, I could see the main deck. It was crowded with men watching in silence. They were dressed in short blue jackets, white trousers. Some wore strange hats. Other people stood down there too—people not dressed in navy jackets and trousers. I thought I recognized their faces.

'Listen,' said Captain Burns. 'The chance is with you, Alex. You just don't see it yet because you're not seeking it. The secret to defeating Octavia is where you are. They've already given it to you. It's with you now. If you find it, your one-man war will make sense, and you will discover your sense of self, your purpose, the most important thing.'

'What is it? What chance? What thing?'

He stood up from the taffrail.

'The Romans can't go to the Goth area of the planet. Why do you think that is? Why can't they go there with all their machines, with all their power. Why won't they dare enter the Goth territory? Why didn't the pilots descend with you to the planet? What is it about the Goth land they don't like or can't endure?'

The sunlight hit the topgallant sails, turning them a brilliant white. Down on the main deck, the ship's bell tolled. I saw the red uniform of a pre-Accord Marine. I saw the Marine replace the small bell hammer and walk back to his station by the helmsman.

'Think, Alex.'

'I'll think if you tell me how to get out from under that Goth.'

He shook his head. 'Even if I knew I couldn't tell you.'

'Why?'

'Because then I'd deny your victory, your reason to become who you are. To appreciate life, Alex, you must face the terror of losing it. Then you'll understand my words. Then you'll know why you wage this fight and others don't.'

'What if I want to lose my life? What if I can't see the point?'

Now, the dawn came racing across the sea from the east, catching the crests of the waves, and striking the mainsail, drenching it with light. And with this light came exhaustion, foul air, pain in my chest, and burning resentment.

'Don't make your father's mistake, Alex. You must hold your life no matter what.'

'What mistake? What about my father? What did he do? Where is he? They won't tell me.'

I thought I saw my ancestor's eyes flick down to the men on the deck.

'Tell no one when you discover it,' my ancestor's voice said. 'Not until you're face-to-face with the monster herself.'

But discover what?

'The secret, Alex. The secret.'

40

'Gwah!' Granak growled.

I was back in the nightmare--back with all its horrors: the choking dust, the pain in my chest, the certainty my ribs would crack and cave, the heat, the baying mob, the foul air, the exhaustion, the weakened limbs, the twisted ankle, the hunger, the impending failure, the likely death, and the monster's dripping red tongue two feet above my face.

But now something else was there: my ancestor's words.

'Gwah,' Granak growled.

Gwah yourself, you foul-breathed monster, I thought, still angry at my ancestor at the same time as being grateful to him. He had insulted me and accused me of self-pity and of neglecting my duty, whatever that was. And he had given only vague answers to my questions of getting out of this mess.

'Gwah!' roared Granak.

'Gwah!' roared the Goth mob behind him.

'Gwah!' Granak roared again, pressing down.

So what's it to be? A painful but quick death or another try at Octavia for reasons unknown, but reasons apparently persuasive enough if you discover them. How could I know? How could I ever be sure? My ancestor's calm tone was reassuring. It made me feel momentarily in control of my destiny, but I was wary of calm, reassuring tones. Too many reassuring voices had told me the Accord always knew best.

So what's it to be, Burns? Certain death or uncertain future, and more failure.

I looked up. Granak's head loomed closer. I could see the awful, pink corrugations in the roof of his mouth. Then, his expression suddenly changed. Something was happening. He had suddenly reached a decision. His snout snapped shut, concealing the lolling tongue. He drew himself up. He was going to end the contest by smashing down with his weight, and his paws and claws, finally breaking my ribs. Then he would rake my neck and face. Then, he would tear out my guts and drag them in the dust. And then he would accept the adulation of the mob and the praise of his king.

So what's it to be, Burns? What's it going to be? How exactly are you going to conduct yourself in the next few terrible seconds?

Give in, whispered my traitorous mind. Give in. Give in. Give in. A few seconds—that's all it will take. A few quick seconds, no longer than it takes to say farewell. Then, a little bit of pain, and it will all be over. Then, you can rest. You can sleep. You can sleep.

'Get out of my head,' I said. 'Get out. Get out. GET OUT!'

Granak pushed himself up for his final, spectacular smash. And without knowing how, or why, I used the tiny gap widening between us to bend my knee, raise my boot, and then with all my fading strength, I drove my heel into the dangling fruit of his enormous genitals.

The impact vibrated all the way through the boot, all the way up my leg, as if I had stomped on two melons. They resisted at first, then squashed hard under my heel against whatever bones or organs lay in Granak's furry abdomen. For good measure, I drew my knee back and stomped all over again.

Above me, Granak's maw opened, but this time, his tongue did not loll obscenely above me. Instead, it curled, like a kid's birthday whistle, rolling back after being blown. He rose high, lifting his head to the sky, but not to smash down on me; it was something else—maybe to beseech Gwanta for guidance or to howl in agony. I didn't care. His weight was off me, and I filled my lungs with the foul air as fast as the breathing device would let me.

Then, I shouted, 'Not this time, pal!'

Granak looked back down at me. He lifted a paw and aimed a raking swipe at my face—but too late. The gap he left was enough for me to roll to the side. The paw and all of Granak's weight hit the sand.

I had survived.

But I was not free.

Granak held me with one paw on my chest and raised the other to rake my neck, or maybe my face. It didn't matter which. The effect would be the same. I struggled and rolled, but the weight of the claw was too much. Well, this is it, I thought. My ancestor might be right. What better way to die than facing fearful odds?

But before the claw could come smashing down, I saw Granak's head snap sideways as the spear tip punched into his ear from the side. It jabbed him once, twice, then a third time, forcing him to reach for balance, and giving me enough space to roll out from under him.

I climbed to my knees, and then to my feet, my ribs shrieking in pain. Close by, swaying in the thick air stood Karz. The spear rested on one forelimb; its base was buried in her chest. She must have run at Granak with it.

'What are you doing?' I said. 'Is this some kind of rule?'

But all she said was 'Gwah,' and dropped the spear.

I turned back to Granak. He was clutching his ear, looking at Karz as if he'd never seen her before, as if she were a new kind of animal. While he was still in shock, I dropped to the sand, grabbed the spear, then ran forward and thrust it deep into his neck. Then I withdrew it before the raking claws swooshed past. Then I reeled the spear in and thrust the tip at him again, going deeper before the claws knocked it away.

I stepped around to his exposed flank. I raised the spear and jabbed it deep. Granak's side was softer, more yielding than his muscular back. He barked and backed away. The spear came out. It had done some damage. His fur glistened with dark blood.

I can kill him, I thought. I can actually kill him. Just keep going. Don't stop. Keep going.

To my right, the king watched on. Beside him stood his equally astonished first lieutenant. Next to them stood Captain Gwawn and the rest of the courtiers. All of them had their mouths open. But none of them seemed to care that Karz had interfered in the fight. They were going to let it continue.

Turning back to Granak, I gripped the spear tighter in my right hand, ready to shove it up into his neck and then into his head, to drive it upwards into his brain, to finish him for good. But at that moment, standing in the dust, in the heat, facing the monster, something unexpected showed up.

An idea.

It came like the opening of a curtain, letting in the light. Or like the moment you finally remember someone's name that you normally never forget. The idea should have been obvious to me, but I hadn't recognized it. I hadn't seen. It had been there, but I hadn't seen it.

Until now.

Everything became clear. I knew what I had to do. I couldn't give up. Nor should I kill Granak. I had discovered something.

'Karz!' I shouted

She looked at me, her faced as surprised as a Goth face could be. She growled something and tossed her head toward the stricken Granak. Behind her, the king's lieutenant stood beside another warrior who must have come from the cave. Was he Granak's second, maybe, ready to restore Goth pride now that another of its soldiers was about to fail?

It didn't matter. I knew what I had to do.

I dropped the spear in front of Karz.

'Gwah!' she roared and swung her snout at my opponent. 'Fight Granak. Fight. Kill!' she roared. 'Kill.'

'No. I want you to help me talk to King Gwantalan.'

'You die,' growled Karz. 'He kill you. Look. He kill you.'

'No, he won't. Not while I can breathe.'

'Gwah?' She didn't understand. 'Fight. Kill. Or they kill.' She tossed her head at the mob.

'No, I won't kill him or them, and they won't kill me either.'

'Not understand. Not understand.'

'Now listen, Karz. I want you to help me talk to the king.'

'Not understand,' she growled.

'You will, Karz,' I said. 'You will.'

41

Every Goth waited to see what would happen.

Karz swayed on her hind legs, clasping her paws in front of her. The king and his courtiers swayed to my right. Granak hunched over in the dust twenty yards away, licking his paw and running it over his face. The Goth mob swayed on the hills, rumbling unhappily.

'Talk king,' I repeated to Karz.

She turned to the king, sniffed, then turned back to me. She unclasped and re-clasped her paws.

'Talk king?' she growled.

'Yes. Talk king.' Then I added, 'Please.'

But her great paws remained on her chest. So, I reached out and took hold of her forelimb. Despite her size and strength, she allowed me to lead her.

The king's lieutenant growled and charged forward to block the way. The rest of the king's retinue dropped to all fours, shuffled forward to join the lieutenant. Then, they stood, like a furry cliff, snarling at me, and at Karz.

'Karz please tell them I talk king.'

'Not understand.'

'Tell king, I can kill Octavia.'

'Not understand,' Karz rumbled, her snout swinging from side to side. But I pressed on.

'Tell king, I kill Roman leader.'

'Not understand.'

The lieutenant growled at Karz this time, but she did not pull away.

'Tell king, I kill Lanalan.'

The sound of the name caused an instant and profound effect. Karz's head ceased its pendulum swing. The lieutenant's mouth opened. I had spoken in the Goth language, and I had spoken its most hated word.

Lanalan.

Karz blinked. Behind his wall of guards, the king coughed.

'Lanalan?' growled Karz. 'Kill Lanalan?'

'Tell king I can kill Lanalan. Kill her. Just me. Kill.'

'Lanalan?'

'Yes. Kill Lanalan.'

The lieutenant sniffed and rumbled at Karz. He wanted an explanation.

'Kill Lanalan?' she growled once more.

'Yes. Kill. I know how kill.'

Then, she stood on her hind legs and turned to the lieutenant and growled my message. The lieutenant growled back at her. Karz growled back at him. She pointed at me, then pointed at

Granak, then pointed into the sky. She raised both forelimbs in what might have been a shrug.

When she finished, the lieutenant and the escort growled. The Goth mob followed their lead. The cliff face rumbled like thunder until King Gwantalan stood on his hind legs and raised his forelimbs in the air. The mob gradually calmed down and each Goth lowered his and her snout.

Then the king growled at the lieutenant. The lieutenant growled at the rest of the guards. They dropped to their four limbs and lumbered aside. The king growled at Karz and Karz padded forward.

After an exchange of low growls, Karz turned to me. 'King say, Goth people never fight Lanalan. Lanalan too strong for paws, claws, and teeth.'

'I know. Lanalan is strong,' I said. 'But please tell king I can kill Lanalan. Kill for Gwanath people. I know how.'

She growled this to the king.

Karz replied. 'King not believe.'

'Tell king, if he stops fight, I tell how I kill.'

Karz relayed this to the king. The king listened. He considered. He looked at the dusty ground. He looked at the flawless sky. Then he growled to his lieutenants. An exchanged of growls followed, along with shaking of heads, raising of paws, and mutters of Gwanta. Then they all stopped, lumbered into their places, their ears cocked to the mob, as if they didn't care, but the ears always flicked back, listening.

'King say you talk, he think.'

'Good. Thank you, Karz. Thank you, King Gwantalan.'

'You talk.'

'OK,' I said.

'You talk.'

'First,' I said, 'tell Granak, we stop fight. Fight over.'

To my left, Granak watched as he licked his forelimb.

The king growled. Karz listened.

'King say how you kill Lanalan? How kill? Rifle no good. Paws, claws no good. Everything no good. How kill? How?'

The moment had arrived.

'The land,' I said. 'The land that kills Ranawah people. The land that stops Ranawah people coming here. Gwanath land can kill Lanalan.'

Karz growled to the king. The king crossed his forelimbs and considered. Then he growled a reply.

'King say Gwanath land not let Ranawah come here.'

'Yes, I know. The land stops the Ranawah. It hates the Ranawah.'

'Goth land hate Ranawah,' echoed Karz and relayed this to the king.

'But which part of land?' I pointed at the gray face of the bluff, at the sand, and at the forest. Then I shrugged as I had seen Karz shrug. 'Which Gwanath land hate Ranawah?'

I had already guessed the answer, but I waited while Karz growled to the king who issued a short, regal bark then turned his head as if the answer was obvious.

'What did he say, Karz?'

Karz said nothing. Instead, she stood on her hind limbs and lumbered toward Granak. She stopped where the spear lay in the sand. Then, after dropping to all fours, she shoved the gray metal rod across the ground towards me.

I knelt down, picked it up, and held it to the sunlight. It glittered and emitted its strange electric hum. Could this be it? Could this be the material so toxic to Octavia, the secret to defeating her?

'Gwantashale,' Karz growled. 'You see. Gwantashale.'

So that was its name. I lifted the spear, sniffed the strange metal, listened to its hum, like a cable bearing strong electrical current. I raised my finger to my mouth to touch my tongue and taste it.

Karz raised a paw and put it on my arm.

'Not,' she said. 'Touch, sick.'

'How sick?' I asked.

Karz put the paw to her chest and mimed the acts of vomiting and staggering.

'Sick,' she growled.

'Kill?'

She scratched her arm. 'Make all sick. Kill some.'

She barked this to the king who growled to the

lieutenant who shrugged.

'Does king think Gwantashale kill?'

'King not know. Only Gwanta know.'

At the mention of the name Gwanta, every Goth's ears twitched, and they all growled.

'I will find out if kill,' I said. 'I will use the Gwantashale on Lanalan.'

Karz relayed this to the king.

'What did he say?'

'King like,' she growled. 'King like.'

'Good. I like too.'

So far, so good.

Then, I said, 'What about me, Karz?'

'You?'

'Will king kill or king not kill?'

Karz turned and growled my question. The king did not reply. Instead, he gazed up at the strange sky, then at the mob of Goths. Then he growled his answer.

'King not kill,' Karz growled, 'if you kill Lanalan.'

'Not kill?'

'Not kill. Not kill if you kill Lanalan.'

So that was it.

I offered a silent thank you to the captain of His Majesty's Ship Hemera.

Meanwhile, the king lifted his head and roared. The escort of Goths roared too. The mob of Goths joined in and then Karz, putting a great paw on my shoulder, lifted her head and roared with the best of them.

'This good,' I said, holding the Gwantashale

spear. 'Good.'

When the roaring ended, I said, 'But Karz, why don't you use this on Ranawah people yourselves?'

'Not understand.'

'Why Gwanath people not use this kill Ranawah?'

Karz shook her head. 'King say already.'

'I missed it. Sorry. Why not fight with Gwantashale?'

'Gwanta not like. Gwanta say only fight with paws, claws, and teeth.'

So there was the answer. The Goths put their religion before everything else, even before destroying their enemies, even before their own lives.

I turned and walked towards Granak. He sat cowed and bleeding. I walked over to him. I held up two palms.

'Granak,' I said. 'Sorry. Friends.'

Instantly, he climbed to his four limbs and issued a warning growl.

Karz came up behind me. 'Not,' she growled.

'But we not fight now.'

'Gwanath people,' she growled. 'King say Gwanath fight Granak now.'

'What?'

'Gwanath people fight Granak.'

'Gwanath people? Why?'

And as she spoke, the king growled and his lieutenants growled and to my horror, the Goth mob came alive, and like a tide of fur and teeth, surged down the hill.

'Must fast,' growled Karz, raising her paw to my shoulder, and tossing her head. 'Must fast. Gwanath people.'

We stepped back. The mob arrived and piled onto Granak in a torrent of growls and raised claws. Each Goth was angry, vengeful, frenzied, and desperate to get at Granak. I watched, horrified. I heard the frenzied roars, saw the terrible heads with their terrible, blood-smeared snouts, plunging and rising with torn flesh in their teeth. When one had torn his share of flesh, he rose and backed out of the pack. Instantly, another Goth would plunge to take his place. And when the terrible mob tore its last piece of flesh and lumbered away, I saw way too much. They had torn Granak to pieces, torn the fur from his flesh, and then the flesh from his bones by paws, claws, and teeth.

'Keep Gwanath people strong,' growled Karz.

I didn't know what to say. I was short of breath with horror. How different the culture of these creatures was to that of the Accord! The Goths and their king and their god despised failure. They punished failure by horrible death. Meanwhile, the Accord and its commissioners celebrated and revered failure. They rewarded failure with gifts of privilege and power. They organized their system of government around failure to make sure every Accord member failed as much as possible--except of course, for the powerful few.

I turned to Karz.

'Thank you for saving me.'

'Gwah.'

'Why did you do it?'

'Not understand.'

By now, the light had faded. The forest cast a dark shadow far across the sand. The Goths dispersed, lumbering back to their caves to lie in front of them and rumble to each other.

I wondered if I would have to stay the night on this planet. The cell back on the Gwantasnarr seemed far more comfortable than a patch of dust in a cave. I turned to Karz to ask her. She was looking up at the sky. So was the king; so were his lieutenants. Soon, every Goth still outside did the same. They all looked up and sniffed suspiciously.

Something strange was happening above the planet.

I looked up too, shielding my eyes against the sunset. There, like an enormous stripe in the sky, a large fleet of ships groaned towards the sun. The word 'armada' might have been a better description. They were the same, huge, transport vessels as the ones that formed the Roman flotilla —the one Octavia had parked beside the moon, the one carrying Romans, Marines, weapons, and colony-building machines. Now, there were so many of these giant ships they cast a long shadow across the Goth land, like an eclipse.

'Ranawah,' growled Karz.

'Where are they going?' I asked.

'Not understand.'

'Go where?' I said, but I guessed there could be only one place this armada was heading.

'Maybe go your home,' growled Karz.

I clutched the shard of spear in my hands. This strange, dull, glittering metal, this piece of Goth land, this Gwantashale—it would soon go to my home too. I held it up and examined it again. Can it really harm Octavia, I thought. Can this small length of rock actually finish her and drive away her ships of destruction?

Before long, I would find out.

PART THREE: HYACINTH

'No member of the Accord Of Nations shall have the right to bear arms, except for duly appointed agents of the Accord Commission.'

The Accord of Nations Constitution

42

The dropship ascended from Gwawanath. Through the viewport, the forests of the Goth lands spread out in green and gray. Then, as we rose higher, they shrunk to a green band running across the arid purple of the Roman lands.

Clouds descended from above, racing down and obscuring the view and forming hills and valleys of white. Then, when the dropship's hull ceased rattling, the planet's great curve emerged beneath the clouds, and every Goth aboard the dropship sighed.

Higher up, the ship accelerated and each Goth and the single human was forced down onto the mattresses and benches. The sighs turned to grumbles as we gathered enough speed to catch the Gwantasnarr in its orbit. When the ship escaped the planet's atmosphere, and the acceleration ceased, I climbed to my aching feet and sat beside Karz. She stood on all fours, gazing at the planet through the viewport, silently mouthing the word Gwawanath over and over.

Unlike Karz, I couldn't wait to leave. I had a new sense of purpose and hope. I touched the pocket of my NWU jacket, probably the fiftieth time I'd touched it that morning. Inside the pocket was the magical lump of Gwanath land that might slay a monster—if the bearer were brave enough, or, if not brave enough, then mad.

'Karz, how long to reach the ship?'

'Sad,' she rumbled.

'No, how long reach ship?'

'Sad,' she rumbled again.

'Why sad? Sad leave home?'

'Sad,' she growled. 'Sad leave Gwawanath. Happy fight Ranawah. Happy, king happy. Happy Gwanta happy. Sad leave Gwawanath. Sad.'

'You'll be back, Karz,' I said.

'Burr happy?' she growled.

'Yes,' I said. 'Happy.'

'Burr sleep?' she said.

'Later,' I said.

'Burr sleep,' said Karz. 'Burr face not good. Burr sleep.'

King Gwantalan had named me Burr in honor of my new role as advisor to the Goth forces. Burr meant 'tree' in Goth—not a specific tree, just tree. Burr, the tree. There were worse names in Goth—worse names such as Lanalan.

'Burr sleep,' growled Karz.

'I'll sleep on the Gwantasnarr, once we get

moving.'

'Then fight Lanalan,' she growled. 'Use Gwantashale.'

'Yes,' I said. 'Fight with Gwanath people and with Gwantashale. Fight Lanalan.'

'Gwantashale secret,' growled Karz.

'Secret,' I replied. 'Only we know.'

I pointed at her, Captain Gwawn, Lieutenant Glathaw, and the few other Goths who had watched the fight with Granak. 'No one else.'

'Secret,' growled Karz.

I touched my pocket yet again. King Gwantalan's courtiers had wrapped a shard of the Gwantashale spear in a heavy cloth and then placed it into a case made from a different kind of rock. The courtiers told Karz the stone would keep the shale's poison locked inside.

Even so, I had many questions. Was the shale really poisonous enough to kill Octavia? If so, would one small case of it be enough? And what was the best way to use it? To simply expose Octavia to it, or to press it on her skin—that's if it were even possible to get close to her? No Goth knew the answers. No Goth had ever used the shale as a weapon. Using shale meant not fighting by paws, claws, and teeth, as Gwanta demanded, and no Goth would ever do that.

So much uncertainty lay ahead. But there could be no going back, no pulling out. I had my chance to stop Octavia and maybe her invasion force too. Now I had to seize that chance, whatever that meant.

Then, there was the other reason I was glad to be carrying the shale, the one my ancestor had implied, the one about myself, the one about my purpose. I still wasn't sure what this meant, but the thought of it gave me comfort. That would have to do for now. I was following my intuition again, just as I had back in the swirling uncertainty of the forest in AON sub-territory California, but this time something was different. I wasn't escaping. I wasn't fleeing with a twisted ankle and a confused mind. I was stepping forward to confront my enemies. And this time, my eyes were open and I was properly armed.

Karz raised a paw at a cluster of lights rolling by on the planet's surface in the grey and purple section.

'Ranaltor, Burr,' she said. 'Many Ranawah, Burr.'

'Ranaltor? Is it a city? A Roman city?'

'Not understand.'

'City—many Ranawah home?'

'Many,' Karz growled. 'Many.'

'You go there? You go Ranaltor?'

Karz growled, 'Many Gwanath people die there.'

'But not you?'

'Two brother me,' she growled. 'Lanalan kill them.'

Lanalan.

Also known as Octavia, Sinistra, and The Lovelorn.

'Sorry to hear, Karz.'

'Gwanath people very hate Lanalan,' she growled.

I asked no more questions, even though I had plenty to ask. How had her brothers died? In what form did the Romans and Octavia exist in their own cities? How big were they? What did they eat? How did they reproduce? Were there even sexes?

Karz would know, of course. Of all the Goths, she would be the one to know. The more I watched her, the more I realized she not only held special status among the Goths but that she was unique. She wore a red neckcloth, like the king. She might even have royal status herself—a princess, maybe, the sister of the king, or his daughter. She could speak Goth, Roman, and an Accord language. She had also saved my life. She was virtuous and kind, a better person than me.

'Karz?' I said.

But she didn't answer, so I kept quiet. Better to keep my thoughts to myself. No, better not to think any thoughts at all. Octavia might read them—even here. If she detected that I carried Gwantashale, the mission would be over. I'd be back to square one, facing fearful odds without a weapon. So, I turned my attention to the receding planet and kept my mind blank.

The dropship drew nearer to the Gwantasnarr. The Gwantasnarr's hull loomed in the viewport, stretching away for a mile or more into space. Then, the ship made contact with the port at the ship's rear. The Goth's ears twitched left and right at the various groans and bangs as we docked. Then the hatch opened and revealed the ramp in the Gwantasnarr's stern.

When the ramp touched the deck, the growling began. A mob of Goths waited for us. They surrounded Captain Gwawn as soon as he stepped from the gangway. Something had happened, apparently, something urgent. The captain listened, his ears twitching. Then he too growled. So did the other Goths from the dropship, and then all of them dropped to their four limbs, turned, and stampeded across the deck towards the passageway.

'What's going on, Karz?'

'Many Gwanath talk.'

'What did they say?'

'Ranawah ships.'

'Ranawah ships? You mean, the fleet we saw is still nearby? It hasn't left?'

'Ranawah ship here.'

'So where did Captain Gwawn go?'

'Go pilots. Tell pilots attack.'

'Attack? No. We can't attack—not if Octavia's not there.'

'Not understand.'

'Lanalan! Not attack if Lanalan not there.'

'They not say Lanalan. Just ships.'

'If she's not there, we've got to stop them. It's no use attacking the ships if Lanalan's not there. Captain Gwawn and the rest will be killed and I won't have a chance to fight Lanalan like I promised King Gwantalan.'

'Not understand.'

'Pilots, Karz. We go pilots. Fast. Stop Captain Gwawn.'

I stepped from the gangway onto the deck, running for the passageway, but I found myself bounding, as if I were running on trampolines. I stopped and tried again, keeping in mind the change in gravity, and my sudden increase in power. I made sure my feet touched the deck before I pushed off. And then I ran down the passageway, Karz loping behind me, and the precious, dangerous, Earth-saving, self-restoring shale safe in my pocket.

43

After a mile of running and lumbering, we reached the door leading to the large stateroom. I pulled the lever, pushed the it open, and stepped inside. The stateroom was in an uproar. Hundreds of Goths stood on their hind limbs, roaring at each other, swaying and shimmering, like an angry pine forest in a gale.

'Keep going,' I called to Karz.

'Pilots,' she growled. 'Go pilots.'

But before we could take a step further, Captain Nolan appeared out of the chaos and stood in front of me.

'You're back,' she said.

'Yes, but I'm in a hurry, Captain.'

'You survived.'

She wore a new expression, a softer, kinder one. It couldn't have been relief, could it? She couldn't be pleased to see me, could she? Surely it wasn't possible.

'Stranger things have happened, Captain.'

'You look different. What happened?'

Karz grumbled up behind me. The Goths around the stateroom sniffed at her. She rose on her hind limbs and growl-warned them away.

'I can't talk to you now, Captain—not with all this noise.'

'But there's blood on your shirt, and what's that in your nose?'

I pulled out the prongs of the breathing device and put it in my side pocket, not the jacket pocket containing the stone case. 'It's something to help breathe down there.'

'Looks too small to be any use.'

How strange it was to hear her speak like a normal human, almost like a friend, a friend concerned for me. Her movements were strange too. She bowed her head slightly and sniffed at my sleeve, like a Goth.'

'What about this blood? Are you hurt?'

'A few scrapes, but I'm OK. You weren't worried about me, were you, Captain?'

For a moment, I thought she might raise a hand to her hip and tell me the name number of the Navy Spirit code that I had most certainly just violated, but instead she reached out and almost touched my sleeve before reeling her hand back in.

'Where is it from?' she said.

'What?'

'All this dried blood and that scratch on your face?'

'It's from the contest.'

'What contest?'

'King Gwantalan's contest.'

'You mean you fought one of the intra-galactic friends?'

'Yes.'

'And you survived?'

'So it seems.'

'It doesn't seem possible. How did you survive?'

'I'll tell you about it later, Captain. Right now I've got to get to the bridge.'

'Wait, Lieutenant. I need to debrief you on what happened down there, as Navy protocol requires. And first, I need to know what's happening here and now. Why are the Goths roaring like they're about to go into battle?'

'Because that's what they're going to do. They're going into battle, unless I can stop them.'

'Why are they going into battle? What did you do, Prisoner 548B?'

So, we were suddenly back to me being Prisoner 548B. I knew her friendly tone wouldn't last.

'I'll tell you after I talk to the pilots.'

She pointed at my jacket. 'What have you got there? What is that lump? It is against Accord values to take souvenirs from other cultures.'

'Can we leave the interrogation till later?'

'No, prisoner 548B, we cannot.'

'Sorry, Captain, but I've got to get to the pilots.'

'You will tell me what happened, Prisoner 548B. You will tell me why our friends are preparing to fight.'

I ignored her and walked towards the forward end of the stateroom.

A guard blocked the door to the passageway, towering above me on his hind limbs. He rumbled a warning 'Gwah.'

But I was ready for him. I had memorized a phrase Karz had taught me.

'King Gwantalan gives me permission to enter,' I growled in my best Goth.

The guard's ears sprung upright. He tilted his head in that weird, dog-like manner I'd seen on Gwawanath. He looked down at me from his great height, his nose frantically sniffing.

'King Gwantalan gives me permission to enter,' I growled again.

'Gwah,' he grumbled, and stepped back. I thought he might even bow to me.

'You speak Goth now, Prisoner 548B?' said Captain Nolan.

'Only a few growls.'

At the end of the passageway, I confronted the next guard.

'King Gwantalan gives me permission to enter,' I growled. The guard didn't even stoop to sniff at me. He turned and thumped on the door. A thump came back in reply and the door opened. I stepped through and into the stateroom.

At the bridge door, I used my Goth command once again. I had to repeat it twice, but the guard understood. 'Gwah,' he growled and then lumbered out of the way. He batted the lever with his clumsy paw. I reached out and pulled the lever for him. The door swung open. I stepped inside and onto the bridge.

Inside, the red-haired pilot and the fair-haired pilot named Janasta sat at the controls. The dark-haired pilot, the officer of the watch, stood before the imposing bulk of Captain Gwawn. He stood twice her height and three times her width. Captain Gwawn growled, his great forelimbs spread wide.

'You're alive?' All three of the pilots seemed to say.

'Mostly,' I said.

'But how?' said the dark-haired pilot.

'King Gwantalan showed me mercy.'

'Mercy? You mean he spared you the contest?'

'Let's leave the contest for now. We need to talk about the fleet of Roman ships that launched from Gwawanath.'

'I agree, but not with you, Lieutenant. You are neither a Goth nor part of Captain Gwawn's forces, though you speak as if you are.'

'It's not the right time to attack the fleet. Please tell the captain.'

'But Captain Gwawn has ordered me to bring the Gwantasnarr alongside the lead ship. He wishes to grapple and board it.'

'Yes, but King Gwantalan's command is to find Octavia first, not attack this fleet.'

'You spoke with the king? You speak Goth now, Lieutenant?'

'Ask the captain. He'll confirm what I'm

saying. Maybe come to his senses, too.'

She growled at Captain Gwawn, who growled a reply that included the word Burr. Then she said, 'You are helping King Gwantalan now. Is that right?'

'Yes.'

'But the Captain says, you're an advisor only. You have no authority. He says he wants to attack that fleet, and then board it with a raiding party and fight with paws, claws, and teeth as Gwanta demands.'

'But the king wishes us to fight Octavia, to fight Lanalan. It's no good raiding the fleet if Lanalan is on the other side of the galaxy. We'll get ourselves killed for nothing.'

At the sound of the name Lanalan, the Goths began growling at each other. I waited till they finished, which took so long that the dark-haired pilot had time to turn and consult the fair-haired pilot and adjust something on the control panel. When she turned back, the Goths were all sniffing as they did at the end of a long growl.

I tried again. 'Lanalan,' I said, 'is not on this side of the galaxy. She's not in that fleet. The king's orders are to find Lanalan. Everything else is secondary.' I was going to add 'even Gwanta,' is secondary, but by now I knew the Goths too well. It was better not to mention Gwanta.

The pilot growled to Captain Gwawn. His snout jerked upward several times. Then, he sniffed at me, opened his mouth, and growled so long and loud, that his breath caused me to take a step back.

'Captain Gwawn says that Lanalan is here, Lieutenant. That's why he wants to attack. I repeat. Octavia is here. Sinistra is here. Lanalan is here.'

At the sound of the name Lanalan, the Goths growled once again, but this time Captain Gwawn raised a paw, silencing them.

'No,' I said. 'She's back on the other side of the galaxy.'

'How do you know that, Lieutenant? Do you also speak Roman as well as Goth? Have you intercepted a transmission from the ships?'

I didn't want to explain that Octavia could speak in my mind and that she told me her plans for Earth through the body of a Roman Marine.

Instead, I said, 'Why would she leave Earth when she is about to be elected a commissioner of the Accord?'

'It doesn't matter, Lieutenant,' said the fair-haired pilot from her seat at the helm.

'Why? Why doesn't it matter? Why would she leave and come here just to greet these ships? They will soon reach Earth.'

'I don't know, Lieutenant, but she is here, and she is near.'

'How do you know? Have you seen her? Has she made contact?'

'We can sense her. We told Captain Gawn.'

'Sense her?'

'Call it a strong intuition, but we can sense her. All Roman people have this ability. She is on this side of the galaxy. So, she can only be aboard one of those ships.'

'Gwah,' roared Captain Gwawn. 'Gwah!'

'And she is probably near the point of acceleration, Lieutenant,' said the dark-haired pilot. 'If we don't move now we won't catch her until she emerges somewhere else in the galaxy.'

'Where will she emerge? In my part of the galaxy?'

'We can't be sure of where she will go, Lieutenant. That is another reason why Captain Gwawn wishes to attack her now, while she is in sight.'

I thought of Octavia, dressed in her blue uniform, issuing commands from the bridge of a flagship. Was she watching us even now, hoping the Goths would attack? And what if we did attack? What if the Goths fought all the way to the great leader herself? Maybe I could confront her. Maybe I could defeat her here on the far side of the galaxy before she could do any more damage to Earth. I reached for the shale in my pocket, but stopped myself when I saw the dark-haired pilot watching my hand.

'Please ask the captain if he would agree to change his tactics,' I said.

'How?'

'From fighting the Roman Marines with paws, claws, and teeth, to finding Lanalan instead.'

The dark-haired pilot growled to the captain, who replied, angrily tossing his snout at me.

'He says no one wants to kill Lanalan more

than he and his Goths.'

'Does that man he agrees with my suggestion?'

'He said the Goths must fight using their traditional methods. There is no other way. However, he is also sending a separate group of soldiers to find Lanalan. You can accompany them.'

I turned to Captain Gawn. 'Gwah,' I growled.

'Gwah!' he growled back. 'Gwah!' he roared to the dark-haired pilot. 'Gwah!' he roared to Lieutenant Glathaw. And then he and the rest of the Goths roared so loudly that none of us saw the fair-haired pilot slump at the controls. Then, the Goths barged out of the bridge and into the stateroom. After growling to the painting of Gwanta, they barreled into the passageway, roaring the news to their comrades aft.

'Karz,' I said. 'Where Ranawah gun?'

'Gwah,' said Karz and lumbered away. I followed her, but Captain Nolan stepped in front of me. 'Burns!' she said. Karz stopped her lumbering to listen.

'What have you just done?'

I said nothing.

'Are you listening to me, Prisoner 548B? I asked you a question.'

Her face was livid. Her fists were balled at the hem of her smock.

'I'll answer you later,' I said.

'I order you not to take part in any more attacks. You are a prisoner of the Accord, not its representative. Your reckless actions will cause

the deaths of our intra-galactic friends and
yourself.'

'Do you speak Goth too, Captain? How do you
know what's going on?'

'I don't need to speak Goth to see you
encourage Captain Gwawn and to volunteer to
join him.'

'Things are different now, Captain. I have to
go.'

'Why? Why are you taking part in this raid?'

'To save lives, Captain. Your life, mine, and
everyone's life on Earth.'

'Can you hear yourself, Lieutenant? This isn't
the savior complex talking. This is something far
worse. A day ago, you said you didn't care if you
lived or died. Now you're some kind… what are
you?'

I reached up to touch my pocket. Her eyes
followed my hand. I stopped myself and put the
hand into my pants pocket, which must have
seemed a strange act in the circumstances, like I
was on a street corner chatting about the weather,
and had just wondered if I had left my Accord
identity card at home, but thought better about
checking my pocket while I was speaking to
someone.

But Captain Nolan had asked the key question:
What was I? Why was I doing this? I thought
back to the gloomy bridge on HMS Hemera and
my ancestor's remark about our family and its
destiny, its role in history, 'the family trade.' I
hadn't believed it, not yet, but I was willing to at

least follow my instincts and find out.

'Gotta go,' I said. 'Ready, Karz?'

But before I could take a step, the Gwantasnarr jolted to starboard. The jolt knocked Karz from her paws and Captain Nolan fell against me so hard that I had to grab her under her arms to hold her up. To my astonishment, she grabbed me as well, and we stood there like a couple in a movie about oppressive forms of recreation in the decadent pre-Accord era.

'Permission to touch the captain,' I said, finding my chin in her hair. She didn't reply. I waited for her to shove me away and fire a Navy Spirit code violation at me, but instead, she held on. She actually pressed her open palms into my back. She actually drew herself closer. Could it be that all her hostility concealed something else?

But then, I felt a prick in the skin on my back. At the time, I thought it was a knot in the NWU stitching, pressed hard against me by Captain Nolan's firm embrace.

Within seconds, this moment of intimacy was over. Captain Nolan stepped back with a blank, clinical face. I was going to say something about meeting after the attack or whatever had caused the ship to lurch, but before I could speak, my vision blurred. The stateroom, the painting of Gwanta, all swirled to the right, and my aching legs would not hold me upright.

'What's going on?' I slurred.

No Goth replied, but Karz growled as fiercely as I'd heard her, and I thought I saw her rise on her hind limbs and throw herself at Captain Nolan, her claws unsheathed, her teeth bared.

44

The shouting woke me up.

It was early. The blinds in my bedroom window showed only the faintest glow. It must have been hours before the morning pledge to the Accord.

But the shouting was loud.

I climbed out of bed and ran into the next room.

Something was wrong.

Kresta was there. Cal was there. Three Harmony Officers were there: two female officers and one male. They wore green uniforms with patches. They carried batons. Handcuffs dangled from their belts. Radios clung to the top pockets of their smocks. The radios squawked with voices asking for 'the situation.'

Cal shouted. Kresta shouted. The Harmony Officers shouted, 'Stop resisting! Stop resisting!'

Two Harmony Officers pulled Cal's hands behind his back. The third Harmony Officer held handcuffs. But Cal was too big. He was too strong for them. They couldn't get his hands behind his back.

It was all wrong. At school, the teachers told us the Harmony Officers protected us. Why were they hurting Cal?

'Stop resisting!' the Harmony Officers yelled. 'Stop resisting.'

But Cal kept resisting. Cal resisted a lot. He was one guy against three. He was bigger than all of them put together.

'What's happening? Mom, what are they doing to Cal?'

'Alex, don't call me… Alex, go back to your room.'

'What's happening?'

'Nothing. Go back to bed.'

But I saw her tears

'Why aren't you helping dad?'

'Accord member,' called the Harmony Officer with the handcuffs. 'Take the young male Accord member out of here.'

Kresta reached out to grab one of my arms. I pushed her hands away. I wanted to help Cal.

'Keep away from them, Alex. Stay here with me.'

But I had already run over to help.

'Why are they doing this, dad?'

'It's all right, Alex. No need to worry anymore.'

'But why? Why are they grabbing you?'

'Don't worry, Alex. It's OK now. No more pills.'

But it wasn't OK. I ran at one of the Harmony Officers and grabbed her arm.

'Get the young Accord member away,' the Harmony Officer yelled to Kresta. 'Get him away or he'll be taken to Re-Orientation too.'

Kresta came over and pulled me away, but I kept yelling, 'Let him go. Let him go.'

Cal broke free. He swung an elbow around and hit

one of the Harmony Officers in the neck. The male one. The Harmony Officer stepped backward and called out 'Now!' to the third Harmony Officer.

The third Harmony Officer, the one with the handcuffs, unclipped something from her belt. It looked like Cal's shaver. She ran around the other side of Cal and pushed the shaver thing into his back. Cal did something I'd never seen before. He stiffened up. His face went all ripply. But he didn't say a word. He stood there, stiffened up.

The Harmony Officer jabbed the shaver thing into him over and over. Cal didn't fall down, but he couldn't move. The Harmony Officer who had been hit in the neck came forward, grabbed Cal's hands, and snapped the handcuffs on his wrists. Then, the three of them, all pulling and straining, dragged him out through the door—all while one of them jabbed at him with the shaving thing.

Outside, a Harmony Office car arrived. The rainbow light on its roof flashed. Two more Harmony Officers jumped out and joined the others, dragging Cal across our front lawn. I still tried to help him. The fourth Harmony Officer grabbed me. He held my two arms. He kept saying, 'Stop it or its Re-Orientation for you too.' I didn't know what they meant.

'Don't watch, Alex,' said Kresta. 'The Accord knows best. No matter how this seems, the Accord knows best.'

But I didn't think she believed what she was saying.

'No. We've got to help him.'

'It's for the best, Alex. I know that's hard to believe, but it's for the best. The Accord knows best. This is the

best for Cal and the best for you. I know it's hard to believe, but this is the best for you both, for all of us.'

I didn't answer her, I shouted to Cal. 'Dad, where are they taking you?'

'Don't worry, Alex,' Cal said. 'It's OK now. No more pills. I've fixed things. If they try to make you take the pills again, don't let them.'

'Are they taking you because of me?'

'No, Alex. Not because of you. It's not your fault.'

'But why are they taking you away? It's because of me.'

'This is not your fault.'

'But why are they taking you away?'

'If I don't see you again, I want you to remember something.'

'Shut it, Burns,' said one of the Harmony Officers. They had dragged him to the car. The rear door was open.

'Don't let them, Cal.'

'Just remember,' Cal said. 'Serve but don't submit.'

'What?'

'Serve, but never submit.'

'Serve or what?'

But one of the Harmony Officers jabbed Cal with the shaver thing and he couldn't speak anymore.

Then Kresta came over to me. She kept saying the same thing: that all this was for the best.

'What are we going to do, Kresta? We can't let them take Cal. Why don't you stop them?'

'Your father... Cal is a good man, Alex, but he's gone too far.'

'But when is he coming back? When is he coming

back?'

One of the Harmony Officers came back to the door.

'Your male child is unruly. He is disrespectful. I'll be reporting his behavior. It's obviously a case of early stage toxic masculinity. The sooner his gender is reassigned, the better. You will hear from us again. T.E.D.'

The Harmony Officer walked back to his car.

'What's he mean, mom?'

But all she could say was, 'The Accord knows best, Alex. The Accord knows best.'

'No, it doesn't. The Accord is taking Cal away.'

'But it's for the best. You'll understand that one day.'

Kresta tried to shut the door so that I couldn't watch the car driving away with Cal in the back seat. It was the worst thing I had ever seen: my father dragged away in handcuffs and Kresta crying, not wanting them to take him away either, but not stopping it from happening.

All because of me.

'It's not your fault,' Cal had yelled.

But that's not how it seemed.

45

The dream faded. I escaped from its grip and drifted in darkness, slowly meeting up with my waking senses. The senses came forward like scouts who had gone out to inspect each body part. They were ready with the damage reports.

My ribs were cracked. My hands were a mess of cuts. My legs and arms were damaged in every quarter. Each muscle ached, every sinew was raw. Each bicep, quadrilateral, and calf seemed to have gone on a grueling, overnight endurance course, and come back next morning in agony, unable to move.

These were the results of my exertions on Gwawanath. They had finally taken their toll.

Next, my memory reported what it knew about the situation, one piece of information at a time: the Goth ship, the bridge, the pilots, the captain's growling command to attack the Romans, Octavia somewhere on the fleet, the heavy lump in my pocket, my collapse while carrying it. Karz growling. The invasion of Earth. My ancestor on his ship. Brave Horatius on the bridge. The Gwantashale. *The Gwantashale!*

With my eyes still gummed shut, I reached up to my jacket pocket, feeling for the small stone case. But I found nothing but the rough, thick cloth of my Navy Working Uniform. The Gwantashale, the secret to defeating Octavia, was not there.

It was gone.

I peeled open my eyes. I was back in the same cabin, as usual, but I was not in the dark. Weak blue light shone in from the passageway, but this time, no hulking Goth swayed at the door.

Something else was different too. My head lay in the lap of Captain Nolan. Through bleary eyes, I looked up at her. She gazed down at me with a soft expression. Her cool fingers stroked my forehead. And I breathed the clean, laundry scent of her JAN smock.

'What's happening?' I slurred.

Before I could say another word, the cool fingers curled under my neck and lifted. She moved her legs from beneath me, then let my head drop to the rubbery mattress. I saw her stand up, towering above me. She straightened her smock. Then she stepped over me and walked away. I sat up on my elbows.

'What were you doing?' I slurred. 'Where's the…?' I caught myself before I said the word "shale." 'What happened?' I said. 'Where are we?'

Captain Nolan was silent. She said not a word:

nothing about the Navy Spirit Code, nothing about toxic masculinity, nothing about my court-martial. She stood at the door, tall, beautiful, and silent.

After watching for a beat, she turned and stepped into the passageway. Her footsteps clipped away forwards, towards the staterooms and the bridge.

'Hey!' I called. 'What's going on?'

But she made no reply.

I sat up, rubbing my face. It was time to get moving. It was time to find out what had happened to me, and time to get back to Earth, before Octavia could land her ships. But before anything else, it was time to find the Gwantashale. Without it, nothing else mattered.

I got to my feet, woozy with drowsiness. I rested against the bulkhead till I could stay upright without staggering. Then, I left the cabin and hurried down the passageway to the head. I splashed my face with water, slapping myself to banish the tiredness.

As I did so, I saw a confronting sight: a reflection in the bulkhead's dull metal. A guy's face stared back at me. The face was older than mine. Its cheekbones stuck out. Dirty blond stubble smeared its jaw, and a long, angry scratch ran from one cheek to its neck, like a zipper. The face looked mad. The eyes were bloodshot and wild. It was an insane man's face, a face belonging to a deranged mind. The distorting metal, I thought. That must be it. Yes, that must be it. The image was distorted by the buckled metal.

I turned away, shaking my head. The time for reflection had passed. The important thing was to find the Gwantashale. Nothing else mattered until I could find that rock.

With a clearer head, I jog-walked to the cabin, checked under the mattresses and along all the shelves.

No Gwantashale.

I found the cabin's light-switch, flicked it on, and went over everything once more. Under the mattresses, along the shelves, everywhere.

No Gwantashale.

I stepped into the empty passageway. Maybe the shale had fallen from my pocket while they Goths carried me, but the passageway remained bare as far as I could see forward and aft.

No Gwantashale.

So as yet, no hope.

A hundred fears suddenly presented themselves: the shale was stolen, it had dissolved in the atmosphere, the pilots had found it and tossed it overboard. The Goths had changed their minds and taken it while I was unconscious. Octavia had detected it and destroyed it—those and many more.

I pushed them away and kept running. I had to get to the staterooms, the viewports and the bridge. If the shale would be anywhere, it would be somewhere forward in the ship.

When I arrived at the stateroom door, I sensed

immediately that something more was wrong. First, there was no guard on duty. Second, no Goth growls filtered from within. I swung the lever, unsealed the door and stepped inside.

As usual, Goths lay on the mattresses scattered about. But something had changed. The Goths were silent. No growling. No movement. No rolling around. No gnawing on bones. No shoving each other over the females. They were sleeping or unconscious.

Or dead.

What was going on? Had they just fought a battle and lost?

'Karz!' I yelled at the Goths. 'Where Karz?'

One of the Goths looked up from his paws. He turned his head and sniffed at me without enthusiasm, then lowered his snout back down and wheezed. I'd never seen a Goth look so miserable or defeated.

'Karz?' I shouted at him, but the Goth said nothing, not even 'Gwah.'

That's when I noticed something else was wrong. The drone from the engines was missing. The ship was silent. There wasn't even a rattle from the hull. What was going on? Had we parked in space? Were we drifting? Was no one at the helm? Or were we traveling through the famous state of acceleration?

I carried on towards the bow and the bridge where the pilots would know the answers to these questions.

At the stateroom's forward end, I reached the

viewport. I expected to see the great globe of Gwawanath glowing purple and green as it had before I passed out. But instead of Gwawanath, the Roman fleet floated off the ship's port side. It was no longer strung out in a column, but had formed into a swarm.

And beyond the swarm, in the distance, floated a planet—not an enormous planet like Gwawanath but a different planet, a small blue planet, the one the Romans called Hyacinth, with its clouds, oceans and continents.

The bows of the Roman ships all pointed at this planet, like nail filings around a magnet. There must have been hundreds of them, maybe a thousand, each the size of a city, and each with colonizing equipment in its holds, and millions of Romans and Marines ready to descend. Ready for 'the occupation of your cities, the annihilation of your people, and the transformation of your seas, rivers, and mountains.'

Perhaps they'd already begun.

To calm my anger, I tried to think positive thoughts. I thought about my ancestor, Captain Burns of the Royal Navy. I thought about his courage, his belief in duty, and the strength he drew from a pre-Accord poem about a brave soldier standing his ground against an overwhelming enemy.

None of it helped.

46

I pressed on from the stateroom and into the forward passageway. No Goth stood guard at the entrance, nor at the forward end. When I entered the forward stateroom, I found more Goths slumped on the deck. None of them growled. None even sniffed. None paid me any attention.

I walked over to a Goth lying on his stomach with his snout pressed into his paws, hiding his eyes.

'Where Captain Gwawn?' I yelled. 'Captain Gwawn?'

The Goth soldier raised his head, sniffed a few times, then lowered it again to his paws and said nothing. I shouted at the other Goths. 'Captain Gwawn?' One Goth looked up. The rest ignored me.

I looked around for signs of an attack, for corpses, smashed bulkheads, damage to the hull, scratches on the deck, bullet holes, and blood. But I found nothing different to before. The bulkheads and decks gleamed their usual dull gray, and the image of Gwanta gazed serenely from his painting.

What on earth had happened?

Maybe the pilots could explain.

I walked to the door leading to the bridge. No guard was on duty. I reached for the door's lever and pulled it down. The lock clunked and the door unsealed. I pushed it open and stepped inside.

Beneath the great viewport, the myriad lights on the control panel blinked. The screens displayed a diagram of the Roman fleet. It was a swarm of green dots surrounding a blue sphere. Other panels displayed the spiral of the galaxy and the Gwantasnarr's path across it. The largest display showed Earth, its oceans and continents crisscrossed by navigational lines.

No pilots sat at the panel. Their seats lay stricken on their sides. Beside them, prostrate on the deck, lay the bodies of the red-haired pilot and the dark-haired officer of the watch. Their mouths were open, their tongues protruded, swollen and black. Their blue uniforms were torn at the throat and the seat.

I knelt beside the dark-haired pilot and touched her shoulder, keeping my head back in case she came violently to life. The uniform's cloth was soft, the flesh beneath it hard. I nudged the shoulder gently. Nothing happened. I nudged again. Nothing. The pilot's body was rigid, like a board, like a mannequin. The other pilot's body was the same: rigid, unmoving, unquestionably lifeless. Both were curiously odorless.

So how had they died? I looked again at their faces. There were no bruises nor cuts, but their tortured expressions implied agonizing deaths. An awful question rose in my mind. Had the Gwantashale killed them? And by bringing it aboard, had I made a catastrophic error?

Behind me, from the other side of the entrance, someone wheezed. I turned around. The blonde pilot, the one who had explained about the Gwantasnarr and the galaxy, sat slumped against the bulkhead, her arms formed into green blades that had burst through her blue sleeves.

I stepped over to her and knelt down. Her mouth rasped a foul odor, almost like a Goth, and her eyelids were closed and trembling.

'Tell me what you need. I'll help you.'

She shook her head.

'Who did this to you?'

She shook her head again and rasped a foul, sewage breath.

'Was it an attack by the Romans—the Ranawah?'

She shook her head.

'A disease? A sudden illness?'

She didn't move.

I wanted to say the word 'Gwantashale' but stopped myself. I'd keep that as a last resort after I had worked through all the other possibilities. Instead, I said, 'Was it poison?'

'No,' she rasped.

'Then what?'

'The Lovelorn,' she wheezed. 'Lanalan, Sinistra. The Lovelorn attacked us.'

'The Lovelorn? Octavia?'

'Lanalan.'

'Lanalan was here?' How? Did she come across from the Roman ships?'

The pilot said nothing, made no movement, except a pathetic and unsuccessful attempt to raise the blade of one arm.

'Rest,' I said. 'Rest till you can tell me what happened.'

Suddenly, her body stiffened and sat upright, as if someone had jerked her up by strings. Her bladed arms rose from the deck and she held them out in front of her, like she was holding a steering wheel or a helm. Before I could ask her what was going on, her mouth opened and she spoke in a clear and confident voice.

'Hello, Alex. Feeling better after your rest?'

Then the pilot's face slackened. The strings had been cut. Her blades dropped to the deck and her chin flopped onto her chest.

I turned around. Captain Nolan stood watching—or at least the figure who resembled Captain Nolan. She leaned casually against the bulkhead between me and the corpses of the other two pilots.

'I love doing that,' she said. 'Oh, Alex! You should see your face.'

47

Captain Nolan had changed.

Her blue, sexless JAN smock was the same, but not the way she wore it. Before, she had let it flop, concealing her figure from my hated male gaze. Now she wore it to reveal and entice. She had cinched the smock's waist and narrowed her floppy pants, so that her legs stretched further from her hips to the deck, and her slender ankles were bare above the tops of her boots.

She stood leaning one shoulder against the bulkhead examining the fingernails of her left hand, tilting her head one way, then the other, extending her fingers, curling them against her palm, then turning her hand over and inspecting the nails from a different angle, as if they were the most fascinating things in the galaxy.

'What happened here?' I said. 'Why are these two dead and that one almost gone? Why are the Goths so?' I searched for the right word.

'So whipped?' she offered, her attention still on her nails. 'So defeated? Why do they cower like they just had their asses kicked, as people once said in your pre-Accord era?'

'Yes. What's wrong with them?'

'Oh, just some travel sickness.'

'What did you do to them?'

'Let's say I grew tired of living by Accord values, especially the one about tolerance. It's so hard to be tolerant when circumstances become so… intolerable, as I'm sure you would agree.'

Beside me, the fair-haired pilot slumped all the way to the deck. Her head hit the gray metal with a sickening bump. Her mouth gurgled green slime. I leaned down, reached out, and closed her eyelids.

Then I stood and faced Octavia, Lanalan, Sinistra.

'What happened to Karz? What happened to Captain Gwawn and the others?'

'Karz? Your shaggy girlfriend?'

'You know who I mean.'

'She's locked in a cabin.'

'Why?'

'So you can watch.'

'Watch what?' I hated this game of question and answer, but I knew I had to stay calm. I knew how dangerous the situation would become if I lost my patience. Better not to confront Octavia. Confronting her could lead to some violent shape-changing, as I knew all too well.

It had been months since I seen her this close and this beautiful. The last time I saw her, she was in her warrior form on top of a skyscraper in

AON sub-territory Hong Kong. Then, she had been as big and terrifying as a moving apartment building.

'What about these pilots?' I said. 'Why did you kill them? They're your own people. They're Romans.'

She frowned at the nails.

'They are traitors, Alex, traitors to their Roman brothers and sisters, traitors to me. They aided the enemy, and not for the first time, either. These three piloted the Goth ship that attacked the Excidium. Remember? You fought the Goths alongside my Marines. You killed their prince. And you killed him to protect me, didn't you, Alex? Surely, you remember?'

'No, I defended Chen and Le Seaux—not you.'

'Le Seaux,' she scoffed. 'She of the thin lips, no hips, too-wide jaw, and terrible, terrible hair. How could you have liked her, Alex? A sexless gwanawwt like that.'

'A what?'

'Gwanawwt. It's a rare word in the Goth language. The Goths don't go much for the gender spectrum, as I'm sure you can imagine. They don't understand it. But they do have some nice words, though, Alex, don't they? Gwah!' she sighed, extending the word until it soothed and coaxed. 'Gwah, Burr. Gwah.'

'How many of the Goths are dead?'

'Some are still alive, Alex. I didn't deal with all of them. I'm not a monster, you know.' She smiled. 'I dealt with the ones who protested after

I confronted the traitors here.'

'Captain Gwawn—where is he?'

'In pieces at the stern.'

'The lieutenants?'

'In bloody shreds beside him.'

'The other Goths—the ones you say you dealt with?'

'Scattered here and there. Walk around and take a big Goth sniff. You'll soon find them.'

'What about the rest?'

'The few who survive are subdued in the staterooms, just as you saw. They're so frightened they won't move. They're terrified of me, Alex. Look through the door and you'll see them skulking down the passageway to escape. It's endearing. Almost. You can never actually like a Goth.'

'Who piloted the ship? Who brought us here through the acceleration?'

'So many questions, Alex. You're as nosey as Captain Nolan.'

'So who piloted us here? You?'

'Well, these three piloted the ship across the galaxy. Then I made them aware of my… presence. That one,' she raised her chin at the dead pilot beside me. 'That one suffered an illness before I got here. I wondered about that, Alex. Do you know anything about it? She collapsed after you returned from your contest. Now, why would that be? Did your handsome new battle scar slay the Roman pilot? Is that what happened?'

She uncoiled herself from the wall.

'You brought something from the Goth king, didn't you, Alex?' Her consciousness searched my mind, like a flashlight shining around in my head. 'You brought back a souvenir, didn't you?'

I willed myself to see nothing, think nothing, hear nothing, to see a tall, stone wall in the dark, and raindrops striking the stones. I couldn't allow myself to picture the Gwantashale or even think of its name. Nor could I allow any feelings about it: the regret of not stowing it; the relief that Octavia had not found it; the question of where it might be now; and my hope that it could stop her once and for all.

Freedom, I thought. Think of freedom. Think of ridding Earth of Octavia and then freeing it of the Accord. Think of defiance. 'Then out spake brave Horatius,' I shouted in my mind, 'the captain of the gate. To every man upon this earth, death cometh soon or late.'

'You know, Alex,' Octavia said. 'Your thoughts sound different to the way you speak. Sometimes they sound like they're from the pre-Accord era. They sound more articulate. They use a larger vocabulary and a different accent. No, they're not *his* thoughts and not *his* voice. They're more as if you draw from centuries ago, or the memory of that time, like you're an old soul. Now why would that be, Alex?'

'I don't know what you mean.' I kept the image of the wall in my mind. Then I changed the subject. 'What about out there—the ships around

Earth?'

'Magnificent, aren't they?'

'Are they carrying all your people?'

'Not all, Alex, but most, plus our Marines and our land forces—ones that aren't exactly Roman in appearance. You haven't seen them yet, have you? Oh, how you would gape at the sight of them, at the damage they can inflict. We also have some people on Earth you haven't seen yet, either. They're a lot of fun, Alex. They're almost human—but just different enough to test an Accord member's love for tolerance and diversity.'

'How many are you?'

'Enough to occupy your planet from New Zealand to Greenland as your Accord pledge states. The remaining Romans will come later.'

'What about the Goths back on Rome?'

'The Goths!' she scoffed. 'They will never leave that planet. They'll be there to the end. They'll stay there till they burn alive.'

'But why come to Earth at all? I said. 'You have never explained your reason. Your own planet is a hundred times the size with varied climates.'

'So many questions, Alex. Why don't you wait until after I've ordered my ships to descend?'

'Tell me now.'

She shrugged and then looked at the top of one shoulder for a moment.

'Rome will be uninhabitable in the near future. No, not because we polluted it, Alex—not because we caused the climate to change. Rome, the planet, is polluting itself from beneath its own surface. We've known this for eons. We've planned for it.'

'Why don't you change it using technology?'

'You've seen the size of the planet, Alex. The forces inside it are beyond our control, just as your Accord can't prevent your planet's cooling climate and falling sea levels. Did I say "your planet"? I meant to say "Our planet?"'

'What will happen to Earth's people?'

She smiled. 'They must accommodate us, Alex, as I told you on your outward journey.'

'Accommodate you how?'

'Don't worry, dear. You'll be with me when it happens?'

'When what happens? What will happen to the people of the Accord?'

She pursed her lips. 'Are you sure you want to know?'

'Certain.'

'They'll become fertilizer, Alex. It will be like a religious act. Ecology and conservation are the Accord religions, aren't they? So, now the Accord members can live their religion and actually become the earth. By then it will all be over.'

'Not if I can help it.'

'Oh, hush now. I've had enough.'

She peeled away from the bulkhead and came swaying towards me, swinging one foot in front of the other. Her every moment was seductive, arousing, and baffling. No woman in the Accord would ever walk in a way so irresistible to male attention. And as usual, and to my shame, she drew a tangle of responses from me. I couldn't let her come closer, but I wanted her to keep walking that way.

'I heard your thoughts, Alex. Should I sway my hips a little more like this? Should I move my shoulders like this? Is that what you like? How about this?' She tore the blue smock's collar. 'You liked Captain Nolan, didn't you? I know you did. Well, now you can have her—as me.'

'Where is Captain Nolan now?' I asked, but she just shook her head as she sashayed up to me and pressed the toes of her boots against mine. Her beautiful face came closer. Her warm hands reached around my neck. The heat of her! The implied weight of her slender body! And the power of my response! I was only human, wasn't I? A male human, subject to the same timeless urges as all men.

'You're so tall,' she breathed. 'So handsome. I like your beard.'

She leaned against me, her face upturned. She was the enemy, the conqueror of worlds, a destroyer of planets, a monster in disguise. And yet, my resolve was weak. No, not weak. It was overcome. I began to lose my reason. I might have even thought of the shale in its stone case. I tried to change my thoughts, but a cinema in my mind had already begun screening personal footage of Octavia from which I could not turn away.

'Out spake brave Horatius,' she whispered, reaching for the collar of my jacket, pulling me closer. 'Kiss me, Alex, while I still forgive you for what you've done. Kiss me. That's right. Gwah! And maybe you'll forgive me too.'

And I almost did. I almost surrendered. I wanted to ask about her about what had happened, to hear her side of things. Maybe I'd been wrong all along.

Thoughts like those killed my will to even question what I was doing. My head swam. My heart thumped. I leaned down to that beautiful face.

'Why do you do it, Alex?'

'What?'

'All this, all you've done. I don't know why you tie yourself in knots when you should just let go.'

But before our lips touched, Octavia changed. Her body stiffened as if I had jabbed her in the back. Her smooth brow creased.

'I've just worked it out,' she said.

'Worked what out?'

'You know what I mean.'

'Know what?'

'You know, Alex.'

I brought up the image of the cold stone wall. I had to stop her from reading my thoughts.

'Oh, you bad, bad Alex.'

I said nothing.

'Bad, bad, ungrateful Alex.'

'What are you talking about?' I said.

'Now I know. I know what you brought back from your visit to King Gwantalan.'

48

'Where is it?'

Octavia's voice deepened. It dropped in pitch to an inhuman bass. 'Where is it?' she boomed.

Her arm swelled, just as the pilot's arm had swelled on the bridge two days ago, tearing the sleeve of her smock, thickening, extending its end into pincers.

'Tell me,' she thundered. 'Tell me, or I will tear this ship up. Then, I'll throw the last Goths into space, including your shaggy, interpreter friend. Especially your interpreter friend!'

Her other arm flung outward, extending from its sleeve. It punched through the rear bulkhead and went on into the stateroom, like an obscene snake pushing into a burrow.

'Where?' her voice boomed. 'Where is it?'

I kept my mouth shut while I thought. What would Octavia do if she found the shale? Would it poison her? Could she touch it? Could she hurl it into space with no adverse effects?

'Tell me!' she boomed. I heard the extending

arm hit the bulkhead at the stateroom's rear. Then, I heard it go smashing onwards into the ship, bulkhead by bulkhead.

'You're not answering me, Alex.'

'What's Gwantashale?' I said, but it was too late to feign innocence. The pincer arm rose. It swayed for a moment, as if deciding which way I would move, then it struck. It shot forward, clamped my throat and held me upright by the neck, lifting my boots from the deck.

'How pathetic! How deceitful! How ungrateful! After all I did for you! After the chances I gave you when I could have crushed you! So, where is it, Alex? Tell me now, of your own free will. Tell me before I destroy this old hulk and the disgusting Goths in it.'

'Why do you want it?' I said. My hands pulled at the pincer's blades, trying to pry them apart, trying to keep the weight off my neck. 'What will it do?' I gasped. But we both knew it was too late. Octavia looked at me, shaking her head.

'So disappointing, Alex.' She tightened her grip. Her other arm telescoped on through the ship. 'I'm going to find it. Then, I'm going to end your one-man crusade.'

'I don't know what you…' I began, but she tightened her grip further. The blades cut into my neck and my grasping fingers. I searched for something to say. It didn't matter what. Anything to buy time. Anything at all. Should I tell her she's wrong? That I want to learn more about her vision for Earth? That I want to go with her?

Instead, I remembered the pilots' words before I descended to Gwawanath. I drew a strained breath and said, 'Why do they call you that name?'

'What name?'

Her beautiful eyes closed as she concentrated on her rampaging arm.

'The Lovelorn? Why do they call you The Lovelorn?'

Now her eyes opened. She turned their full blue beam on me.

'What?' she boomed. 'What did you say?'

'That's what they called you, right? The Lovelorn. They said everyone on your ship called you that.'

'What?' she boomed. 'What?'

'The Lovelorn. The… Love… lorn.'

'What?' she said again, as if she couldn't believe that I could utter the name.

'What happened to you, Lanalan?'

Her unblemished skin mottled to a reptilian green. Her deep voice became two voices of two different pitches as if two people spoke at the same time.

'Who told you?' the voices boomed.

The pincer tightened its grip. My boots rose higher from the deck. My throat tightened and my breath wheezed. I had to do something to break free. With my back against the bridge's starboard bulkhead, I raised my left boot and stomped at Octavia's slender waist. As always, I hated attacking a woman, but I had to keep reminding myself of the creature underneath the beauty: not a woman, not Captain Nolan, and definitely not a human.

The force of the boot shoved her backward. The pincer slid from my neck and snapped shut with an obscene click. Octavia stood there, blinking. Her right arm still telescoped through the ship, the pincer coiled for another strike.

Then her mouth closed into a pout. She appeared to have reached a decision. Her gentle approach to interrogating me was over. Force would now be applied. I prepared myself to confront the Lovelorn, the other version of Octavia.

Her left arm shot out for me once more. I stepped out of its way. It cannoned past into the bulkhead behind me. Then, while both her arms were busy, I lowered my shoulder and ran at her as hard as I could. My shoulder hit her middle with a great thump.

The impact would have knocked any man off his feet. But it caused Octavia's delicate ankles no more trouble than a backward step, a slight adjustment of her weight. Within a second, she stood, long legs apart, reeling in her left arm from the bridge's bulkhead. It coiled behind her for a moment and then once again struck at my throat. This time, I caught it and held onto it, one hand on each blade.

Now she tried a different tactic. She flung the arm across her body, dragging me with it, dragging me right off my feet and tossing me through the hole she had made. I landed on the stateroom deck.

As soon as I hit, Octavia pounced. Her free hand grabbed my throat yet again. Amazingly, her other arm still telescoped outward, smashing through the ship. It had been her right arm; now it was her left arm. How had she switched them?

'What else did they say?' she shouted in that two-tone, bass voice. 'What else did they call me? What else did they say about me?'

'Don't you remember, Lanalan?'

'Tell me what they said,' she hissed.

If only I had the Gwantashale in my pocket, I could have shoved it into her green and bubbling face.

'Tell me, Alex. Now!'

Suddenly there was a bang at the back of the stateroom. The passageway door swung open with a bang. I heard the clatter of enormous claws on the metal deck. Octavia twisted her head over her shoulder to see what it was.

'Gwah!' came a deep growl. 'Gwah!'

49

I looked up to see who or what had entered the stateroom with such force.

Then, I saw Karz lumbering across the deck.

She swayed on her hind limbs. Her teeth were bared, and her claws were extended and splayed. Her forelimbs were folded across her chest, cradling the stone case containing the Gwantashale. The case was open. The lump of poisonous rock glittered inside. Karz must have found it or hidden it when Octavia began her attack. Now, the shale was exposed to the very creature it was meant to kill.

'Gwah!' Karz roared.

Octavia watched her. She still had one pincer on my throat and one arm extending deep into the ship, but her eyes focused on the advancing Goth. She released the pincer grip on my neck. Her telescopic arm, now deep into the ship, came telescoping back. When it came crashing back into the stateroom, Octavia turned and advanced at Karz, growling and barking in Goth. Karz answered with growls and barks of her own, as she lumbered to meet Octavia with three heavy, shaggy steps.

Octavia would win this battle. Karz was huge, but Octavia had just killed Captain Gwawn and hundreds of other Goths by herself. She had the power to change her shape, to swell her size, and to form all manner of blades and spikes and other unimaginable weapons. Whereas Karz, despite her claws and strength, could only shove, rake, stomp, rip, and bite.

'Stay back, Karz!' I yelled, knowing she would not listen. With one paw, she raked at Octavia's neck. Octavia easily swayed out of its way, letting the claws slice past. Then, Karz tried to bite Octavia's head from above, but failed when Octavia ducked from under her. Octavia was too fast, and Karz too slow. The fight looked certain to end in seconds with Karz sliced or tripped or stabbed or beheaded or whatever tactics Octavia has used to kill the Gwantasnarr's crew.

But it was not over for one reason: the Gwantashale. As Octavia swelled and changed into her monstrous other self, the glittering shale weakened her. She rose up, but then her body slackened. She expanded and deflated. Her pincer arm slumped to her side, her knees bent, and her mouth dropped open as she sank towards the deck.

Karz ceased her growling. She closed her maw,

twitched up her flattened ears, and watched Octavia sag beside the long yellow claws of her hind limbs.

'Karz, give it to me!' I shouted. 'Give the Gwantashale to me.' But Karz did not listen. Her ears and snout pointed down at Octavia, Lanalan, Sinistra, the hated, ancient enemy of the Gwanath people.

'Give me Gwantashale!' I said. 'Give Gwantashale me!'

But Karz had no time. Octavia was down, but not out. Her left arm swung up and knocked the Gwantashale case from Karz's forelimbs. It hit the deck and rolled through the door and into the passageway.

Instantly, Octavia's strength returned. She rose from the deck, lifted her bladed arms to Karz's shaggy chest, and shoved. Caught on her hind limbs, Karz could not hold her ground. She stumbled backward, trying to keep her balance, but each time she stood up, Octavia shoved her back.

They reached the passageway door. Karz fell in a rolling, furry heap, but climbed to her four paws before Octavia could drop on her. The two of them faced off, Goth and Roman: one the warrior admiral; the other the bear-wolf princess.

Octavia spat a series of Goth words into Karz's face. Karz growled in reply. But down on the deck, her right rear paw had quietly hooked the case of shale. As Octavia poured out invective, Karz kicked the case. It slid forward over the metal and stopped beside Octavia's feet.

Octavia stopped shouting. She closed her mouth, blinked several times, and backed away, placing one hand on her stomach and another behind her, reaching for an imaginary rail. Then she staggered back, throwing out one hand to fend away the poison, but it did no good. Her knees bent and she slumped and wilted.

I watched, astonished at the shale's sudden and devastating power over Octavia's mind and body. It was an invisible force that not only sickened her, but actually repelled her and stole her energy.

She slumped against the passageway bulkhead, then looked up at me with an ugly, twisted face, part monster, part Captain Diana Nolans, and spoke in a voice of normal pitch without the booming bass.

'You can't live with these animals, Alex. And you can't survive without me. I'm the only friend you have in the entire galaxy. You just don't know it. You don't know that you need me. You'll always need me. And now you're about to find out how much.'

She straightened up. Her face winced in pain. Then, with a great swing of her right elbow, she smashed a hole in the Gwantasnarr's port side hull one-third of the way along the passageway. A chunk of the hull swung out into space. It wavered as if caught in a breeze, and then it broke from the Gwantasnarr and went swirling away into the void, leaving a hole the size of a large dinner table.

Instantly, black space filled the breach and depressurization began. Fragments of the smashed bulkheads rose and drifted towards the passageway. They kept low as they reached Octavia's feet, as if sneaking away from the fury, the hatred, and the violence.

Octavia turned to me one last time. Her expression softened and her arms reformed into hands. She touched her lips with two slender fingers and smiled. Then, she bent her knees as gracefully as a ballerina from the pre-Accord era, and leaped over Karz toward the hole in the hull.

And into space.

50

I stood, mouth open, too shocked to move, unable to comprehend what I'd seen. Of all the bizarre and strange events I'd witnessed on this voyage, Octavia leaping into space was the strangest. She hadn't tripped into space. She hadn't fallen. She hadn't been sucked out by the depressurization. No. She had jumped, like diving to her death from a cliff.

My mind swirled. Did that mean she would die? Did it mean I had won?

I pictured Octavia's corpse tumbling along the Gwantasnarr's hull, bumping into its hatches and rails, and then floating to the stern and on to oblivion. Then, my mind drifted further, to the Roman fleet itself and the Roman officers realizing their leader was dead. I saw them nodding in solemn agreement. Without Octavia to coerce them, they would see that the invasion of Earth was a mistake. Then, I imagined the fleet of ships turn their bows and steer thoughtfully away.

But I knew it was was too much to hope for. Octavia would never end her life so casually. Surely she would know how to survive, and she would know how to reach her ships, as impossible as it seemed. And the invasion of Earth would proceed as she planned.

And yet, maybe she hadn't survived. Maybe the brief exposure to the shale had done more damage than I thought. Maybe it warped her mind as well as poisoning her body. Maybe jumping into space was partly an act of madness as well as a way of trading one form of agonizing death with another.

Maybe.

But what about the casually blown kiss? She hadn't seemed in pain then, had she? She had acted like she had a plan. So what was most likely? Was she killed by the shale? Or was she killed by space? Or was she swimming her way across ten thousand miles of nothingness to her nearest ship?

I felt a gentle knocking against the backs of my knees and saw debris drifting along the deck. Somewhere an alarm sounded. It growled in Goth or pre-Roman. I knew I should do something, but for the moment, I drifted in a space of my own, astonished at what I had seen, and troubled by thoughts of what I would have to do if Octavia were alive and we met again.

Soon, a blue light came alive and flashed urgently in the stateroom's corner. Still, I didn't move. My mind moved to thoughts of about open space and its dangers. How deadly and mysterious it was! The Accord had forbidden the study of astrophysics, but the research of the pre-Accord scientists still existed. It lay deep in the Accord library at AONT sub-territory Los Angeles. My Slingshot instructor had even read one of the forbidden files.

'Space,' he said, 'will kill you in seconds if you're not wearing a protective suit. The first thing to happen is that all the oxygen in your lungs expands, causing pain, organ destruction, and hazardous chemical reactions. Then, depending on whether you're in sunlight or shade, your body burns or freezes. Either way, all of this would happen in a matter of seconds. Before that, the fluids in your brain would gurgle and you would pass out before the nasty stuff began—like your eyes exploding.'

Could that mean Octavia's eyes would explode?

Without thinking, I took a step toward the breach. I had to find out for myself where Octavia had gone and if she had survived. The passageway and the breach waited across the stateroom deck. That's where I would go. The alarms and the flashing lights could wait.

But my boot slid across the gray metal. I looked down and saw the floating debris smacking the heavy cloth of my NWU. Then, the debris flowed away towards the passageway door where it paused, swirled into eddies like water in a stream, then rushed outside.

I drew a breath, but my lungs didn't fill. Something was wrong. Very wrong. I came out of my daydream. I looked around. Floating debris from the smashed bulkheads floated over the deck like a knee-high blizzard. The growling alarm was deafening. The pull on my uniform was strong. The pull towards the breach!

I stepped back. Now my boots seemed to have no purchase on the metal at all. My jacket billowed. My deepest breath would not fill my lungs. Everything not nailed down drifted towards the passageway.

Soon, larger objects joined the debris. The painting of Gwanta bulged on the forward bulkhead. His serene face puckered out. Then, one corner came loose, then another, then the whole painting flew from the wall and flapped to the passageway like a startled vulture.

Next, and to my horror, the two pilots's bodies tumbled out from the bridge. Like big dolls thrown into a wind, they sailed backward over the deck, their limbs dragging behind them, their hair streaming, their faces still twisted in agony. Both corpses hit the doorway and lodged in the jambs. Then they gave up and fell through and out into space.

I turned and fought my way over to bridge door. It was like wading chest-deep against a receding tide. I took hold of the lever and the wheel and hung on. The artificial gravity had faded with the atmosphere and my legs rose from the deck. Soon I was horizontal among the flying junk.

By now, the atmosphere was so thin that even the alarms faded to distant growls. My deep breaths sucked in almost no air. So I took one deep gasp, inhaling as much of the thin atmosphere as I could, because I knew that next breath, there might nothing left but space.

I held on, my legs out behind me, the debris floating past. After ten seconds, I writhed like a drowning man. After thirty seconds, my mind clouded. After sixty seconds, I lost my grip. My hands slipped from the door's lever. Then it was my turn to go flying across the deck.

I braced myself for the crash into the doorjambs. I gritted my teeth in anticipation of the broken bones. I flung out my arms, ready to catch whatever I could grab to stop me from rushing through the breach and into the void.

To nothingness.

And failure.

51

But I did not go flying through the breach.

Instead, I thumped into an enormous, shaggy back. One poor Goth had come hurtling from the rear end of the passageway and got stuck. His great limbs straddled the gap. His claws gouged the bulkhead, holding him back from the yawning blackness outside.

Now we were two beings on a precipice. Neither of us said a word. He couldn't growl. I couldn't speak. There was no atmosphere, only danger. One slip and one of us would be dead.

I threw out an arm toward the edge of the breach. If I could grab and hold it, I could pull myself inside. I could also take my weight off the Goth. Maybe he would survive too, but I didn't have much hope for him.

I was right. The Goth soon departed. His claws slipped from the jagged edges and space pulled his great bulk outside. He tumbled into the void, slashing and clawing at nothing. Then he was still. I watched him go, waiting for his eyes to

SHALE

explode.

But by then, it was my turn. The breach was three yards across, too wide for me to straddle. So, I hung on to one cold, jagged edge. If I could hold on long enough, maybe the pull would end, and the space outside would become the space inside. Maybe I could swim to the stateroom and close the door, creating a seal.

Maybe.

If I survived the freezing cold.

If I stayed conscious.

I flung out my hands to grab at anything I could find inside. I found nothing. My legs swung outside into space. My ankles ached with cold.

Then I found something else.

The thick shaggy forelimb of Karz.

On the aft side of the breach, Karz clung to a loop of electrical cable. Her other limb now clung to me.

I would have yelled, 'Thanks,' if I could. Instead, I silently mouthed the word 'Gwah.' She watched me over her bleeding snout. Selfless brave Karz! Once again, she had saved me from death.

But there was no time to mouth any more words of thanks. At the far end of the passageway, a mattress and a Goth corpse came tumbling through the door. If they hit us, they would knock Karz and me into space.

The mattress came first. It hit Karz on her rump. Then the corpse crashed into the mattress.

The double impact was too much for Karz's cable. One end of it came free from the bulkhead, turning it into a strand. Karz lost her grip and fell forward, pushing me ahead of her. The mattress and the Goth corpse came next, stuck to Karz's back. All four objects rushed towards space, with me in the lead.

But the objects also created an opportunity. The impact had been so great that we had pitched across the breach itself. I found another cable loop in the smashed hull, got my elbow into it, and held tight. Now, it was my turn to offer a helping hand, and it was Karz who dangled at the precipice with the mattress and Goth corpse.

With one desperate pull of my left arm, I somehow dragged Karz away from the breach just enough. The Goth corpse and the mattress slid from behind her, but instead of bursting out into space, they lodged across the gap, mattress first with the Goth corpse pressing against it.

Together, the two of them created a partial seal.

No sooner had this blocking up of the breach taken place, when the atmosphere changed. The debris flying along the passageway slowed to an ankle-high drift. No large pieces of debris came after them. The depressurization had been temporarily halted and the air was devoid of suck.

By that time, I was gasping, straining to breathe, barking like a mute seal.

The ship's air pumps forced atmosphere back

into the passageway, but not fast enough. There was only one way to survive. I had to get out of the passageway and into the forward stateroom where the pumps could refill the atmosphere faster.

I pointed to the forward door. Karz was roaring or snarling behind me, but making no sound. It wasn't just because of no air. I couldn't hear over the tiny bells ringing in my ears.

I crawled, one slow hand in front of the other with my lungs in agony and black spots gathering in front of me. I gulped at the thin air, crawling and fading till I reached the end of the passageway, and the doorway to the forward stateroom.

Karz crawled behind me, shoving me with her snout. Then, when we both reached the stateroom, I turned, kicked the door into its jambs, turning the levers to dog it shut. Now, the fore section was sealed, except for the hole in the rear bulkhead left by Octavia's punch.

Through the door's viewport, I saw the mattress and the Goth corpse break free and sail away into space. They were gone, but Karz and I were still alive.

Just.

As I gasped for breath, Karz nudged me with her snout. She nosed something at me—some kind of object. It was a thick red cloth in which something was wrapped.

I looked down this object and smiled. Wrapped in that cloth was the one thing in the galaxy that could defeat Octavia—if she still existed.

It was the dull, gray length of Gwantashale.

The sight of it was worth a lungful of air.

52

I sat slumped against the bulkhead, sucking thin air into my lungs as fast as I could manage. Breath by breath, over several minutes, the spots in front of my eyes dwindled to dots; my heart stopped thrashing against my ribs; and the bells in my ears tried to ring on, but eventually they too faded to a distant jingle. The only physical reminder of my brief time at the breach was cold feet.

Once I could breathe easier, I scanned the surrounding deck. Then I found it—the precious lump of Gwantashale. I picked it up and unwrapped it from its cloth. I held it in both hands and gazed into its dull glitter, wondering at its power to hurt Octavia. Then, I clutched it to my NWU as if it were the most precious material in the galaxy which, of course, it was.

Karz stood on all fours, watching me.

'Me sit on it,' she growled. 'Keep inside.'

'Good, Karz. Very good.'

Karz tossed her head up and down, the Goth

way of smiling or chuckling.

'Thank you, Karz.'

'Not thank. Gwanath people hate Ranawah. Hate Lanalan. Very hate Lanalan.'

'OK. Good,' I said. Then, I unwrapped and re-wrapped the shale, pushed it into my jacket pocket, and buttoned the pocket tight.

Karz lumbered back to the door leading to the passageway. She lowered her head and pressed it to the glass porthole.

'Bed gone,' she growled. 'Gwanath gone.'

I went to the door. Karz lumbered away from it. The breach showed nothing but space and the distant Roman fleet. But at the far end of the passageway, something had changed. The door was sealed shut, just like the forward door. It had either slammed shut as a result of the depressurization, or one of the Goths had closed it, which meant the Goths in the main stateroom might still be alive.

'We go there,' growled Karz.

'We can't,' I said. 'Not safe. We'll go after we land. Must hurry.'

'Not understand.'

'I go bridge. Help save Gwanath people.'

'Gwah,' she growled, nodding.

'Help Gwanath people,' I said again, and then, 'And save Earth.'

At the bridge, I assessed the damage. The helm remained in place. The panel of screens and controls seemed intact. They hadn't been damaged by the depressurization or the flying debris. The navigation charts were gone, but I wouldn't be needing those. The Earth already loomed through the bridge viewport.

At the starboard side of the bridge, the third pilot, the fair-haired one that Octavia had used as a puppet, sat in a slump, wedged behind the door. Her uniform had snagged and spared her corpse an undignified drift into space.

I went to the pilot's seat and sat down. The screens revealed the same situation as before. The Earth floated blue and white. The Roman transports and warships, waited to invade.

I tried to work out the controls. Which of the myriad of small black levers or green buttons or touch screens fired the engine? Which stopped it? Which activated the thrusters? Which de-activated them? There were so many questions, including the biggest question of all: How will I ever fly this thing to Earth? That's if it could even land it. That's if I could even move it.

'Gwah,' said Karz.

'Yeah,' I said, staring at the controls.

'Gwah.'

'Sure. Gwah!'

'GWAH!' she roared. This time she put a great paw on my shoulder. She tossed her snout toward the viewport.

Three large ships in the invasion force had begun to move.

53

Now what?

As usual, I had to make my plans as I went along, which was totally against my training and my nature. Successful missions required planning and preparation, especially practice of the necessary skills. Yet, all the actual combat I had seen in the last few months had been the opposite —sudden, strange, impossible to predict, and carried out through improvisation and trial and error.

All my decisions had been made in the heat of the moment, under pressure, with little information, and against the most bizarre enemies. Not 'Ready, aim, fire,' but 'Ready, fire, aim.' Then repeat. Now, I found myself once again in a situation I could never have imagined. I sat at the controls of an alien spacecraft; the spacecraft was over a mile long; and I didn't have a clue how to do so much as to switch on the lights.

Through the bridge viewport, the three Roman

ships gathered headway. At first, I thought they were heading towards the Gwantasnarr, but as the minutes passed, their true destination became clear: the blue and white globe in the distance called Hyacinth.

Meanwhile, the Gwantasnarr was going nowhere. It drifted through space with a damaged hull, smashed bulkheads, no crew, an uncertain engine status, a pilot with zero experience, and time running out.

Not good.

I examined the instrument panel for recognizable controls. Apart from the helm, the other controls formed a bewildering display of levers, touchscreens, flashing symbols, pulsing buttons, and instructions in a language I couldn't read.

Any of them could have started the engines just as any of them might have fired the ship in the wrong direction, perhaps even into the state of Acceleration to other parts of the galaxy.

'Hyacinth!' I commanded, using the Roman word for Earth. Speaking it aloud had worked once before on a Roman ship. Maybe it would work again.

'Hyacinth,' I commanded.

Nothing.

'Hyacinth!' I shouted.

Nothing.

'Hyacinth! Hyacinth!' I shouted closer to the panel.

Still nothing. The various lights and

illuminated shapes ignored me, going about their business.

Time to try something else.

I put a finger on the touchscreen and moved the symbols around. I raised a finger above a cone-shaped symbol. The symbol reminded me of a propulsion jet. Maybe it started an engine of some kind. But before I could press it, Karz lumbered up behind me.

'Go where?' Karz growled. 'Go Gwawanath?'

In the rush to get moving, I had all but forgotten about Karz and what she might want. It hadn't occurred to me that she might no longer care about the mission. With her comrades dead, she would want to go home to Gwawanath. I thought she was like the rest of the Goths: born to fight Ranawah, born to die for the glory of Gwanta by paws, claws, and teeth, but I was wrong.

I dabbed the cone-shaped symbol.

'Where go?' growled Karz again.

The symbol flashed. The ship shuddered. Nothing more. So, I dabbed at arrow symbols. The ship's bow nudged to starboard. The view through the viewport showed the moon, the Roman fleet, the Earth, and then dark space. A three-dimensional compass glowed on a separate screen. It showed the Gwantasnarr rotating. I dabbed at the symbol again. Nothing happened.

'Where go?' growled Karz.

'Nowhere. Not if I can't work this out.'

'Not understand.' The growl sounded

impatient.

'I can't talk now, Karz.'

'Go Gwawanath,' she growled. 'Gwawanath.'

'Can't go Gwawanath. Not know how.'

'Go Gwawanath. Many Gwanath die. Go Gwawanath.'

'Sorry, Karz. I don't know how.'

This was the truth. I couldn't fly to Earth let alone across the galaxy. But maybe the ship could go Gwawanath after all this was over. I should have explained my thinking to Karz. Instead, I dabbed at the panel, a green triangle. This time, the ship jolted. We began moving forward. The display confirmed this.

A start.

'Go Gwawanath,' growled Karz.

I tried one of the joysticks, moving it to port, hoping it would counter the rotation. Instead, it caused the ship to roll. Now we gained headway, but rotated to starboard and rolled, like a ride at an amusement park. I slid from the seat onto the bulkhead, then onto the underside of the deck above, then across it and onto the starboard bulkhead. The dead pilot slid with me. So did Karz, all four limbs flailing, claws out, scratching at the dull grey metal.

We flopped back to the deck. I ran back to the controls, jumped into the seat, snapped the harness into place. Then I nudged the joystick back. The roll slowed and stopped, but the rotation continued.

'Go Gwawanath,' snarled Karz. She stood to

my right, one great paw around the back of the other pilot's chair. I ignored her again, concentrating on the mystifying control panel symbols. Which to choose next? That pulsing green one—did it control the main thrust? I raised a finger. Here goes, I thought.

Before I could press the button, the Gwantasnarr's atmosphere suddenly changed. The pressure dropped. An alarm sounded deep in the ship. The lights in the bulkhead corners flashed. The remaining debris went skidding out of the bridge toward the passageway. The dead pilot splayed flat against the bulkhead with her fair hair fanned out. Then, everything settled down again as quickly as it had started.

'Whatever that was, I think it's over for now.'

But Karz wasn't there.

'Karz?' I called.

But there was no Karz on the bridge and no Karz in the stateroom.

'Karz,' I called. 'You OK?'

No response. No growls.

'Karz,' I called.

Nothing.

I unsnapped the harness and stepped over the pilot's corpse. I walked into the stateroom. Nothing and no one there. Then, with a chill, I sensed what had caused the ship to depressurize.

I walked to the door and its small port window. At the far end of the passageway, the far door gaped open. Karz must have gone down there to check if any Goths were alive. When she opened the door, the depressurization had started all over again.

I watched through the port for any movement. Karz did not appear, nor did any other Goth. There was nothing I could do to help and no possibility of running down there without the risk of falling through the breach.

I gave up and walked back to the bridge, telling myself that if we could get to Earth, I would find a way to send the ship back to Gwawanath and take Karz home. That is, if she were in the stern, and if she were still alive. But, as usual, I was making it up as I went along.

I walked to the bridge viewport, dreading the sight of Karz tumbling past. But I saw nothing and returned to the control panel. How could I get the ship moving forward? I dabbed and nudged at this control and that. The ship began to roll again. The harness tightened as I turned upside down. The view slid by the viewport. The hull joints groaned. The three-dimensional compass turned. The display images whirred.

Not again, I thought.

I selected a button on which a blue cylinder appeared. Maybe it would turn off the thrusters and the engines so I could regroup and try again.

Be the one, I thought, raising a finger over the button. But just before I could press it, someone spoke in a rasping voice.

'Don't,' rasped the voice. 'Don't dare touch that symbol. It's not the one. No, don't touch the red square, either. You're not even close to the right control.'

I turned to face the source of this voice. Behind me, the remaining pilot slid back and forth with the rotation of the ship. Her damp hair stuck to the gray metal. Her eyes were open.

'You're alive?'

'Don't push that button, Lieutenant. Please.'

'You're alive. Can you help me?'

'Just… don't… push… that… button.'

'So, which one is it? Which controls take us to Earth?'

She lay slumped and wheezing.

'Tell me which one,' I said. 'Tell me which controls.'

'First,' she rasped. 'Get rid of it.'

'Get rid of it? Get rid of what?'

'You know what I mean, Lieutenant. Get rid of it or you'll be going nowhere.'

54

My finger hovered over the blue cylinder.

Who was it that had spoken? The pilot or Octavia playing puppet-mistress again?

'The symbol you are about to press,' the pilot wheezed, 'will begin the Acceleration. The ship will head into deep space. Very deep space. Earth isn't far from the galaxy's edge, Lieutenant. And intergalactic space is very lonely.'

'I thought you were dead.'

'The appearance of death,' she wheezed.

'How can I be sure it's you and not Octavia?'

'You can't, but while you are wondering, the shale will kill me.'

'Tell me how to stop the ship's rotation.'

'First, throw the shale into space.' She paused to draw a slow, hoarse breath. 'Then, I'll help you. I just want to save the Gwantasnarr. It's King Gwantalan's only ship, Lieutenant. His only ship.'

'I'm not throwing away the shale.'

'Please. Walk across the deck to the

MM HOLT

passageway. Open the door. Throw it into space.'

'Sorry, pilot. The shale is staying here.'

'Don't be so foolish as to believe you can kill Lanalan, Lieutenant—if that's what you are planning. Throw the shale away and save yourself the trouble. Then we'll all survive, including the ship.'

'Sorry. I'm keeping it.'

'Then it's the end for everyone: for you, for me, for whichever Goths are still alive, and the people on your planet.'

'So you won't help?'

'Not won't, Lieutenant. Can't.'

The ship rolled and rotated. Through the viewport, the parade carried on: Earth, the moon, and the mass of Roman ships and round again.

'I'll take it to the back of the stateroom,' I said. 'Will that do?'

'Not far enough,' the pilot wheezed.

'I'm not throwing it away.'

'Then take it to the stern.'

'No atmosphere back there, as you well know. And I don't have time.'

'It's the sensible course to save the ship.'

Her head slumped, and a green bubble expanded at the corner of her mouth.

'Pilot?' I said. Can you hear me?'

She said nothing. So, I got out of the seat and crawled over to her. I touched her shoulder. Nothing. I nudged her. Nothing. She was still as death.

So, with reluctance, I half-crawled, half

staggered with the roll and rotation of the ship to a far corner of the stateroom. Then, I took off my NWU jacket, rolled it into a bundle and tied it to the rear bulkhead railing by its sleeves. She shale was still buttoned inside the large pocket.

Then, I staggered and crawled back to the bridge, snapped myself back into the harness, and turned to the pilot.

'Better?'

'No. The shale is still too close. As I told you, it must be thrown away.'

'You're not listening. I'm not throwing it away.'

'It's a simple choice,' she wheezed, but not as weakly as before. 'You keep the shale and we both die. You throw it away and you'll live to fight another day.'

'How do I know you're not Octavia?'

'As I said, you don't, but I'm not.'

'Is she still alive?'

'We're resilient creatures, Lieutenant. We can endure a lot, but not even Octavia can survive in space for long. If she is alive, one of her ships must have collected her.'

'So, you saw her jump?'

'No, I could sense her, just as I sensed her presence before. But I was deceived. My senses told me she was far away in space, not on board the ship in the form of your friend.'

'So can you sense if she's still alive now?'

'Throw away the shale first and I'll tell you.'

What a situation! I was damned if I did and

damned if I didn't. I needed the pilot to get to Earth, but I couldn't secure her help without throwing away the shale.

'I can't throw it away.'

'You are already the cause of so much death on the Gwantasnarr, Lieutenant. Don't be the cause of the ship's destruction, too. King Gwantalan spared your life. Don't repay him this way. Don't destroy his ship and his cousin too.'

'His cousin?'

'Lady Karz.'

'Listen,' I said. 'Help me stop the roll and rotation, first. Then we can talk.'

She said nothing. The parade of Earth, the moon, and the Roman ships went by in the viewport. Then she spoke.

'All right.'

'So, you'll help?'

'You must activate the side thrusters to stop the rotation,' she wheezed. 'Sit in the port side pilot's seat. The small rotating lever by your left hand—move it to port for half a second.'

I climbed to the seat and snapped the harness on. Then I reached for the lever.

'No, Lieutenant. That's the forward thrust. The lever to the left.'

I found the lever among the clutter of controls and nudged it. The ship shuddered. The parade of Earth, the moon, and the Roman convoy slowed but did not stop.

'More.'

I nudged the lever again. The parade slowed

further till Earth and the moon passed by at a more leisurely pace, still upside down, then right side up.

'Now, use the lever by your right hand to stop the roll.'

I nudged this lever. The spinning Gwantasnarr slowed and then came level.

'Now push the symbol that looks like a blue circle.'

'What does it do?'

'It resets the Gwantasnarr's controls.'

'I'm not resetting anything.'

'Push it.'

'Why?'

'Because I don't know what you've done, Lieutenant. Every wrong setting must be reset.'

It took me several seconds to even find the icon with the blue circle.

'This one?'

'Is it next to a symbol shaped into a twelve-pointed star?'

'Yes.'

'That's the one.'

I pushed the symbol. Nothing happened. Then, the control panel lights went out, as did all the lighting on the ship, and we sat in darkness with no sound, not even the hissing of the atmosphere pumps.

For ten terrible seconds, I expected a pincer at my throat, a blade to my head, a wheezing breath in my ear, and some terrible words of revenge.

But there was nothing.

Then, the lights flickered on. First, the lanterns around the hull's exterior lit up. Then the control panel lights blinked on, as did the lighting in the bridge and the stateroom. I imagined lights blinking on in the passageways and cabins too, running all the way to the stern, a mile away.

'OK?' I said.

The pilot slumped like a discarded doll.

'OK? Are you OK?'

'OK,' she breathed. 'We are drifting now—still affected by Earth's gravity, but drifting.'

'Would you like to sit up?'

'I can't.'

'Wait there.'

I unsnapped the harness once more and walked over to her, wary that at any moment, a pincer might rise, or that she might change shape.

'Do I have your permission to lift you?'

'Strange question, Lieutenant.'

'It's an old habit.'

I reached down and grasped her beneath her arms. The weight of her. Roman women weighed many times more than humans. She must have weighed three hundred pounds. But up she came, and I soon had her sitting upright with her back against the bulkhead and her legs stretched along the deck in front of her.

'I'd offer you something to eat or drink, but there's nothing up here—not even any of those gray bones.'

She shook her head. Romans apparently

neither ate nor drank.

'Now,' I said. 'Tell me about the controls. Which one will get us moving towards Earth?'

But she shook her head.

'Nice try, Lieutenant.'

'So you still won't help?'

'No, Lieutenant. Nothing more will be said. Not until you get rid of it.'

I walked back to the pilot's seat, sat down, and strapped myself in.

Then, I found the lever, I'd nudged earlier. It was the only one I knew, but it would get us moving forward towards Earth.'

'What are you doing, Lieutenant?'

'Will you help me if I tell you?'

'No, not until you…'

'Yeah, I know.' I nudged the lever forward.

The Gwantasnarr responded. From way back in the ship's stern, there came a rumble. The ship's main engines fired—the same engines that took us across the galaxy.

'How do you…?' I began to ask how to avoid gaining too much speed, but I knew what the pilot's answer would be. So, I closed my mouth, gripped the helm, and tapped at the lever. The great ship responded again, slipping faster through space. The displays reported the increase in velocity with a surge of grey characters on blue screens. I couldn't read them. Maybe it didn't matter. The important thing was that we were moving.

Then I turned to the pilot. 'This is easy, like

flying a Slingshot.'

She didn't laugh. She sat in misery. I didn't blame her. But I couldn't let her have control, not until I was on Earth.

'Lieutenant,' she said.

'Don't bother. The shale is staying here.'

'Not the shale,' she wheezed. 'Out there.' She raised a drooping hand at the viewport.

'What's out there?'

Then I saw.

55

The blast from the enemy ship lasted five seconds.

Blue, straight, and as thick as a highway, it streamed across the bow, filling the viewport and the bridge with light. Then, the beam disappeared, and I imagined it racing onwards into space, going on forever, out from the solar system, on and on, until it blasted onto the surface of a planet or an asteroid in another solar system, in another galaxy, in a billion years' time.

Seconds later, another beam lit up the bridge all over again. It was thicker than a highway this time, closer too, looming in the viewport like a great blue pipe. It was a shot across the bow, warning us to stay put.

I checked the displays on the panel. They revealed giant ship detaching from the rest of the Roman fleet and heading towards the floating shape of the Gwantasnarr. Had they suddenly decided to board us?

'Not going to happen,' I said aloud without realizing.

'What did you say?' wheezed the pilot.

'Nothing,' I replied.

'You can avoid them, Lieutenant, if that's what you're thinking. Your only chance to save this ship is to give me the helm.'

'Here it is. Take it.'

'First get rid of the shale.'

That was the end of the conversation.

Without waiting for more complaints or advice, I nudged the lever controlling the Gwantasnarr's engines. The ship surged forward so fast that I fell back in my seat and the pilot slid into the bridge's rear bulkhead.

A streak appeared on the display, followed by an alarm. Then, there was a loud bang like a hammer blow on the hull. The ship's bow lurched to starboard. The view of Earth and the moon slid to port. Another streak appeared. The alarm sounded again, and a second blast hit the stern, knocking the bow to port, sending the view of the moon and Earth to starboard.

'Get rid of the shale,' wheezed the pilot. 'I can help.'

'No.'

'You are a fool, Lieutenant.'

'Anything's better than nothing,' I said.

'Are you sure?'

Now, the Gwantasnarr's comms came alive. A voice spoke a series of growls and shrieks. Then, the shrieks changed to a female voice speaking

English in a pre-Accord accent.

'Rebel ship Herculaneum,' the voice said, 'this is the Roman ship Carthage.'

'That's us,' wheezed the pilot from the deck. 'They're hailing us. We're the Herculaneum to them.'

'Halt your progress!' the voice commanded. 'You will be intercepted, then boarded by our Marines. Halt your progress immediately. If you do not comply, we will sink you. Acknowledge your understanding. Over.'

I reached for the lever controlling the engines, nudging it further forward. We slid faster through space. I nudged the lever further still. The ship responded. forward. The engines hummed. I felt the ship vibrating through the seat.

The comms came alive again. 'Herculaneum! This is the Carthage. Halt your progress. We repeat. Halt and prepare and surrender your vessel.'

'Where is the comms equipment?' I said.

'Why?'

'Just tell me.'

'No. You will say something foolish, something to antagonize.'

So, I hunted around the panel till I found the equipment. Meanwhile, the comms spoke again.

'Herculaneum. Final warning! Acknowledge compliance. Over.'

I turned to the pilot. 'What's Latin for "No?"'

'What?' she wheezed.

'What's Latin for "No?"'

'I haven't spoken it since I defected. And speaking Latin won't do you any good. They'll…'

'Look, we're moving now. If we keep going, we might be able to avoid being boarded. If we stay put, it's certain they'll catch us. What's the word?'

'No, Lieutenant. It's better to say nothing. We must protect the king's ship from destruction.'

'Then, I'll tell then in an Accord language.'

'Nullum,' wheezed the pilot.

'Nullum!' I shouted. 'Nullum!'

'Nullum?' came the reply over the comms. The strange accent sounded amused. 'So be it, Lieutenant Burns. Vos elegit te feci. Nunc nec corpus portabit.'

Yes, so be it.

I performed a mental stock take.

The Gwantasnarr was faster and more maneuverable than the Roman transports, but I could never evade the enemy ship. I didn't have the skills. I didn't even know to fire the Gwantasnarr's weapons.

So what to do?

If we went straight towards Earth, could we outrun our attackers?

How fast were we traveling? And how much time and space would be required to slow down when we got to Earth. If we got to Earth.

As if reading my thoughts, the pilot said wheezed, 'The only thing to do is to throw away the Gwantashale.'

'What?'

'The Gwantashale—throw it away. Then, I'll help.'

'You can read my thoughts?'

'I can read some of them: your thoughts of panic and freedom, and your more disturbing thoughts.'

'What thoughts?'

'Listen to my voice. Throw the Gwantashale into space and I'll help you. Do it while there's still time.'

'How many times must I tell you it's not going to happen?'

'Lieutenant, even if you evade that ship, which you won't, you'll crash into your planet, destroying the Gwantasnarr while killing yourself, me, and any remaining Goths. You have no alternative. So do it now. Throw away the shale.'

'Why can't I use the Gwantashale against the Romans—if they board us?'

'Against how many? They'll send as many Marines as it takes.'

'Are the Marines immune to the shale?'

'No, but they have weapons. You have none.'

'I have the rifle.'

'The rifle is in the stern armory with the other weapons. You cannot access it, and even if you could, it would take you too long to go there and back. Better to throw away the shale. Better to let me help.'

'I need the shale. It's all I've got to fight Octavia.'

'It's all folly, Lieutenant. A fantasy of your troubled mind. You can't defeat Octavia, shale or no shale. You're just one man. She's an army; she's a navy; she has Roman technology. And she's herself—dangerous, ruthless, and without conscience. You're one man, Lieutenant—and a man with a conscience. You can't win.'

'So you keep telling me.'

'Yes, but you don't understand. You can't defeat her.'

'Can't defeat Octavia? That's strange coming from someone who aids an army of her enemies who fail every time to even slow Octavia down. So, unless you can give me a better idea, I'm keeping the shale.'

The pilot's expression turned sly.

'I know where there is more shale. I'll take you to it before we're captured.'

'Where? On Rome? On Gwawanath? Sorry, but we're staying on this side of the galaxy.'

'No. I don't mean Gwawanath. I mean Earth.'

'There is no Gwantashale on Earth.'

'Oh, but there is.'

'Where?'

'Someone put it there centuries ago.'

'Why would Rome do that?'

'You'll have to ask the Lovelorn. She served as a lieutenant on the failed mission to take it back.'

'How did she and crew not die from exposure to it?'

'Some were made sick. Sinistra herself was poisoned. But at first, they were safe because they sealed it in a case lined with black stone.'

'How big is it? How much is there?'

'The case is the size of a sailor's sea-chest—a chest from hundreds of Earth years ago. There was more than enough to kill Octavia, Lieutenant Burns. Enough to kill armies.'

'Where is it and how do you know it's still there?'

'It was buried on the coast of your AONT Africa by the crew of a pre-Accord warship.'

'Why did they bury it? Why didn't they keep it?'

'The more questions you ask, Lieutenant Burns, the less time we have. You have only one choice: throw the shale away or be captured all over again. You can't fight Octavia from a cell on her ship.'

The pilot lay flat on the deck again. Her skin had turned yellow. The green drool congealed on her chin. It might have been an act. For all her suffering, she never went all the way and died. She always managed to just hang on. But she was also right about the shale. It was no good dying just to save it.

Damned if you do, Burns, I thought. Damned if you don't.

The impact alarm sounded again, and another shot struck the Gwantasnarr. It hit the stern again with a great clang. The ship yawed, like a car performing a handbrake slide. On the instrument panel, a light flashed over and over. An alarm repeated a single syllable that I couldn't understand. It sounded like 'Gliss! Gliss! Gliss!'

'Herculaneum!' said the comms. 'You have three minutes.'

'Now or never, Lieutenant Burns,' wheezed the pilot. 'Now or never.'

56

I unsnapped the harness and got to my feet. Then, I stepped out of the bridge. I walked across the stateroom, over to the rear starboard bulkhead. The lump of Gwantashale hung from the rail, wrapped in its cloth inside my NWU jacket. I untied it and carried it over to the passageway door.

I peered through the small porthole, saw the breach in the hull, the yawning blackness outside. At the far end of the passageway, the port window in the door revealed no activity. No Karz. No Goths. No life.

I unwrapped the bundle, put my blue NWU jacket back on, and then I held the length of shale in one hand and the cloth in the other. I took a deep breath, grabbed the lever, and unsealed the passageway door.

The stateroom began to depressurize. Any remaining debris came drifting towards my boots.

I held the shale in my left hand. Then, I placed

it on the doorjamb and slammed the door shut. I checked the shale. Not even scratched. So, I slammed the door a second time. The result was the same: no scratches, not even a groove. But on the third slam, the shale broke. A large piece fell down into the passageway, bounced on the deck, and then flew out into space—gone forever along with its power to stop Octavia.

But I still held a small lump in my hand about the length of my thumb.

That's all.

It wasn't much. Maybe it wasn't enough. But it would have to do.

I wrapped the shale in the cloth, doubling the folds. Then, I buttoned it back into my NWU jacket pocket.

When I got back to the bridge, I knew something was wrong.

The pilot stood at the controls. She was upright and beautiful again. Her skin glowed. Her hair was disheveled but shining, like she had just woken up from a long, refreshing sleep.

When she saw me, her right arm began to swell.

'This is more like it,' she said.

'It's gone. You got what you wanted. Now, get us out of here. Take me to Earth, like we agreed.'

The pilot smiled and shook her head.

'Change of heading. The Gwantasnarr is returning to Gwawanath.'

57

The pilot watched me, a curl to her lip. How different she was to three days ago to the shy woman who stood with her eyes lowered to the deck! I knew power could change people, but I didn't know it could change them so fast. The way she smiled, she could have been Octavia.

'To Gwawanath?' I said.

The air had thinned after I had opened the passageway entrance. It difficult to draw a full breath, at least for me. The pilot, of course, had no trouble.

'You didn't think I'd actually endanger the Gwantasnarr, did you, Lieutenant? You didn't think I'd actually take you to Earth and risk destroying King Gwantalan's only ship?'

'Now I know, ' I said, finding the air suddenly thin again.

'Know what, Lieutenant?'

'Why… Octavia… wanted… to… kill you.'

'Oh, and why is that?'

'You betray… people's… trust.'

'Ha, ha,' she laughed, tossing her hair over her shoulders. 'You know nothing about me, Lieutenant Burns. You know nothing at all.'

'I don't need to know. Your actions… speak so loudly.'

Her hands dabbed and twisted at the controls. 'You don't think it's something else, Lieutenant? Maybe you think you know me because you recognize something of yourself.'

'The difference between you and me,' I said, 'is that I'm still fighting for my people. You are trying to defeat yours.'

'I know exactly why I fight, Lieutenant. Many Roman people lost their lives because of Octavia, including my family. She's a tyrant. She must be defeated, one way or another, even if that means fighting alongside her enemies. That's why I do what I do. You, however, don't know why you fight at all, do you?'

'I have my reasons.'

'Do you? That's not how it seems.'

'Like I said, I have my reasons.'

'Careful, Lieutenant. Without enough reasons, or the right reasons, you won't go the distance. There's nothing to drive you on through adversity. You'll give up. Either that or you'll get yourself killed. Not that it matters now. Your battle is over.'

I ignored her. 'Why not help me out?' I said. 'We're both fighting Octavia.'

'No, Lieutenant. King Gwantalan and the Goths are fighting her. I am helping them. In any case, there are not enough soldiers left aboard. I'm going back to Gwawanath.'

'You could still attack. You have the ship. I can help you.'

'Help, Lieutenant? You? Without the Gwantashale, you can't even help yourself. I'm going back to Gwawanath while there's still time. You can come too if you like, but I don't recommend it. King Gwantalan won't like to hear what happened. He showed you mercy last time. Next time, he won't.'

'I'm not going back to that planet.'

'No? Then you can always wait here in space. Maybe Octavia will send a ship to pick you up before you freeze… or burn.'

She reached for the controls.

'You're interesting, Lieutenant. You're foolish, but you're brave. You're like a Goth soldier, but smarter. And handsome—for someone in human form. I can understand why Sinistra likes you. Who knows! If you choose to come with me, perhaps we might become friends—if King Gwantalan lets you live.'

'At least let me find the Gwantashale,' I said.

'The Gwantashale? The shale you just threw away?'

'No, the Gwantashale on Earth. Or is that a lie too?'

'No, it's there, but I'm not going to Earth. Now step back.'

I didn't move.

'Step back, Lieutenant, or you'll feel this

around your neck.'

The seams on her shirt sleeve burst as her arm flattened out into a blade. The blade split into two, forming a pincer.

'There's no need for that,' I said.

'I disagree. I am about to put the ship into acceleration. Now get back into the stateroom, for your own safety. Trust me, you won't want this around your neck when we enter stage three.'

But no sooner had she spoken when a blast hit the ship's port side, shoving the Gwantasnarr to starboard.

'Time to go!' the pilot shouted.

Then a bigger blast hit. The midship section took the impact. The ship seemed to flex along the mile of its length, like an archer's bow. In the bridge's viewport, Earth slipped to starboard, and the screen filled with blurred stars and black space. Then, as the ship snapped back straight, Earth streaked across the bridge and out of sight.

The blast knocked the pilot to starboard, but not from her seat. The snap-back knocked her all the way to the deck. It threw me into the port bulkhead. My shoulder hit first so that I bounced off and was on my feet again while the pilot was still climbing to hers. That's when I seized the moment.

The pilot had climbed halfway to her seat and was pushing at the controls. The engines groaned. The ship lurched, gathering headway. I took two steps forward, pulled the shale from my pocket and held the bundle close to the back of the pilot's head.

Nothing happened at first. The pilot didn't flinch. She actually sat down and dabbed at shapes and nudged joysticks. The pincer swayed distracted by her side.

So, I exposed the shale further. I unwrapped the lump from the insulating cloth and brought it to within a hand's width of her beautiful neck.

This time, she noticed.

Her body stiffened as if she had been stabbed in the back, or jolted with electricity. She sat upright, her chin high, her face contorted, her teeth clenched. Her left hand froze in the air. She was like a pianist about to play a chord.

'No,' she gasped. 'Please. No.'

Her right arm, the pincer swung up, rising as high as her shoulder. There it came to a sudden stop and trembled.

'Take it away. Please take it away.'

'Don't touch a thing on that panel,' I said, moving the shale closer. 'Don't move that pincer, either.'

She stiffened further, rising higher in her seat.

'You threw it out,' she hissed. 'I sensed it. You threw it out. You threw it…'

'Yes,' I said, 'but not all of it.'

'Please. Please take it away.'

Her complexion began to mottle, returning to a sickly green and yellow.

'Please,' she said again.

'The sooner you take me down to Earth, the sooner you'll get away from it.'

'It will kill me.'

'No, it won't. You didn't die before.'

'It's on my skin. Please. I can't move.'

'Yes, you can.'

'It cramps my muscles.'

'Muscles? Is that what they are?'

'Please.'

I withdrew the shale an inch. The pilot's body slumped. She clutched her chest with one hand and then reached around to the back of her neck and pressed her fingers over the newly formed welt.

I couldn't help but pity her. She was only being loyal to King Gwantalan. And I hated the act of tormenting a woman, even an alien woman, even one with a pincer for an arm.

Even Octavia.

But neither of them were Earth women. Both were killers. I had to keep reminding myself.

'Now,' I said. 'Try anything more and I'll shove the shale into your ear and keep on shoving till it burns your brain. Got that?'

She lowered her head but said nothing.

'Got that?'

She nodded a feeble nod.

'Good. Then, let's go to Earth before they intercept us.'

'They will fire even more beams at the ship.'

'I don't care. Let's get going.'

Her left hand drifted towards the icon of the blue cylinder.

'No, not that one.' I moved the shale close to

her neck again. She shriveled away from it.

'I'm going to keep this here until you line up the ship's bow with Earth.'

She withdrew her slender hand from the button with the blue cylinder. Then she moved it to the thrust lever and then the helm. The engines groaned, and the Gwantasnarr turned to port. Earth slid back across the viewport, but not to its center.

'Why aren't we heading straight at it?'

'The Earth orbits the sun at six thousand miles an Earth hour, Lieutenant. We have to allow for its movement.'

'OK. Whatever it takes. But let's try again.' I withdrew the shale.

'No,' the pilot sobbed. 'Take it away.'

'If you try to roll the ship, or plunge its bow, or try any sudden movement that will throw me around the bridge, or, if you try to switch off the air pumps. . .'

'I won't. Please. Just take it off me.'

'There's one thing more.'

'What?'

'Change that right arm of yours. Change it to a human hand. I don't want to see any pincers, blades, claws, fangs, or anything except a human hand.'

I watched the pincer reform from a smooth, mottled green weapon, back to a slender woman's arm.

'That's better. Now how much time do we have?'

'None.'

'Then, let's go. Let's get to Earth fast as you can.'

She nudged the lever controlling forward thrust. The vibration of the great engines shook the deck. The hull's joints rattled and moaned. Bits of the bulkhead shook loose. But we were on our way toward Earth and Octavia.

'Why are you doing this, Lieutenant?'

'What?'

'Why? You say you have reasons. What are they?'

'To stop Octavia. If I can stop her, I can stop the invasion.'

'But why you? Of all the people on your planet, why are you, Alex Burns the one holding the shale?'

An image flashed in my mind of my ancestor aboard HMS Hemera. 'You are meant to wage this fight just like your ancestors have fought,' he said. 'Call it the family trade.' His words made no sense, of course. How could such a thing be a family trade? Maybe it was something from the pre-Accord world. Some kind of duty or service, like my father said about the navy. No, it didn't make sense. Not completely. And yet there I was, holding a piece of alien rock on an alien ship hurtling towards yet another confrontation with Octavia. Was duty making me do it?

'What did you say, Lieutenant?'

'Huh?'

'You said something. It wasn't in one of your

Accord languages, so I didn't catch it. What was it?'

’Just get me down to Earth.’

'I'm interested. What did you say?'

‘Earth,’ I repeated. ‘Earth.'

’Why Earth? Octavia is with her ships. You haven't thought this through.’

’Just get me there.’

‘That’s easier said than done, Lieutenant.’

We would soon find out if she was right.

58

The Gwantasnarr surged forward. Earth loomed in the viewport. The Roman ship blinked menacingly on a screen displaying the view from the stern. Now that we had defied their command, they were back to threatening us with more blasts of their beams.

I stood behind the pilot, the shale ready in my right hand.

'What's your name?' I said.

'You know my name. You have heard it already.'

'Tell me again.'

'It's Janasta in Goth, Flavia in Roman.'

'Which should I use?'

'Janasta. I am more Goth than Roman now.'

'OK, Janasta, can you fire on them?' I said. 'Can you hit them before they hit us again?'

'No. Impossible.'

'Why?'

'We'd have to use the stern cannons.'

'So, use them. Blast their bow. Destroy them

completely.'

'First, one blast is not enough. The ship has shields just as we do. Second, to fire the stern cannons requires a crew. I can only fire from the bow, Lieutenant. We can't hit them unless we turn around.'

'Then, what can we do?'

'I can try to evade the blasts until we reach Earth's atmosphere. They won't bring such a large ship down to Earth. Not yet.'

'OK. Do it. Make your maneuvers and then let's get down there.'

'Get down where exactly? You haven't told me.'

'First show me where this sea-chest of shale is buried. Then, take me to AONT USA sub-territory California. Drop me in the forest near the coast where I met the Goths.'

'That's two places.'

'Right.'

'You said one.'

'I changed my mind.'

'The Gwantasnarr is not built to land, Lieutenant, or drop you anywhere. It is designed to remain in space. Have you seen the size of it?'

'You flew it across the galaxy. You'll find a way.'

She hunched over the controls, shrinking from the shale, one slender arm in a blue shirt sleeve, the other bare to her shoulder.

On the screen, the image of the lumbering Roman craft began to flash urgently.

'They're going to fire again,' Janasta said. 'I'm going to make the evasion maneuvers. Nothing violent, Lieutenant. I'll roll the ship to port, then starboard. It won't dodge every shot, but it will minimize the damage. I have a duty to the ship, to keep it safe for King Gwantalan.'

'OK,' I replied. 'evasive maneuvers, but no acceleration.'

'I don't think evasion will be enough.'

'Don't worry, Janasta. They want to capture me. Not kill.'

'Are you sure?'

'Call it intuition. They just want to disable the ship, not destroy it.'

'It comes to the same result.'

'So just get us down there.'

'I am trying, Lieutenant.'

Suddenly, I felt a strange buzzing in one of my pockets. At first, I thought it must be the shale, its strange hum. Then, I realized the buzzing came from a different pocket. It came from my handheld, the one handed to me by Ricci in the forest.

'What is that noise?' said Janasta.

'It's my comms device. The satellites must have picked it up.'

I took the handheld from my pocket. Janasta turned to look, then glanced at the shale and turned away.

'Why do you frown at it so intently, Lieutenant?'

'The number of messages coming in.'

'What did you expect?'

'Not this many.'

'It's been three years, Lieutenant. That's a long time on your world.'

'Three years? What do you mean three years? It's been a week.'

'That's how long you've been away, Lieutenant. A week or so for the Gwantasnarr; three years down there. It's all due to time and space and the speed of light. But then, you don't know about those things, do you?'

The Gwantasnarr had reached the upper atmosphere of Earth without another significant hit. The stern view revealed the ship falling back.

Janasta lowered the bow. Streams of sparks soon flowed over the bridge viewport, following by licks of flame. The ship began to shake and rattle.

'The Gwantasnarr is not meant for this,' she said.

'Just keep going.'

'As I keep telling you, it is not a dropship. It's not designed to support its own weight. The hull might buckle and there's no guarantee that I can hover in your atmosphere. The downward thrusters are…'

'Then, we'll hover over the sea and I'll jump into that. Whatever it takes, just keep going.'

The ship shook violently for the next few minutes and the licks of flame left black streaks on the viewport. Then, all of a sudden the viewport filled with mist. Then, almost as quickly, the mist vanished, and we raced over a vast, sandy desert with great dunes rippling all the way to the horizon.

Janasta read my thoughts.

'No, I can't go any slower, Lieutenant. This isn't a sightseeing ship. It has to be this velocity.'

At the desert's furthest western edge, the AONO Atlantic waited—a great block of blue-green against the desert's dull yellow. When we flew over it, Janasta said. 'The sea-chest is there, outside a coastal town named Essaouira. That's what they called it in your pre-Accord era.'

'That's a big area. Tell me the navigational location.'

'The Roman navigational location?'

I brought out my handheld again. 'Tell me the Roman coordinates, then tell me the coordinates for somewhere else. The front steps of the AON Headquarters in AON sub-territory Los Angeles. Tell me those. If I can work out the location for one set of coordinates, I can work out the other.'

She spoke them aloud while I held the handheld near to her face.

'OK, Lieutenant?'

'Yes, now, get me to AONT sub-territory California.'

The Gwantasnarr surged away from AONT Africa. Its shadow raced us on the ocean below. Occasionally, it slid over the decks of AON vessels stacked with shipping containers.

'Better climb out of sight,' I said.

Janasta raised the bow. Clouds filled the

viewport, then vanished, and we cruised along great canyons of white cotton.

We approached AONT USA. The clouds faded away. We flashed over the coast, heading west, rolling across the land like the pioneering Accord fighters centuries before, defeating the armies of the pre-Accord powers at the Battle of Albright in the country's middle regions.

These regions were now dotted with giant gray warehouses. Gray towers reached up, and gray vehicles crawled between them like large beetles. The warehouses and towers stretched north and south, almost as far as the horizons.

'Is it all Octavia's military equipment?'

'And building equipment.'

'For cities?'

'My guess is that it's for everything.'

'What's everything?'

'Do you really need me to tell you, Lieutenant? Hasn't Octavia described what's she's going to do to the mountains, oceans, and forests?' Then she added. 'And the people.'

'Why this planet? There must be another planet she could occupy? There's a whole galaxy of them.'

'There is, Lieutenant. There's a more suitable, larger planet they call Elysium which is uninhabited.'

'So, why doesn't she choose Elysium? Why doesn't she save herself the trouble of killing the natives?'

'We have explained it to you already,

Lieutenant. Earth was discovered first. The Lovelorn was on some of the early missions.'

The Gwantasnarr raced west, streaking over vast plains, dragging up teardrop-shaped craft in its wake. Soon, the mountain range AONMR Newsome rose in the viewport. AON sub-territory California lay on its far side, beyond AON sub-territory Nevada.

At this point, I made a phone call. I pulled the handheld from my pocket. With one hand still holding the shale beside Janasta's neck, I used my free hand to flick through the list of missed calls, all from the same number.

I dabbed at the redial button. Three long ringtones sounded, then four, five, six, and finally someone answered.

'Who's this?' said a hostile voice. It might have been Adams, the guy from the forest, but the voice sounded guarded. 'Who's this?' the voice said again. 'You think I've got time to waste?'

'Adams? It's Burns. Alex Burns. Remember? The helicopter crash in the forest outside AONB Holder… after the court-martial. Can you meet me at the same place?'

Silence. Then the voice said, 'Yeah, right. You think I'm stupid?' The phone blipped. He'd hung up. I pressed the number again. The ringtone sounded. No answer.

'We are approaching the border of your AONT sub-territory California,' said Janasta. 'As I warned, it's…'

I didn't listen. Instead, I tapped the number

again. The call went through to voicemail. A robot voice that could have been male or female asked me to leave a message. 'Adams, it's me. I'm back. I have news. Call me, ASAP.'

I hung up. I didn't hold much hope for Adams, Ricci or their group. Three years ago they were hopeless or lying. Now they might be worse. But they were also all I had—them and the small lump of Gwantashale held in my right hand behind Janasta's neck.

'Entering the territory now,' she said.

In the pre-Accord era, California, as it was known then, had led the way in promoting the Accord's new policies. It was the first state to ban men from holding positions of authority; it was the first to raise taxes to ninety-five percent; and the first to outlaw civilian weapons. It also claimed to have no borders, but at the same time, forbade its residents from leaving for other sub-territories. California was also the first place to make Accord values the law. Now, it would be the place where the final battle would be fought.

'See what's waiting.' Janasta nodded at the screen. It showed a network of hovering teardrop-shaped craft. 'Those things can do worse damage than anything the Gwantasnarr can inflict.'

She turned around in her seat. She looked at my hand and the small lump of shale.

'Do you understand, Lieutenant? There won't be any escape this time.'

'And as I told you, Octavia wants to capture

me, not kill me. They won't fire on the ship. Trust me.'

'It will be a form of suicide.'

'Suicide. Got it. Now let's keep going.'

59

Janasta brought the ship to a halt.

'What are you doing?' I said. 'Keep going.'

'You have not understood. Those ships have the same weapons as we do, which they will use if we proceed. They will knock us from the sky. There can be no evasion tactics now.'

'What if you ram them?'

'Ram them, Lieutenant? Drive the Gwantasnarr into them—bow first.'

'That's what ramming means. We could take them by surprise. They won't be expecting it.'

'It would break the ship. Then, we would crash to earth, or onto a city west of them. The result would be your death... and the deaths of whichever of your people we hit.'

'Ram. They'll get out of our way.'

'I'll ask you again, Lieutenant. Are you aware of the size of the Gwantasnarr? It is a frigate in your naval terminology, but it is many times larger than one of your aircraft-carrying ships. It would cause immense damage.'

'You mean aircraft carriers.'

'You know what I mean.'

'So what would you do? What's your plan?'

'Climb. Leave the atmosphere. Leave the planet. Accelerate. Head to Gwawanath. Survive. Preserve King Gwantalan's ship.'

'No time. We can't spend years going there and back. I might only have days until Octavia lands the rest of her forces.'

'Then we should turn back.'

'No turning back. Ram the ships. Or fire on them.'

'You aren't listening, Lieutenant. If we fire on them, they will fire on us. At this range, we will lose the battle as well as the Gwantasnarr, and you will lose your life.'

'Can you contact them, send a message?'

'To tell them what?'

'That we don't want to engage. We only want to pass them, not attack.'

'No, Lieutenant, they will fire on us whatever we do. They'll fire on us because this ship is theirs. We stole it when I defected.'

'They won't fire. Octavia's wants to capture me not kill me. '

'You can't rely on that. Octavia is unpredictable and capable of anything, the worst things. The only way out is back into space.'

And she reached for the controls.

'No.' I brought the shale closer to her neck. Instantly, she stiffened and her hands froze over the panel.

'Please. Don't force me to destroy my ship. It's my life.'

'Then let's try something else. Lower your altitude, Janasta. Go beneath them.'

'It is a mistake.'

'Just do it. Please.'

She winced. I saw her right hand morphing into the pincer again, before changing back to a human hand. I sensed she was approaching her limit, but For the moment, she obeyed. She lowered the morphing hand to the side of the chair. I readied the shale over her neck and waited for the strike.

The comms came alive. A voice spoke in a series of growls and shrieks.

'Sounds like Goth.'

'It's Roman,' Janasta replied. 'They say to halt and await a boarding party.'

'Or?'

'They didn't say anything more.'

'Tell them, no thanks.'

'That will only provoke them.'

'Say it politely. Say please.'

She spoke into the comms. The same shrill language.

When she finished speaking, I said, 'Now go under them or fire on them.'

Janasta lowered the Gwantasnarr's altitude until we slipped beneath the swarm. The shadows of the hostile ships passed over the viewport, sending us into shade, then light, then shade again. The same shadows dappled the land below, into which the leviathan shadow of the Gwantasnarr merged.

All was strangely still, strangely peaceful.

The calm before the storm.

No sooner had I thought this when an alarm went off in the back of the bridge: a short, shrill syllable, a Roman word, repeated over and over.

'The first shot has been fired, Lieutenant. Just as I said it would.'

The shot struck somewhere amidships on the starboard side, causing the ship to yaw. A second shot hit the port side, throwing us back the other way. A third hit closer to the bridge, causing the bow to pitch down and Janasta to slide forward in her seat.

'Keep going.' I saw the change in Janasta's face and I knew that she would use the strike to make her move.

'The hull can resist only so many times. Why don't you listen to me?'

'Get a move on. Reduce altitude, go further beneath them. Get me to that forest. Then you're free.'

She watched the screen as two enemy ships dropped from their formation and came alongside like escorts. They had no visible ports, but I knew who would be aboard: Roman pilots and the tall, armor-clad Roman Marines.

'It's over, Lieutenant. We're too big to go this low. The only thing to do is to climb.'

'Fire on them. They are an illegal occupying force on Earth. Fire on them. Use the bow chasers.'

'I can't risk the ship. I've given up everything for this. I'm not letting you destroy us.'

'Fire on them! Now!'

I pushed the shale into her neck. She stiffened, then reached to a set of switches and buttons at the top of the panel. She chose a dial covered by a small hood. She unclipped the hood. Then she turned the dial forty-five degrees.

'You ordered the ship do this, Lieutenant. Not me.'

'Get on with it.'

She pressed her thumb onto a switch. Instantly, the viewport filled with blue light. The Gwantasnarr's bow slid to starboard. When the blinding flash of light vanished, I saw both of the teardrop vessels rocking backward, listing and wobbling like bees in a breeze. Then they dropped, falling from view, plunging into the shadow below. We heard one explosion, then the next, and saw the orange flames rise from the dark.

'Now you've done it.'

'Just keep going.'

The comms came alive. No great volley of shrieked aliens syllables this time, just five measured and threatening words.

'What did they say?'

'What I told you. They will destroy the ship.'

'No, they won't. Just keep going towards that forest.'

But no sooner had I said these words when the

MM HOLT

ship was rocked by several teeth shattering hits.
'Move!'

I thought Janasta might finally fling the pincer,
but instead, she forced the Gwantasnarr forward
and down.

Then, a new alarm rang, then a second alarm
began—one with a different pitch and warning.

'What is it?'

'There is a fire. A fire amidships, and also on
the stern's starboard quarter.'

'Keep going.'

More blasts hit the Gwantasnarr. They
knocked the stern heavily to port, then down, so
that the viewport filled with the undersides of the
craft above us.

'What will we do when we get to this forest?'
Janasta said. 'If we get there.'

'Just get me there. I'll handle whatever's
waiting.'

The alarms rang on. Another blast hit closer to
the cabin, and then a massive strike of two
thunderous blasts hit directly above us, and for
the first time, smoke curled from the joints where
the deck met the bulkheads.

'Return fire. What are you waiting for?'

But Janasta said nothing. Her tearful face
glowed a dull white. Deep furrows creased her
forehead. Her skin was yellow-slick. The hinges
in her jaw bulged.

I had pushed her too far.

Her beloved ship was falling to pieces.

She would take no more orders and she

406

wouldn't care what happened to her.

The pincer strike I had been expecting would come at last.

60

'Just a little longer,' I said. 'Then we'll be free,' but Janasta had already twisted in her seat, bringing out the pincer from beneath the console.

And swung it at my face.

I raised my right elbow. The pincer struck it at an angle, but it did not glance off. It carried straight on, knocking me off my feet and into the bulkhead. My back hit first; my head hit second. I slid down to the deck. Then, I struggled to my feet just as Janasta stepped out from behind the pilot's seat, the pincer raised and menacing.

Think fast, I thought. In a microsecond, she would be on you. The pincer will snap shut on your neck, or ribs. Or it will rise up and slam down on your face.

Janasta raised the pincer and took a step forward. A screech from the comms stopped her. Several shrill sounds blared out from it. She stopped and listened, but kept her eyes on me. Then she shrieked a reply.

'What did they say?'

'The usual. Last chance or we'll destroy you.'

'So you're going to surrender?'

'Why would I do that? I'm getting out of here —if that's still possible.'

'But that's not what you told them, is it?'

'No, I offered to give them you if they would stop firing.'

'Did they agree?'

'They didn't say. They're checking higher up.'

'Checking with who… or with what?'

'Checking… with her.'

'Then use the time to do something. Drop me off. We're in an atmosphere. I can get to the stern. Let me have the dropship, like the one that went to the planet.'

'The dropship? You think you could fly it?'

'No, but you can fly it from here.'

'I'm not doing anything but getting out of here —out of your solar system and gone.'

'Then drop me somewhere. Drop me in the sea. The coast is not far. I'll swim from there.'

'You are deluded, Lieutenant, yet again. You'll die in impact or you will drown or die from exhaustion or exposure. I don't have time for your fantasies. I only have time for the Gwantasnarr and getting away.'

The pincer shot forward, knocked my defensive arm out of the way again, and closed on my neck. And then it kept on closing. I twisted to break free, but the grip tightened on my windpipe.

But before it could crush, I slapped the piece of

shale on the pincer and pressed it hard.

But it did nothing. Nothing at all.

The pincer kept on crushing. Obviously, I had to get the shale closer to Janasta's head—or body, or inside her mouth. If only I could break free.

Then the comms came alive. Not a series of shrieks this time. Instead, a calm, measured voice spoke a long sentence of Roman.

Janasta halted the pincer's crushing grip.

She knew whose voice spoke.

So did I.

61

Janasta turned and shrieked a series of syllables at the comms, probably telling Octavia she would hand me over. But would Octavia believe her?

Within seconds, another blast struck the ship, then another, then another. All of them clanging like great discordant bells. The ship's stern swung with each hit. More alarms sounded. Debris dropped from the bulkheads. The smoke curled and thickened on the deck.

The blasts knocked Janasta to her knees. She used the grip on my neck to steady herself, pulling my head down to pull herself up. But when the final series of blasts hit the Gwantasnarr, she fell to her knees once more, and the blades slid away, snapping shut with the usual obscene click. I lunged away as they snapped again, slicing the front of my NWU.

I climbed to my feet, holding the shale in my right hand. Janasta saw it and kept her distance. She sent pincer arm slashing the air in front of me, a double-bladed snapping knife with a thrust range of two yards. It swung left and right, in and out, as if selecting vulnerable places to stab—my ribs, my legs, or my stomach.

My instincts told me to run. My conscious mind whispered a second idea: to wait, if possible, until the next blast then get inside the pincer's range. The idea made me think of Granak, circling around me, trying to find a way inside the range of my spear. He had done it by dodging the sharp tip and then charging as soon as I stumbled. Maybe I could do the same.

'You forget that I can read your thoughts, Lieutenant,' Janasta sneered. 'Your stupid tactic won't work. I'm not Granak, and you can't make a move without me knowing.'

And as she said that, I thought of an idea. Rather than trying to dodge the pincer, I would try to something else: to disorient her with thoughts.

'Do you know what I'm thinking about now?'

I formed an image of her acting out the moment in her life that I guessed caused her the most pain: the moment she had betrayed her own people.

I conjured an image of her fighting against other Romans—beautiful women like herself. I imagined her own face twisted in shame for the countrymen she had killed. Then, I imagined her in a moment alone, slumped in a cabin, bowed by heavy remorse.

I had no idea of course whether any of this

happened, but I imagined it vividly and with plenty of shame, regret, and self loathing. When I emerged from this miasma of remorse, I saw her watching me with her head on one side. The pincer had ceased its probing. It wavered in the distance between us.

Now, I thought. Now or never!

I dropped beneath the pincer, but instantly, Janasta came alert again. The pincer coiled back and reared up at me. I stopped my charge, and we were back to the standoff. 'Nice try,' said Janasta. 'Almost worked.'

But as she spoke, three blasts from Octavia's fleet hit the Gwantasnarr's bridge from above and from the side. They knocked us both from our feet onto the deck. Now it was a race to see who would get up faster.

Before Janasta could rise, I scrambled on hands and knees, all the while keeping the shale in one fist. I ducked beyond the pincer's blades and reached Janasta's boots. Then, I grabbed the cloth of her uniform, pulled myself up her body and thrust my fist towards her face.

The pincer swung violently behind me. A slender fist hit my ear, but by then, I had a firm grip on the blue shirt. I shoved the shale at Janasta's face. She raised her chin, twisted her head, squinted horribly. I shoved the shale at her mouth, missed, but managed to get it into her left nostril.

Then, I pushed it up as far as I could force it, pushing like I settled the breathing device into my nose on Gwawanath. Pushing until I hit cartilage, or whatever it is that aliens are made of.

She stiffened. Totally. Already weakened by the shale's presence, she was now powerless, overcome with poison or radiation or whatever it was the shale sent forth into her body. She couldn't even move her left arm to push me away. The pincer slumped against me, tried to wrap around me, writhing like a defeated snake.

Then, it too went rigid.

I pressed harder with my right thumb and used my left hand to grab the hand flailing uselessly at my ear. Then, Janasta's body began to shake. The pincer came to life again, smacking the bulkhead between the bridge and the stateroom. She couldn't speak, but her eyes pleaded with me to stop.

But I didn't.

Horrible.

'Tell me the name of the Roman who broke Octavia's heart?' I said. 'The reason she is called the Lovelorn?'

She said nothing.

'The Roman's name. What did he do to her? Tell me.'

I released the pressure on the shale until she gasped.

'Please take it away.'

'Tell me the guy's name first.'

'Ranant. His name was Ranant.'

'Ranant.' I mimicked her pronunciation.

'Thank you. And what did Ranant do?'

'Please.'

'What did he do?'

'He rejected her and chose her rival instead.'

'What was her rival's name?'

But then the pincer came swinging. I shoved the shale back into her nose. Her back arched. The pincer froze in mid-swing, trembled in the air, then dropped to the deck where it quivered. Minutes later, Janasta's arched violently one last time. Then, it went slack and slumped onto the deck.

I lifted my thumb from her nose, but left the shale wedged in place, just in case.

'Sorry,' I said. 'I wish it could have been different.'

I dragged the heavy, beautiful, lifeless body to the side of the stateroom, and laid it on the deck in the smoky mist, as if she were a warrior princess from a forbidden fairy tale. I tore a strip of her blue sleeve and tied the pincer arm to her left arm, just in case it might come back to life.

Then, I stood over her, sick with revulsion at what I had just done, and not because of any Accord nonsense about being intolerant, but because of something else, something to do with being human or having a spirit. I couldn't say what.

As usual, I didn't have time to think. I never had time to think. Or plan. Or consider. Or reflect. To reflect! How nice that would be—and how dangerous.

Instead, I got up and looked around the stateroom. The ship was in chaos. Alarms sounded astern. Smoke billowed overhead like a thunder cloud. I had to do something. I had to get back to doing my… my what?

I stopped and thought.

'I have to get back to my duty.'

62

I stepped across the smoky deck and onto the bridge. The view through the viewport was dark. The sun had dropped beneath the horizon. The Gwantasnarr's flashing bow lanterns shone in the gloom. The panel of controls blinked and swirled. The two pilots' seats were empty. I was suddenly conscious of my predicament: I was alone aboard a mile-long spaceship hurtling through the dark.

One step at a time, I told myself. It was my usual phrase in times of uncertainty. One step at a time. Don't think of everything at once, just the next step. Keep in mind whatever is going right. The enemy craft had stopped firing. That was something good, wasn't it? You're back on earth, too—almost.

I shoved all bad thoughts aside and dropped into the pilot's seat. After snapping the harness buckle tight, I drew a deep breath and confronted the controls.

First things first. I scanned the panel. Which of the instruments were the altimeter, attitude indicator, and which showed the airspeed?

None of the flashing, swirling symbols made sense. So, I switched to what the Navy called VFP —Visual Flight Protocol. In other words, I peered through the viewports for points of reference on the land. Not that I could see any. The darkness hid the land below and its roads, coasts, mountains, and forests.

But not everything.

There was a city in the gloom ahead, its street light radiating outward from its center in the classic Accord, circular layout. But which city and in which part of AON sub-territory California. If Janasta had been heading for the correct forest, the city should have been AON sub-territory Omar, population, five-hundred thousand.

Not where I wanted to be, but not too far away, either.

I gripped the helm and pulled. I felt the bow lift and the ship climb. So far, so good. But the Gwantasnarr pitched forward again when the engine thrust could not maintain the climb at such a low speed.

'The ship is not designed to land on planets,' Janasta had said.

So, I nudged the starboard thrust lever. The Gwantasnarr had no wings. It couldn't bank in the air. Rocket engines and thrusters had to shove it forward and back, up and down.

To my relief, the lights of AON sub-territory Omar slid to starboard, and the port window filled again with blackness. On the control panel, one of the visual displays outlined the shape of the coast ahead. The AONO Pacific came up as a vast and dark blue region. Beside it lay the dark green of the AON sub-territory California National Park. That's where I would head.

Through the window, the forest was a dark, lumpy region. Good. No lights meant no people. I coaxed the Gwantasnarr's engines down while gently pulling the helm. The Gwantasnarr's hull complained in a series of metallic rips. The altitude dropped, and the airspeed decreased as we sank into the dark.

I kept throttling down while keeping the ship's nose high.

And held on.

Hoping.

Down we sank. On the screen, I could see the forest coming closer and then very close, and I heard no sounds except moans and groans deep in the ship and engines' drone. Soon even these faded as we dropped into the gloom until there was only a whistling silence.

And then it happened!

Wham!

Trees, branches, more trees, more branches, and more trees again. They thwacked the underside of the hull, scraping and cracking, bending and breaking as the unimaginable weight and size of the Gwantasnarr struck the forest canopy and slid across its top.

I throttled back even further. The great ship dropped. The thwacks of branches gave way to shrieks as we slid into the tree trunks themselves.

Tree trunks!

The trees fought the hull, striking it as the Gwantasnarr rammed and plowed its way forward.

I pulled the thruster lever back completely, hoping to stop the engines. The trees and warning alarms drowned out all engine noise. But I knew the ship was slowing down because I slid forward in the seat, and the harness straps dug into my chest.

Then the Gwantasnarr dropped even further into the trees, sinking lower and lower until occasional branches and leaves thwacked at the viewport and a new rasping sound surged up from below.

Soon, the small port window on my left filled too. Branches and tree trunks flung themselves left and right. Sprays of gray dirt plumed into the viewport as the Gwantasnarr's bow hit the earth.

And then, with a great groan of rendered timber and screeching metal, the Goth frigate Gwantasnarr—the ship that had just traveled across the galaxy and back again—slowly, painfully ground its way to a halt.

And lay still.

I sat in the harness, listening. I was certain something more was coming: a sudden drop, a list to one side, an explosion, another blast from the ships above.

Or even Janasta rising up with her pincer

snapping.

But there were only noises, a whole cacophony of them: the hull's groan at carrying the ship's weight; the whirr of hidden mechanisms in the bulkheads; the winding down of the great engines a mile to stern; the tick-tick of hot gray metal in the bow; the distant crashes of objects falling in the cabins, holds, and staterooms; and at least three different alarms.

And something else.

It sounded like hundreds of boots thrumming on the deck, as if the Roman Marines were boarding the ship.

I listened more closely.

Not the thrum of boots.

Something worse.

The roar of fire.

Time to get out. Time to get away from the ship.

I unsnapped the harness, stood up, and stepped into the stateroom. The soles of my boots felt warm. I found Janasta still prostrate, the pincer open but lifeless. Surely she was dead this time, not just unconscious but well and truly dead.

'I'm sorry,' I said once more.

Then, I dropped to one knee, prodded the dark lump from the corpse's nose, wrapped it back in its cloth, put the cloth into the top pocket of my blue NWU jacket and buttoned it.

Then, I stood up and thought about what to do next. As usual, there was never any time to think too long. New alarms had joined the old alarms, and the Gwantasnarr, exhausted from its ordeal, listed to port.

63

Time to leave the Gwantasnarr.

I left Janasta's body and walked across to the passageway door. I took a breath, pulled the hot lever, and pushed the door open. Cold air rushed in through the breach in the hull. I stepped through the door, past the breach and the smashed tree trunks bulging into it like broken bones, and walked to the door at the passageway's end.

In the larger stateroom, I found a horrible sight. A mountain range of Goth corpses against the forward bulkhead. The Gwantasnarr's sudden stop must have forced them there. I walked along this grim pile of fur, claws, open maws, and dead eyes, bending down every few yards to look for a Goth with a red collar.

'Karz!' I yelled. 'Karz!'

Nothing.

'Karz! Karz!'

Nothing. Not a Growl. Not a bark. Not a faint rumble of Gwah or Burr. All the Goths were dead. Karz's body must have been buried among them.

With the smoke rising to my knees, I left the Goths and went through the next passageway down past the cabins, and storerooms, and slop rooms. I kept walking for the whole mile to the stern, calling out Karz's name as I went.

But there was no answer. Nothing. No Karz. No living Goths. No one.

At the stern, the dropships floated above their stations. Smoke drifted beneath them. The limbs and heads of Captain Gwawn, Lieutenant Glathaw, and other Goths lay scattered around. Octavia had not been lying about what she'd done.

I went to the port bulkhead and ransacked every shelf, locker, and cabin until I reached the stern port. Then, I crossed over to the starboard bulkhead and ransacked every locker, shelf, and cabin there too.

Until I found the armory.

Inside, I found only a single item snapped into the wall clips.

The heavy Roman rifle. My old friend.

I gently lifted the rifle from its clip, slung it over my shoulder by its strap, and stepped outside. By now, the smoke had thickened and I had to cover my mouth with my elbow.

Time to get off the Gwantasnarr.

I hurried between the dropships to the ramp at the stern port. The port was sealed tight. I ran my hands along the bulkheads on either side until I found a panel of switches. I pressed all of them. Got no response. Then pressed them all over again, slowly, and one at a time until a motor whirred unseen and the port unsealed from the deck and the ramp lowered itself down.

So far, so good.

Last time I had been in this part of the ship, the planet Gwawanath floated outside. This time, I saw a forest at night—one transformed by the sudden arrival of the Gwantasnarr.

The ship had bulldozed a deep furrow in the soil. It was deep enough to drive a truck along. It ran way back into the forest gloom. Either side of it, smashed tree trunks reflected a throbbing orange glow. Sparks flew up like fireflies into the canopy. Cracks and hisses issued from the forest edge as the sap in the trees bubbled and boiled.

I stepped onto the ramp and crossed to its far edge, twenty yards above the furrow's base, and an ankle-twisting drop. I wouldn't be risking that again. Instead, I tightened the rifle's strap, crossed to the port side edge of the ramp, and then leaped to the nearest tree. Then I climbed down, branch by branch, till I could drop to the forest floor. No twisted ankles.

The view forward shocked me. The great spaceship with the childish sounding name listed to port like a wreck on the bottom of the ocean—dark, enormous, and lifeless. Its days of traversing the galaxy were over.

I stood there watching the fire overtaking the ship, thinking of the Goths and Romans I had met on the bizarre voyage to the galaxy's far side. And especially of Karz and her heroism.

Then, I thought about my return to Earth and all that I hated about the Accord: the Oppression Hierarchy, the emphasis on victimhood, the re-writing of pre-Accord history, the veneration of failure, the suppression of masculinity, the rejection of motherhood and families, the lies and betrayals of Accord Commission, and the greatest betrayal of all: the appointment of Octavia to a position of power.

All of these thoughts came rushing in on me, like the heat from the Gwantasnarr's fire.

But not for long.

My reverie ended as soon as I saw one of them —one of the things I would eventually call the Swamp Creatures. They were the other kind of Romans, the ones Octavia had boasted about.

The ones 'living among you.'

64

'Hi there, friend,' said a voice behind me.

It was a male voice, the first male voice I'd heard speaking an Accord language for two weeks. It sounded deep, rich, smooth, and sly.

'Hi there,' it said again, oozing like molasses.

I said nothing.

'Does your Accord sub-territory branch officer know you're out here, friend?' the voice asked. 'Didn't you see the message? They sent out a text to all handhelds. They said to stay inside your home. It's a lockdown, like the one we had for the virus. Remember that? So that means everyone's got to stay inside—except for those people whose culture is affected by this spaceship incident, which is my culture, by the way, not your culture.'

I unslung the rifle and spun around. I held the muzzle level at hip height, my finger on the fire button. I saw the creature in the gloom, tinged with flickering orange firelight. It was about my height and swayed on long legs, ten yards away.

It was dressed in a dark blue smock with an Accord flag patch on one arm.

The face was not human. It was gray, like the Gwantasnarr's hull, but unformed and unfinished, like an abandoned sculpture. The eyes were wide, the head totally bald, and the face too long. The body was the same, especially the legs. And the posture was languid and stooped. His arms hung in front of him like they carried heavy buckets.

'Easy now,' oozed the creature, holding up its long arms. Skeletal gray wrists extended from the blue sleeves. 'You're breaking a few rules here, friend. That weapon you're carrying—it's a forbidden weapon, right? And from what I can tell, it belongs to my culture, which means it must also be a stolen weapon, too. I see you're also wearing an Accord of Nations Navy Work Uniform with a brig patch on the chest, which must mean you're an escapee from one of the Navy's prisons. Very interesting, wouldn't you say, friend?'

I kept the rifle level, my finger on the fire button, ready to blast this thing to globs of goo. After the fight with Janasta, I had no inclination to be polite.

'If I were you,' the creature said, 'I'd drop that big gun and step away from it before you break any more laws. Believe me, it's for the best, friend. But don't worry. You can hand that rifle over to me before you do any harm. Just take your finger off the fire button first. When your finger is clear, lift the strap over your head, and hand the weapon over to me—stock first, if you don't mind.'

I didn't move. The creature annoyed me, especially the tone. He talked as if this were his planet and I were the alien who didn't know the law. I checked the catch on the rifle's stock. The warning light blinked in the dark.

'Easy, friend,' said the creature. 'That's a very dangerous thing you have in your hands. Very, very dangerous. You do know that in addition to carrying that particular weapon, it's forbidden to flick the switch to arm the weapon, and then point the weapon at someone. Very forbidden. Extremely forbidden. Big trouble from the Accord local branch if they find out, which they will. Big, big trouble, especially when it's pointed at a friendly visitor, such as myself. I'm a visitor and a friend. You can trust me.'

'You're no friend,' I said down the length of the rifle's barrel. 'And you're no visitor.'

'No? Then, what am I, friend?'

'You're an invader and an enemy.'

The creature shook its mournful head.

'Now you're using forbidden words too. Where have you been, friend? Haven't you heard? It's totally against the new Accord protocol to insult visitors. It's written in the new Accord Roman Synergy. That's the name of our new treaty. And you just othered me too, friend—othered me intentionally. I guess you haven't been around for a while, have you? Otherwise, you'd know how things have changed. I guess you came down with that big ship there, didn't you? Now you're trying to escape before you're captured, aren't you? You're trying to escape before they catch you and drag you back to that court-martial you escaped from three years ago. Am I right, Lieutenant Alexander Burns?'

The friendly smile morphed into a crooked grin.

I raised the rifle from my hip.

'Get back or I will help you escape to the afterlife or wherever you freaks go when you're dead.'

The creature didn't move. It just swayed in the dark with one palm outstretched.

'And you're aggressive, too. Tell me what's making you unhappy. Perhaps I can help. You need assistance. You need a shave too. Beards, you know, are also forbidden by the local Accord protocol. They're too male, too oppressive. They reinforce stereotypes. Surely you know about that, friend, in which case you also know that the Accord doesn't like males to be aggressive. They might get the wrong ideas about men and women and power—and also about friendly visitors. But maybe you're wearing a beard for that very reason. Or maybe you have permission. I've heard about you, Lieutenant Alexander Burns. Oh, yes. I know quite a lot about you, and everything you did.'

We stood facing each other in the glow of the flames—wild man and protocol-quoting alien. We held each other's gaze. Then, I saw the slightest twitch of the creature's head. I turned. Behind me, tall shapes crept silently in the orange light. When I turned back, the creature stood in front of me, his long arms raised at neck height.

'Nice try,' I said, quoting Janasta.

The creature opened its mouth to speak again, but before it could utter a word, I pressed the fire button on the weapon—the weapon made by this creature's own culture.

The blast threw it ten yards backward, tearing a hole in its middle, and kicking up a plume of earth behind. The creature howled 'Awooo!' and then thrashed about in the soil, making a noise that sounded like 'Ack! Ack! Ack!'

The rifle's recoil also knocked me backwards, but not over. I kept my feet because I knew I had to fire again. With the creature attempting to stand up, I steadied myself, found his green shape in the crosshairs, and fired once more. 'Splodge' went the shot in the dark, knocking the thing backwards. It thrashed in the soil spluttering 'Ack! Ack! Ack!' all over again.

Then I swung the rifle around to my other enemies, the barrel moving like a turret gun. The creatures were rushing at me, pack style, hoping to reach me before I could fire. I put the crosshairs on the creature in the lead. Before he could take two more lunges, I pulled the fire button.

The rifle boomed. The muzzle climbed. The blast knocked the creature into the three others behind him, sending them scattering like ninepins. Then, all the creatures stopped in their tracks, their arms flung out. They gawped at the writhing bodies of their comrades. Then, they gawped at me, their sloppy mouths opening and closing as if this had all been a terrible misunderstanding, as if the meek and compliant earth creatures could never be possible of such violence.

They couldn't have been more wrong—especially about this Earth creature. I was capable of more violence than their warped alien minds could ever imagine. And I was in a murderous, vengeful mood. I detested the idea of my home world being occupied by aliens. Now, seeing the reality, I hated it with hot blood.

Before any of the invaders could take a lunge further, I dropped to a kneeling stance and fired twice more. I hit one of the creatures to the left, spinning him around, and knocking him to the ground. Then, I fired through the group at one of the back runners, flinging him backward for several yards into the dark. Then I hit the creature on the right. The blast swept his legs from beneath him, and his gloomy and then astonished face dunked into the damp earth as if he had been shoved in the back of the head.

Then I swept the group with the virtual sights.

The blasts had done their work. The creatures left standing backed away, hands raised, calling out, 'Hold your fire, friend. We aren't here to harm you. This is all a mistake. We're visitors.

We're your friends.'

'You're no friends. Keep walking and don't stop. Keep going all the way to Rome.'

Two of them dropped to the ground, grabbing the limbs of their fallen pals. They pulled them along, dragging them down the furrow towards the stricken Gwantasnarr.

I kept the rifle level and my finger on the fire button, wondering whether I should have finished them—if that were possible.

But I was also wondering how many more would I have to shoot. I concentrated so hard that I didn't hear the handheld ringing in my pocket.

65

I reached down, pulled the handheld from my pocket, pressed the green 'answer' button.

'Adams?'

A pause, and then a male voice.

'That's no way to greet someone in the Accord.'

'What?'

'Where's your salutation, Accord member? Where's your T.E.I.D?'

'I'm not saying that.'

'Everyone must say it. You think you're special? You think you're excused from saying it?'

'Cut it out, Adams. Time's running out.'

For about ten seconds, there was only the roaring fire and trees sighing as the sap boiled.

'OK, so it is you.'

'And you're Adams, right?'

'Say it louder, Burns. They can't hear you in AON sub-territory Alaska.'

'OK, but you're the guy I met in the forest near AONNB Holder three years ago.'

'Who else would I be?'

'I remember your voice, your phrasing.'

'What's that supposed to mean?'

I drew a breath and counted to five. 'Last time we met, you said you would help me. Does your offer still stand?'

'You had your chance three years ago, Burns. If you wanted help, why did you turn it down? We've been here flying the flag of resistance alone. You've been hiding under a rock or something.'

'I was away.'

'And that's supposed to make everything fine?'

'No, but things have changed. They're much worse. A lot has happened. I'll explain later. Where are you? I just came down in a Goth spacecraft. It landed in a forest near…'

'You think we don't know, Burns? The whole sub-territory saw that thing.'

'Right. It's already set the forest on fire. That's one of the reasons, I need your help. The other is the new kind of creature out here.'

'You think we don't know about them too?'

I waited before answering. 'What's going on, here Adams?'

'What do you mean?'

'Can you help me or not?'

'That's not a very polite way to talk.'

'Can you help or not? Tell me yes or no because I don't have time to play twenty questions.'

'We could be persuaded.'

'Persuaded?'

'Start with an apology.'

And with that, I hung up. The guy wanted to score points, not help. I wasn't going to play games. Not when I still had doubts about the resistance or whatever they called themselves. So, I hung up. I'd take my chances alone.

I set off again. I kept the moon at my back, heading north. I threaded through the smashed trees, deeper into the forest. If I kept going, I'd eventually see the lights of AON sub-territory Omar. And when I reached it, well, I'd work out what to do when I got there. In the meantime, I'd stay out of sight and keep the weapon unslung and the shale buttoned tight in my pocket.

I hadn't gone far when the handheld rang again. 'What happened?' said Adams's voice.

'Listen, Adams. Can you help me or not?'

'What makes you think I won't tell the Harmony Officers and the Navy MAs where you are?'

I took the phone from my ear and stabbed the red button. Then, I dropped it to the forest floor and raised my boot to stomp it to pieces so it couldn't be tracked.

But then it rang a third time. My boot was still in the air. I left it there for a good four rings. Then, I decided I'd give Adams one last chance.

'OK. We can help. Take it easy. You're so thin-skinned, Burns. I thought you were supposed to be some kind of rebel.'

'Where are you?'

'We're here. We're tracking you with a thermal

imager.'

'Where is here and who is we?'

'Relax. It's just me and Ricci. You met her already back in the forest.'

'How did you get here so fast? It's only been thirty minutes.'

'It's been hours, Burns. Hours at least. You must have hit your head.'

'How do I find you?'

'Just keep walking the way you're going— away from the fire and the ship. Visitors are crawling all over the mess you made of their pals at the stern. That wasn't smart, Burns. Not smart at all.'

'How will I find you?'

'Just keep walking.'

Adams sounded a bit too much like one of the creatures himself for my liking. Maybe I should have stomped on the phone after all.

'Here, Burns,' a voice said. It came from the trees on my right side.

I swung the rifle around.

A human form stepped towards me. He wore the same old-fashioned army khaki uniform as three weeks and three years before.

Beside him stood Lieutenant Ricci with the same pixie haircut.

I lowered the rifle's muzzle, but kept it ready, just in case.

'We've got a truck waiting about half a mile away,' said Adams. 'We better get there before they find us.'

But I didn't move.

'What's wrong now, Burns? What's the holdup?'

'You look different to three years ago.'

'It's us, Burns,' Adams said. 'Now put the rifle down. If you fire again, you'll just end up in another mess with the visitors. Or, the Navy MAs will show up. Then, you'll be in AONNB Holder again before you can say the word "inclusion."'

'That will never happen.'

'You don't think so? Believe me. Anything can happen these days.'

'He's right, Lieutenant,' said Ricci. 'You better come with us.'

From the north, the xylophone tones of the emergency vehicles drifted over the forest. To the south, the fire blazed orange in the night.

'Now or never,' said Adams. 'Join us in overthrowing the Accord or fight alone. Your choice.'

I wanted to inform him that it was Octavia, not the Accord who was the biggest danger. But this wasn't the time to argue. I was tired, hungry, and alone.

I made a decision.

'OK.'

'OK what?'

'Let's get to your truck.'

Adams turned and led the way.

Inside the truck and heading away, I said, 'Just how bad is it now compared to three years ago?'

Ricci sat in the front passenger seat beside

Adams.

'See for yourself,' she said.

The headlights lit up a roadside poster. It showed Octavia, as beautiful as ever, flanked by no less than three Accord commissioners: Commissioner Genet, Commissioner Rule, and Commissioner Gul, all in unisex Accord smocks, all smiling benignly. Around them loomed the gormless smiles of a dozen of the creatures from the forest.

The poster's headline read, 'Greater diversity. Greater strength. On 26 Avital 249, T.E.D. goes intra-galactic.'

'What's that about? What's 26 Avital?'

'It's a new international holiday this week.'

'But what's Avital?'

'It's the new name for April,' said Ricci. 'The Accord renamed all the months after pre-Accord feminist scholars. Next year, they'll announce the new names for the days of the week. The seasons too.'

'What's the holiday for?'

'To celebrate Intra-galactic Diversity Day,' said Ricci. 'Admiral Octavia will finally have her swearing-in ceremony.'

'But didn't all that happen three years ago?'

'No, Burns. Didn't you know she went away?' said Ricci. 'She left for three years, like you. And then when she returned, the Accord commission decided to hold the whole thing all over again next week: the Intra-galactic Diversity Day, the official launch of the new greeting, and the swearing in of Octavia. They also decided to make it the same day as the opening of the new territories.'

'The new territories?'

'The new territories set aside for the visitors.'

'How many territories?'

'Forty, at least.'

'Forty?'

'Yep. Some are the size of the former states.'

I sat there as the car rolled through the night. So much had happened. So much needed to be thought out. The Accord had scheduled its ceremony to take place in a few days' time. It would be just Octavia's style to make it the same day on which she landed her forces and began the destruction of the cities, rivers, oceans, atmosphere, and native inhabitants.

'Burns!' said Adams's voice.

'What?' I said.

'Are you asleep?'

'I'm here. What's going on?'

'Why do you keep reaching up to that pocket, Burns? What's in it?'

I didn't answer.

'Burns? Did you hear me? What's in your pocket? Look! You're touching it again. It's like you've got a nervous complaint. You're twitchy. You can't keep your hand away from it. What happened to you up there?'

I didn't want to talk about my pocket. The closer I came to Octavia, the more dangerous it was to even mention the shale. I didn't want to even think about it. Thinking about it meant that she would know about it too. She would read my mind, or at the very least locate me. I couldn't let that happen. Not yet. Not after all that had happened. Not after all the deaths.

'Burns!' Adams said. 'What's in your pocket?'

'Nothing.'

'That's a lot of attention you're giving to nothing. What is it, Burns?'

He wouldn't let it drop. I was too tired to lie. I was also hungry, exhausted, and pissed at the way an invasion had already begun by stealth.

So, I said, 'It's the stuff that freedom is made of.'

'And what's that?' Adams scoffed.

'I'll tell you when this is over.'

'Over? When what's over?'

'Octavia,' I said, not meaning to say the name. 'When Octavia is over.'

PART FOUR: SINISTRA

'All lives matter, however, some lives matter more than others. The lives of intra-galactic visitors matter most. The lives of people descended from the pre-Accord West matter least, and the lives of males in this category matter least of all.'

The Accord Roman Synergy Treaty,
Year 250, The Accord of Nations Era

66

I met Adams and Ricci in Adams's kitchen in
what he called his 'safe house' on the fringes of
AON sub-territory Pankhurst about twenty miles
from the outskirts of AON sub-territory Los
Angeles and about forty miles from the AON
Headquarters where the Intra-Galactic Diversity
Day Celebrations would take place.

Adams and Ricci sat at a table watching the
Unity TV news. The news anchor reported that
the meteor sighted over AON sub-territory
California overnight had crashed to earth in a
wilderness area near AON sub-territory Omar.
The local Harmony Police declared the area off-
limits to Accord members. Designated groups,
however, could access it, but so far, the only
group permitted to go theres was 'intra-galactic
visitors.'

Someone else was also in the kitchen. One of
the 'resistance' members stood at the stove
stirring a pot with a wooden ladle. He was in his

forties, maybe, and in good shape, slim, and almost my height. He wore a t-shirt and pants with pockets that had loops on them.

He offered a smile. 'U.A.D., Lieutenant.'

'Morning,' I said. I had forgotten what U.A.D. meant.

'Soy porridge OK?' the guy asked.

'Soy porridge? Great,' I lied.

'We can't get any other kind if that's what you're wondering, but at least it's the best.' He held up a box. It had the brand name 'Soyalty,' and an image of several young Accord members standing with their hands on their hearts in front of the Accord flag. No families or parents present, of course.

'Soy porridge is fine with me,' I lied again. It wasn't the time to be choosy. I had to get busy.

'Coming up,' said the guy. 'I'm Rourke, by the way.'

'Thanks, Rourke. I'm Burns.'

'I know who you are. We all liked what you did in AON sub-territory Hong Kong.'

'Thanks. So you saw it?'

'Saw what?'

'The creature in the harbor—the monster?'

'What creature in the harbor? I didn't see any creatures in the harbor. We just liked the way you stole the Slingshot off the ship.'

'Have a seat, Alex,' said Ricci. 'Did you sleep OK?'

'Best sleep in years. What's U.A.D.?'

'It means "Until the Accord is defeated."'

445

'Until the Accord is defeated,' I said.

'You don't like it?' said Adams. 'Well, too bad.' His resentment was up bright and early.

'I didn't say that. Anything is better than T.E.D. and T.E.I.D.'

'That's your comment? It's better than T.E.D.? That's all? So, I guess you don't like it.'

I let this pass. I needed Adams's help. Getting him worked up wouldn't make him any more helpful.

'You shaved off your beard,' said Ricci.

'I'm glad to be rid of it. It drove me crazy with itches.'

'It's amazing,' Ricci said. 'You look just like that movie actor—the one who always plays the bad guys. Even with that scar.'

I sensed Adams's resentment rising, so I decided to head him off. 'Thanks for the razor, Adams, and the clothes.' I patted the shirt and stroked the sleeves. I also patted the top pocket for the twentieth time that morning. The lump of shale waited in its cloth.

'The shirt's too small,' said Ricci. 'The sleeves don't cover your wrists.'

Rourke put a steaming bowl of soy porridge onto the table in front of me. I dipped in a spoon. As usual, the soy porridge tasted like defeat. 'Delicious,' I said. Then I turned to Ricci. 'What's the news?'

'You don't know?' said Adams.

I had been away for three years and didn't know what day it was, let alone what the morning headlines said. Adams didn't wait for a reply. He turned up the volume on the TV.

We all watched in silence. Up came a story featuring the mournful creatures I'd seen in the forest. This time they had joined with a commissioner in opening a Centre for Anti-Toxicity and had dressed their long and droopy limbs in Accord rainbow smocks, pants, and Accord unisex peaked caps.

'Are those things all over AONT USA now?'

'Not everywhere,' said Ricci, 'just the cities the commission designated as being sanctuary cities. Pankhurst is one of them. Those "things," as you call them, are all over town. Look out the window. Sooner or later, you'll see one.'

Next came a series of Accord adverts, all made to strict guidelines. As usual, cisgendered men acted as carers for children or gave testimonies for gender transitioning services. Those who identified as female acted as Harmony officers and military personnel. They never appeared inside homes, and never, ever as mothers with families.

'What am I supposed to be watching?'

'Nothing,' said Adams. 'It's just the news.' He turned the TV volume down. Then, he said, 'Do you want to talk about the resistance group's capabilities now? You want to hear about personnel, locations, and weapons? We're up to a thousand trained fighters now.'

I pushed the bowl of soy porridge away.

'OK. Can the group get me close to Octavia

during the initiation ceremony?'

Adams sat in silence, frowning at me.

'You don't want to know about the group. Don't you know what's at stake?'

'I know what's at stake.'

'Don't you know what we're about? Rourke gave you a clue: U.A.D. It means until the Accord is defeated. That's our aim. What's wrong? You don't like it?'

'Sure. It's a great aim. The Accord must be overthrown, but.'

'But what?'

Time to stop being pleasant.

'It's no use overthrowing the Accord now.'

'Oh, and why's that?'

'We're going to be ruled by the Romans or the visitors or whatever they're called these days, not the Accord.'

'The visitors! They're not a problem. They'll go along with whatever government we choose. They just want their sanctuary areas. The admiral said so herself. The visitors are not the problem. The problem is the Accord, the same as always.'

'Are you sure? Octavia's about to become a commissioner. More Roman commissioners will be elected. They'll make laws to suit themselves. Then what will we do?'

Adams sat up in his chair and pulled it closer to the table.

'You think you know everything, don't you? Well, you don't, Burns. You haven't been here for three years. If you had, you would know that the problem is not the visitors. It's the Accord. That's who we're fighting. The Accord. That's who we're planning to take down.'

'Listen, Adams. I want to be free of the Accord as much as you do, but we've got to see the major problem here: the invaders.'

'Invaders? You mean "the visitors."'

'They're invaders, Adams. Visitors leave. Invaders stay and take over. That's what's happening here. We've got to be free of them first before anything else. Despite what the Accord says on Unity TV, this not a time for tolerance. The invaders are not friendly. They don't believe in Accord values. They will not integrate. They will organize, gain political power, and then sweep us aside.'

'Sweep us aside?' said Ricci. 'That's a bit dramatic, isn't it?'

'Maybe it's not dramatic enough. I can put it in more detailed terms. How about they'll kill us, exterminate us, eradicate us, just like pests, and then they'll start on the planet, changing the oceans and forests.'

'You're paranoid, Burns. None of that can happen. For one thing, the visitors want to integrate. Second, they need our help.'

'Need our help how, and for what?'

'Admiral Octavia said they need our advice on how to live here harmoniously both with the people and with nature. She said they don't want to repeat any mistakes they made on their own planet with global warming.'

'Well, that's not what Admiral Octavia said to me.'

'And what did she tell you?' said Adams.

'She said they don't need us and don't want us. Not even to serve them. They just want the planet so they can change it to suit themselves. We're in the way. Also, global warming didn't happen on their planet. She's lying to flatter the commissioners.'

'But what about T.E.D.? She said they admire our values.'

'Their idea of progress isn't the same as the Accord's. Just because they're an older civilization doesn't mean they value T, E, and D. They'll get rid of us when it suits them. You should see what's waiting in their flotilla out there in the solar system. Believe me, it's not Accord smocks and goodwill.'

'But they're all about harmony, aren't they?' said Ricci. They live with the Goths on their own planet. They know about tolerance and living in peace with others.'

'No, the Goths retreated to a part of the planet the Romans can't go.'

'What do you mean "can't go"?'

'That part of the planet is toxic to them.' I reached for my top pocket again.

Adams shook his head. Apparently, I just didn't get things.

'So you think we can just get rid of the visitors, Burns? Just like that. We just tell them to go away? Is that it? Or maybe, you'll take them all on with a PQ47 and then they'll pack up and go.'

'I'm working on an idea.'

'An idea! Oh, great! An idea! Now we can all relax. Would you care to tell Ricci and me about your idea, or aren't we experienced enough to appreciate its brilliance?'

It had been a mistake to mention my plans. The more I talked about them, the more likely it was Octavia would find out. I should have known any idea would sound crazy to Adams and Ricci. I should have walked out of the kitchen. But I couldn't. I needed Adams's help. As much as I wanted to work alone, I needed his help to be ready in time for Octavia's ceremony.

'I'm sorry. It's not that I don't want to tell you. It's that I can't. Not yet.'

'Why not?'

'I can't explain. I'd tell you if I could.'

'Why can't you explain?'

'I just can't. It would affect the mission.'

'Oh great. So, you want us to change all our plans and priorities, but you can't tell us your own plan. What is it? Just you against them? You're one guy, Burns. Hasn't anyone told you that?'

I ignored him. Time was wasting. The ceremony was in two days. 'Do you have a gunsmith?'

'A gunsmith? Why would we need a gunsmith? We use stolen ordnance—from the Navy base.'

'No gunsmith?'

'You think this is the pre-Accord era, Burns? That we melt our own metal and make our own bullets?'

'OK. So, you don't use a gunsmith. Got it. But do you know where I could find one?'

'But we do have a gunsmith,' said Ricci. 'Or we did. But we don't need his services now because of all the ordnance.'

'Does he live near here?' I asked.

'The other side of town, I think.'

'Can you message him?'

'We don't use texts in case we're monitored. It's better to just go talk to him.'

'Good. Got any ammunition here with you?'

'Some.'

'OK. Grab all the PQ47 rounds you have. Then, let's get going. Thanks for the porridge, Rourke.'

'More if you want it.'

'No. No, thank you.'

'Shouldn't you rest longer, Alex?' said Ricci.

'I'll rest when it's over.'

'Wait a minute,' said Adams.

I sighed, sensing another argument coming, but instead, Adams said, 'You ought to listen to this, Burns.'

He turned up the volume on the TV. Octavia came up, talking to a reporter. She stood in front of the Accord headquarters in AON sub-territory Los Angeles. She wore one of the Accord Commission smocks. Her hair was up in its familiar bun shape. She was beautiful, as always.

I sat down to watch.

'I'm looking forward to meeting again,' Octavia said. 'I know you're here, so it won't be long.'

The reporter's microphone tilted from Octavia.

'You mean the commissioners, Admiral?' the reporter asked. 'The commissioners are here.' The microphone tilted back to Octavia.

'I'm looking forward to so many things, especially to some big surprises which I'll announce right after I'm sworn in.'

'Big surprises, Admiral? Can you give us a hint?'

'I'd like to, but everyone will have to wait a little longer. However, I can tell you this: that the first Intra-galactic Diversity Day will be unforgettable, a day everyone will remember. I'd like also to restate how much I'm looking forward to meeting you again. Very, very soon.'

'Did she say what I thought she said?' This was Ricci speaking. 'If I didn't know better, I'd say she was talking to you, Alex, like she could see you through the TV screen. Did you see it, Adams, or is it just me?'

Rourke spoke from over at the stove. 'How can she look like that but the rest of them look like swamp trees?'

Adams ignored him, but he must have noticed something. 'What are you not telling us, Burns?'

'Like I said, I'll tell you all about it when this is over.'

'Where were you the last three years? Why can't you tell us what you did and what you saw?

If we're going to help you, we have a right to know.'

'Can you turn that off, Rourke?' I said.

When the TV screen was blank, I turned to Adams. 'I'm sorry, but I can't tell you till it's over.'

'And when will that be?'

'That depends on how fast you get me to that gunsmith.'

'Why do you need him? Or can't you tell us that either?'

'OK,' I said. 'I can tell you that much. I want him to make me PQ47 bullets using a new kind of metal.'

67

A day later, we drove from Pankhurst to AON sub-territory Los Angeles, after collecting the ammunition from the gunsmith, an older guy Ricci and Adams called Sky.

Sky hadn't liked the sound of the job. He squinted at the shale as I held it out to him in its red cloth, and then he squinted up at me and my new scar, and said, 'What is this stuff?' and then, 'Where do I know you from?' and, 'Who or what are you going to shoot?'

Ricci stepped in. She told Sky the shale bullets would aid the cause of U.A.D., and that it was safer for him if he didn't know what the 'stuff' was or who I happened to be.

So, shaking his head, Sky consented. Then, Ricci repeated what I'd told her on the drive there. She told Sky to be careful to use only half the metal lump, not to waste even a scraping, and not to sniff it, and especially not to taste it, and to wash his hands afterwards with disinfectant soap.

After hearing that, Sky changed his mind. He said, 'You'll have to find another gunsmith.' But Ricci asked me and Adams to leave for a few minutes, and then after some quiet words, Sky changed his mind back again. Ricci's pixie looks were hard to resist and Sky was only a male after all.

Afterward, he sawed the shale in two with a hacksaw, and handed me one half. We left him to his task and returned later to collect twelve shale bullets packed in a small cardboard box in three neat rows of four.

Meanwhile, I carried the leftover lump of shale in my top pocket, wrapped in its cloth. I tried not to think about the shale and the bullets and whether twelve rounds would be enough for the task. They would have to be enough. They were all I had. There was no other way.

We parked Adams's Rainbow van at a lookout high in the hills. I borrowed Adams's binoculars and scanned the city, searching out the location where the Intra-galactic Diversity Day celebrations would take place, and where I could hide with the PQ47, the alien rifle, the shale bullets, and take my aim at the Accord of Nations' newest and first intra-galactic commissioner.

The city of AON sub-territory Los Angeles was mostly low-rise buildings spreading west all the way from the foot of the hills to the AONO Pacific. It was hard to say whether the trees dominated the buildings or the other way round.

The trees and the light brown houses were evenly mixed, like bread cubes in a green salad.

Downtown, a cluster of curious buildings rose above the rolling green and brown. Some of these buildings were tall, others low and wide, some rounded, and some like cubes with their edges sanded to gentle curves. The buildings made up the city's administration zone and were homes for the innumerable Accord departments.

All the buildings were in the TEDIST architectural style. The TEDIST philosophy rejected pre-Accord-era ideas of building design of thrusting, sharp-edged towers that oppressed everyone who lived in them, or looked at them.

TEDIST buildings respected oppressed peoples. Their curved sides were as unimposing as possible—no thrusting spires; no excessive height; no sharp corners, no harsh-reflective glass.

At the center of the TEDIST cluster stood the Accord of Nations Headquarters, the epitome of the TEDIST philosophy. It was curved and non-masculine, like a narrow egg with its top sliced off into a plateau. No one dared say what the building actually resembled, which was a forbidden pre-Accord-era sex device.

The AON Headquarters was at the center of the city's famous circular web of streets that had been built after a severe earthquake devastated the city in 183 AONE. Its address was the most famous in the city if not the entire Accord: The Steps to Equity, 2020 The Avenue of

Revolutionary Feminists.

The headquarters loomed in the binoculars, standing tall in a clutter of buns, cups, upturned plates, and hats—not that anyone dared call these famous structures anything but 'inspiring.'

'You think you'll find a vantage point, Alex?' said Ricci. 'The area around the Steps to Equity will be swarming with Harmony Officers. They'll be on every street corner and rooftop.'

'And how will you do the deed?' said Adams. 'That PQ47 isn't a sniper rifle and those bullets are no good over a long range. Do you honestly think you could hit the target, even up close? If you do, your brain is more damaged than I thought.'

'I'm a reasonable shot.'

'No one's a reasonable shot with a PQ47,' said Adams. 'What will happen is that you'll fire, you'll miss, and you'll end up hitting a commissioner. Then, every Harmony Officer in the country will come searching for me, Ricci, and our group. You see that, don't you?'

I put the binoculars down.

'For what I'm planning, I don't need to be far away. I just need a clear view of the target.'

'The target?' Adams smirked. 'You think the target's going to come up to you and say, "Shoot me, Burns. Shoot me. I'll put my hands up for you"?'

'No, but I think I can get close enough to complete the shot.'

'How, Burns? How will you get that close?'

'I can't tell you. Not yet. But I will when it's over, like I said.'

'And what if you succeed, Burns? What then? The Romans, the visitors—they'll just pack up all the equipment they unloaded over the past three years, and go somewhere else?'

'I don't know. But they won't do anything unless we force them.'

'What if they don't have anywhere else to go?'

'They do have somewhere else, a more suitable planet than ours.'

'How do you know?'

'That's what they told me, or at least, what one of them told me.'

'Brain-damaged,' said Adams. 'It's too much, Burns. And it's not right. It's not what our resistance group is about. To be honest, I don't think we should have any part of this any longer. And if you take my advice, neither will you.'

I turned to Ricci.

'Do you also think I'm brain damaged?'

'I agree with Adams. You overestimate your chances and your abilities. The odds are against you, Alex. You're just one guy. If you fail, we'll be the ones to suffer the consequences.'

I looked at the cluster of buildings, keeping my mouth shut.

'So why don't you wait?' Ricci said. 'Then we can get more people involved. We can plan. We can distribute authority. We can multiply our efforts. You know what they say: "The individual is nothing. The group is all."'

'There's no time. It has to be tomorrow before Octavia's announcement, her big surprise, which I think will be her order to attack our cities and land her transports.'

'You sure?'

'Almost certain.'

'Why can't you tell us about that chunk of metal in your top pocket?'

'Like I said. I want to but I can't. Not till it's over.'

'Why?' said Adams. 'Do you think we'll warn her? That we're spies? Is that it?'

'Are you spies?'

'Just tells us what's going on, Burns.'

'Not till the ceremony's over.'

'When you've failed, you mean. When you've brought the Harmony Officers down on us?'

I ignored him. 'Let's get going.'

'You haven't even scouted a position,' said Adams.

'I know.'

'But where's your vantage point? Which rooftop? Which building? What street? How will you avoid the Harmony Officers? How will you get close enough carrying a bag of guns?'

'I won't need to.'

'What are you going to do, fly?'

'I don't have a J-Pack if that's what you mean.'

'So, how?'

'You two just get me as close as you can. I'll take it from there. Your group doesn't have to get involved. You can just melt away. You never saw me. You never heard from me.'

'So you're going to shoot from street level? Is that what you're saying? You're going to walk up the Avenue of Revolutionary Feminists carrying two rifles, one of which is an alien bazooka, and then with thousands of Harmony Officers and thousands of military personnel all around, and the whole of the Accord watching on TV, you're going to drop to one knee, take aim and hit your target from two thousand yards away, and your target just happens to be the Accord's VIP guest and the first intra-galactic commissioner? Is that the plan?'

'Let's just get moving,' I said.

'Brain-damaged,' said Adams. 'Wherever you've been for the last three years, it's messed with your head. You're just one guy and you think you're going to change the course of history. You know that, right? You're just one guy, and one guy who is going to fail.'

'So they tell me.'

68

The night before Intra-galactic Diversity Day, I cleaned the PQ47 rifle and loaded the magazine with the shale bullets.

I sat on a table outside another of Adams's safe houses. This time in Smollett Canyon, another section of the hills behind AON sub-territory Los Angeles.

As usual for AON sub-territory California, the temperature was cold—cold enough for Ricci to hand me one of Adams's crew-necked, synthetic wool sweaters. The Unity TV weather forecast for Intra-galactic Diversity Day tomorrow was for heavy rain.

But I didn't want to think about tomorrow. Not because I didn't have to prepare as much as possible, but because I didn't want Octavia reading my thoughts. What a paradox! I had to plan the attack, but I couldn't plan in detail. I couldn't even think about a vantage point from where I'd take the shot.

I would have to improvise on the run, as

usual.

As I cleaned the PQ47, I tried to think of other things—of anything at all. I thought about the PQ47 and its habit of slipping from semi automatic to burst mode; the Goths charging into gunfire without fear; Karz's heroism; Ricci's pixie hair; Ricci's lingering hand as she offered me Adams's sweater; the sickening sight of Granak's eye fluids soaking the hot dust; the leviathan Gwantasnarr groaning in the dark forest; Octavia's beauty; Octavia's power; the outrage in her voice when she discovered the secret.

Octavia! How much did I really know about her? I knew some things for sure: that she was dangerous, unstable, and obsessive. I also knew that she wasn't entirely mad either. She had led her people from Rome to a new home planet; she had charmed the Accord Commission through flattery and reason; and she commanded millions of sailors and Marines on thousands of ships. No, she wasn't entirely mad; she was sane-mad, or mad-sane, which made her far more dangerous.

What about the rest of the Romans—did they support her or was there a chance they would rebel, like Janasta and the other pilots? Maybe they too believed that Elysium was the better planet colonization. And what of Octavia's lieutenant, Drusilla, and her officers aboard the Excidium? Would they rebel if pushed too far?

I reassembled the PQ47, then put the rifle aside and took in the night view below. The great city of AON sub-territory Los Angeles spread far and wide. The strands of low-wattage streetlights radiated to the north, and to the foot of the Smollett Hills here in the east. To the west, they reached almost out of sight.

I thought about all the millions of Accord members in all the houses and apartments. If Unity TV could be believed, these people all welcomed Octavia, just as every Accord member around the world welcome her too. They eagerly anticipated her arrival and millions like her—all without the least awareness of the imminent destruction. The Accord told them Octavia was a good thing, and the Accord always knew best.

At the web's center, the cluster of buildings had been lit to mark the occasion of Intra-galactic Diversity Day. The tall egg of Accord Of Nations was visible even from the Smollett Hills thanks to a series of animated projections on its curved sides.

First came images from the new Accord flag. Rainbow stripes, doves, and planets swirled around each other, then came together to form the new flag itself: a dove sitting on a rainbow, surrounded by planets on a brown background. The view zoomed out to show the flag rippling in the breeze.

Then the flag faded away. The faces of Accord commissioners came forward, one by one, in order of their rank on the Oppression Hierarchy. First came the disabled transgender commissioner from AON Friedan Isles. Next came the image of the intersex commissioner from AONT Nadler (known in the pre-Accord era as Antarctica). And on they came all the way through to the very last commissioner to step forward, the commissioner representing AONT Eurabia.

And then came the finale: an image of Octavia Caesar herself. There she stood, feminine and approachable. Beside her, the other commissioners looked shabby, pale, and sickly. Normally, such obvious beauty drew accusations of internalized patriarchy, but in Octavia's case no one would dare. Octavia was a visitor, and therefore so diverse that she ranked at the very top of the Oppression Hierarchy, along with the Goths. She was beyond criticism.

For a moment, we gazed into each other. She, the stateswoman with all the power and corruption of the Accord commission behind her; and me, the outsider with two rifles and the illegal belief that the world would be better off without Accord commissions and alien invaders.

I picked up the heavy, alien rifle and checked the magazine. The less I thought about Octavia, the better. Same with the visual display of the Accord commissioners and the new flag. It had been a mistake to come outside at all.

I was about to take the rifles inside when footsteps padded across the lawn. Ricci sat beside me. She held up two glass tumblers, each filled with a swirling brown liquid, and clinking ice cubes.

'Here, take this,' she said, but her eyes were on

the image of Octavia. 'Look at her. She's such a beautiful female-identifying person. Surely her intentions are good. Are you really sure you're doing the right thing?'

69

At another time, I could have made a joke about Ricci's last remark. It was against Accord values to assume women were kind and good-hearted. It was also against Accord values to comment on a woman's appearance, especially in praise. It was even worse to link good looks with good intentions. But now wasn't the right time to make jokes. Instead, I held up the sports bag holding the rifles, the only things that mattered for the moment.

'It's getting late,' I said.

'Wait. Don't go yet, Alex,' said Ricci. 'Try this first. It'll help you relax.'

She held out the tumbler.

'What is it?'

'It's called rum. Try it.'

'It's called what?'

'Rum. It's a pre-Accord alcoholic drink. It's made by distilling sugarcane juice. Our contact, Green Forest gets it from another contact in AON sub-territory Jamaica. It's illegal, of course, just like all sugary drinks. Take a sip. It'll calm your nerves.'

'I'm calm. See my hands?'

'Come on. Just try it. One sip.'

I set the bag of rifles beside the chair and sat down. Then, I took the glass from Ricci's long, cool fingers. I lifted it and tilted it. The ice cubes rattled. The rum burned like fuel, but after a few moments, it tasted sweet.

'Thanks.'

'Have some more.'

'I'll have some later.'

We sat in silence. I opened the bag and took out the PQ47 again. I pulled the cleaning cloth from my pocket and ran it over the stock and barrel. Ricci watched me for a while, then said, 'So, you're still convinced?'

'About what?'

'About tomorrow—that it's the right action.'

'It's the only action.'

'Doesn't it bother you that no one else would agree, that people in the Accord like the Romans and the diversity they bring?'

'No. They won't like anything about them when they know the truth.'

'Have you heard there's even talk of the Accord opening restaurants serving visitor food? That's got to be a good thing, right?'

'Romans don't eat. They must be lying.'

'That's not what Admiral Octavia said. She told the commission that people would love Roman restaurants.'

'People won't like the Romans or their restaurants when the visitors start killing everyone.'

'But you don't know that, Alex, do you?'

'That's Octavia's plan. She told me. Twice.'

'She hasn't acted on it. You might do all this for no reason. Imagine if you're wrong.'

'I'm not wrong.'

'But you might be.'

'I'm not.'

'Adams says you're not thinking straight. He thinks you're suffering from burnout or some stress-related illness from your experiences in space. What's so funny?'

'Burnout!,' I said. 'I don't believe in burnout. It's just another word the Accord uses to coerce people or coax them into thinking they need more help from the Accord. It's like when they say they want to keep us safe for some reason, and then impose a lockdown of some kind.'

'Isn't being kept safe a good thing?'

'It's matter of degree. Driving a car isn't safe. Swimming in the sea isn't safe. Being alive isn't safe. If all we wanted was to be safe, we'd never leave our homes, and we'd never do anything. And that's not living. Living is doing things. Living is taking calculated risks. Living means accepting that there might be consequences of actions. Living means being responsible for the consequences if the actions turn out bad. That's living. That's being alive. Safe!—how I hate the word. And how I hate the abuse of it by the

Accord.'

'Hey! Calm down! You're getting worked up. I'm with you. I don't like the Accord either. What do you think Adams and I are doing with our lives? We're with you, even if you push us away.'

'Sorry,' I said. 'I'm tired. That's all.'

Ricci took another sip of the rum and watched the display on the Accord Headquarters go round its cycle of the flag, the commissioners, and Octavia's serene gaze.

After the night air soothed away the tension, Ricci said, 'And what if you fail?'

'I don't think I will.'

'Yes, you do.'

'If I fail, I'll know that I served the people, and that I didn't submit to the Accord or the aliens.'

'Serious words for a twenty-nine-year-old.'

'Twenty-six.'

'Even more serious.'

'These are strange times, I said. 'We have a corrupt government oppressing the people. We have a population that craves being oppressed. We have alien invaders waiting to bring in billions of their own who'll kill us all; and if that's not enough, we have rampant bear-wolf monsters tearing around in spaceships. All of us should talk seriously, as seriously as we can, as seriously as people have ever talked about anything.'

She smiled. 'I'm just wondering why.'

'Why what?'

'Why you?'

That question again, the same as Janasta had

asked, and the same question I asked myself. I imagined my ancestor on the deck of his great ship, watching and waiting for my answer, wondering if I believed what he told me about 'the family trade.'

I pushed the image of him aside.

'Because no one else will and then it will be too late.'

'OK, but what if you didn't try? What if you chose not to go out there tomorrow? What if you stayed alive instead? What if you waited to find out what happens first?'

'I know what will happen.'

'You're still convinced?'

'I have to be.'

I set the PQ47 down. I wanted Ricci to believe. I could make her believe if I told her what I'd seen and heard. But I was too tired, too travel-weary, too angry, and I had a traitorous mind. If I stared arguing now, I might lose my resolve.

'I have to be,' I said again.

Ricci watched the display on the AON Headquarters. Octavia came up again, smiling and irresistible. 'She's very beautiful,' Ricci said, ignoring Accord values again. 'Her long hair. No cisgendered female has hair that long in the Accord. Do you like it that way?'

'No, I like your hair.' I was going to mention its pixie quality, but kept quiet. Ricci might have been a member of her Accord resistance group, but that didn't mean she wouldn't denounce me for sexual harassment.

'I'm talking about Octavia's hair,' she said.

'Don't be fooled,' I said. 'She's dangerous.'

'But why? Why is she dangerous?'

'Something from her past. The pilot on the ship told me about it. That's besides being an alien, of course—an alien with different values from ours. She and the other aliens don't believe in T.E.I.D., no matter what she says. Her culture is a military culture with military objectives which are to leave their home planet, conquer ours, and transform it.'

'What thing from her past?'

'I'll tell you when tomorrow's over.'

'You say you have spoken to her. Did you ever try reasoning with her?'

'You can't reason with her.'

Ricci smiled.

'What?'

'I can understand why she likes you.'

'Why?'

'For one reason, you really are just like that actor. I've told you that already, right? The guy from the movies about the pre-Accord era. Everyone says so, don't they? What's the guy's name again?'

'I don't know. Holistic someone or Diversity somebody. One of those respectable, actor kinds of names.'

'Why don't you come a little closer?'

Ricci put her arm around my neck and pulled herself towards me. The ice in her rum glass clinked.

'Why are you holding your hands like that?'
she said. 'You think I'll accuse you of sexual
assault? Well, don't. I'll sign the release form. I
promise.'

'No.'

'Then what?'

'Machine oil.'

She smiled. Our lips touched. She reached for
my shirt. Her fingers curled just beside the pocket
holding the shale. Then she pulled herself closer.
She was beautiful and gentle. Any man would
want her. And yet, even at that moment, my
thoughts drifted to that other woman's beauty,
her desirability, the heat and strength of her.

'I liked you since we first met,' Ricci
whispered. 'Even in that cell.'

But then, that other woman's voice spoke in
my head.

Her voice.

Alex! it said. Alex.

'What's wrong?' said Ricci.

'Nothing,'

Alex. I see what you do.

'What is it? Something's wrong.'

'No. It's… it's…'

'Are you OK?'

'No. I mean, yes, I'm OK. It must be this
drink.'

I stood up.

'The rum?'

'Don't worry. It's not you, Ricci. It's…'

'Is it her? Is that what you mean?'

Across at the Accord of Nations headquarters, Octavia's giant image shone out in the dark.

'Is she's doing it again, like in the kitchen yesterday?'

I see you.

She was deep in my mind.

I'm looking forward to meeting you again.

I picked up the rifle.

'Hey!' said Ricci.

'Let's get away from that.'

'From what?'

'From that.'

'It's just an image on a building, Alex.'

'Yeah. Wouldn't it be nice to think so?'

70

'But where is he?' I asked.

'He's gone away, Alex.'

'But where? Where has he gone?'

I was back at my childhood home again. We were in the kitchen. Kresta was there. It was after school. She had just been talking on her handheld. Now, she was kneeling in front of me, her hands on my shoulders. It was two days since the Harmony Officers took Cal away.

'Where?' I asked. 'Where did they take him?'

'I don't know, Alex. They wouldn't tell me.'

'Why not? Why wouldn't they tell you?'

'Sometimes the Accord is like that. They keep things secret for our protection.'

'But why?'

'It's to keep us safe.'

'Aren't we safe already?'

Kresta got up and walked to the kitchen bench. She pulled a tissue from the box and dabbed at her face. 'Why don't we have something to eat?' she said. 'I have those new tofu burgers. You like those, don't *you?'*

I had been doing my homework on the kitchen table. The homework was about Oppression Hierarchy. I had to color in a drawing of the different kids in the Accord and where they were on some kind of ladder thing. The one kid that looked like me was at the hierarchy's bottom. He was smiling, which was weird because the other kids, the ones higher up the ladder, looked sad, like they didn't want to be there.

'Alex, you like the tofu burgers, right?' Kresta said. It was so weird how she didn't look at me, and that she didn't she tell me about Cal? 'After dinner, we can watch Unity TV. Have you heard there's a new channel for young Accord members?'

'No.'

'I think it's called U Kids. You know, like "Unity kids," but also "You kids." Funny, right? They say the first episode is about the Accord and its path to happiness for every young member to follow.'

I had been coloring the drawing with a green crayon. I put it down.

'Why did they take Cal away?'

Kresta looked through the window, then went back to the stove. She opened the refrigerator and pulled things out.

'They said he has to learn about the Accord again. That's all.'

'Why can't he learn about the Accord here with us?'

'I don't know. That's what they said.'

'When is he coming back?'

She put the frypan on the stove.

'Kresta, when is he coming back?'

She turned a nob on the stove. 'I don't know Alex, but they said a while.'

'How long? Next week?'

'No longer than that.'

'The week after?'

'Alex, enough.'

'Well how long?'

She switched off the stove and walked around. She knelt down in front of me again. Her face very serious.

'A long time. A very long time.'

'Longer than my next birthday?'

'Longer than that Alex. We might not ever see Cal again.'

I didn't say anything. I was confused. I had a million more questions and didn't know what to ask. We wouldn't see Cal anymore. It couldn't be true. The room seemed to freeze. Kresta stood up and went to the kitchen again and pulled a tissue from the box and put it up to her face. Then, she opened another drawer.

'They had some other news, Alex. Some good news.'

'About dad? Can we go and see him?'

'Don't call him that.'

'About my father?'

'Please, Alex. I've told you about those words.'

'About Cal? Why can't we see Cal?'

'I got a call from Dr Iqbal. He said you don't have to take the pills anymore. The quota has changed. Cal did something to make them change their minds.'

'What's a quota?'

'It just means you don't have to take the pills.'

'Did Cal tell Dr Iqbal I don't have to take them? Is that why they took him away?'

'I don't know, Alex. Maybe.'

'Is it my fault they took him away?'

'No, Alex. Of course it's not your fault. Don't even think that.'

'When is he coming back?'

'Alex if you keep asking that I'm not going to answer you.'

'But why? Why can't you tell me why?'

'Because the Accord knows best, Alex. That's why.'

'No, it doesn't. Cal said the Accord never knows best.'

I picked up the crayon and smeared the drawing in green from top to bottom. Then, I looked up at Kresta. She looked angry or maybe frightened.

'Don't ever say that, Alex.'

'Why not?'

'Don't ever say it. Not at school, not to your friends, not to me, not even in your own thoughts.'

'But it's what Cal said.'

'Listen, Alex. If you keep doing what Cal said, you're going to end up in trouble like Cal's in trouble. There's a lot of things you don't understand. But you will when you're older. Right now you have to trust your . . . you have to trust me to keep you as safe as I can. It's not easy in the Accord for people like us.'

'Cal said I should join the navy. He said it's what our family always did. He said our family were heroes in the pre Accord.'

'Don't say hero and don't say pre-Accord either. You will get us both into trouble'

'He said I had to serve but not submit.'

'You don't know what that means.'

'But I will. I will understand.'

'It's all right, Alex. You can cry if you want. It's all right.'

'No. Boys don't cry.'

'Yes, they do, Alex. Of course they cry.'

'Well, they shouldn't. Ever.'

'Did Cal also tell you that?'

'I'm going to be in the navy.'

'No, Alex, you're not. It's not safe. I know it's hard, but you're young. Please trust me. Promise you'll never join the navy.'

I didn't say anything. I had another crayon out, the blue one. I didn't want to say anything more. Anything I said made Kresta go to the box of tissues. So, I said nothing.

After a while she said, 'What are you drawing?'

I put another big streak across the whole page of the Oppression Hierarchy, like I was covering it up. A big blue one, that took up the top third of the crayon. Then, I put the crayon on the kid at the bottom, the kid who looked like me.

'I don't think he's supposed to be colored blue, Alex.'

I colored him blue anyway, and I drew a blue hat on him. Then, I drew hard blue dots on him like he was wearing my father's uniform. Then I drew straight line under his feet and then sloping lines going down, and then wavy lines at the bottom that looked like water, and I kept on drawing and saying nothing and smearing more and more of the blue crayon onto the kid who was supposed to be me, and I didn't even notice when Kresta put a hand on my shoulder and *said wasn't I going to eat something.*

71

I woke at five-thirty a.m., six hours before I would fire the shale bullets at Octavia's upturned smile. I shook off the dream's grip. Then, I dealt with the first of the morning's obstacles: the heavy presence of dread.

Dread!

The one good thing about never having time to reflect before a battle was that dread had no time to whisper in my ear. The fight with Granak, the battle with the Roman Marines, and with Janasta —all of them had been thrust on me before dread could show up and start talking.

Not this time. Dread crouched by my bed in the dark, waiting for me to open my eyes. Now Dread started talking. It started warning me that if I went ahead with my plan, I would suffer, or worse, I would be captured, and then die decades later in a lonely cell in AONNB Jenner. Dread also showed me images of Earth under Octavia's merciless control.

I shook my head. I had to ignore Dread. I had

to take a sword to Dread, or maybe a spear. I had to kill it or I could never kill Octavia, the most dreadful enemy of all.

I got up, stretched, and dropped to the floor. Then, I strained my way through forty pushups and forty stomach crunches. My muscles complained and resisted. They were sore from my day and a half on Gwawanath, but I forced them to keep up, all the way to the last press of my knuckles into Adams's brown carpet.

I felt better when the pushups were over. Maybe it was because I'd followed my old routine, the one from AONNS Harmony, three months, and a lifetime ago. I knew that my old life was long gone and I could never turn to it, but the old drill gave me a sense of, I don't know, normality, I guess, which was something I hadn't felt for months.

Pushups and crunches done, I re-checked the weapons. The PQ47 and the alien rifle lay in their sports bag together, both gleaming. I almost wished them good morning. The two of them were my comrades in this struggle, and I imagined they too were preparing themselves for the day of dread.

Rifles preparing themselves! Next, I'd give them names: Destroyer for the PQ47; Devastator for the alien weapon; Liberators for the three kinds of ammunition. Together, the Destroyer, the Devastator, the Liberators, and I would complete our dangerous mission.

I stood there for a moment savoring this

daydream. Then I shook my head. It wasn't the right time for daydreams. I had to get my thinking straight. I had to get my mind right.

But I stood a moment longer in another kind of daydream. This time, my father Cal's words came back to me. 'Serve but don't submit,' he had shouted as the Harmony Officers dragged him away. 'Serve but don't submit.' I hadn't thought about that morning for years. Why had the memory come back to me? And why at that moment?

I shook it away. I'd think about it later. For the moment, I had other things to do. I picked up the PQ47 and checked its mechanism and the magazine loaded with the twelve shale bullets. All good. Then I lifted the alien rifle. Nothing to check, no ammunition to load, and no mechanism. I inspected its parts anyway: the heavy stock, the fire button, the long barrel, the various sights.

So far, so good.

Everything was ready—except my mind.

I zipped up the bag, put on Adams's civilian clothes, made sure the remaining lump of shale was wrapped up tight and buttoned into the top pocket where I could reach it. Then I went in search of Adams and Ricci.

Ricci wasn't in her room. She wasn't in the kitchen either. I saw her through the kitchen window, back out on the lawn, her back to me. She stood gazing over AON sub-territory Los Angeles and at the Accord headquarters. I went to the kitchen counter where a teapot stood waiting. I found a mug and poured myself a cup and then a second cup. Then, I went outside. Ricci turned and smiled a wary smile.

'Sleep well?' she asked.

'Enough.'

'You're tired.'

'I'm OK. Here, take this.'

'Thanks,' she said. 'Any bad dreams?'

'No. Why do you ask?'

'You like the tea?'

'Is that what it is?'

'It's the new blend called Comfort Tea. The finest in the Accord. What's the matter? Don't you like it? Maybe you should add some soy milk. It takes away the bitterness.'

'I don't drink soy milk, especially not today.'

We checked the weather. Heavy clouds had sailed in overnight from the AONO Pacific. They darkened the sky. The sides of the Accord Headquarters glowed bright and significant in the gloom. The video display was the same, looping over and over: the new flag, the parade of commissioners.

And Octavia.

Ricci spoke. 'The IDD celebrations have started in other time zones. Unity TV started showing them overnight. They broadcast from AON subterritory Kinshasa. Huge ceremony. Flags. Millions of people. Captain Drusilla. She gave a speech. She said great things are about to happen in the Accord. You've met her too, right?'

'Where is Adams?'

'Gone.'

'Why?'

'He didn't want any Harmony Office attention if things went wrong.'

'Do you think there's a chance he might have told the Harmony Officers about me?'

She frowned. 'Why would he do that?'

'Because he thinks I'm wrong. Because he's excluded. Because he doesn't like me. And because he likes you.'

'I don't think he would, Alex. He just didn't want to stay. He's worried about the group.'

'But you stayed.'

'Yeah,' she replied. 'I stayed.'

'So you agree with me now.'

'Yes, and no.'

'Which means?'

'It's yes, I agree with some things and no I don't agree with others.'

'It's a pity you're no longer in the Navy. With an answer like that, you'd be an admiral.'

'OK. I mean yes, if what you say about this Octavia is true.'

'It *is* true. Will you believe me when the first of the transport ships drops from the clouds, each one about the size of the city? That's what will happen.'

'But if they do come down, they'll be going to the new sanctuary territories, right?'

'Maybe, but I think they'll come here.'

'Why?'

'Octavia will want a big display of force."

'And so it's up to you and you alone to stop them and the only way to do that is by eliminating… the target. I know how it goes.'

I said nothing. Octavia was nearby. Better not to talk about the plan. Better not to even think about it.

Seconds later, a large raindrop hit my shoulder. Moments after that, two more drops smacked down, one on my neck, the other in Ricci's tea. Lightning flickered in the west, beneath the thunderheads.

'It's going to rain on the parade,' said Ricci.

'Good. It'll keep the crowds away.'

'Funny.'

'What is?'

'It's nothing to do with today.'

'So what is it?'

'Just something from the PAE—something people used to say.'

'What did they say?'

'That it never rains in the south of AON sub-territory California. It was a popular song way back then. But look at it now. It always rains, and it's usually cold.'

Time to go. I took one last look at Octavia's image on the Accord building. She stood there, tall and beautiful, gazing back at me, as if to say, 'See you soon.'

Ricci's phone rang. It was Adams. He told her that back in Pankhurst the swamp creatures were breaking into homes and attacking people in the main street. They had even vandalized the monument to the famous pre-Accord revolutionary, Emily Pankhurst after whom the town was named. Then they'd set fire to the statue of Ariel Hoskins, Captain Nolan's famous ancestor. The Harmony Officers hadn't stopped them. Unity TV ignored it all, of course. They would never 'other' the visitors by reporting on their crimes.

Today, it seemed, would be the biggest test yet for T.E.D.

And for me.

72

At midday, we drove the Rainbow van to the fringe of AON sub-territory Los Angeles. Above us, the rain clouds hid the network of teardrop-shaped ships in the sky. Beneath the clouds, Unity TV helicopters flew towards the Accord of Nations Headquarters. Other helicopters flew away from it. At least four more cruised at various heights.

We peered through the windshield at the drowned streets. Ricci was at the wheel. I was in the passenger seat. The rifles were in the sports bag in the back.

'So, where now?' she said.

'Turn here,' I said.

'Here? But this takes us straight to the Accord HQ.'

'Exactly.'

'You're really going through with this, aren't you?'

'Right.'

'It's not too late to rethink, Alex.'

'If you want to, just leave me here. I'll get there some other way.'

'I'm not bailing out yet.' She pressed the accelerator and turned the van into the Avenue of Revolutionary Feminists.

'Thanks,' I said.

'So where's your vantage point? Where are you going to take your shot?'

I didn't answer.

I didn't know.

The Avenue of Revolutionary Feminists lead directly to the Accord of Nations Headquarters. It passed through the whole TEDIST cluster of buildings and ended at the Steps to Equity.

'See the crowds in the distance, Alex? That's a lot of people. Even the rain hasn't kept them away. How will we ever get close enough?'

'Just keep going.'

'That's your plan? Just keep going?'

'Right. Just keep going, all the way, as close as you can get.'

Ricci shook her head. 'Failing to plan,' she said, 'is planning to fail? Every sailor knows.'

'Just keep going.'

'What if you don't find a vantage point, Alex?'

'But I will find one.'

'And what if you don't?'

'Then, there's always another way.'

'Why not try again when you have a plan? You told me you don't like thinking on the fly.'

'I don't. Never have. I hate it. But there's no time for anything else, and too much planning would only make this harder.'

'How?'

'Because then she would know?' I raised my chin at the watery image in the distance of Octavia's giant, serene face on the side of the AON HQ.

'How would she know? Can she read your mind?'

'Don't worry about my lack of plan. I'll find a way. Security won't be tight. They're not expecting any trouble. I'll be able to get close.'

Ricci shook her head.

'Alex, maybe Adams has a point.'

'Stop!' I said. 'Stop right here.'

Ricci pulled the van over.

'Listen. I know how it sounds. The plan or lack of plan is crazy, not thought out, doomed, reckless, a suicide mission. I get it. Completely. But that's the plan I'm following, for reasons I can't tell you yet. I don't expect you to come with me. I don't expect you to help. I'll understand if you want out of this. I'm grateful for what you and Adams have done. Take the van and go. Let me out here. I'll be fine. But if you want to stay, don't tell me to pull out.'

We faced each other: sane woman and wild man. Ricci put out a hand and touched my cheek with her fingers. Then, she turned back to the wheel, placed the van in gear, and drove on.

A mile along the Avenue of Revolutionary Feminists, we met the first of the roadblocks. Two Harmony Office patrol cars waited, their rainbow lights flashing. Two officers stepped into the middle of the avenue as we approached. One of them held up a palm and then pointed at a side lane with elaborate stabs of a finger. We slowed the van and pulled into the lane.

'Leave this to me,' said Ricci. 'I know how they think.'

'Don't say any more than you have to,' I said.

The Harmony Officer appeared to identify as a female of Ricci's age. She wore a rainbow slicker, streaming with rain. She leaned down to speak through the driver's window while the rain pattered on her hat. Then, following the Accord protocol, she ignored the male in the van and spoke to Ricci.

'T.E.I.D.,' said Ricci. 'It's a great day for the Accord and Accord values.'

'T.E.I.D.,' said the Harmony Officer. 'Yes, Accord member. A great day. The greatest day yet.'

Then, the Harmony Officer turned to me.

'T.E.I.D.,' I said.

'We made a wrong turn,' continued Ricci. 'We'll get out of your way. We didn't know there'd be roadblocks around the Accord headquarters.'

She reached for the gearshift.

'Wait,' said the Harmony Officer. 'A couple of things first.'

Ricci kept her hand on the wheel. 'Sure.'

'You're alone with a male without a third person present. I need to ask a few questions.'

'But everything's OK. We can just get out of your way.'

'Stay where you are. I have to ask the questions. You might be in this van under duress.'

'Sure, if you have to, but it's not necessary.'

'Did this male force you to drive this vehicle against your will?'

'No. I follow the Accord requirement that those who identify as females should never take a back seat. I'm driving because I want to drive. Females are better drivers, anyway, as we all know.'

'Has this male inflicted any unwanted sexual advances towards you today?'

'No. No unwanted sexual advances.'

'Good. We have to check that too. Trust and verify, right?'

'Trust and verify.'

'When any male is alone with a female, we have to investigate. You should know that, Accord member.'

'You're right,' said Ricci. 'I'll remember next time.'

'It's for your safety.'

'My safety. Right. Well, if that's all.'

'Wait!' said the Harmony Officer, placing a forearm on the window ledge. 'This male is familiar. I've seen him somewhere. What's his name?'

Ricci smiled. 'Yes, everyone says that about him. It's because of that actor. You know the one who plays the bad pre-Accord characters in the movies—the toxic male guy, the handsome guy?'

The Harmony Officer leaned closer. 'May I know your pronouns and your names?'

'My pronouns are zee, zer, and zaam. My name is,' Ricci hesitated. 'Inclusion. Inclusion Roberts. And this guy's pronouns are…'

'You used the word handsome,' said the Harmony Officer. 'Handsome is a non-approved pre-Accord-era word, zaam. It legitimizes the male gaze. If you know the Accord constitution, zaam, you'd also know about that word.'

Ricci made no reply.

'But yes,' said the Harmony Officer, 'he is like that pre-Accord actor guy. But I still need to check his ID. Show me your I.D., Accord member.'

'That's OK,' said Ricci. 'We'll get out of your way.' She reached for the shift and slotted it into reverse.

'Wait! I need that I.D.'

'We've taken up too much of your time. We'll get going.'

'Wait!' said the Harmony Officer. She'd just remembered a name—one that had been on top of a list three years ago and had dropped from interest. Now, here it was, back on top again.

'Stop the vehicle! Turn off the engine.'

'No need, Officer,' said Ricci. 'We're going now.'

'Stop the van! Now!'

She reached through the driver's window, grabbed the keys, and twisted them. The engine was electric, of course, so we didn't hear it cut out, but the dashboard lights went blank. Meanwhile, the Harmony Officer's other hand rose to her mouth. Her radio was clipped to her smock cuff. She didn't reach for a weapon. Harmony Officers usually didn't need them because civilians had been denied weapons for centuries.

So, instead, she shouted into her other sleeve. 'I need support!' she said. 'Now!'

'Regine!' squawked a speaker in the Harmony Officer's raincoat. 'Regine' was the new Harmony Office word for the toxic pre-Accord male radio communications words, 'Copy' or 'Roger.'

'ASAP,' said the Harmony Officer.

Until this point, I had done nothing except sit in the passenger seat and watch Ricci. Now it was time to be more active. It was time for the guy who resembled the pre-Accord villain to do something.

I unsnapped my harness.

'Sorry,' I said. 'We've got an appointment.'

'Stop!' shouted the Harmony Officer.

I ignored her, and flung my right arm over Ricci's chest, and reached down to the ignition. I grabbed the officer's wrist. 'Sorry about this,' I said. 'It's not sexual assault, you understand. We just need to get going.' With my other hand, I grabbed the radio and yanked it from her cuff, and tossed it onto Ricci's lap.

'Alex, I wouldn't…'

'I know you wouldn't.'

With one hand holding the officer's left, I caught her right hand with the other and held on. The officer raised a boot to the van door. The plastic panelling buckled as she drove the boot into it, trying to pull free from my grip. She was strong and her wrists were slippery. But I was stronger. Much stronger. Toxic male stronger. Compared to fighting aliens like Janasta and Granak, this was nothing.

'Sexual assault!' she yelled. 'I'm being assaulted by a male wanted by the Harmony Office.'

I shook the keys from the Harmony Officer's slippery hand.

'There,' I said to Ricci. 'Let's get moving.'

'I can't. Not while you're holding her through the window.'

'I'll let her go before she's hurt! Now, step on it before she bites me.'

Ricci pushed the start button and slotted the gearshift into reverse.

'Help!' the officer yelled. 'Assault! Sexual assault!'

Ten yards away, the other Harmony Officers looked up.

'Help! Okafor! Help!' the Harmony Officer screamed.

One of the officers came striding through the rain, chin up, chest out.

Then he broke into a run.

'Get moving!' I yelled to Ricci.

Ricci reversed. The Harmony Officer trotted

495

sideways next to the car with both hands through the window. Her steps would have looked dainty if her eyes weren't so wide and her mouth so gaping. The second officer, who I guessed was Okafor, was running flat out to catch up.

Ricci stopped, put the van in drive, then put her foot down. I released the Harmony Officer's hands. She staggered, but kept her feet, then faded into the rain. Okafor stood beside her, but not leaning down to help nor putting an arm around her shoulder. He was following the Accord protocol by asking permission first.

Meanwhile, the Rainbow van sped away, back along the Avenue of Revolutionary Feminists.

'Well, that didn't work out well,' Ricci said. 'Where now?'

'First, talk into this,' I held the Harmony Officer's radio in front of her face. 'Say these words: "False alarm. Stand down. Cancel back up."'

'False alarm. Stand down. Cancel back up.'

'It might buy time before they get here.'

'And then what?'

Through the van's streaming windows, I saw two Unity TV helicopters thump by. They were flying away from the center of town, away from the Unity TV headquarters.

'Are you listening?' said Ricci. 'Where should I go? Or should we just give it up, Alex? Let's just give it up. Fight another day. I'm not saying I won't drive you where you want to go. It's just…'

'Too late. They'll be searching for us.'

'But we can hide,' Ricci countered. 'I know a place in AON sub-territory Alano. It's in a forest. No one goes there.'

'We'd never reach it.'

'Then what do we do?'

'I've worked out the vantage point.'

'Where? From a cell in the AON LA Harmony building?'

'Not funny.'

'Then where?'

'Hear that?' I said.

She frowned, listening. 'What am I listening for? The rain or the sirens?'

'Look over there.' I pointed through the windshield at a row of apartment buildings. Above them, the two Unity TV helicopters hovered in the rain. Then they descended behind the buildings and out of sight.

'There's a stadium behind there,' I said.

'So?'

'They're using the field as a staging point to fly to the AON Headquarters. If you haven't noticed, there have been four helicopters in the air all morning, which means there must be a fleet of at least that many. The spare helicopters are waiting their turn on the ground somewhere in the city. I think they're in that stadium.'

'So your vantage point's in the air, from a stolen helicopter?'

'Yes.'

'Let's just try for Alano, Alex. They haven't caught us yet.'

'You don't have to come with me. Just drop me off as near as you can to the stadium. Then, tell the Harmony Officers the toxic male went rogue and forced you at gunpoint to do as he wanted. They'll believe you.'

She looked in the rear vision mirror, then at the road ahead. She bit her lip and turned to look at me and then stopped. Then she shook her head, gripped the wheel and looked at the wet road through the windshield.

'I can't believe I'm saying this,' she said. 'What's next?'

'Turn right,' I said. 'The first chance you get.'

73

As the Rainbow van pushed on through the rain and the sirens grew louder, I worked on my plan.

If we could get to that stadium before the Harmony Officers stopped us, and if there were helicopters parked on the field, and we could steal one of them, then we could have a better chance at Octavia.

As long as we weren't shot down first.

As long as I could keep the chopper steady while I fired.

As long as the engine's thump didn't ruin my aim.

But if no helicopters, what then?

Yes, what then?

Well, I'd cross that bridge when I came to it. For now, I had to stay in motion. I had to complete the mission. I had to take the shots at Octavia. No matter what.

'Can you go faster?'

'We're in a Rainbow van, Alex, not a

Progressive. It's got no power.'

'OK. So, just get us to the sports stadium.'

We drove along the Avenue of Revolutionary Feminists, lurching between the four lanes, overtaking slower cars. Each car carried one or two occupants—no families, as usual. They were all going to watch the ceremony at their friends' houses at IDD parties—or so I guessed.

Up ahead in the rain, more rainbow lights flashed. Four Harmony Office cars parked nose to tail across the road. Harmony Officers waved fluorescent paddles to direct cars through a gap on the left. For now, the traffic flowed through them. I knew it would soon stop when they got the call to block the road.

Meanwhile, rainbow lights flashed from three Harmony Office cars in pursuit. Above us, a helicopter thumped, no doubt with a camera aimed at us, relaying everything to Unity TV and the Accord.

'Now what?' said Ricci.

'Turn off the road.'

'I can't. The barrier is too high. We'd just hit it and bounce back or roll and crash.'

She was right. The safety barrier rose as high as our doors, and the Rainbow van could never get over it or through it.

'OK,'

'OK, what?'

'Let's try something else.'

'Like what?'

'Accelerate at the roadblock.'

'They're moving another car into the gap, see?'

'So put your foot down.'

'What! And crash into it?'

'We won't have to crash it.'

'Then what?'

I reached behind into the van's cargo hold. I grabbed the bag carrying the two rifles, unzipped it, and slid out the heavy alien weapon. I pulled it into the cabin. Then, I had to push it back into the hold again so I could turn it around to get the muzzle pointing the right way.   'You're not going to fire that thing in here.'

'No, I'm not. If you had fired this thing, you'd know that's not a good idea.'

'So how will you fire it? Don't do what I think you're planning.'

Before Ricci could protest any further, I raised my right boot, drew it back, and stomped hard at the windshield, heel first. I stomped once, twice, three times. Then, a crack line appeared in a hubcap-sized section. I stomped a few more times till part of it broke free and flapped out in the wind.

With the rain hitting my chest and face, I raised the weapon, pushed the muzzle through the windshield, and sighted the four cars in the roadblock. To the side of them, Harmony Officers stood waiting. Two waved light paddles back and forth, like waving hello or goodbye. Then they saw the van. They drew their weapons: Equality Pistols, probably. They were powerful enough to kill, but only if the Harmony Officers could aim them.

We would see.

I squinted through the rifle's sights.

'Keep this speed,' I said, 'and cover the side of your face.'

She raised her right hand and cringed behind it.

'Or block your ears. Your choice.'

The road block waited two hundred yards ahead. I aimed at the road ten yards in front of it to allow for the van's forward motion. Then I pressed the fire button.

The shot went out, the muzzle climbed, bashing a channel through the windshield's upper third. Meanwhile, the recoil was so great, I broke the seat and found myself lying on my back.

I sat back up and checked the barricade. No good. The shot had struck the road in front, blasting out a crater. The cars stood undamaged.

Meanwhile, the Harmony Officers decided now was the time to use their pistols. Through the rain, their pistol hands jerked like they'd been given small electric shocks. Two bullets tonked on the van's metal.

'Are you OK?'

'What?' Ricci said. 'I can't hear anything?'

'Are… you… OK?'

'No but yes,' she shouted. 'Shouldn't we swerve to avoid the bullets?'

A hundred yards to go.

'Just keep us steady.'

I raised the weapon and pressed the fire button. Ricci flinched. The van swerved. But the blast struck one of the cars amidships, right in the Harmony Office logo—the one with the twelve clasping hands of various hues. The shot had blasted a hole through the metal and sent the seats inside bouncing. But the blockade remained in place.

Not good.

Better try something else.

With more shots from the Equality Pistols tonking on the van and a hundred yards to go, I aimed at the rear quarter of the car in the middle of the blockade, right at the pre-Accord fuel tank. The rifle boomed, the muzzle climbed, the windshield shattered, and I flew out of the seat into the back of the van itself, tearing Adams's pants on the harness buckle.

'Still OK?' I called to the back of Ricci's head.

But I didn't hear her reply because of the explosion up ahead. A great boom filled the air, followed by a flash of brilliant orange.

I climbed into the cabin to see the damage. The blast had done its work. The car had exploded. It had also climbed up the car behind it, like it was playing piggyback.

But it had also left a gap in the blockade, a gap too small for a Rainbow van.

'We won't fit.'

'We'll make us fit. Put your foot down.'

Ricci shook her head and frowned, but she put her foot down all the same.

We hit the gap between the two cars. The metal screeched as the van scraped the fender of the car on the right. The fender on the left screeched even louder. It gouged into the van's side and yanked out one of the side panels from the parcel section.

It didn't stop us. We came out of it and lurched into a sideways skid. One of the front wheels growled like a Goth.

But we got through the barricade.

'I can't believe I'm doing this,' Ricci said. 'Adams and the group—we never…'

'Just keep going.'

More sirens and flashing lights joined the chase. More helicopters thumped overhead. The Accord was closing in, but we were on our way. The stadium loomed between the apartment buildings on the right. We would reach it.

But then a voice spoke in my mind.

'I'm starting my speech, Alex. Don't miss it. It's going to be something no one will ever forget.'

I threw up the image of the wall. I focused on its stony bricks, hard and impenetrable, streaming with rain, just like the rain streaming across the van's broken windshield and into our faces.

'No. Not yet. Not yet.'

'What? What not yet?' said Ricci.

'Just keep going.'

'Is something wrong? Something else, I mean?'

'No.'

'Then what?'

'Not now.'

And we kept our wobbling course for the stadium and for Octavia.

74

At the stadium entrance, the next obstacle waited. A boom gate blocked the road; and steel rails funnelled us towards it. The Harmony Officers must have radioed ahead with a warning we were coming. Two guards stood in front of the boom, dressed in rainbow slickers, their hands waving at us like broken windshield wipers.

They jumped out of the way as Ricci accelerated towards them. We hit the boom at fifty miles an hour. The boom turned out to be more solid than it appeared—not wooden as booms used to be, but steel. It rested between two posts: the post on which it tilted at one end, and the other side of the road in which its arm rested.

And so, the boom didn't shatter or break in two. It flexed like an archer's bow. The two ends of it stayed put. The van's grill crumpled and its rear end bucked. Ricci's airbag exploded as her head slammed forward. The sports bag containing the rifles flew into the windshield. Then, the van's rear dropped back to the road with a crunch, and Ricci and I were left sitting in the furious rain with the airbag sighing, the helicopters thumping overhead, and the three tones of the xylophone sirens booming behind us.

'Are you OK?' I said to Ricci.

'What?'

'Anything broken?'

'No, I'm… I'm… I'll be OK. Let's… let's get going.'

But she wasn't OK. She picked at her khaki shirt, fascinated by the raindrops soaking it. Then she turned to me with a creased brow, as if I were a stranger. I doubted she'd be going anywhere.

Meanwhile, the tones of the Harmony Office cars grew louder and louder and then stopped. Rainbow-colored lights flashed in the van's side mirror. Car doors slammed. Radios squawked.

I reached out and turned the side mirror. It showed four Harmony Office cars and at least six officers crouching behind the open doors, each clutching Equality Pistols. A female voice shouted through a loud hailer.

'This is the AON sub-territory Los Angeles Harmony Office. Step out of the van. Keep your hands up and lie face down on the ground. Comply or we will use AON-approved persuasion methods. Open the door to signal you understand.' A moment of silence passed before she added, 'We already know your preferred pronouns.'

I looked through the broken windshield to the stadium. It was two hundred yards away across a carpark in which Unity TV vans glistened in the rain. If we could get to the vans, we could take cover behind them, and then reach the stadium and the helicopters.

And Octavia.

First things first. I needed to buy time for Ricci to recover.

I picked up the alien rifle from the footwell, checked the sights, and the mechanism. It was good to go.

With Ricci rubbing her head, I twisted in the seat and aimed through the parcel section at the van's back doors. l checked on my target through the side mirror. Two of the Harmony Officers crept forward, crouching with Equality pistols raised in the usual two-handed grip.

I fired the weapon. One blast, then a second. After that, there was no need to check the rear vision mirror any more. The shots blew the van's rear doors out. Light, air, and rain came in. I could see the devastation. One Harmony Office car was a wreck. The other was on fire. The two creeping officers cringed in the rain, their hands over their heads.

Ricci slurred a few words. 'I can walk, I think. Let's go.'

'Are you sure? You don't have to do this.'

'I want to. I believe you.'

'You hit your head and now you believe me? I'm sure there's a compliment in there.'

'It's too late to go back,' she said. 'Let's keep going.'

Good enough, I thought.

'OK. You take the bag. Run towards the stadium entrance. Use the Unity TV vans as cover. I'll stay here and distract these guys while you go. Then I'll follow. Let's meet just inside the stadium at the entrance to the field.'

She picked up the bag carrying the PQ47 and the ammunition. Then, she stepped out of the van and slipped around to the front, out of the line of fire. Then she ran towards the parking lot and the stadium. Her groggy feet veered left. She stopped, corrected her course, and set off again for the parking lot.

'And Ricci,' I called.

She stopped, turned back.

'What?'

'Don't fire the rifle. We need every round.'

'Got it,' she said, then ran for the cars.

'Every round!' I called again.

I turned back to the Harmony Officers and their cars. I fired two more blasts, setting a second car leaping.

Then I followed Ricci.

In the stadium, I found her taking cover behind a shipping container. She waved when she saw me enter.

'Which helicopter do you want?' she said. 'Two just took off. The pilots know we're here. They're trying to get everything in the air.'

'Where are the guards and the TV people?'

She held up the PQ47.

'They ran when they saw this.'

And then I knew something was wrong. I was going to ask her about the rifle when I saw Harmony Officers creeping through the stadium entrance. One of them raised a loud hailer and ordered us to get on the ground.

What a surprise!

'Let's get that one.' Ricci pointed to a small helicopter with a perspex canopy.

'No. Let's get that one over there.' I pointed at a helicopter on the far side of the field.

'Why that one?'

'It's the only type I've flown.'

We set off. I walked backward, pausing every twenty steps to fire another blast, before picking myself up and hurrying on.

On the helicopter's canopy, the Unity TV logo streamed with rain. Beside it was the helicopter's number, Unity 47, and a name, 'Raechel Meddows.' Probably the name belonged to a pre-Accord social justice activist or journalist, or both. In those days, journalists and activists were the same, always working to bring about the end of the pre-Accord world.

We climbed inside. Ricci still had the bag of ammunition and the PQ47. I had the alien rifle. With the rain drumming on the canopy, I reached for the start button, found it, pressed it, and waited. The main rotor blades turned, first powered by the battery, which then gave way to the engine. The blades turned faster, the tail rotor spun behind us, and the canopy shuddered.

'They're coming,' Ricci said, pointing at the

Harmony Officers advancing through the rain. 'Their guns are out.'

'Don't worry. They can't hit anything—not with pistols, not at that range.'

'Can they hit something with that?'

'With what?'

'With that!'

Through the rain, I saw a small armored vehicle. It came rolling out of the stadium entrance, its rainbow paintwork glistening, the six wheels shiny, and the small cannon bouncing in its turret.

'Where'd they get something like that?'

'Must have been from the food shortage protests a year ago.'

'OK. Don't worry,' I shouted. 'We're almost there. Just have to wait a little longer.'

But I saw, to my horror, that Ricci had lifted the PQ47 and aimed.

'Stop! What are you doing?'

'Firing warning shots.'

'Wait! Don't fire! Ricci! Stop!'

I flung my arm across the cabin. I grabbed Ricci's arm and pulled it from the rifle. The helicopter lurched like a drunken bee. Then, I grabbed for the rifle itself. My fingers snatched the stock, just above the trigger guard. But I was too late. The rifle barked and reared in my hand. Big ripples formed in the water-soaked playing field beside us, going away like a stone skipped across a lake. Then, almost immediately, smaller ripples formed as the rain came down and washed the larger ones away.

Ricci had fired.

Not once.

Not twice.

Not three times.

But nine times.

Nine of the twelve precious shale bullets were gone.

75

I pulled Ricci's right hand from the trigger and held it hard by the wrist.

'Hey!' she said. 'Let go.'

'I need those bullets.'

'What? Why?'

She must have been still dazed from the airbag's punch. Unless this woman beside me wasn't Ricci. And if not Ricci, then who? But there was no time to think. The Harmony Officers and their armored vehicle had crept within a hundred yards. Time to get moving.

I let go of Ricci's wrist. 'No more shooting, OK,' I said. She looked at me like she'd never seen me before. I turned back to the helicopter's controls. I twisted the throttle and flicked on the governor switch. Then I reached for the cyclic and raised the collective. The Rachael Meddows rose but then pitched forward, like a dragonfly stooping to drink.

I pulled the cyclic back. The Raechel Meddows lurched in reverse, but kept rising. I gentled the cyclic and the anti-torque pedals till we leveled out. Then, I pressed down on the right pedal, rotating us around until we faced the center of town and the distant cluster of TEDIST buildings. I pushed the cyclic away from me. The Raechel Meddows's nose sniffed the rain. The blades forced us forward, and we lurched towards the Accord of Nations headquarters.

In the distance, the display on the building's side glowed through the downpour. The screen now showed one image only: the statuesque, poised, beautiful, and deadly figure of Octavia. She smiled as she spoke, enunciating each word. Her lips pouted circles. Her white teeth shone. I tried to lipread her, and thought I saw the words 'occasion' and 'momentous,' but she could just as easily have said, 'honored and grateful,' or maybe even, 'Let the invasion begin.'

Behind Octavia, ranks of gray marines glistened in the wet. Flanking her were the smiling faces of famous Accord Commissioners. The display then switched to the rows of lesser commissioners and AON military leaders, all watching from beneath a canopy at the base of the Steps to Equity. But the star of the show was Octavia. The camera soon returned to her face and her mouth speaking to the city and the world.

And me.

I touched the alien rifle. It was ready as always. Then I reached up and checked my top pocket. The lump of shale waited there. Thank goodness.

Nine of the shale bullets were gone, but this small lump remained. If my last three shots missed, and all else failed, at least I had that lump, even if I didn't know how I would use it.

'Why aren't you going higher?' yelled Ricci over the engine noise. Her voiced sounded childish. She was like someone in disguise whose accent had slipped. 'Why so low, Alex? Why so low?'

With horror, I thought she might be one of Octavia's puppet bodies, like Janasta or Captain Nolan. I looked at her. She smiled back at me. What would I do if she were now Octavia? Shove her through the hatch to her death?

'You'll see why in a moment,' I said. 'We'll have some friends up here with us any minute now.'

'Who?'

I knew that AONAF Slingshot fighters would soon come streaking upward from AONAFB Lynch. Each would be armed with guided missiles. I also knew that they would only fire on us if they could avoid hitting civilians, which they couldn't at low altitude.

'And what's that? That thing up there?'

I ignored her. I knew what that thing up there would be: one of the Roman transport ships descending through the clouds, as big as a city, and with a hold full of hostile aliens, machinery, and weapons, all waiting for Octavia's final orders, when she would announce her 'great surprise' to the Accord.

'Can you bring up the ceremony on your handheld?' I shouted over the chopper's thump.

'You want to hear what your girlfriend is saying?' she said. Her voice, like her smile, didn't sound right.

'No, I want to check out the security before we get there.'

She reached into her pocket. Then, she dabbed at her handheld with her index finger. The sound came up. I could just hear Octavia's voice over the engine and the rain.

'… stand here before you on this momentous day,' she said, 'to join with the people of the Accord of Nations as we go forth to a future in which the peoples of Earth and Rome celebrate in unison… celebrate the values of tolerance, equality, and the intra-galactic diversity of our two…'

A Unity TV helicopter came thumping along beside us, the camera aimed our way. The reporter beside it talked into a headset.

Ricci lifted the rifle.

'No.' I placed a hand on her arm, pushing the rifle down. 'The bullets. We need them.'

'I'm just warning them off.'

'It's a good idea, but not now. Please. Not now.'

'Why won't you tell me what's in the bullets?'

'I will, but not until the mission is over.'

'Mission. Makes it sound like what we're doing is Accord-approved.'

'The Accord will thank us when this is over.'

But I knew it would not. The Accord would

never admit to making an error, let alone a catastrophic one. Nor would it admit to problems with its ideology. It couldn't. It never would. That's why it would have to be overthrown. One day.

But for now, first things had to come first.

'There is no going back,' said Octavia's voice from the handheld. 'Our two worlds' have reached a turning point…'

You're right, I thought, touching the rifle. No going back.

I waited for Octavia's next grand statement. What words would she say? A glorious future, perhaps? Unprecedented harmony, maybe?

But no.

Instead, she said, 'Stay calm, everyone. We're about to receive a visitor in a helicopter. Lieutenant Alexander Burns is trying to disrupt the course of history. That's what you're trying to do, isn't it, Alex? That's why you're here.'

But we hadn't even arrived yet. We were still on the far side of the headquarters, approaching the screen with Octavia's image still gazing out into the rain. She smiled out at me. I thought she might have winked again.

Meanwhile, down along the street, the ceremonial formations had seen us. Their various colored smocks shuffled and mixed in panic. The green and red smocks of the Harmony Officers mixed with the rainbow smocks of the Department of Diversity; the olive smocks of the AON Army mixed with the light blue smocks of

AON Air Force and the dark blue smocks of the AON Navy. I wondered if Admiral Zhou stood among them, or even Captains Odilli and Paine. And maybe even Captain Diana Nolan from the Judges Advocate Navy. Captain Diana Nolan! The thought Octavia duping me by using Captain Nolan's body almost made me ill. But I shook the thought away.

And focused on Octavia.

I brought the helicopter around the AON headquarters until the Steps to Equity, the podium, and Octavia lay below us. I focused so much on her I didn't see the fading light. I didn't hear Ricci yelling at me. 'It's not Slingshots,' she yelled. 'It's not the Slingshots?! Why aren't you looking? They're up there in the clouds.'

'Take the stick,' I said.

'What?'

'Take the stick. I'll work the pedals. All you have to do is keep us still.'

'But I don't know how.'

'Take it anyway.' I reached across the Ricci's lap and grabbed the PQ47. I raised it and looked through the sights at the scene below on the Steps to Equity. Everyone had scattered. Only the Roman Marines and Octavia remained. She looked up at me through the rain.

The moment of truth had arrived.

76

The PQ47 was light compared to the alien rifle. Its usual rounds would cause no more harm to Octavia than a pinch. But I reminded myself that this particular PQ47 could sting with Gwantashale, the mere presence of which forced Octavia to slump onto the Gwantasnarr's deck. True, the shale back then was longer than my hand, but if the small bullets could pierce Octavia's skin or her shell, they might have an even greater effect.

Maybe.

And 'maybe' would have to be enough for now.

'What do I do?' cried Ricci over the thump of the rotor blades. 'I don't know what to do?'

'Just hold steady.'

'I don't think I can. I'll crash it.'

'Twenty seconds. That's all I'll need.'

'I can't! Alex, I can't.'

'Just hold it!'

For a moment she did. She held the stick. We

stayed level.

I flicked the PQ47's fire setting to single shots. I couldn't afford to spend the last three rounds in one pull of the trigger.

Ricci was still nervous.

'Alex, we've got to get out of here.'

'You're doing great. Just keep us still. Twenty seconds. That's all I'll need.'

'It's something else. Look what's up there. Can't you see them? Look what's up there.'

'Just hold us steady.'

But the helicopter pitched forward, and I had to put the rifle in my lap and take the cyclic back. I steadied the Raechel Meddows and then used the anti-torque pedals to bring my side around to Octavia. Then, I handed the cyclic over to Ricci's trembling hand.

'Try again. Keep it steady. Twenty seconds. Just twenty seconds.'

She took the vibrating control with two hands and held it between her knees. We stayed level for three seconds, then five. So far, so good.

I turned away from Ricci, lifted the PQ47 and looked through the sights at the scene a hundred and fifty yards below.

Octavia stood waiting. The Marines stood in ranks behind. The Accord commissioners had vanished, probably to a safe space deep inside the HQ. They might have been corrupt, but they weren't stupid. Nor were the members of the military. They had fled from the Steps to Equity. Now they streamed along the The Avenue of

Revolutionary Feminists like a river of small panicking rainbows.

But not Octavia. She wasn't going anywhere.

She gazed up at me defiantly, her hands clasping the sides of the lectern. She looked as if she were about to resume her speech after a round of applause. She might even have been enjoying herself. She had certainly never appeared more beautiful. Not even a hundred and fifty yards of downpour could diminish her power to attract and beguile.

When I fixed the crosshairs on her chest, she smiled, as if this was just a game, as if earth bullets could never hurt her, and that she would absorb them, or repel them. They'd bounce off her like the raindrops.

She and I would both soon find out.

I touched the trigger, but once again, I choked on the revulsion of shooting at a woman—even an alien disguised as one. Octavia appeared so human in appearance. It was easy to believe the disguise and forget about what lay beneath: a monster much larger and dangerous than a Goth.

Alex, said the voice in my head. Alex. It sounded tender and forgiving, like a lover's voice after an argument. Alex, it whispered as if she was about to say, 'Come, now. You know this is wrong. Put the gun down. You're making a fool of yourself.'

I shook the voice away and resettled the crosshairs over the Accord flag on Octavia's blue smock—on the breast of the dove perched on the rainbow arching across the blue star field. But the helicopter rattled and swayed so much the sights would not stay put. With nine bullets in the magazine I might have taken the risk and fired, but with only three, I had to make sure I hit.

And then, for the briefest of moments, the helicopter settled.

So, I squeezed the trigger.

And fired.

The shot went wide. I saw it spark on the shoulder of the Marine behind Octavia's left.

The helicopter lurched.

'Steady now. I'm almost there.'

'I don't know how,' said Ricci. 'Can't you see what's up there?'

'It won't attack. It's not here for us.'

'How do you know?'

But there was no time to explain.

I fired the PQ47 a second time. The same target: dove and rainbow patch on Octavia's chest. This time, the helicopter swung to face down the street. My fault. I'd pushed one of the anti-torque pedals by mistake. The shot went wide again. Octavia didn't move. She didn't even blink.

'Last shot,' I shouted.

'And then what?' Ricci yelled.

I ignored her. I knew how it seemed. I also knew Ricci would agree with me in a quieter moment—if there would ever be a quieter moment.

I put my eye to the sights. This time, I settled the crosshairs on Octavia's mouth. But the helicopter pitched forward. Ricci was about to lose control and all of this would come to nothing. Or worse! It would come to capture.

So, I focused again. Octavia smiled even more —smiling as if she knew about Ricci, and about the shale. She smiled like she knew I had one round left.

Nothing to be done, I thought, and I pulled the trigger one last time.

The rifle bucked. The muzzle climbed. I smelled the gun smoke. The crosshairs rose out of view, then settled back in front of my eye. I checked the scene below.

Nothing.

Not a flinch.

Not a blink.

The shot had gone wide again.

But not astray.

I saw a tuft of cloth flicker on Octavia's shoulder. The shot must have ricocheted from the stone wall behind her, nicking her uniform, just above her collarbone. But had it entered her body where the damage could be done?

I waited for the next few seconds, watching.

And then, as if in slow motion, Octavia's expression changed. Her smile faded. Her mouth opened. Her knees slowly bent. She slumped at the lectern, holding its edges to keep from falling. Her head lolled. Her lips mouthed a command. One of the Marines left the ranks behind her, clomped forward, and took her arm.

'Let's get out of here,' shouted Ricci. 'You fired

your shots. Let's go! Take this stick and let's go!'

But I couldn't go—not till I knew that the Gwantashale poison had done its work. I watched Octavia drop, her knees giving way. The Marine knelt beneath her. He held her with one arm above the glistening steps. Her head flopped to her chest. I imagined her agonized thoughts and pictured her cursing me as her life and all her plans for Earth faded away, just as the plans of her former comrade, Janasta, faded on the hard metal deck of the Gwantasnarr.

But I also knew it would never be that easy. Octavia would never go quietly. She was too powerful. There was too much at stake. And just as I feared, Octavia was far from defeated.

'What on earth is that? Alex, what is it?' Ricci shouted. This time she wasn't shouting about the transport ships. 'What is it?' she yelled. 'What is it?' She was hysterical, and I could understand why. Down on the Steps to Equity, Octavia had risen from her prone position at the lectern. Her body slowly boiled into a new shape, bursting the stitches of her blue uniform, twisting and swelling, turning shades of purple and green. She rose up and up. She wasn't smiling anymore, and we both knew what would happen next.

77

I dropped the PQ47. It fell till it clattered on the street below. The sights shattered on impact. The fore stock broke from the barrel. Farewell, Destroyer

I took the cyclic from Ricci, put my feet on the pedals, and steadied the helicopter. I lifted the collective. The engine groaned as we rose above the giant form billowing up beneath us.

'What is that thing?' cried Ricci once more.

'You can see what it is,' I shouted.

'But what is it?' she yelled.

'That,' I said, 'is a glimpse of reality.'

'A glimpse of what?'

'It's what I've been warning you about. It's what nobody wants to talk about, or can't talk about because that would mean using honest words, not the deceptive Accord words like visitors and othering. That's an alien, Ricci. That's a monster. That's an invader and a killer. That's our future.'

'Get us away from it,' screamed Ricci. 'Just get

us away… from it.'

'Sure,' I said. 'Just hold on.'

'Go behind the hills. Go as far away as possible.'

'No time. They've started.'

'What's started?'

'You saw the ship, right? In the clouds?'

'So where can we go?'

'I'll put you down somewhere nearby—somewhere you can get away.'

'And what about you?'

I said nothing.

'Alex, what about you?'

The answer was that I would find a place to confront Octavia alone with the lump of Gwantashale. I didn't know where. As usual, I was improvising. All I knew was that the shale bullets had failed. Now there was only one chance left.

'It won't be long,' I said, trying to sound calm, but even I could hear the strain in my voice. My nerves were raw in a way they hadn't been during the worst of the trip on the Gwantasnarr —not even when Granak smashed down on my chest.

'I can't believe it,' said Ricci.

I felt sorry for her. She hadn't asked for this. Despite her bold talk about the resistance and rebellion, she was like everyone else in the Accord: she thought she knew all about the world and all about the visitors.

Until she didn't.

She thought she knew about tolerance too.

Now she had glimpsed the intolerable.

'Just get away from that thing,' she said.

'Tighten your harness,' I said. 'And don't look back.'

I urged the helicopter upward. The rotor blades thumped. We climbed higher into the hammering rain. And Octavia rose with us, changing color, forming a scale-like exterior, emitting a rubbery snapping sound, a terrifying hiss, and a foul stench.

Her face swelled into something inhuman. Gone were the beautiful smirk, the high cheekbones, the amused smile. They had been replaced by an open maw.

'Ahhhlexxxxxx!!!!!' the Octavia creature roared, drowning out the growl of the helicopter's engine and the thumping blades. 'Ahhhlexxx!!!'

When we reached a height above the Accord building, the way through the various buns and cups of TEDIST architecture lay clear. I swung the cyclic to port and set us going north, just as Octavia's claws snatched at the skids, causing the helicopter to tilt so much that Ricci grabbed hold of my shirt.

Beneath us, chaos ruled the streets. The ranks of VIP guests, the heads of nations, and senior military officers ran down every avenue and lane, and through every park and tunnel. Running from the monster.

'So where, Alex? You still haven't told me where?'

'In a minute.'

'Where?'

'Just hold tight for now. We'll find somewhere.'

I glanced over my shoulder at the Accord headquarters and the display on its side. The images for Intra-galactic Diversity Day were back. The flag rippled, the commissioners came forward, and Octavia smiled as beautiful as ever. Now the giant beast Octavia towered beside the images, running with slow, ponderous steps, each step a block long.

I reached up to my top pocket. The lump of shale was still there, thank goodness. But now it felt so small and insubstantial, no bigger than a pebble on a beach. But it was all I had. It was all that stood between a free earth and whatever future was in the transport ships glowering above.

Would it be enough?

'Alex. It's following us. Alex?'

Not us.

Me.

78

As if on cue, the next problem showed up.

A red light flashed on the helicopter's instrument panel: a silent, tiny, insistent flash demanding attention. At first, I ignored it. A light that small couldn't mean anything important: a safety harness warning or a reminder to shut the hatches. Nothing to worry about.

But it kept on flashing. I looked closer at it. A small symbol beneath the light showed its function. The small symbol was a capital 'F.'

'F' for fuel.

Ricci watched me. I just shook my head. Who could ever imagine that a cliche from the worst of the Accord movies could happen in real life? Who could imagine it would happen at the worst possible moment?

'How long?' Ricci asked.

'Maybe ten minutes,' I answered. 'That's how long it is in Slingshots.'

'How do you know it's ten minutes?'

'It'll have to be.'

Through the canopy, I could see nothing but streets and houses. No sports field except for the stadium where we'd stolen the Raechel Meddows, which by now would be swarming with Harmony Officers.

So where to go?

If we had to, we could land on a street—but only if we gained enough distance from Octavia first.

'What's happening back there?' I yelled.

Ricci turned around and craned her neck outside for a moment. The wind whipped her short hair. When she came back, her pale skin streamed with rain. 'It's still coming, and it's worse.'

I turned to check. After months of horrifying sights, this was the worst: Octavia, as tall and thick as a building, stomped over the streets, her arms swinging forward like wrecking balls, her feet crushing cars, crushing people from every rank on the Oppression Hierarchy. At one point, her claws slipped on the wet street—slipped in the rain, or on people unlucky enough to be in the way. It was horrifying.

But the most horrifying sight was her face.

'What have you done?' yelled Ricci. 'There must have been a better way to stop her than this?'

'If there is, I'd like to know.'

'But see what's happened. You'll never stop her now—not when she's like that, not when she has those ships up there.'

'I can stop her.'

'With what?'

'In my pocket.'

'That's it?'

'That's all I'll need.'

Ricci opened her mouth to speak, changed her mind, then turned and checked behind.

'She's closer now. You better climb.'

But I couldn't climb. I couldn't risk running out of fuel at altitude, and I couldn't risk drawing the Slingshots.

'What about there?' Ricci pointed in the distance. I saw nothing at first. 'There,' she said again. Then, I saw it, a tall, flat-roofed tower about forty floors high. If we could land on that roof, it would allow Ricci to escape and give me a chance to stay out of range of those stomping feet.

Maybe.

I squinted at the building through the rain. It was pre-TEDIST, shabby, and old. The rooftop bristled with junk. Not a fitting place for a showdown with Octavia. I'd imagined the top of a mountain, or the middle of the ocean, or high in the sky, surrounded by black storm clouds. But this old building was where it was going to be. The blinking fuel light demanded it.

'OK. We'll go there,' and I pushed the cyclic forward, urging the helicopter on. The fuel light flashed. Then the comms came to life. A female voice spoke.

'Lieutenant Burns. This the AON sub-territory

Harmony Police communications tower. You are ordered to land and surrender to the Harmony Officers who are pursuing you by road.'

I pulled the microphone from its clip and pushed 'TALK.'

'Not this time,' I said. 'Keep your orders to yourself.'

I reached for the comms button and switched it off. Then I urged the Raechel Meddows onward towards the old building, willing it to make it before the fuel ran out.

Am I ready, I wondered. After all that's happened, am I ready? And can anyone ever be ready for something like this? With so much at stake? When facing such fearful odds? Or are they always ready when they're following the family trade?

Within minutes, I would find out.

79

We hovered over the tower block, searching for a place to set down. The roof spread as wide as several pre-Accord tennis courts. But that's as far as the comparison went. Clutter dominated every square yard. Satellite dishes, air conditioner intake units, pipes, exhausts, clusters of aerials, and various junk grew like a rusty garden of wild, alien trees.

On the north side, a four-armed teeter-totter waved at us. On each arm, someone had painted a name: oppression, equality, tolerance, and intolerance. The helicopter's downdraft flung the arms about, turning the teeter-totter into an allegory of the Accord's historical struggles. Oppression and tolerance rose and fell. Equality and intolerance banged up and down. And everywhere, the raindrops bounced on the concrete.

So where to land?

The Raechel Meddows decided for us. Warning alarms joined the red flashing fuel light. Six rapid electronic gongs sounded, as if summoning us to our last meal. Then, the engine spluttered, and we dropped heavily into the clutter.

One skid hit before the other. It smacked the tolerance arm of the teeter-totter. The whole craft rolled to starboard. The blades thwacked and gouged the concrete and smashed the teeter-totter's oppression and equality arms, flinging them away into the rain.

Then, the helicopter's cabin scraped the through the mess in widening circles, like a stricken Goth biting at a wound. We went crunch and crash as the blades pulled us away from the ruins of the teeter-totter, and dragged us past the stairwell hutch to the roof's limits.

When the blades finally smashed themselves into shards, and the engine died, we found ourselves tilting over the building's edge, gaping through the hatches at the raindrops going away and the street forty floors below. Only Ricci's harness straps kept her from joining the rain drops plunging into the precipice. Her right hand held the cyclic, her left hand flailed.

'Don't look down,' I said. 'Don't move, either. We'll get you out of this.'

'If you say so,' she called, but she looked down anyway. When she looked back, her face was so twisted by panic, she couldn't speak.

'First things first,' I said. 'Hand me the rifle. Slowly. Keep hold of the stock. We'll climb out together. You come through the cabin as I step out of it. Keep holding the rifle. Don't let the rifle go, even if the chopper slides.'

As I climbed from my seat, the helicopter groaned and tilted. If I stepped outside, it would swing over the edge, falling to the street with Ricci inside.

Ricci let go of the cyclic, lifted the rifle and held it for me. The muzzle pointed at my chest. I took hold of it with my right hand, steadying myself on the cabin with my left.

'Ready?' I said

'Be careful,' Ricci replied. 'I'll be torn to bits.'

'Just take it one step at a time. Keep hold of the rifle and unclip the harness.'

With her left hand, she unclipped harness. Her weight was now partly on the seat, partly on the rifle. I climbed from my seat onto the wet roof, keeping a hold of the rifle's muzzle.

It was a mistake.

The change in weight distribution tilted the cabin further over the edge, slowly at first, then faster, like water pouring over a fall. Ricci kept hold of the rifle as the cabin dropped around her. The collective lever snagged on the knees of her khakis pants, tearing them with an obscene rip, but the cabin fell past her and she came through the starboard hatch, like a diver coming up for air. The cabin dropped away and plunged with the raindrops to the street.

As the helicopter smashed below, I pulled Ricci onto the roof. She clutched my shirt so hard I thought she might rip the shale from my pocket. The moment could have been romantic in another place, at another time, on another day.

But not now.

Right on cue, a bellowing roar came through the rain.

'Ahhhhhlleeeexxxx!'

'You better get going,' I said. 'Go down the stairs. Don't go out onto the street until you know she's up here with me, not down there.'

'Can I help? I could stay out of sight and shoot when the moment comes.'

'No use. Not anymore. And you've forgotten. We don't have a PQ47—not that it would do any good.'

'What is it with her? Why this obsession with you?'

'When this is over, I'll tell you all I know.'

'Surely, you don't have to do this today. There's always another day.'

'There's no more other days. It's now or never.'

'But you're just one guy, Alex.'

'So people say.'

'But it's horrible.'

'I know. Don't look.'

The footsteps stomped closer, shaking the building itself, causing ripples in the puddles on the rooftop. Then the footsteps stopped. Sounds from the city filled the silence: the distant thump of helicopters, the chimes of Harmony Office sirens, and the rain beating on the concrete, punctuated by occasional 'tings' as droplets hit the broken symbol from a junked drum kit.

Seconds later, the building moved, shaking like

one of AON sub-territory Los Angeles' infamous earth tremors.

But this was no earthquake.

It was Octavia climbing.

'Go,' I said to Ricci.

'Tell me we'll meet again.'

'We'll meet again.'

Ricci reached up and kissed me, then turned and ran toward the stairway hutch, stumbling and falling to the glistening cement as the building shook. Then picking herself up, again. She turned back to me one last time. Then she opened the shaking door of the stairway hutch and stepped inside.

And disappeared.

I walked to the center of the roof, the furthest point from all the edges. Then, I faced north toward the Smollett Hills, the direction in which the building dipped its edge with each pull of Octavia's claws.

I drew a slow breath, held it, and breathed out, readying myself. Then, without realizing, I spoke some old, pre-Accord words.

'And how can man die better Than by facing fearful odds, For the ashes of his fathers, And the temples of his gods.'

Then, the building's rooftop stopped dipping towards the hills and started lurching. The clutter of junk slid north along the wet concrete. An old washing machine sailed by, escorted by wires and cans. A satellite dish slowly rotated as it scraped past. The teeter-totter's arms rolled among the cans and wires collecting at the building's edge.

There was a pause. The building was still. The raindrops bounced among the clutter. For a moment, I hoped Octavia had slipped and fallen to the street where she lay broken and burst. Or better yet, that the shale's poison had finally killed her, and she had expired with her claws hooked into the building's side.

But I knew this was too good to be true.

Seconds later. The building shook again and the junk on the roof rattled. There would be no escape, not for Octavia, not for me. The moment had come. The only thing to do was to see it through to its horrible end.

And then Octavia arrived.

First, one clawed-hand rose over the building's edge, followed by an enormous scaly forelimb. The claws stretched forward, dropped down, and dug into the roof, crushing a cluster of aerials. They gouged into the concrete until they held. A second set of claws rose, dark and shiny, and slammed down into the rooftop, sending up plumes of concrete chips.

The forelimbs strained. Veins in the creature's wrists pushed up from under the skin, like cables. Then Octavia's head appeared, forehead first, then her face itself. There was no trace of the beautiful woman who smiled in the rain at the podium. This was a monster.

She said nothing as she heaved herself onto the roof like a swimmer climbing from a pool. One knee appeared, followed by a clawed foot, covered in scales. A second clawed foot clomped onto the roof. Finally, all of Octavia stood above me like a colossus, almost like another building itself. Then we faced each other: the towering alien monster and the rain-drenched human.

'Hello, Alex,' she said, her pre-Accord accent now a booming bass that rattled the satellite dishes and rippled the puddles.

'Hello, Octavia.'

I reached for my top left pocket. But instead of finding the familiar lump buttoned inside. I found nothing but a flap of cloth.

The shale had gone.

80

I checked the other pocket, the right one.

Nothing.

I checked the knee pockets and back pockets.

Nothing and nothing.

I checked the tops of my boots, then the wet concrete in front and behind me.

Nothing, nothing, and nothing.

The shale must have fallen out when the Raechel Meddows fell over the building's edge. So, maybe the shale lay in the wreckage down on the streets. Or maybe it lay beside the edge itself, twenty yards away.

Twenty yards away!—too far away for me to go back and search.

So what now?

The shale wasn't just my best plan; it was the only plan. No shale, no hope of defeating the monster. No shale, no hope of ridding Octavia from the world.

No shale, no survival.

I took a breath, pushed these thoughts away,

and thought instead of brave Horatius at the bridge, facing fearful odds. Like him, I wouldn't turn and run. I would see this ordeal through with or without the shale.

I turned back to Octavia. She watched me, the slightest of smiles on her hideous face. Then, she spoke in her booming voice, 'What are you doing, Alex? Trying to find your screechy, no-hips friend?' Her voice changed in pitch and she mimicked Ricci.

'Oh, Alex! Tell me we'll see each other again.' Ricci's voice ended and the booming bass voice returned. 'So pathetic, Alex. So pathetic.'

Then, she crouched to her knees, crushing old chairs and boxes beneath them. Her head loomed above mine.

'You shot me with Gwantashale.'

I didn't speak.

'Shot me, Alex! Me! The one who cares for you.'

I kept quiet.

'Where is the rest of it?'

I said nothing.

'Didn't you hear me? I said, where is the rest of it?'

'Gone.'

'Gone where?'

'I threw it from the Gwantasnarr—out into space?'

'Why?'

'So that Janasta could recover enough to fly to Earth.'

'Liar!' she roared. 'Where is it?'

'Ask your fleet out there in space to look. They're closer to it.'

'No, Alex. I think it's nearby. I can sense it.' She leaned forward, sniffing at me with great nostrils. 'I can tell it hasn't been long since you touched it.'

'It's the shale bullets. That's what you can smell.'

'More lies. Tell me where it is,' she commanded.

'Find it yourself.'

'Don't force me to do something you won't like, Alex.'

'Like what?'

She leaned back and looked into the sky. Above her, a transport ship hovered in the rainclouds, huge and threatening, like a black asteroid suspended above the Earth. Beside it, bristling battleships hovered in the mist. Octavia raised a great, scaly arm. The transport ship came alive with light. Seconds later, beams shot forth from the ship's port and starboard cannons. They hit the western slopes of the Smollett Hills, the swept across the city, going all the way to AON sub-territory Manhattan Beach. They lit up the streets like a lightning strike. The buildings and streets turned bright white and the most distant highways were as clear as the closest lane.

Octavia lowered her forelimb. The beams ceased. The ship's lanterns switched off and the great craft lay silent and motionless except for the flames around its gun ports and a solitary light in its bow. Octavia looked down at me. We stared at each other, listening to the raindrops on the roof and the cacophony of other noises now joining in: distant car alarms, explosions, falling rubble, screams, and what sounded like the wail of an Accord Airliner.

Octavia said, 'When will you learn, Alex? When will you understand that you can't stop my ships, and you can't stop me?'

I kept quiet, willing my mind to think of something I could use to fight her.

'You are embarrassing yourself,' Octavia boomed. 'Do you really think you can save them —the people down there? Why are you certain they want saving? Believe me, Alex, they don't care. They want me here—me and my people. They say they love diversity. Well, I'm as diverse as it gets.' And the monster laughed.

'Only because they don't know what you'll do to them. They think you'll be joining them in the morning pledge. They don't know about your plans.'

She laughed. 'How wrong can you be, Alex! They'll love it. They already love being oppressed. They're what the Accord has made them. All over the world, in every city, people yearn to rise higher on your Oppression Hierarchy. They want to go as high as they can, all the way to being the ultimate victims. They long for submission and failure, but I suppose you might be right in one sense. They don't know about the pain. They don't know about the suffering. Not yet.'

Behind her, the enormous transport ship crouched. I imagined the alien invaders aboard it and the masses of weapons and machinery in its holds. The same leviathans no doubt glowered over the Accord's other great cities: the AONT sub-territories of Beijing, Tehran, New Delhi, Kinshasa, London, and the rest. I imagined the people in those cities, gazing up at the sky. How many of them now saw the truth?

I turned back to Octavia.

'I'm going to stop you.'

'Oh,' smiled Octavia. 'You are going to stop me? That's interesting. Why do you care anyway? You don't have a friend among these people—not even your little pixie, Lieutenant Ricci. They hate you. They want to imprison you. They think you are an enemy of their precious Accord values.'

'You are an invading force. The people don't know it yet, but they will. They'll know everything the word invasion means.'

She looked at me with pity. 'I've wondered why you care, or at least why you pretend to care. At first, I thought you were merely trying to make up for your frustrated career, which was understandable. Then, I thought it might be because you don't want to see your planet destroyed. I can understand that too. But now I know your real reasons, Alex. Big, personal, frightening reasons.'

'You don't know anything about me.'

'Really? Are you sure? Then, let's hear

someone explain it to you.'

Her face froze. Her eyes rolled back, revealing bright, pure white. Her mouth opened, and she spoke in my mother Kresta's voice.

'Your father's a good man, Alex,' Kresta's voice said through the rain. 'He's a good man. He just got hold of the wrong ideas. That's all. You can't believe what he says, but you can believe the Accord. The Accord knows best. It always will.'

'Stop that.'

'Am I getting closer?'

'No.'

'I think I am.'

She crept to within touching distance. Her face froze again. Her mouth opened, and she spoke in the words of my father—his call to me as the Harmony Officers choked him and dragged away. 'It's not your fault, Alex. It's not your fault.'

Her face unlocked. She mock-frowned. 'I never get the words right. But I'm close, aren't I? You do all this because you believe it is your fault. All of it—your father's arrest, his shattered career, the waste of his life, your mother's torment over choosing the Accord. If you hadn't caused so much trouble, both of them might still be around. And now you try to save people because you believe that will make the pain go away.'

'No.'

'No? Then, let's see for ourselves.'

Before I could react, she shot out a claw and grabbed me like a toy. The rough skin scraped my neck, the knuckle joints bent around my ribs, and then the scene faded away. We vanished from the rooftop and reappeared in a small room—one from decades ago. The figures from the dreams stood there: the Harmony Officers, Cal and Kresta.

The action played out, the same as in my dream. This time, the Harmony Officers grinned as they jabbed my father with the stun gun and its horrible snap. I saw Kresta's anguish, her confusion, trying to convince herself the Accord knew best when she knew it didn't. Letting it all overwhelm her own judgment, not shielding her child from it.

'Enough!' I shouted.

And we came back on the building top in the hammering rain.

'In a way, I've done you a favor.'

'No.'

'Oh yes. I gave you your chance to ease your guilt. If I had never arrived in the Excidium three years ago, where you would be today? You would still be stuck, Alex, a lieutenant O-2, training for non-existent missions, groveling to officers who despise you, taking courses that require you to disbelieve your senses, detesting yourself, and all because of what happened long ago.'

'No,' I said again, holding back my anger, and holding back my mind. I had to keep thinking of the truth: The Accord is oppressive. Octavia is an invader. Defying her and the Accord is the right thing to do, no matter what happened to me. No matter how many people believed the opposite. No matter what had happened in my childhood. It was my duty to do it, the family trade.

'I'm so glad you're coming to your senses, Alex?'

'Are you sure that's what I'm doing?'

'What choice do you have? You can be kind to me and live a life you could never imagine, or you can go back to that other life—the frustrating life, the life of no power, no achievement, no freedom, only failure, guilt, and resentment. You'll rot in a Navy brig till you die bitter and unfulfilled—and beyond my power to forgive you.'

'Is that all you have to say?'

'First, I'm going to make you watch some more, Alex.'

She raised her arm again. The ship came alive once more. Lights flicked on around its hull. I imagined the same lights coming on along the crouching ships all round the world.

'When I lower my arm, Alex, the end will begin. The capital cities will burn, the people will die, the land will be cleared. Then I'll move the ships inland to other cities.'

'Don't to it.'

'Don't do it? Is that all you can say?'

'Don't do it. Let the people live. They won't be in your way.'

'Don't make me laugh.'

The fight was lost. I knew it. I couldn't stop Octavia. I had no shale, and her mind lay beyond the reach of moral appeals.

So I tried one last time. It was a long shot, but if the truth could hurt Octavia the way it hurt me, there might be a chance.

'You think I'm the only one with a past, Lanalan? Or should I also call you by your other name? Surely you know the one I mean.'

Her arm remained high in the sky, unmoving.

'What?' she boomed.

'I already know that Lanalan is your Goth name? Remember, back on the Gwantasnarr? But I also know your Roman name: the name they called you before your terrible humiliation.'

'What?' her voice boomed again.

'Hello, Sinistra,' I said.

And I knew I'd hit a nerve.

81

'Sinistra!' I shouted.

'Stop!' she boomed.

'You too were a loser in your nation's navy,' I said. 'You were Sinistra, the one your shipmates called The Lovelorn, and the Goths called Lanalan.'

'No,' she boomed, her breath hot and foul, and I knew the mere mention of the name caused an ancient humiliation to come rushing back at her.

'I know what happened, Sinistra. You and Ranant. Remember him? The shipmate who dumped you. Remember?'

I saw her body swell, saw the scales readjusting, sliding around on her flesh like the scales on a giant snake.

'He rejected you!' I shouted. 'Threw you over! Dumped you. Wanted nothing to do with you. He knew you were obsessed! Crazy! What did Janasta say? You were too…'

'You know nothing,' she fumed.

'I know about this story, Sinistra. It's your own

personal creation story. It's the reason you do what you do. Isn't it, Sinistra? The pain and humiliation are crippling, aren't they Sinistra? This guy, Ranant—he was your infatuation, your obsession, and he rejected you.'

'I am Octavia Caesar, admiral, and commander of the forces of…'

'The truth is that you don't want me. I'm just one Earth creature. You don't even want my ancestor, do you? You want Lieutenant Ranant or something you imagine is like him.'

'Don't say his name,' she boomed. 'You know nothing about Lieutenant Ranant. You're not fit to speak his name.'

'You killed him, didn't you, Sinistra?' I said, guessing. 'Killed him because he didn't want you. Killed the one you loved. And then you killed whoever he chose over you. And yet you are so sick, you still want him. Don't you?'

'I'm not going to…'

'Sinistra!' I called. 'Sinistra! Sinistra. SINISTRA!'

She threw me to the concrete. Then she appeared to change again, turning from a giant to a four-legged creature, with an enormous maw, like a lizard's. I've done it now, I thought. I've pushed her over the limit—for better or worse.

I hadn't known how the Ranant affair had turned out. I'd guessed she'd killed him, and I'd guessed right. Now she was furious.

I stepped back, bringing the alien rifle around on its strap. I knew the rifle couldn't save me, no matter how powerful its blasts, but at least it would give me the chance to die with a weapon in my hands.

'Ingrate! Betrayer!' Octavia's voice rippled the puddles beneath my feet. 'How dare you!' she roared. 'How dare you! How dare you!'

'What are you going to do, Sinistra?' I called. 'What are you going to do? Your secret's out. They'll be laughing at you up there in the sky. The Marines are laughing. Your officers are telling jokes about you. Those swamp creatures you sent to Earth—they'll laugh at you too, if they can. Everyone finds you a joke, Sinistra. What are you going to do about it?'

'What am I going to do? I'm going to make you suffer just as I suffered.'

'To suffer like you, I would have to be as insane as you.

Her body swelled.

'I,' she said, 'am going to make you watch what I do to your planet.'

The flesh rippled beneath her scales.

I stood my ground, keeping the rifle level. No matter what she did. No matter what she said. I would not move. The stair hutch waited behind me. The door invited me in. I could reach it with ten steps. But I stayed put. This had to be decided now.

Or never.

Octavia crouched. She raised a giant claw, as if taking aim. Then, with incredible speed for a creature so huge, swung the claw to snap me up.

But I was ready.

I fired the rifle, hitting the clawed hand in the palm. Octavia roared and snatched it back. I fired a second time, hitting her shoulder. She boomed a mighty howl as she clutched the wound with her free arm.

The rifle had done its work—for now. But I knew that even the most devastating blasts wouldn't stop her for long. Any moment, she would change her mind about letting me watch. She would kill me. But for now, I carried on shooting and shouting.

'Rejected!' I shouted at her. 'Sinistra, the rejected! Sinistra the tossed aside! Sinistra, the not good enough!' I shouted anything I could think of to taunt and wound her.

Then, I fired the rifle a third time, aiming at her eyes. She raised a great limb to shield her face. The blast went out, but this time, it missed. The rifle's wet stock had slipped against my shirt, and the shot went over Octavia's head and away through the rain into the clouds.

But the rifle's recoil punched back as hard as ever. The backs of my knees hit a raised pipe, and I fell over it and onto the wet concrete.

Octavia removed her forelimb. She dropped to four limbs and placed a great claw beside my head. With her free claw, she reached for me all over again.

I kicked myself away, pushing and pushing with my legs, like a swimmer backstroking, sliding along the wet concrete, all the while, trying to bring the rifle up to fire again.

I had a half-second before the claw would reach me, and crush me, or pull me apart, or smash me, or throw me over the building's edge, or whatever idea came to Octavia's deranged and evil mind. Maybe she would eat me. Who could say?

First things first, Burns. Get away from the claw and keep firing.

So, I pushed myself further away. The heels of my boots slipped, the rain smacked my face, and the claw hovered above me, waiting to snatch.

But in all that chaos and closeness to doom, I felt it. I couldn't believe it, but I felt it.

The small lump under my back.

82

It was a lump all right, but was it *the* lump?

On that cluttered rooftop, it could have been anything: a metal bolt, a toy, a clod of mud, a shard of the helicopter's rotor blade.

Or the shale.

This particular lump was hard but soft, like it was wrapped in cloth, just as the hard lump of Gwantashale had been wrapped in cloth.

Maybe all was not lost.

I rolled to one side and swept my hand over the wet concrete until I found whatever it was that had pressed into my back. I worked the thick cloth around in my hand.

And I knew.

Octavia watched, nostrils flaring.

I climbed to my feet, my mind racing to answer a single question: How can I use this small lump to maximum effect?

But I already knew the answer. I just didn't want to say it to myself. No, I couldn't even think it. Octavia would listen to my thoughts.

So, to buy time, I said, 'What's the matter, Lanalan? Searching for your lost dignity.'

She appeared to reach a decision. She raised one claw to the sky, looked up at the giant ship and then looked back down at me. She opened her mouth to speak. No doubt she was about to tell me it was the end for the Earth or something like that, but before she could utter a word in that horrible voice, I lifted the rifle, aimed, and fired at her maw. The blast blew open a gaping tear in her flesh.

Where toxins could enter.

I dropped the rifle and grabbed the shale. Do it, I thought. Shove the shale in the wound. Do it before she sees you. But I hesitated. Octavia would block me, raise her head, swat me aside. Or she would spit the poison out. That's if she didn't bite me in half first.

No, there was only one thing to do—one thing to end this once and for all. I had to get the shale where she couldn't spit it out.

I lifted the rifle a second time.

'Lanalan!' I called. 'The Lovelorn.'

As the great maw opened to speak, I fired the rifle once more. Then, I ran forward, the shale in my right hand. I held it in front of me, holding it high like a symbol of defiance, like an ancient warrior advancing against overwhelming odds.

And I jumped from the rain-splattered concrete.

Into Octavia's maw.

83

The jaws clamped shut, slamming me into suffocating, slimy folds.

The outside world vanished. No more rain, light, or cold. No more damaged city. No more leviathans crouching in the clouds. Instead, I saw thick darkness and heard the monster's body sounds of rushing breath and fluids coursing through wet flesh.

I imagined the view from outside: the rooftop in the rain, Octavia stunned among the junk, eyes bulging, one claw clutching at her throat, the other three slowly gouging the concrete.

What did she think? Should she spit me out? Should she swallow me? And when would she detect the Gwantashale? Would it begin as a strange taste in her mouth, different to the oily taste of human clothes and skin? Or would she feel nausea or pain or a spasm?

'Work!' I shouted to the shale in the muffled, slimy dark. 'Release your poison, or whatever it is you do!'

No response came from Octavia, not a cough, not a gag, not a shake of her head. Had the shale done its work already? Were her jaw her muscles locked and her organs already shutting down? All from one small shale lump?

Still, I waited.

Nothing.

A minute passed.

Still nothing.

But then, something. A slackening of the jaws, then a tightening, then shivering as if Octavia had contracted a fever. The shivering intensified into shaking, then violent shaking, and then to uncontrollable thrashing.

Her body rose until it stood erect. Her head jerk backward. Her throat constricted. Her jaws locked so hard that her teeth cracked. I clutched the shale in my fist, not daring to let go in case the poison faded. I told myself the tighter I squeezed it, the more potent it became. I held on through every jerk, jolt, doubling up, and sickening constriction of her throat.

Then I felt Octavia falling. She must have toppled over the building's edge. I felt my own organs rise in my abdomen. Then I felt the heavy crash to earth as I slammed against the slimy curve of her teeth.

Next, I sensed Octavia stand up again and stagger. Her giant limbs transferred her weight from one side to the other. I could feel the vibrations from her joints rippling up to her head. I imagined a monster in agony stomping through the city, its head writhing, its claws at its throat.

Boom! Boom! Boom! came the internal sounds of Octavia's bones striking the street. Boom! Boom! Boom! The movements became more violent. I felt her lurching, falling down, climbing up, running, falling again, staggering up, and running once more.

And all the while, her head shook, flinging me from side to side, into wet flesh, into the sides of her great teeth, then wet flesh again. I expected to crack my head. I drew up my knees and covered my face with one arm. With the other, I held the shale in my fist.

Boom! Boom! Boom!

Were the sounds in my head or were they explosions? Or both? Had the invader ships fired at the Accord's capital cities? Were they destroying buildings, burning houses, clearing the way for the transports to land and disgorge their soldiers and weapons of destruction?

I couldn't tell. The only thing to do was to hold on as Octavia raged across the city.

To hold on and wait for the end.

Octavia's or mine.

Or both.

84

But then Octavia stopped running.

Her head slumped forward and then all motion ceased. Her furious breath roared around me. Time passed. The breathing slowed. The washing-machine surge of fluids faded away. Was this the end at last?

Apparently not.

Her head rose. Her body was in motion again. Not running. Not thrashing. Something else.

Climbing.

It began with an upward lunge. Then there came a pause, followed by another upward push. Although I could see nothing but dark, I imagined the great limbs reaching and pulling while her monstrous legs pushed from below.

And all the while, her breathing rasped in and out. The outward breath became foul with a tinge of copper, as if her body's vessels had burst inside her.

But where were we? Had Octavia called down a transport ship? Was she climbing into its cavernous hold? Would alien surgeons pry open her jaws? Would they cut open her throat and pull me out?

I hung on in that damp, fleshy cave, hoping the shale would finish its work and end her life, but she stayed alive, climbing higher and higher.

Eventually, she stopped once more. Then, she fell to the side with a great whump. Her head hit something hard, throwing me against her teeth, knocking the shale from my fist.

Then she settled.

Her breathing faded until it I could barely sense the foul vapors passing over me. There was nothing except my own panicked breaths and tiny colored lights blinking in front of my eyes.

I had to get out. I squirmed backward, pushing against whatever I could find: soft flesh, hard pallet, strange spurs of cartilage—all of it sickening. Worse! Without Octavia's breath rasping in and out, I now had no air to breathe myself.

I kicked, twisted, pushed, and punched, but the jaws stayed shut. So I kicked and twisted all over again. All to no use. The jaw stayed locked. The maw was becoming my tomb.

I stopped struggling. I needed to think while I could. I had to get this immense weight off me. I had to escape or I would die. I was sure of it.

Stop struggling, I thought. Yes, that's what I should do. Rest. Stop squirming like a swimmer against the waves. Rest. Then I'd be OK. The escape, my mission—all of it. I could work it all out, but first I needed to rest. I needed to rest. These tiny colored lights twinkling around me— where had they come from?

My mind drifted. My consciousness faded. Octavia's death would also be mine. I tried to stay awake, to do something—anything. To kick once more, to push, or even call to Octavia for help. But like hands pulling me underwater, exhaustion seized my mind and shut it down, and then it forced my body to surrender.

And then, I wasn't there at all.

85

I awoke to a different scene: the deck of a great sailing ship at night. I stood on the ship's forecastle, high above the dark sea. The three great masts stood behind me. The air was so fresh, the space open and vast. I could breathe the glorious salty air. And yet, I was not pleased to be on that ship. I sensed that this time would not be like the others.

The man in the pre-Accord naval coat appeared amidships. He stepped from the gloom and came towards me. Out of sight, the ship's bell tolled. Then the lookouts reported from around the ship. 'All's well,' came the reports. 'All's well. All's well.'

My ancestor spoke. 'Alex,' he said. There was none of the usual taunting quality there. It was something else, something I didn't like— sympathy. 'Alex,' he began again.

'No,' I said. 'Not this time. I don't need you. Whatever advice you're going to give, whatever pre-Accord poem you're going to quote—I don't need it. Not now.'

'What makes you think I'm going to advise you?'

'When have you ever not advised me? You always give me some half explanation and then leave me to work out the rest for myself. That's the way it goes, right?'

'Not this time. Not anymore.'

'Good. I don't need any advice. I'll work it out alone. I'm almost there, anyway.'

'No, Alex. You won't… work it out.'

'I'll work it out like I did on Gwawanath. I've killed Octavia. Don't you know? Didn't you see? I killed her with the shale. And if I've killed Octavia, I've freed Earth. If I can do that, I can free myself. I can do whatever comes next. I know it now. I did it. Just as you said. The family trade.'

'No, you don't know that you've done either of those things. Nor do you know you'll get yourself free. I'm sorry, Alex, but this time, you won't.'

'It's not true.'

'It's a difficult thing to hear, Alex. The most difficult of all. But it is the truth.'

'No.'

'It's time.'

'Time? What do you mean "time"? Time for what?'

'You'll be joining my crew. Then we'll have all the time we need to explain about the family, about your mother and father, everything.'

'No!' I shouted.

'Listen to me, lad.'

'No. Don't call me that.'

'All right, Alex, Lieutenant Burns. It's time. You've done enough.'

'No,' I shouted. 'Who are you to decide what happens?'

'I decide nothing, and yet, it is decided.'

'What does that mean?'

'Why are you so surprised to be here? Not thirty minutes ago, you jumped into a monster's jaws expecting to die, maybe even wanting to die, wanting your own death.'

'I was wrong. I'm not ready. My mind. I'm so tired.'

'You fought bravely. No one could have done more.'

'I'm not ready. I haven't worked it all out. I'm not ready to leave.'

'It's too late, Alex.'

Down on the main deck, a crowd of people gathered. Some wore modern civilian jackets and hats. Some were children.

'They're not the crew.'

'No. They're not the crew.'

'Then, who are they?'

'I think you know who they are, Alex.'

I saw the two darkened figures at the front of the crowd: a man and a woman in modern clothes. Accord era clothes. The woman wore a smock. I didn't need to see its color to know it came from the Accord of Nations. And the man was… the man was…

'Are they?'

'Are they what?'

'Are they who I think?'

'Yes, Alex. All of us are your family. We're here to welcome you.'

'No.'

'It's time, Alex.'

'I'm too young,' I shouted. 'It's not time. I'm not meant to be here. I've got to get back.'

'It's over, Alex, but not in the way you think.'

'Why? Why is it over?'

His eyes looked to the rigging, then back at me.

'"There are more things in heaven and earth, Horatio, than are dreamt of your in philosophy."'

'More Horatius and the bridge?'

'Horatio, Alex, not Horatius.'

'I don't need your quotations.'

'Calm down. Get a hold of yourself. You'll have the answers to all your questions—why you fought Octavia, all of them.'

'Don't tell me to calm down.'

'You must if you're to…'

'To what?'

'To accept.'

'I'm not accepting anything. I'm getting out of here, out of this. Now that Octavia's gone, I know what to do. And this is just a dream. It's always been just a dream not some dimension between two times.'

'It's too late,' my ancestor replied, and as he spoke, the sails above us flapped. The cutwater smacked the sea out of sight beneath us.

'Shouldn't you adjust your sails? You're spilling your wind.'

'Aye,' he replied. 'Lieutenant Collins will attend to the sails. For now, I'm here to talk to you about what happens next.'

But I didn't want to talk to him. I'd talked enough. I had to escape. I had to get back. There were things I had to do. I didn't know what they were yet, but I knew I had to get back.

Over the port gunwale, the dark ocean rose and fell, rolling away to some distant coast out of sight in the dark. What lands existed in this dream world? Surely if seas existed, then lands must too. And if not, then maybe the sea itself might be an escape.

My ancestor already knew my plan.

'Don't be foolish, Alex. I know what you're thinking. It won't help you. Let me save you from embarrassment. You can't succeed—not that way.'

'Can't?' I said. 'Can't? I've heard that word all my life.'

'This time you must heed it. Greater things await if you'll just listen to me. Did you hear me, Alex. It's not the end.'

But I ignored him. I climbed onto the gunwale and grabbed the shrouds, the taught net of ropes that held the foremast firm. Then, I stood over the limitless dark of the ocean, my thoughts racing. I'm improvising, as usual, I thought, always improvising, never having time to plan, never knowing why.

'Alex!' my ancestor called. 'Don't be a fool. You'll only delay the inevitable. You'll make it worse.'

I didn't answer.

'Alex!' my ancestor called.

Too late.

I jumped. The wooden rail creaked beneath my boots. I went up and out into the cold air, out into the freedom and the dread. The dark water waited down where the ship's hull curved beneath.

It came rushing to meet me.

86

Nothing had changed. I was still inside Octavia's maw, unable to breathe, unable to move, struggling to think. The tiny colored lights sparkled in front of me and my pulse boomed in my ears.

If I could just get the corpse to flinch or roll. If I could only get it to unlock its jaws. I kicked and pushed at the congealing flesh, but it was as unyielding as clay. The outside world lay feet away, but it may as well have been light years.

For a moment I lay still, fascinated by the green, red, and purple lights. They were like a glimpse of the quiet galaxy at night. The more I gazed at them, the more I forgot the pain in my chest—the pain like a stripe—a hot stripe pressing on my ribs.

A hot stripe of pain!

And then, I realized. There was no hot stripe of pain. It was the rifle laying across my chest. The rifle! My old friend. How could I have forgotten it? I inched my hand up between Octavia's pallet and the damp cloth of my shirt until I found the trigger guard. Then, I found the fire button and reached a tentative middle finger over it. I turned my starry gaze to the side and squinted. The galaxy of colored stars shone brighter and multiplied.

Then I pressed the fire button.

In such a confined space, the blast had nowhere to go. The heat, the blast noise, and the recoil were all confined in the heavy squash zone. And as predicted, the blast went nowhere. Except into Octavia. The recoil shoved the rifle along my chest, tearing my shirt, gouging my sternum, and snapping my finger in the trigger guard. But the most important thing was that Octavia the monster had flinched.

She was still alive! Maybe only just, but still alive!

The body winced in pain, rolled and tossed its head, turning it enough for me to slide the rifle around so I could fire again—this time back at the way I had entered this trap in the first place. I reached out with my left hand and found the trigger guard. Then I turned my head and squinted all over again.

And fired.

The blast shot forward. The recoil sent the rifle sliding past my face. Now, my ears rang with the clash of a gong, deep and shattering. I felt Octavia's body move, either through pain or reflex.

My eyes had been closed against the blast. I

slid a palm between them and the wet flesh and opened them, not knowing what to expect.

But then I saw it.

Light. A weak glow came from beyond the toes of my boots. And air, too. Just enough for me to draw a breath and not retch.

I drew up my knees and clawed with my hands, pulling myself towards the light and away from death. I squeezed myself through the fleshy blast wound, feet first, then hips, then torso, until I slid out, like a pre-Accord baby in the days before compulsory stomach births. Out into the world and the light and the wet concrete. Then, I lay there on my back, letting the blessed rain hit my face, letting it roll down my neck and under my shirt.

I was alive. I was back in the world of the living.

Octavia lay behind me, a fallen giantess, still and lifeless, her face shattered, her glistening scales as unmoving as house tiles.

I got to my knees, reached back inside the wound, grabbed the rifle's hot muzzle, and pulled it out. Then, I stood up, drew a breath of cold, fresh air, and tried not to think about the dream of my ancestor. It could wait till another time.

Instead, I looked around and tried to work out where Octavia had brought me. I was on a building rooftop. Around me were the curved sides of TEDIST buildings. Beyond them lay the spread of AON sub-territory Los Angeles rolling away to the sea. I recognized it all, even though I'd never seen it from this height or this position. It could only be one place: the flat roof of The Accord of Nations Headquarters.

Octavia had staggered all the way back here from the apartment building where we'd played out our showdown. She must have stomped her way through the streets, one claw at her throat, the other held out in front of her for balance, trampling cars, and lampposts, all the way across town, and then somehow climbed the building's slippery curved side. But why? To make a defiant gesture? To show what she had once dominated?

And what of the invasion? Yes, what of that?

I looked again at the city and the famous circular streets. All around the headquarters, the city lay devastated; the buildings lay smashed or burning on almost every block north and south. Great channels lay striped across the roads and the houses where the beams, shot from the sky, had strafed from the mountains to the sea. But not everywhere. Parts of the city were untouched. And if not all of AON sub-territory Los Angeles was destroyed, then other cities might have survived too.

I turned back to the corpse. It lay shattered in the rain. Octavia, the world conqueror, the grand admiral, the insane leader of a great military force, the astonishing beauty, the tyrant, had finally expired. I lowered my head. If this was victory, it was hollow. Octavia had been an enemy, a dangerous one. But she had suffered in her own way. She deserved respect.

I felt a strange sense of… I wasn't sure what, but it felt like relief, like recognizing myself again for the very first time.

I slung the heavy rifle over my back and headed for the stairs. When I got to the door of the hutch, I unslung the rifle and turned around to take one last look at the rooftop.

It was a bizarre scene! The slumped enormity of Octavia's corpse; the dark heavy clouds; the glow of distant fires; and the chimes of emergency vehicles like dinner gongs; and the teardrop-shaped craft silently descending from the clouds to hover beside their slain leader.

I watched them, fascinated, knowing I should go, but wanting to see what they would do. The craft spread out and took up positions around and above the rooftop. Others hovered over the roof itself. Their hatches opened. Platforms descended carrying ranks of armed Marines.

What would they do? Now that Octavia was dead, did that mean her orders no longer applied? Were the Marines coming to guard the corpse or to take revenge on the killer.

I watched them step from the platform onto the glistening concrete. Some clunked around Octavia's body towards her head. Others lowered their weapons and came directly toward the stair hutch and to me.

'Lieutenant Burns!' a male voice said in a pre-Accord accent. It sounded strange all over again to hear that accent from a male. 'Stay where you are. You will not be harmed. I repeat. Stay there. You will not be harmed.'

Yeah, I thought. Sure I won't.

I raised my weapon at the closest Marine and fired. The blast knocked him down with a great clatter. The other Marines stepped over him and kept coming. More descended from the teardrop-shaped craft.

I slung the rifle and turned to the stair hutch. I could not allow myself to be captured, not after all that had happened.

I had to get out, to stay free, forever.

But as usual, that was easier said than done.

87

Inside the stair hutch, I clattered down to the next floor. There, I found a rank of six elevators. All their displays showed numbers rising. I guessed that each carried Roman Marines or Harmony Officers bearing stun guns and handcuffs.

Not this time, I thought. Not ever. Never again.

I found the door to the stairwell and tried the handle. Locked. So, I stepped back, lifted the rifle, and, using my third finger, pulled the fire button.

I kicked the shattered door aside and dropped down the stairs, jumping two at a time, then three at a time, then each flight in two leaps, risking a twisted ankle all over again.

Keep going, I told myself. Only fifty flights to go.

Aye, but what then? What then?

Twenty flights down, the sound of many footsteps thrummed up from below. Beams from helmet-mounted flashlights swung left and right, up and down, seeking and probing.

The Harmony Office must have deployed their Equity Squad. The Equity squad was trained to use special weapons and tactics—so they said. Well, we would soon see how effective their training had been.

When I reached the twenty-fifth floor, I checked whether anyone had crept up the stairs. Sure enough, Harmony Officers waited two flights below, staring up at me. Meanwhile, from above came the heavy clatter of the Roman Marines.

A voice came up the stairwell.

'Lieutenant Burns,' the voice called. 'Harmony Officers! Captain Kholi speaking. You are under arrest. Stay where you are. Put down your weapon, step back from it and lie face down on the landing.'

That command—yet again.

'Put down the weapon!' the voice called again. 'We have four rifles aimed at you. If you do not comply, we will use force.'

'To kill?' I shouted back. 'Will you use force to kill?'

A pause, as if Captain Kholi had taken out the Harmony Office field manual and leafed through its pages.

'Killing Accord members is against Accord policy and Harmony Office values.'

'Mine too,' I shouted.

'Then, put down your weapon.'

'But I still have another policy,' I called back.

'And what's that?'

'I'm never going to let you arrest me.'

I upended the rifle and fired down the stairwell. As a first move, it was impressive. The full horror of the alien weapon revealed itself to the Harmony Officers. The terrible noise, the blinding flash, the ear-shattering echo, all descended on them, stunning the air.

I shouted. 'How about you put your weapons down, Captain? How about you step away? How about you lie face down on the steps? Comply with my command and then we won't have any trouble. Disobey and I will blast the stairs from under you.'

No reply.

'Tell you what. I'll make it easy for you. Turn around and go back the way you came and no one will suffer.'

'You're under arrest, Lieutenant,' came the hesitant reply.

'Have it your way.'

I leveled the weapon at my hip and went down the next flight of stairs, two steps at a time, firing the weapon, firing at walls, railings, whatever came into view. Every blast was ear-shattering. Every pull of my middle finger on the fire button smashed craters in the walls and caused chunks of concrete to plunge to the stairwell base.

After three flights, I stopped and picked myself up. I saw the lights of the Harmony Officers' helmets going down the stairwell.

So far, so good.

Just to make sure they got the message, I fired once more, down at the base of the stairwell. The blast sounded like a Navy depth charge from the pre-Accord era. When the echoes faded away, I patted the rifle while I listened for footsteps. Then I walked down the stairs, one step at a time, like a free man.

At the last flight of stairs, no Harmony Officers waited, but the Marines clattered down the stairs above me. They hadn't yet fired a shot. Maybe they were ordered not to kill me after all.

But who had issued the orders? Had Drusilla, Octavia's second in command, taken over the landing force? And what would she decide? Would she now want to capture me and try me in a court for murder, as the Goths had done?

'Not going to happen,' I said to no one.

I pulled the stairway door open. I saw the enormous lobby with its glistening marble, high ceilings, Accord flag, and statues of former commissioners.

At the street entrance, there was a wide floor-to-ceiling window revealing the terrace and the famous Steps to Equity where Octavia had stood at her podium not one hour before. And waiting on the other side of the glass was the full force of the Accord's regional law enforcement resources and military police.

Harmony Officers, Equity Teams, Navy MAs, Army MPs—all of them stood watching me with their weapons raised.

A loudspeaker squelched. Out came the voice

of Captain Kholi.

'This time, there's no escape, Lieutenant Burns. Put your weapon down on the floor in front of you, then step aside from it and kneel with your hands behind your head.'

Just one week, I thought. One week, I'd like a break from that command.

'Now, Lieutenant.'

Just one day, I thought. I'd even take one day's break from being told to get on the ground.

'Now, Lieutenant,' the voice said again.

'No,' I replied. 'Not this time.'

And instead of lying face down, I raised the weapon once more.

And fired.

The blast hit the glass of the great window. It knocked a hole the size of a Rainbow van. A second later, the whole window shattered, cascading in glittering shards to the floor. Meanwhile, the blast carried on and went above the heads of the assembled Harmony Officers all the way to the building opposite, shattering its windows, sending sheets of glass plunging down onto the Avenue of Revolutionary Feminists.

It was a magnificent show, a spectacular display. Every soldier, Harmony Officer, MP, MA, and civilian cringed and covered their ears—if not their heads.

But it was also too late.

The Roman Marines exploded through the stairwell door behind me. They clattered around on the marble floor, with weapons raised. They surrounded me, saying nothing. They didn't need to speak. There would be no escape this time.

'Glad to see you actually do something, guys. It is guys, right? Here in the Accord, we have to check?'

I let the rifle slip from my hand until the stock butt clinked on the marble. Then, I let it drop to one side, like a falling hero.

The Marines were silent. One of them swung his rifle towards the smashed entrance way indicating I should walk.

And so we marched outside. Me and my escort of alien Marines. We stepped through the shattered window and onto the terrace. Weapons were raised again. Everyone faced my direction: every MP, Harmony Officer, and soldier.

But No one said a word. Not even Captain Kholi of the Equity Team. Everyone stood there, weapons drawn and waiting.

The Marines ahead of me stopped. I stopped too.

'What's going on?' I said.

No one answered. Not even Captain Kholi uttered a word. Everyone looked up at the top of the building.

The strangest event of that astonishing day was about to take place.

88

The rain had dried up; the explosions had ceased; and the transport ships no longer blocked the sun. But the street darkened all the same. The sunlight vanished. A shadow darkened the street for an entire block. Although I couldn't see what was coming, I guessed what it must be.

The air whistled with the plunge of a great object, pushing air in front of it, dragging air behind. Everyone on the street, from the MAs to Captain Kholi waited and watched, mouths open, suspended in disbelief, or horror as the carcass of the slain Octavia slipped from the rooftop and plunged down from fifty floors above.

Down, down to the street below.

For the second time that morning, I escaped death. Before Octavia's carcass smashed onto the Steps to Equity, two metallic hands gripped my shoulders and pulled me into the shelter of the building's entrance. A robotic voice said something that sounded like Octavia's original name.

'Sinistra. Oh, Sinistra.'

And then, the most sickening crash.

The impact devastated the street. It annihilated every car, tank, streetlamp, traffic light, dog, bird, tree, insect, and any other life form unfortunate enough to be in the way. It smashed down with the thump of a thousand sacks of meat. It caused a tremor in the sidewalks and a smashed a crater into the road.

Then, a fraction of a second later, before people could close their gaping mouths, the corpse exploded with a deep boom. Out surged a tsunami of scales, viscera, chunks of flesh, shards of bones, claws, and sinews. Green bile splashed the sides of the buildings, splattering anyone and anything in hot, stinging juice.

It was over in ten seconds.

89

Eventually, the survivors emerged from the detritus.

Harmony Officers and Navy MAs crept out from behind body chunks. They stepped onto the street and slunk toward the shattered corpse, crouching down to check beneath it for their comrades.

Captain Kholi came forward. She stood up from her crouch, brushed some bloody chunks from her splattered uniform, and climbed the steps.

'Now's not the time, Captain,' I said.

But she ignored me and greeted the Marines.

'T.E.I.D. Intra-galactic visitors,' she said.

None of the Marines replied. Their helmets remained closed and silent. Captain Kholi was undeterred.

'Please let me express our condolences on the loss of your great admiral,' she said. 'Our thanks, too, for capturing her murderer, Lieutenant Burns. We'll take him off your hands now, and make sure he faces the full extent of the Navy's codes of behavior, and the laws of the Accord of Nations.'

Typically, she mentioned nothing about the attacks on the city by Octavia's ships. She would believe they were examples of another nation's culture, and therefore deserving of tolerance and praise.

'Save yourself, Captain,' I said. 'It's not going to happen. Help your comrades sort out the mess down there instead.'

She turned her head and spoke over her left shoulder.

'Take Lieutenant Burns from our intra-galactic friends.'

Two officers stepped forward. One carried handcuffs. The other held a PQ47 rifle. Both grinned.

'We'll take it from here, intra-galactic friends,' one of them said.

The Marines said nothing. Their metal hands remained clamped on my shoulders.

'Please hand us the prisoner, intra-galactic friends,' insisted Captain Kholi. 'This traitor and murderer is ours. It's a matter of Accord jurisdiction. He committed his crimes here at the Accord of Nations headquarters and in the Accord of Nations sub-territory of Los Angeles, not in your new sanctuary states.'

The Marines said nothing.

Captain Kholi grew impatient.

'Take the prisoner.'

'No one is taking me anywhere,' I said, 'especially not these guys.'

'The traitor will remain quiet.'

'You're out of your league here, Captain.'

'Shut it or we'll gag you, Burns.'

'I'd like to see you try.'

'Gag the prisoner.'

The officer with the cuffs put them back on his belt. Then he pulled out a rubber gag from his pocket. He stepped forward, gag ready.

'Don't try it, pal.'

'Or what?'

'Or you'll find out.'

When he came within a foot of my face, there was a great crunch of metal behind me. I thought the Marines might have been about to intervene. But instead they snapped to attention with a great clang of hundreds of metal boots on stone.

The guy with the gag stopped.

'What's going on?' said Captain Kholi.

'Look up in the sky,' I said.

We all turned to watch as one of the teardrop Roman craft descended.

'It's the new admiral arriving, Captain,' I said. 'If I were you, I'd wait before doing anything to insult the new leader of the visitors, especially on Intra-galactic Diversity Day.'

'You aren't me, Burns, and you are going to a damp, cold cell at AONB Holder. Then you'll face a second court-martial for the code violations you committed today.'

'Things have changed,' I said.

The teardrop ship cast a shadow over Octavia's corpse. The shadow slid over the shattered body and collapsed head. Then, it stopped beside the Steps to Equity, hovering low over the splattered street.

A hatch opened in its side. A gangway telescoped down to the street. Two Marines emerged at the hatchway and clanked down it steps. Then they stood at attention with their rifles shouldered. A beautiful woman emerged from the hatch wearing the blue uniform of the Roman Navy.

As I expected, it was Captain Drusilla, Octavia's second in command. She descended to the street, paying no attention to the Harmony Officers, the MAs, and emergency workers. Without looking left or right, she approached Octavia, her old shipmate and commanding officer. She bowed and then spoke several words we couldn't hear. Finally, her duty done, her respects paid, she withdrew. Her escort of Marines came forward and together they stood at the base of the steps, waiting.

Then, she spoke to one of the Marines beside her. He turned and barked a single word to the Marines holding me captive. They clomped their feet a second time. Two steel hands nudged me forward and we crunched down the Steps to Equity to the street with Captain Kholi protesting all the way until we reached Drusilla and her escort, where she composed herself and saluted.

'T.E.I.D., Captain Drusilla,' said Captain Kholi.

'T.E.I.D.,' Drusilla replied, 'although my rank is not captain anymore. It's admiral.'

'T.E.I.D., Admiral.'

Drusilla turned to me. 'Good afternoon, Lieutenant Burns.'

'Good afternoon, Admiral. My condolences on the passing of Admiral Octavia. She was a great and inspiring leader.'

'Admiral, we would prefer if you did not speak with this prisoner,' said Captain Kholi.

Drusilla ignored her. 'Thank you, Lieutenant Burns. Your tribute is welcome and well said.' She turned to Captain Kholi.

'Captain, you wish to say something?'

'Yes, Admiral.'

'Please, don't bother. We will relieve you of Lieutenant Burns. He must come with us now.'

'My apologies, Admiral. Lieutenant Burns is wanted by the Accord of Nations Navy and the Harmony Officers of AON sub-territory Los Angeles. He's wanted for the murder of the admiral and many crimes and code violations from before that. He must face a court-martial and if found guilty, he must be sentenced and serve his time in one of our Navy land brigs.'

'I'm sorry, Captain, but we require Lieutenant Burns aboard our flagship.'

'My apologies again, Admiral, but Lieutenant Burns committed these crimes in our jurisdiction. It would be a different matter if he committed the crimes and violations in your sanctuary areas.'

'Don't worry, Captain. We won't keep

Lieutenant Burns forever. Also, you see our Marines and aircraft. I believe we have the first claim on him by way of military prominence. I hope you won't try to prevent us from escorting Lieutenant Burns to our ship.'

Captain Kholi frowned. The gears turned behind her forehead. Maybe she hoped an Accord Commissioner would show up to explain things. She turned to the street below, but found nothing but the dull metal of the teardrop ship and ranks of gray Marines.

No one would come to her rescue.

'If that's what you want, Admiral, but we must have Lieutenant Burns returned to our custody as soon as possible.'

Drusilla made no reply. She turned and walked away. The Marines unclamped their metal hands from my shoulders. I followed Drusilla across the street to the gangway of the hovering craft.

Just before she climbed the first step, she turned and looked at my torn and soiled clothes, my gore-smeared face, my crooked, broken finger, and other injuries I didn't know about yet.

'Are you all right, Lieutenant?'

'Yes, Admiral.'

'You have suffered since I saw you last. Your mind has suffered as well as your body.'

'I'll survive.'

'Our medical officer will examine you.'

'There's no need.'

She turned and ascended the gangway.

'Admiral Drusilla?'

She turned.

'Yes, Lieutenant.'

'I wish it could have been different with Octavia.'

'Save your wishes for your own people, Lieutenant.'

I didn't reply. So she turned once more and climbed the steps, but I stayed down on the street.

'One thing more, Admiral.'

She stopped. 'Last question, Lieutenant.'

'OK. Last question. Do you also want to imprison me?'

'No, Alex. I'm not going to imprison you.'

'Then what?'

'I'm going to give you a gift.'

'A gift, Admiral?'

'Something you appear to be willing to die for.'

'And what's that?'

'Your freedom.'

'Freedom, Admiral?'

'Yes, freedom, Lieutenant. Freedom from your court-martial, from prison, and, if you wish, from the Accord of Nations. As you know, the Accord Commission and the people will never forgive you.'

I made no reply.

'And if they knew all you'd done, they might even thank you. I see by your smile that you are amused, Lieutenant.'

'What will you do now that Octavia is dead, Admiral? Will you complete her plans?'

'Her plans?'

'Octavia's plans for earth, for the Accord, for the people?'

'No, Lieutenant. I believe you know the answer to that question already. You have heard of the planet we call Elysium.'

'Yes, Admiral.'

'Then you know. Anything more? Please hurry, Lieutenant. It is late.'

'Yes, one more thing. Why are you helping me after what I did to the admiral — if helping is what you're doing?'

Drusilla raised her beautiful chin and looked across the street to the ruin of Octavia. Then she turned back to me.

'Call it our way of repaying a favor. You solved a problem for all of us, not just for earth. But let us talk later, Lieutenant. Now is not the time. Here is not the place.'

'Talk about what later?'

'Our plans, your future, misconceptions about our treatment of our co-inhabitants the Goths, and many other topics you might wish to understand.'

Then she turned and ascended the final steps. 'Don't take too long to think about it, Lieutenant,' she said, before stepping inside the hatch. The Marines behind me clomped their boots on the street. They too were ready to board.

And so, covered in gore and slime and blood, and with my ears ringing, and my broken finger pointing to somewhere far away, I ascended the gangway and entered the alien craft.

Epilogue

'What can you see?' said Ricci.

'Nothing. Not a thing.' Adams turned the focus wheel on his binoculars. 'Not a thing, except Harmony Officers and rainbow tape across the street.'

'Is that all?'

'Well, the Harmony Officers carry weapons now. Can you believe it?'

'And what about the… you know… mess?'

'Gone. The visitors must have cleaned up the whole thing—the head, the gore, the claws, everything. It's all gone.'

'There's nothing at all?'

'Might be a stain on the side of the Cohesion Building.'

'Let me try,' said Ricci, holding out her hand.

'You think you'll find something I didn't?'

'I don't know, but we've got to keep trying.'

'Why don't you face facts?' Adams said. 'He's in a cell at AONB Holder for life. Either that or he's dead.'

Ricci raised the binoculars and scanned the street. She saw the Steps to Equity exactly as Adams had described. Nothing remained from Intra-galactic Diversity Day—not even the bullet holes on the buildings opposite the Accord Headquarters. She put down the binoculars.

'Was he right?'

'No. He was dead wrong.'

'Why?'

'He should have attacked the Accord, not the visitors. Like I told him. The Accord is the problem, the same as always. But did he listen? No, he did not. And now we're back in the same place we've always been.' Adams shook his head. 'We should never have listened to a kid. He's twenty-six. What could he know about the world?'

Ricci saw something over Adams's shoulder.

'Put these in your pack.' She handed him the binoculars. 'Quickly.'

'Why?'

'Harmony Officers. Behind you.'

Without turning around, Adams unzipped his small backpack and dropped the binoculars inside. He zipped the pack up and slung it over his shoulder.

'You two!' a voice called.

'Start walking,' said Ricci.

'You think they won't catch us? We better stop.'

Two Harmony Officers came up. They wore the usual green smocks. The patches on the front showed the new Accord flag and each officer's name. One patch read 'Daw,' the other read 'Ibori.' Daw was tall. Ibori sat in a wheelchair.

'T.E.D., officers,' said Adams.

'T.E.D.,' said Ricci.

'Haven't you heard?' said the officer named Daw.

'Heard what?' said Adams.

'It's not T.E.D. It's T.E.I.D.' said Ibori from the wheelchair. 'Nothing's changed. It's T.E.I.D. You should know that, Accord member.'

'But they're gone, right?' said Ricci. 'The sky's clear. The ocean's clear. No one's seen a visitor in weeks. Not even the ones in the sanctuary towns.'

'Did you hear that on Unity TV?' said Ibori from his chair.

'No.'

'Did the Accord Commission announce that the visitors had gone?'

'I don't…I'm not sure.'

'Did you hear an official announcement about anything at all?'

'No, but…'

'Then nothing's changed. Our intra-galactic friends are still part of the Accord.'

'OK,' Adams said. 'If you say so.'

'The Accord Commission says so, Accord member.'

'OK, got it. We'll get out of your way.'

But the officer named Daw hadn't finished.

'State the proper greeting.'

'What?'

'Say it.'

'Say what?'

'The official Accord greeting. Say it.'

'Why?' said Adams.

'So we know you've understood. It's the law, and the law enforces the Accord values. You don't want people thinking you don't respect Accord values, do you?'

Adams drew a breath.

'T.E.I.D.,' he said.

'You too,' Ibori said to Ricci.

'T.E.I.D.,' said Ricci.

'That's better. Now tell us what you were doing?'

'When?' said Adams.

'Just now,' said the officer. 'And watch the tone, Accord member.'

'We wanted to see the site of the… incident,' said Ricci.

'What incident would that be?' said Harmony Officer Daw.

Adams smiled at the officers' blank faces.

'You know what incident we mean. Everyone knows.'

'What does everyone know?'

Ricci interrupted Adams. 'He means the celebration to mark the first Intra-galactic Diversity Day, don't you?'

'Yes,' said Adams. 'The I.D.D.'

'Why don't you just watch the replay on Unity TV?'

Adams was about to say that the Unity coverage cut out as soon as Lieutenant Burns fired his first shots. Ricci interrupted him.

'We will. We wanted to see the site for ourselves, to make it more memorable.'

'No one is allowed near the Steps to Equity— not until the Accord allows it.'

'We didn't know,' said Ricci.

'Everyone received a text message.'

'Oh, we didn't check our handhelds.'

'Well, you should. The commission might send a message at any time.'

'We'll check more often in the future.'

'Make sure you do. Now leave the area and don't come back until you receive a text message from the commission saying you have permission to be here.'

'We won't,' said Ricci.

'Let's go,' said Adams.

'One last thing,' said the officer named Daw.

'Yes,' said Ricci.

'Show us your Accord Member identification.'

'Why?' said Adams.

'Because you appear to be a cisgendered male accompanying a female without an escort. That's why.'

Adams reached between the buttons of his shirt. The card hung from a lanyard.

'Yours too.'

Ricci's reached into her pocket and held out her

card. Officer Ibori ran a scanner over it.

'Now leave!' said Officer Daw. 'Next time, make sure you have a third person present.'

They walked away, back towards Adams's new Progressive van.

'They're worse than ever,' said Ricci.

'All the more reason to start the revolution,' said Adams.

But Ricci said nothing. She knew that whatever Adams said, he could never start a revolution. Someone else would have to start it—someone who acted rather than talked.

Their handhelds pinged with incoming messages.

Adams pulled his handheld from the holster on his belt. Ricci pulled hers from her jacket pocket. The screens displayed a familiar caller ID.

'Did you get the same message I did?'

'Yeah,' said Adams.

'From the same sender?'

'Looks like it,' Adams said.

'What's your message say?' Ricci asked.

'Until the Accord is Defeated,' said Adams. 'Until the Accord is Defeated.'

'So where could he be?' said Ricci, looking to the sky.

— The End —

A few words from you
could make all the difference.

Thank you for reading SHALE. I hope you enjoyed it.

If you have a few spare moments, would you please do me a huge favor and post a brief review where you purchased it.

Reviews are critical for encouraging people to read the book, especially for new authors like me who do not have the resources of large publishing houses to support them.

No reviews, no readers.

So if you enjoyed the book, would you please revisit the page from where you downloaded it, and scroll down to the button that says, 'Write a review.' Then, type, 'This was amazing.'

I'm only kidding. I know you'll put what you think best. On the off chance you didn't like the book, could you contact me with your thoughts. I would love to hear them. Email me at mmholt548@gmail.com

My sincere thanks,

M.M. Holt.

Like to be notified when M.M. Holt releases a new book?

It's easy. Visit the address below and enter your email address in the signup form. You'll receive updates on works in progress, access to deleted scenes from the Burns Series, and snaps from my relentless travels. But no spam.

mmholt.com

If you have any problems, email me at mmholt548@gmail.com. I'll put you on the list.

Thank you,

M.M. Holt.

You've reached the end of the series to date, but did you start at the beginning?

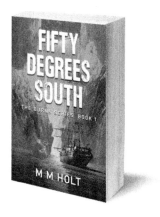

The Burns Series Book 1
The astonishing adventure
that started it all.

If you enjoyed Alex Burns's clash with Octavia in the Accord of Nations era, you might also enjoy the battle that started it all when Alexander Burns the elder met Octavia six hundred years earlier in 1803 AD.

Read on to discover what it's about.

At the end of the earth, we fought an enemy from beyond the stars.

1803. The Napoleonic War. A Royal Navy warship is ordered to pursue an enemy frigate to the frozen waters far south in the Indian Ocean. There it must capture the enemy ship and retrieve a mysterious sea-chest, contents unknown. Failure not permitted.

For the determined young captain and his crew, this already dangerous mission turns into a battle with a mysterious vessel that appears not in the sea, but, unbelievably, impossibly, in the sky above them.

And it is not friendly.

Embark on an astonishing adventure in 'Fifty Degrees South,' the action-packed, science fiction adventure novel that readers around the world can't put down. Reviewers describe the story as **'Brilliant,'** and **'A unique science fiction novel.'**

Check out the sample chapter on the following pages or go straight to Amazon and search for 'Fifty Degrees South,' by M.M. Holt.

'Fifty Degrees South'

The Burns Series Book 1

Chapter 1

WHEN THE FIRST blue beam struck the sea just ahead of HMS Morgause, none of the seventy sailors in the first watch saw it. Instead, they were concentrating on the task known as wearing the ship, changing its heading from southwest to southeast.

At the ship's helm, Jessop, the quartermaster, turned the wheel clockwise, and great ship came into the wind. The Morgause's bow swung to starboard and the compass in the binnacle wobbled around to west-south-west, then west where it paused as Jessop waited for the next command. He was so engrossed in his task of feeling the ship's movement, he missed the sight of the blue beam entirely.

Forward of Jessop, on the main deck, the crew stood ready, the thick ropes in their hands, waiting for the commands to heave the yards of the main mast around to coordinate with Jessop's turn of the helm and with the other crewmen hauling on ropes at the foremast and the mizzen mast.

They too missed the blue beam as it hit the water, thick as a four barrels, and curiously light as it went down into the depths.

High on the mainmast, Trinity Evans was scouring the south for the enemy vessel, the Besançon, which the Morgause had been desperately pursuing for seven long weeks in heavy seas. But when he turned west with the movement of the Morgause's bow, he too missed the blue beam. He didn't see the three-second long blast from the sky, the cylinder-shaped shaft of light, wide and smooth, smacking the dark sea, going through it and straight down and distorting, like a twig in a glass of water. Nor did Trinity Evans hear the hiss of steam that followed.

On the quarterdeck, the view forward was blocked by the mainsail. The officer of the watch, Mr Kyte concentrated on Jessop's shouted compass readings. Mr Kyte didn't see the beam either, nor did he see the smoldering carcass of an enormous white squid surfacing ahead of the Morgause and sliding along its hull to be churned in the ship's wake.

But when the ship hard worn to her new southeast course and was pushing through the dark and swelling water at a good eight knots, the blue beam struck again.

And this time, it was noticed.

Trinity Evans ducked, held up an elbow, and thought it was lightning coming to strike him dead, but this was not like any lightning he'd seen before. For one thing, it was bright blue; for another, it was straight. It also wasn't flashing. It struck sixty yards ahead of the Morgause and blazed for a full five seconds. No lightning ever did that—not in Trinity Evans's experience. Not on your life. Not even after ten too many mugs of grog—the extra strong stuff.

He watched the beam, fascinated. The way it went right down into the water. Only when it finally ceased did he prepare to hail the deck. But still, he hesitated, wondering what he should say. This wasn't a regular sighting. It certainly wasn't the sighting of the Besançon, nor any other ship. This was something else entirely. It wasn't even in his list of hails, which was long. Still, he had better hail something before someone on the deck noticed it first. He slapped a hand to the side of his mouth and peered down at the darkened figures way below.

'On deck there!' he called. 'On deck!'

'Yes, Evans,' came the reply. 'Is it the Besançon?'

'No, sir. Strange light, sir! Strange light.'

'Where away?' came the reply but only after a few moments.

'Straight ahead!' he called.

As he said this, another beam hit the sea. Same place—directly ahead. Same thickness. Same intensity, it was the color of the blue in the plate

glass windows back in his church in Penzance—
which made Trinity Evans wonder. Was this a
sign from the Almighty? Was the Second Coming
at hand? Was this something mentioned in the
book of Revelations? It certainly didn't look like a
friendly light. Tomorrow, he thought. No more
grog. No more ale.

'On deck there!' he called again.

'We saw it, Evans,' someone called back.

'Something new!' Trinity Evans countered.

'What?' came the reply.

'The strange light—it came from that big dark
cloud.'

On the quarterdeck, Mr Kyte walked to the
taffrail and looked up into the gloom at the gray
cloud that had settled off the ship's port side,
huge and glowering, almost like a ship itself, a
ship of the air, with curious bulges. A ship of the
air, he thought, then shook his head. His
overactive imagination was at work again.

My Kyte made a note of the time. It was three
bells in the morning watch, just as dawn was
fighting off the night. Possible enemy activity
sighted. A strange blue light.

'Did you see it, Poole?' he said to the youth
beside him, one of the ship's young midshipman
who were training to become officers, just as Mr
Kyte himself had trained twenty years ago.

'Yes,' said Poole. 'I saw it, port bow, a quarter
cable length away.'

'You mean, "Yes, sir,"' said Mr Kyte. 'You're in
His Majesty's Navy, Poole, and we are at war.'

'Yes, sir,' said Poole. 'Beg pardon, sir. The light, sir—it made me forget myself.'

Mr Kyte scanned the darkness again. Nothing but the swelling sea in the soft dawn. Nothing but the shush of the water along the hull, and the creak of ropes as the ship rose and fell. He looked down at the main deck. The seventy men of the morning watch, dressed in their blue jackets and white duck trousers stared into the darkness. Others looked up at Mr Kyte—waiting for a command—and an explanation.

Then, without warning, another blue beam shot from the dark cloud. It was closer this time. He could see it clearly. It was a thick blue shaft of light, straight as a sun ray, coming from the dark cloud, going straight down into the sea, illuminating the underwater world beneath for a good sixty yards or so, and going down into the depths.

Trinity Davies was already hailing him from the upper deck when a second beam struck the water. Same straight blue shaft of light. Same point of origin in the dark cloud above. Two beams. One to port. One to starboard. They were like a ceremonial gateway of light.

Mt Kyte turned around. Poole was behind him, crouching.

'Stand up straight, Poole,' he said.

'Yes, sir,' said Poole.

'The men must see that you are unafraid, that you are fearless.'

'Yes, sir,' said Poole. 'Beg pardon, sir.'

'Never again, Poole.'

'No, sir. Never again. Fearless.'

'Fearless of even the strangest things produced by war and the heavens.'

'Yes, sir.'

Mr Kyte turned back to the beams.

'Are we going to beat to quarters, sir?' said Poole.

Is was a good question. Beating to quarters meant the bosun's whistle would blow, drums would pound, commands would be shouted, and the crew would scramble for battle, the one hundred and thirty men asleep in the hammocks below would rush to join the men already on the main deck. The gun crews would rush to the cannons ranged along the sides of the Morgause, untying the ropes that held them fast on their wooden carts, readying them for the gunpowder and the cannonballs. The Marines would climb with their muskets into the tops. The powder boys would scramble to the magazine, deep inside the ship, and rush upward with buckets of powder for the gun crews. The wicks would be lit and set in tubs beside each cannon. The boarding crews would assemble for the armourer to hand out the cutlasses, rapiers and pistols. The gun ports on the main deck and below would swing open and the Morgause would be ready to unleash thunderous hell and utterly smash any ship within range.

Beating to quarters.

Mr Kyte made his decision.

'Yes, Poole,' he said. 'Give the order. Beat to quarters.'

Poole almost broke into a run before checking himself. He was eager for something to be done about the beams.

'Mr Pound!' he called to the bosun.

'Sir,' Mr Pound called up from the main deck.

'Per Mr Kyte, we shall beat to quarters.'

'What?' said Mr Pound.

'We shall beat to quarters!' called Mr Kyte.

'Aye,' said Mr Pound.

Instantly, the mood of the ship changed. Mr Pound's whistle piped its shrill two tones, and the ship came alive.

Mr Kyte watched the blue beams and wondered.

The year was 1803 in the Napoleonic war. The location was the Atlantic Ocean in the lonely waters far south the equator, off the west coast of Southern Africa on His Majesty's Ship, Morgause. Seas moderate to heavy. Wind from the northeast. Time at sea: sixty days. Mission: to capture the enemy frigate Besançon and retrieve a certain sea-chest, contents unknown, and return said sea-chest to the Admiralty in London.

Failure not permitted.

'Mr Poole,' said Mr Kyte without taking his eyes off the beams.

'Yes, sir.'

'Pass the word for Captain Burns.'

—/—

To continue reading, search Amazon for 'Fifty Degrees South,' by M.M. Holt. I know you'll enjoy this book.

Acknowledgments

My sincere thanks to the many friends and family who encouraged me to persevere with this novel and the others in the series.

A special mention to authors Peter Boghossian, James Lindsay, and Helen Pluckrose for their academic paper, "Human reactions to rape culture and queer performativity at urban dog parks in Portland, Oregon." This hoax paper was the inspiration for the news item to which Alex Burns listens in his cell at AONNB Schumer.

I would also like to acknowledge the mysterious gentlemen known as Awww, Rrrr, and The Hobgoblin. Their encouragement and advice have been invaluable. Yes, the pseudonyms are necessary. All three know the Accord will never forgive them.

M.M. Holt.

About M.M. Holt

M.M. Holt is a mysterious figure who lives partly in the real world, but more often in his imagination.

He writes science fiction, horror and adventure novels, often involving a Navy lieutenant named Alex Burns who struggles to keep his sanity in a future world gone mad with political correctness. This same Alex Burns also fights alien invaders. Sometimes Burns's great seafaring ancestors also appear in the books. They are also named Alex Burns, and in their owns times they also battled invaders from beyond the stars. Battling aliens and dystopian regimes is like a family tradition.

M.M. Holt is a relentless traveler. He can usually be found writing in cafes by the sea, or in a bar on the edge of a crowded street, usually in far flung cities. If you see him, he'll be the handsome yet enigmatic stranger pounding the keyboard of his laptop, pausing only to sip black coffee and glance warily over his shoulder. He knows the Accord Of Nations is always one step behind.

Contact M.M. Holt

mmholt.com

mmholt548@gmail.com

Facebook
(Search for MM Holt, author)

@MMHOLT3

Instagram
Search for mmholt548

Printed in Great Britain
by Amazon

39551639R00344